DAVID MORRELL

The Protector

WARNER BOOKS

An AOL Time Warner Company

Warner Books, Inc., 1271 Avenue of the Americas, New York, NY 10020

Visit our Web site at www.twbookmark.com

 An AOL Time Warner Company

Printed in the United States of America

First Printing: May 2003
10 9 8 7 6 5 4 3 2 1

Library of Congress Cataloging-in-Publication Data

Morrell, David.
    The protector / David Morrell.
        p. cm.
    ISBN 0-446-53068-9
        1. Illegal arms transfers—Fiction.   2. Bodyguards—Fiction.   3. Scientists—Fiction.
    I. Title.

PR9199.3.M65 P76 2003
813'.54—dc21

2002038001

To Henry Morrison, who has been my agent since 1968,
almost a lifetime ago. My heartfelt thanks
for your friendship and guidance.

Acknowledgments

Much of the tradecraft in *The Protector* has not appeared in fiction before. I learned it from a great many people who have firsthand experience in the high-risk activities depicted here and who were kind enough to teach me. The tactical uses of duct tape, lead fishing sinkers, chamois car-washing cloths, and partially serrated shotgun shells are only a few of the things I was taught. My thanks to the following:

Linton Jordahl, former U.S. marshal. The U.S. Marshals Service ranks with the Secret Service and the Diplomatic Security Service as one of the premier protective units of the United States government.

Don Rosche and Bruce Reichel of the Bill Scott Raceway's Executive Security Driver Training course. Various U.S. government agencies, including the Diplomatic Security Service, send their personnel to BSR to learn defensive and offensive antiterrorist driving techniques. Rather than provide a recipe for committing felonies, I left out a small but important step in hot-wiring vehicles.

Lt. Dave Spaulding of Ohio's Montgomery County Sheriff's Department. Lieutenant Spaulding's department contributed to the high-level security for the 1995 Dayton (Bosnian) Peace Accords. He is one of America's foremost firearms instructors. See his *Handgun Combatives* and *Defensive Living*, the latter cowritten with retired CIA operations officer Ed Lovette.

Karl Sokol, master gunsmith. Many military and law-enforcement personnel credit their lives to the dependability of a Sokol-modified firearm. The refinements made to "the protector's" Sig Sauer 225 are typical of his craft.

Ernest Emerson. In addition to being one of the best manufacturers of tactical knives (his CQC-7 is featured in this novel), Mr. Emerson is also a top-level blade instructor who works with various elite military and law-enforcement units.

Marcus Wynne, former paratrooper with the Eighty-Second Airborne, former federal air marshal, and first-rate thriller novelist. See his *No Other Option* and *Warrior in the Shadows*. As a young man, Marcus was one of my literature students when I was a professor at the University of Iowa. Years later, he returned the favor and taught me many aspects of the world of high-risk operators.

Dan "Rock" Myers, former member of U.S. Special Operations/military intelligence and former contract officer for the Diplomatic Security Service.

The Protector also features nonlethal tradecraft, and for that, I am grateful to Jake Eagle and the staff of NLP Santa Fe, practitioner trainers in neuro-linguistic programming. Years ago, when I learned that the CIA and other intelligence services, as well as some elite military units, require NLP as part of their training, I took certification classes in it.

In all these matters, if I got the details right, it's because of my teachers. If the details are wrong (always remembering what I said about not supplying recipes for felonies), I'm the one to blame.

David Morrell
Santa Fe, New Mexico

No passion so effectually robs the mind of all its powers of acting and reasoning as fear.
  —Edmund Burke, *On the Sublime and Beautiful*

PROLOGUE

State of Emergency

1

RIOT POLICE DISPEL PROTESTORS

St. Louis, Missouri, April 14 (AP)—What officials feared would be a third day of rioting ended this morning when two thousand armor-clad policemen used batons, pepper spray, and tear gas to dispel ten thousand protestors. The riots disrupting the World Trade Organization conference here had turned downtown St. Louis into what amounted to a war zone, with damage from fires and vandalism estimated at $15 million.

The protestors claim that WTO ignores environmental and labor abuses in undeveloped countries. Although similar demonstrations in Seattle four years earlier had alerted St. Louis authorities about what to expect, police still found themselves overwhelmed. "We prepared for six months," Police Chief Edward Gaines said at a press conference. "But these anarchists are even more organized than they were in Seattle. Thank God, we finally wore them down."

2

"Anarchists." The think-tank supervisor considered the word. "Nicely chosen."

"Al suggested the police chief include it in his statement," the Army general said.

"But the chief has no idea what really happened. A perfectly successful operation," the military analyst said.

Two lieutenant colonels and a tall, sinewy woman filled out the group. The "Al" (short for Alicia) to whom the general had referred wore a khaki pantsuit that resembled a uniform. She sat with the others in a darkly paneled drawing room. Their high-backed chairs were arranged before a large screen, onto which an overhead television projector beamed videotaped images of the crisis.

Highlights from NBC's coverage had just ended. Now a condensed version of CNN's began. The initial sequences showed the first day of rioting. Protestors stretched all the way from Busch Stadium and the Federal Courthouse to the huge America's Center, where the World Trade Organization was holding its conference. By nightfall, downtown St. Louis was paralyzed. On the screen, rioters smashed every window they came to. They overturned vehicles and set fire to them. Flames reflected off sidewalks covered with shattered glass.

The second day's edited sequences showed more protestors cramming the streets, damaging anything they could find. At a press conference, the mayor declared a state of emergency, ordering all civilians to avoid the downtown area.

But on the third day, the outnumbered police, joined by state troopers and the National Guard, organized a counterattack. The screen showed them using tear gas to funnel the rioters along Market, Chestnut, and other downtown streets toward Memorial

Park. There, in the green space around the towering Gateway Arch, retreating protestors trampled a tent city they'd erected.

A reporter spoke urgently as a camera in a helicopter peered down on the rioters being pushed beyond the Arch. Protestors threw rocks and bottles at the relentlessly converging policemen. One bottle was filled with liquid and had a rag stuffed into it. As a young man lit and threw it, the camera whipped to show it crashing into flames. Gas masks, helmets, shields, and body armor made the police resemble "an army of Robocops," the reporter breathlessly announced. Ignoring the burning gasoline and the rocks, the police fired tear-gas canisters. So much haze spewed around the rioters, they could barely be seen.

A camera on a Mississippi barge now showed the action. The rioters stumbled from the haze. Bent over, coughing, they looked as frightened as they'd looked angry moments earlier. Police in gas masks emerged, pounding with batons, pushing with shields. Coughing harder, the protestors panicked and lurched in the only unimpeded direction available: the Mississippi. Thousands tumbled into the river, struggling to stay afloat as the dark figures of the police reached the bank and stood guard.

"I'm sure you noticed the man who threw the Molotov cocktail," the general said. "Some liberal commentators are claiming he's part of a group of agitators. The theory is that the corporations whose policies are under attack paid thugs to instigate the violence. The police fought back, and the legitimate protestors had to defend themselves, eventually becoming rioters and discrediting their cause."

"A conspiracy theory." The think-tank supervisor sighed. "There always has to be a conspiracy theory. But in this case, they happen to be correct. It's just not the conspiracy they imagine."

The general nodded. "And it was right there on television for everyone to see. On every network. As plain as day. But nobody noticed."

"As I said"—the military analyst made a congratulatory gesture to the four men and the woman seated near him—"a perfectly successful operation."

3

ARMY RANGERS DIE ON TRAINING MISSION

CAMP RUDDER, Florida, April 24 (AP)—The commander of Camp Rudder, headquarters for the Army Sixth Ranger Training Battalion, confirmed that fifteen Army Rangers had drowned in a swamp two nights earlier while on a training exercise. The announcement had been delayed, he said, so that family members could be notified.

"We're still trying to determine what happened," Lt. Col. Robert Boland said. "We train in that area all the time, but we almost never have problems. Granted, last night was unusually cold for this time of year, and recent rains had made the water unusually high. But these men were Rangers. At this stage in their training, they'd already been taught to endure much more difficult conditions. All we know is they didn't make radio contact when they were supposed to."

4

The swamp is my friend, Braddock insisted to himself.

Holding his M-16 above his head, wading through the cold chest-high water, pulling his combat boots out of muck, he repeated the mantra his survival instructors had drilled into him long ago when he'd joined the Rangers.

The swamp is my friend.

A lot had happened since then. Braddock had been through combat in Grenada, Panama, Iraq, Afghanistan, and in numerous unpublicized missions, often in jungles. Now *he* was an instructor, and as he slogged through the darkness, leaning slightly forward to compensate for his sixty-pound pack, he hoped that every man in his squad had made "The swamp is my friend" their mantra, as well.

The alligators are my friends.

The snakes are my friends

Don't think.

Just repeat it and believe it.

Ignoring what felt like a sunken log that shifted under him, nearly causing him to lose his balance, Braddock focused on those words to live by, hoping that his men would also.

They'd been in the swamp for three hours, with another two to go. You're more than halfway through, Braddock wanted to assure them, but he couldn't. This exercise was being conducted under strict voice silence. Even their radio transmissions every half hour to their companion squad a quarter mile away were voiceless, composed of electronic pulses. As a further deprivation, none of them wore night-vision goggles, on the theory that sophisticated equipment was a luxury they shouldn't rely on.

The darkness is my friend.

This night had been chosen because it didn't have a moon. As a bonus, thick clouds from yesterday's storm lingered, blotting out the stars. Hulks of dead trees loomed in the darkness, gray against black, only the slightest gradations at the lowest end of the light spectrum providing an indication of Braddock's surroundings. Under such sightless conditions, the streaks of green-and-black camouflage grease on their faces might have seemed unnecessary, but Braddock had warned them to plan for every contingency, saying that even on a night mission, camouflage grease was mandatory.

His drenched, cold uniform clung to his legs, hips, and chest. He saw a slight glow ahead as the squad's scout checked a luminous compass and shifted direction, the other men following. Braddock would have to discipline him for that, confine him to barracks, make him run extra miles. I shouldn't have seen the glow from the compass, he thought. A sniper out there would have seen it, too.

Despite the insect repellant Braddock wore, mosquitoes settled on his face, drawing blood, making him itchy. He ignored them. Insects are my friends.

He listened to the ripple of water as his squad waded onward through the barely visible dead trees. His upraised M-16 cramped his arms. The fetid swamp rose to his neck. Under the water, something nudged against his left side. He smelled rotting vegetation.

He shivered.

That troubled him. Accustomed to much worse conditions, Braddock accused himself of starting to lose his edge.

A gray mist drifted over him, a pungent odor beginning to irritate his nostrils. As the water felt colder, he shivered harder. But the numbness in his legs and the tightness in his chest didn't matter. More important things occupied him.

Any second now, Braddock thought.

His sense of timing was perfect. Overhead, flares burst. Haloed by smoke, their harsh light pierced the darkness. Braddock's men stared up in surprise, the descending glares reflecting off the scummy water. Although Braddock had known about the flares, he'd been under orders not to tell his men.

Anticipate.

Don't be surprised by anything.

Part of the point of the exercise was to make Braddock's already-stressed unit feel unexpectedly threatened. At once, three fighter jets streaked over the skeletal trees, their approach so swift that only after the jets passed could they be heard, their thunder deafening. Braddock wore a waterproof electronic location transmitter so that the pilots knew where not to shoot. Ahead, the jets fired rockets and 50-mm tracer bullets into the swamp. Two hundred yards away, the night became alive with explosions and fire.

"Jesus," somebody said.

No! Braddock mentally shouted. *You're not supposed to talk!*

"What the—" somebody else demanded. "Don't they know we're here?"

Braddock surged through the water toward the second man and glared. Shut your mouth, Braddock's eyes said.

Smoke from the flares drifted over them, smelling of cordite and dead things, almost making Braddock gag.

"Christ, those rockets almost hit us," a third man said.

Braddock splashed urgently toward him, glowering him into silence. Damn it, keep control. Obey orders, he wanted to shout.

The water seemed colder. As another soft thing nudged against Braddock's left side, he shivered harder. His heart pounded. His breathing quickened.

"Nobody mentioned anything about *rockets*," a fourth man said, his voice wavering.

Furious, Braddock surged toward *him*, then stopped as the descending flares hissed into the water, spewing more smoke, darkness overcoming everyone. Braddock shivered so hard that his teeth chattered.

At the same time, his stomach felt on fire. Unaccountable fear crept up his torso, cramping his muscles, spreading heat around his heart. His breath came so fast, he couldn't control it. Inhale, one, two, three. Hold it, one, two, three. Exhale, one, two, three. Inhale, one, two, three. Hold it, one, two, three.

But his chest kept heaving, refusing to obey. He didn't understand. After the numerous combat missions he'd been through, this was nothing. The swamp is my friend. The darkness is my friend. *What's happening to me?* he wanted to scream.

One of his men—the toughest of his trainees—*did* scream. "Something bit me!"

No! The man sounded as out of control as a civilian would have been. It didn't make sense.

"A snake!"

A log—or *something*—bumped against Braddock's side.

"An alligator!"

"*Something's under my—*"

Suddenly, one of Braddock's men fired full-auto at the darkness, muzzle flashes illuminating ripples in the water, bullets shredding dead trees, men screaming as they, too, fired at the night. A bullet seared Braddock's right arm. He lost his balance and fell back, greasy water flooding into his mouth and up his nose.

The rattle of the M-16s sounded hollow beneath the surface. Keeping a tight grip on his weapon, Braddock fought against the weight of his pack and struggled upward. As he broke into the air, desperate to breathe, the multiple gunfire suddenly became loud enough to make his ears ring. Smoke and the smell of cordite swirled around him.

Muzzle flashes blinding him, he shouted, "Cease fire! Cease fire!" He barely recognized his voice, so severely had fear seized his throat, making his normally husky tone a shriek.

A bullet struck his left shoulder, slamming him backward into the water. Fangs seemed to pierce his neck. *No! The swamp is my friend! The alligators, the—*

When he scrambled upward again, resurfacing into the panic of screams and gunfire, a bullet blew the back of his head away.

PART ONE

Threat Assessment

1

Shoes and watches. Cavanaugh had learned a long time ago that one of the secrets of being a capable protective agent was to pay attention to shoes and watches. Loafers, for example. Somebody wearing them was unlikely to be a trained kidnapper or assassin because an experienced runner-and-gunner knew how easy it was to lose loafers in a chase or a fight. Only boots or lace-up shoes were acceptable. Thin soles were a further indication that someone was unlikely to be a serious threat, thick soles being mandatory in a fight. Of course, somebody wearing loafers or thin-soled shoes could still be a threat, but at least Cavanaugh would know he was dealing with an amateur.

Similarly, watches told Cavanaugh a lot. Many operators trained in the 1970s and '80s wore either Rolex diver's watches or Rolex pilot's watches. The rationale was twofold. First, those watches had a reputation for functioning under rugged conditions, an essential requirement for a runner-and-gunner. Second, in an emergency, a Rolex became portable wealth, easily sold for cash.

Not that everyone wearing a Rolex aroused Cavanaugh's suspicions. They had to be in their forties or older, fitting the age profile of someone who'd been trained during the seventies and eighties. Also, operators from that era tended to prefer sneakers, jeans, T-shirts, and windbreakers (often leather) for their casual street clothes. The windbreaker would be loose, capable of concealing a handgun. To the untutored eye, someone who fit that description wouldn't seem unusual, but to Cavanaugh, that person caused concern.

Operators trained in the 1990s and afterward had a different profile. They were younger, of course, and the watch they preferred was cheap and anonymous but capable of taking a beating, the sort of rubber-coated diver's watch that had a timer function and could be bought in any decent sporting-goods store. They preferred hiking boots (tough, thick soles), loose-fitting camping pants with baggy pockets (to conceal a weapon), a loose pullover (to conceal a weapon), and a fanny pack (to conceal a weapon). Given the poor fashion sense of most people on the street, anyone who matched this profile didn't stand out, except to a protective agent like Cavanaugh, who instantly placed them under suspicion.

Watches. So much could be revealed by them. Cavanaugh had once been on a protective detail in Istanbul. His assignment had been to help provide security for an American billionaire who had gone to Istanbul to negotiate a corporate merger, despite threats against the man's life because of his much-publicized financial support of Israel. Before the billionaire's jet arrived at Istanbul's airport, Cavanaugh had checked the busy concourse and the area outside. The variety of clothes that the crowd wore—traditional Arab robes as well as numerous types of Western dress—made it hard to find a telltale common denominator. But watches, Cavanaugh knew, seldom lied. When he noticed half a dozen men in their thirties who wore dissimilar but baggy clothes, who appeared not to have anything to do with one another but who all had similar thick-soled shoes and the same type of sturdy black rubber-coated athlete's watch, alarms went off inside him, warning him that he had to find another way to get his client out of the airport.

It wasn't something Cavanaugh did consciously. It was his reflexive way of seeing the world, much as the legendary security expert Col. Jeff Cooper advised everyone to maintain a state of vigilance that Cooper called "Condition Yellow" (White being the average person's lack of awareness, Orange being intense alertness in response to danger, and Red being a fight for one's life).

In Condition Yellow, then, observing shoes, watches, and other indicators, Cavanaugh got out of a taxi at Columbus Circle and walked into Central Park. The time was around two in the afternoon. The route he took through the trees avoided paths and was intended to let him know if he was being followed. He exited at West Seventieth Street and crisscrossed blocks at random, heading south, eventually climbing the steps from Columbus Avenue and starting across the huge open area in front of Lincoln Center.

One benefit of this cautious frame of mind was that it kept him solidly in the moment, appreciative of each second, not only aware of the crowd that was typically in front of Lincoln Center but also aware of the unusually clear sky, of the pleasant feel of the sun on this splendid May afternoon. He crossed to the famous fountain, sat with his back to it, and considered what was going on around him. Two young men threw a Frisbee back and forth. Students, presumably from nearby Juilliard, sat on benches, reading textbooks. Busy-looking people crossed back and forth from the various buildings. Couples chatted. Turning, Cavanaugh saw a businessman sitting behind him on the edge of the fountain. The man had a briefcase in his lap and glanced at his watch.

Out of habit, Cavanaugh shifted so he could pay closer attention. The man was in his thirties, of medium height and weight, with short dark hair. Any number of businessmen fit that profile. His black suit looked expensive and fit him perfectly. No place to hide a weapon. The man's black briefcase also looked expensive and was shiny enough to be brand-new. When the man crossed his legs, Cavanaugh was able to study one of his shoes. A sturdy black Oxford, so new that the sole was barely scraped. And as for the watch . . .

Cavanaugh didn't mind that it was one of those shiny types with all sorts of dials and buttons. True, a certain level of businessman preferred to be unostentatious, but others liked to indulge themselves with gadgets, and a watch capable of being a timer while it also indicated the hour, minute, and second in two different time zones could be amusing for a certain type of mind. No, what bothered Cavanaugh was that the watch was so thick, the shirtsleeve around it had to be unbuttoned, looking sloppy in contrast to the man's otherwise-impeccable appearance.

The man checked his watch again, then directed his attention to the left, toward the entrance to Avery Fisher Hall, one of the buildings in the complex.

At that moment, Cavanaugh sensed someone coming toward him and peered up at a tall, slender man who had a slight mustache and a wide-brimmed hat that Cavanaugh knew hid thinning gray hair. Although the man was in his fifties, he exuded the wiry strength of someone much younger. His shoes were so polished that they reflected the movement of people walking past. His gray pinstriped suit gave the impression of a uniform. His white shirt was heavily starched. The only colors were the red and blue of his tie, which didn't relieve his pallor.

"Duncan." Cavanaugh smiled and shook hands with him. "You look pasty. You need to get outside more."

"Bad for my health." The brim of Duncan's hat cast his face in shadow. His last name was Wentworth, and because he'd spent much of his life outdoors as a member of Special Forces and later as the head instructor for Delta Force, he'd had three operations for serious skin cancer. "You're far too tan. Put on more sunblock."

"Yeah, the ozone layer's getting thinner. One more thing to

worry about." Cavanaugh glanced again toward the man in the black suit sitting behind him on the edge of the fountain. "Anyway, it's too nice a day to be indoors. I figured since you were supervising the new security arrangements at Lincoln Center, we could meet here instead of at your office." He referred to the Madison Avenue headquarters for Global Protective Services, a security agency Duncan had established when he'd left Delta Force. After only five years, the agency had branches in London, Paris, Rome, and Hong Kong, with another soon to open in Tokyo. Its reputation had spread because of the quality of the protective agents Duncan hired, all of them having been special-operations personnel, many of them Duncan's former students.

"How are your injuries?" Duncan asked.

"Healed."

"The ambassador sends his regards."

"He's very lucky."

"Yes. To have had somebody as good as you running interference for him."

Cavanaugh couldn't resist grinning. "Anytime you start buttering me up, it means you want something."

Duncan gave him a "guilty as charged" look. "Do you think you're ready to go back to work?"

Taking another glance over his shoulder, Cavanaugh noticed that the man in the black suit looked more intense as he checked his watch yet again and continued staring toward Avery Fisher Hall. The open cuff around the thick watch became more bothersome.

At once, the man saw something that made him sit rigidly. With the briefcase on his lap, he placed his hands on the buttons that would open it.

"Excuse me a minute," Cavanaugh said to Duncan. He stood and rounded the fountain, following the man's gaze toward Avery Fisher Hall and a red-haired woman who had just stepped out. In her thirties, well dressed and pleasant-looking, she was with a man, whom she gave a "see you later" kiss on the cheek. Then she started across the open area. In ten seconds, she would pass through the crowd and be close to where the man in the black suit sat staring at her.

Cavanaugh came up on his blind side as the man opened the briefcase just enough to reach inside it.

The woman came closer and glanced in the man's direction, amazing Cavanaugh, inasmuch as most people never noticed anything around them. She froze as the man dropped the briefcase, revealing a pistol in his hand.

Several things happened almost at once. The woman screamed, the man moved toward her, and Cavanaugh darted behind him, shoving his arm into the air. He wrenched the pistol from the man's hand, dragged him backward, tipped him into the fountain, and pressed his head underwater.

Duncan came over to him. "Yes, you're certainly feeling better."

"Are you just going to stand there enjoying yourself, or would you mind calling a cop?"

Duncan pulled out a cell phone. "Don't you think you should let him breathe?"

"Not really, but I guess we'll never hear his story otherwise."

"She told him she wanted a divorce—something like that—and he couldn't take the rejection, of course," Duncan said.

"Of course. But I want to know why he dressed up. He doesn't normally wear a suit. You can tell, because his watch is too big for the cuff on a dress shirt."

"If you don't let him breathe pretty soon, you'll never know."

"Spoilsport." Cavanaugh pulled the man's face from the water, watched him splutter, and demanded to know about the suit.

With a little more submersion, the man was persuaded to explain. After shooting his wife, who had indeed asked for a divorce and who'd been going to meet him at her lawyer's office, he had planned to shoot himself. The black suit, like the shoes, was new. He had left instructions that they were to be his burial clothes.

"Just when you think you've heard everything," Cavanaugh said.

But there was more. The man had kept checking his watch because he'd known when to expect his wife to leave work and go to her appointment with her attorney. One of the three dials on his watch indicated the current time. Another dial showed the amount of time that had elapsed since she'd told him she wanted a divorce; a third counted down the remaining seconds that she'd had to live.

Cavanaugh shoved the man's head underwater again.

"So what do you think?" Duncan asked.

"About?"

"Are you ready for another assignment?"

2

The Warwick Hotel had recently been renovated, but its marble and dark wood lobby still evoked the tradition and character of a Manhattan landmark. Cavanaugh turned left and entered the hotel's quiet bar, where an attractive woman with green eyes and an intriguing expression sat at a corner table. He approved of her choice of location—her back to an inside wall, away from the bar's numerous windows—although if he'd believed she was in any danger, he wouldn't have let her appear in public in the first place.

Her name was Jamie Travers, and until recently, she had lived in seclusion with him at his ranch in the mountains near Jackson Hole, Wyoming, from where he had periodically set out on security assignments, taking care that her weapons training was up-to-date and that colleagues in need of R and R were there to watch over her when he had to go away. Two years earlier, she had testified about a gangland killing she'd witnessed. The mob boss who'd gone to prison had put out a contract against her. Twice, despite police protection, she'd nearly been killed, prompting Cavanaugh, who admired her determination, to step in and arrange for her to disappear. The contract had finally ended when the man who'd ordered it choked to death while eating spaghetti and meatballs in a federal prison. Despite the seeming innocence of the mob boss's death, Jamie had been convinced that Cavanaugh had had something to do with it, but he continued to deny any involvement, even though he had once told her that the only way to stop the mob boss from being a threat was to kill him. "Kismet" was all Cavanaugh would say about the supposed accident. Shortly afterward, they had married. Now they continued to base their lives in Wyoming, but for its beauty, not its seclusion.

Shoulder-long glossy brunette hair made the beige pantsuit and the emerald blouse she wore perfect choices. Admiring his wife, he moved a chair so that he could sit in the corner with her. The location allowed him to survey both entrances to the room as well as the pedestrians passing the windows along Fifty-fourth Street and the Avenue of the Americas.

"What are you drinking?" he asked.

"Perrier and lime."

He tasted it, savoring the lime. "How was your afternoon? Enjoying being a tourist?"

"Love it. I haven't been to the Museum of Modern Art in so long. It was like seeing an old friend. And how was *your* afternoon?"

He told her.

"You accepted another assignment?" Jamie looked surprised.

"We planned to fly home the day after tomorrow, so this won't interfere with much, especially since you're seeing your mother again tomorrow. I didn't think you'd mind going home ahead of me. I'll join you in a week."

"But you're barely healed from the last job you did."

"This one's easy."

"That's what you said the last time."

"And the money's good."

"I've got more than enough money for both of us," Jamie said.

Cavanaugh nodded. His protective agent's income allowed them to stay at the Warwick, which was comfortable without being palatial. But if they'd used Jamie's money, which came from the sale of a promising dot-com company she'd founded during the Internet frenzy of the 1990s, they'd have stayed in a master suite at the Plaza or, at the very least, the St. Regis.

"Why don't you let me take care of you?" she asked.

"Foolish male pride."

"You said it. *I* didn't."

He shrugged. "People need protecting."

"And that's what you do. I shouldn't have bothered asking." She hooked an arm around one of his. "So what makes *this* job easy?"

"The client doesn't want anybody to shield him."

"Oh?" Jamie looked surprised again. "What *does* he want?"

"The same as *you* did. To disappear."

3

Cavanaugh got out of the car, a two-year-old Ford Taurus that Global Protective Services had supplied. Apart from its special modifications, including a race-car engine and a suspension to match, it had been chosen because its dusty gray color and ubiquitous design made it so nondescript, it was almost invisible among other sedans. Sunday afternoon, however, it was the only vehicle in this abandoned industrial area of Newark, New Jersey. He scanned the graffiti-covered warehouse: a sprawling three-story structure that had most of its windows smashed. Rust-streaked doors hung open, revealing what at first appeared to be garbage but turned out to be a city of homeless people. As far as was visible into the building, battered cardboard boxes provided shelter. Black plastic bags held whatever possessions the inhabitants treasured.

Dark clouds cast a cold shadow. On the river behind the warehouse, boat engines droned. A tug blew its horn. Thunder rumbled. Cavanaugh pressed his right elbow reassuringly against the 9-mm handgun holstered on the belt beneath his jacket. The Sig Sauer 225 held eight rounds in the magazine and one in the firing chamber. Not a massive amount of firepower, not the sixteen rounds that a Beretta was capable of holding, but he'd found that a pistol containing that much ammunition was slightly large for his hand, affecting the accuracy of his aim, nine well-placed shots being better than sixteen that went astray because of a poor grip. Plus, as the federal air marshals had decided in the late 1980s, the Sig Sauer 225's lighter weight and thin, compact design made it an ideal concealed carry weapon. But just in case, he had two other eight-round magazines in a pouch on the left side of his belt, beneath his jacket.

A chill wind strengthened, redolent of approaching rain. At the gaping entrances to the warehouse, a few grizzled faces squinted out.

Cavanaugh took his cell phone from his jacket and pressed the "good for today only" numbers Duncan had given to him.

As the phone rang on the other end, more grizzled faces appeared, some apprehensive, others assessing.

On the other end, the phone rang a second time.

"Yes?" a man's trembly voice asked, sounding like he was in an echo chamber.

Cavanaugh supplied his half of the recognition sequence. "I didn't realize the warehouse was closed."

"Ten years ago," came the other half of the sequence, the voice continuing to sound unsteady. "Your name is . . ."

"Cavanaugh. And yours is . . ."

"Daniel Prescott. Daniel. Not Dan."

This exchange, too, was part of the sequence.

More haggard faces studied him, an army of rags trying to decide if the newcomer was an enemy, a benefactor, or a target.

Isolated drops of rain struck the greasy pavement.

"Global Protective Services has a reputation for being the best," the voice said. "I expected a fancier car."

"One of the reasons we're the best is we don't attract attention to ourselves and, more important, to our clients."

Heavier drops struck the pavement.

"I assume you can see me," Cavanaugh said. "As you wanted, I came alone."

"Open the car doors."

Cavanaugh did.

"Open the trunk."

He did that, too. The man evidently had a vantage point that allowed him to look into the vehicle.

The dark clouds thickened. A few more drops of rain struck around him.

Cavanaugh heard faint echoing metallic noises on the phone. "Hello?"

No response.

"Hello?" he asked again.

More faint echoing metallic noises.

Thunder rumbled closer.

A few derelicts stepped from the warehouse. Like the others, they were scruffy and beard-stubbled, but the desperation in their eyes contrasted with the blankness and resignation Cavanaugh sensed in the others. Crack addicts, he assumed, so overdue for a fix that they'd try taking on a stranger who was unwise enough to visit hell. "Hey, I came here to help you," he said into the phone, "not to get soaked."

More metallic noises.

"I think we both made a mistake." He shut the trunk and the

passenger doors. About to get into the car, he heard the trembly voice say:

"Ahead of you. On the left. You see the door?"

"Yes."

It was the only door still intact. Closed.

"Come in," the unsteady voice said.

Cavanaugh got behind the steering wheel.

"I said, 'Come in,' " the voice insisted.

"After I move the vehicle."

He drove along the cracked concrete parking area. Near the door, he turned the car in a half circle, facing it in the direction from which he'd come, ready to leave in a hurry if he needed to.

"Entering," he said into his phone.

He got out of the car, locked it with his remote control, and sprinted through the drizzle. Sensing movement with his peripheral vision, he glanced to his left along the warehouse, toward where more crack addicts stepped into the increasing rain and watched him. Wary of what might be behind the door (more crack addicts?), he put his phone into his jacket and did something that he hadn't planned: drew his pistol. As he turned the knob, he noted that although the lock was coated with grit, there was a hint of shininess underneath—the lock was new. But it wasn't engaged. Pulling the heavy, creaking door open, he ducked inside.

4

As swiftly as the door's protesting hinges allowed, Cavanaugh closed it. No longer a silhouette, he shifted toward the deepest shadows and took account of where he was. At the bottom of a dusty concrete stairwell, metal steps led up. Cobwebs dangled from the railing. On the left, a motor rumbled behind an elevator door. The place smelled of must and gave off a chill.

Aiming his pistol toward the stairs and then toward the elevator, he reached behind him to turn the latch on the sturdy lock and secure the door. But before he could touch it, the lock's bolt rammed home, triggered electronically from a distance.

He concentrated to control his uneasiness. There wasn't any reason to suspect he was in danger. After all, Duncan had warned him that the potential client, although legitimate, had eccentricities.

Prescott's merely being cautious, Cavanaugh tried to assure himself. *Hell, if he's so nervous about his safety that he feels he needs protection, it's natural he'd make sure the door's locked. He's the one in danger, not me.*

Then why am I holding this gun?

He pulled the phone from his jacket and spoke into it. "Now what?" His voice echoed.

As if in response, the elevator opened, revealing a brightly lit compartment.

Cavanaugh hated elevators—small sealed boxes that could easily become traps. There wasn't any way to know what might be on the other side when the door reopened.

"Thanks," he said into the phone, "but I need some exercise. I'll take the stairs."

As his eyes adjusted to the shadows, he noticed a surveillance camera mounted discreetly under the stairs, facing the door. "I was told you wanted to disappear. It seems to me you've already done that."

"Not enough," the unsteady voice said. This time, it came not from the phone but from a speaker hidden in the wall.

Cavanaugh put away his phone. A vague pungent smell pinched his nostrils, as if something had died nearby. His pulse quickened.

No matter how softly he placed his shoes, the metal stairs echoed loudly as he climbed.

He came to a landing and shifted higher. The pungent smell became a little more noticeable. His stomach fidgeted as he faced a solid metal door. Hesitating, he reached for it.

"Not that one," the voice said from the wall.

Nerves inexplicably more on edge, Cavanaugh climbed higher and came to a door halfway up the stairs.

"Not that one, either," the voice said. "Incidentally, am I supposed to feel reassured that you're coming with a gun?"

"I don't know about you, but under the circumstances, it does a world of good for *me*."

The voice made a sound that might have been a bitter chuckle.

Heavy rain hit the building, sending vibrations through it.

At the top, a final door awaited. It was open, inviting Cavanaugh into a brightly lit corridor, which had a closed door at the other end.

This is the same as stepping into an elevator, he decided. The pungent smell seemed a little stronger. His muscles tightening, he didn't understand what was happening to him. A visceral part of him warned him to leave the building. Abruptly, he wondered if he *could* leave the building. Even though he always carried lock picks in his jacket's collar, he had the suspicion that they wouldn't be enough to open the downstairs door. Breathing slightly faster, he had to keep telling himself that *he* wasn't the one in danger—Prescott was, which explained what Cavanaugh hoped were merely security precautions and not a trap that had been set for him.

He glanced up at a security camera in the corridor he was expected to enter. To hell with it, he thought, annoyed by the nervous moisture on his palms. If Prescott wanted me dead, he could have killed me before now. Regardless of the insistent pounding of his heart, a strong intuition told Cavanaugh to surrender to the situation. Something else told him to run, which made no sense, inasmuch as he didn't have a reason to believe he was in danger.

Impatient with himself, he came to a firm decision and holstered his weapon. *It's not going to do me any good in that corridor anyhow.*

Entering, he wasn't surprised that the door swung shut behind him, locking loudly.

After the gloom of the stairwell, the lights hurt his eyes, but at least the pungent smell was gone. Managing to feel less on edge, he walked to the door at the end of the corridor, turned the knob, pushed the door open, and found himself in a bright room filled with closed-circuit television monitors and electronic consoles. Across from him, bricks covered a window.

What captured his attention, however, was an overweight man in his forties who stood among the glowing equipment. The man wore wrinkled slacks and an equally wrinkled white shirt that had sweat marks and clung to his ample stomach. His thick sandy hair was uncombed. He needed a shave. The skin under his eyes was puffy from lack of sleep. The dark pupils of his eyes were large from tension.

The man aimed a Colt .45 semiautomatic pistol at him. Its barrel wavered.

Cavanaugh had no doubt that if he had still been holding his pistol when he'd entered, the man would have fired. Doing his best to keep his breathing steady, he raised his hands in reassuring submission. Despite the big gun that was nervously aimed at him, the uneasiness Cavanaugh had felt coming up the stairs seemed of no importance compared to what *this* man must be feeling, for, outside of combat, Prescott was the most frightened man Cavanaugh had ever seen.

5

"Please remember you sent for me," Cavanaugh said. "I'm here to help you."

As Prescott continued to aim the Colt, his pupils got larger. The room became more sour with fear.

"I knew your one-time-only phone number and the recognition code," Cavanaugh said. "Only someone from Protective Services could have had that information."

"You could have forced those details from the person they were sending," Prescott said. As on the phone, his voice was unsteady, but now Cavanaugh understood that it wasn't an electronic effect—Prescott's voice shook because he was afraid.

The door behind Cavanaugh swung shut, its lock ramming electronically home. He managed not to flinch. "I don't know who or what you feel threatened by, but I hardly think one man coming here would be the smartest way to get at you, not the way you've got this place set up. Logic should tell you I'm not a threat."

"The unexpected is the most brilliant tactic." Prescott's grip on the .45 was as unsteady as his voice. "Besides, your logic works against you. If one man isn't much of a threat, how can one man provide adequate protection?"

"You didn't say you wanted protection. You said you wanted to *disappear.*"

Sweat marks spreading under his arms, Prescott studied Cavanaugh warily.

"My initial interviews are *always* one-on-one," Cavanaugh said. "I have to ask questions to assess the threat level. Then I decide how much help the job requires."

"I was told you used to be in Delta Force." Prescott licked his dry, fleshy lips.

"That's right."

The classic special-operations physique involved muscular shoulders that trimmed down to solid, compact hips, upper-body strength being one of the goals of the arduous training.

"Lots of exercise," Prescott said. "Is that what you think qualifies you to protect somebody?"

Trying to put Prescott at ease, Cavanaugh chuckled. "You want my job stats?"

"If you want to convince me you're here to help. If you want to work for me."

"You've got this turned around. When I interview potential clients, it's not because I want to work for them. Sometimes, I *don't* want to work for them."

"You mean you have to *like* them?" Prescott asked with distaste.

"Sometimes, I don't like them, either," Cavanaugh said. "But that doesn't mean they don't have a right to live. I'm a protector, not a judge. With exceptions. No drug traffickers. No child abusers. Nobody who's an obvious monster. Are you a monster?"

Prescott had a look of incredulity. "Of course not."

"Then there's only one other standard that'll help me decide if I want to protect you."

"Which is?"

"Are you willing to be compliant?"

Prescott blinked sweat from his eyes. "What?"

"I can't protect someone who won't take orders," Cavanaugh said. "That's the paradox of being a protector. Someone hires me. In theory, that person's the boss. But when it comes to protection, *I'm* the one who gives the orders. The employer has to react to me as if *I'm* the boss. Are you willing to be compliant?"

"Anything to keep me alive."

"You'll do what I say?"

Prescott thought and then fearfully nodded.

"So, okay, here's your first order: Put that damned gun away before I ram it down your throat."

Prescott blinked several times, stepping back as if Cavanaugh had slapped him. He held the gun steadier, frowned, and slowly lowered it.

"An excellent start," Cavanaugh said.

"If you're not who you say you are, do it right now," Prescott said. "Kill me. I can't stand living this way."

"Relax. Whoever your enemies are, I'm not one of them."

Cavanaugh surveyed the room. To the right, in a corner, past the electronics and the monitors, he saw a cot, a minifridge, a sink, and a small stove. Beyond was a toilet, a showerhead, and a drain. The type of food on the shelves made clear that Prescott didn't worry about being overweight: boxes of macaroni and cheese, cans of ravioli and lasagna, bags of chocolates, candy bars, and potato chips, cases of classic Coke. "How long have you been here?"

"Three weeks."

Cavanaugh noticed books on a shelf below the food. Most were nonfiction, on subjects as various as geology and photography. One had a photo of a naked woman on the cover and seemed to be a sex book. In contrast, another volume was *The Collected Poems of Robinson Jeffers*, with a few books about Jeffers next to it. "You like poetry?" Cavanaugh asked.

"Soothes the soul." Prescott's tone was slightly defensive, as if he suspected that Cavanaugh might be mocking him.

Cavanaugh picked up the book and opened it, reading the first lines he came to. " 'I built her a tower when I was young— Sometime she will die.' "

Prescott looked more defensive.

"Knows how to grab my attention." Cavanaugh set down the book and continued scanning the place. Videotapes sat next to a small television. Prescott's taste had no consistency: a Clint Eastwood thriller, an old Troy Donahue–Sandra Dee teenage-romance tearjerker. . . .

"I've seen worse places to go to ground." Cavanaugh thought about it. "Homeless people and crack addicts as your cover. Smart. How'd you know about this warehouse? How'd you set up this room?"

"I did it a year ago," Prescott said.

"Whatever your trouble is, you saw it coming?"

"Not this particular trouble."

"Then why did you . . ."

"I always take precautions," Prescott said.

"You're not making sense."

"In case," Prescott told him.

"In case of what?" Movement on a TV monitor abruptly caught Cavanaugh's attention. "Wait a second."

6

"What's wrong?" Prescott spun toward the monitor.

On the screen, a gray image showed a dozen ragged men plodding through the rain, converging on the Taurus.

"Jesus," Prescott said.

"Crack addicts are amazing," Cavanaugh said. "No matter what it is, if it's left alone, they'll try to steal it. I once knew a guy who stole forty pounds of dog food from his father so he could buy crack. What's *more* amazing, his drug dealer took the dog food, rather than demanding money. For all I know, the drug dealer ate it."

On the screen, the ragged men, drenched with rain, tugged at the side-view mirrors or used chunks of metal to pry at the hubcaps.

"Have you got a way to hear what's going on outside?" Cavanaugh asked.

Prescott flipped a switch on a console. Immediately, the sound of rain came through an audio speaker.

Cavanaugh heard the distant scrape of metal as the ragged

men worked in the downpour to try to disassemble his car. "Get a job, guys."

He took the car's remote control from his jacket pocket. It was more elaborate than usual, equipped with half a dozen buttons.

Prescott looked puzzled as Cavanaugh pressed one of the buttons.

Suddenly, the audio speaker filled the room with an ear-torturing siren that came from the Taurus and made the men drop their makeshift burglary tools, fleeing like drenched versions of the scarecrow in *The Wizard of Oz.*

Cavanaugh pressed the button again, and the siren stopped.

"Are you ready to get out of here?" he asked Prescott.

"To?" Prescott looked apprehensive.

"Somewhere safer than this, although, Lord knows, this place is safe enough. After my team arrives, after we get organized, we'll give you a new identity and relocate you. But first I need to know what kind of risk level we're talking about. Why are you so frightened?"

Prescott opened his mouth to answer, then frowned at the monitor.

Four of the men were back, heading for the Taurus.

"At least they get points for persistence," Cavanaugh said.

He pressed another button on the remote control.

Gray vapor spewed from under the wheel wells. Despite the rain, it blossomed, enveloping the crack addicts. Coughing and cursing, they stumbled back. Bent over as if they were going to be sick, they pawed at their eyes and staggered away.

Cavanaugh pressed the button again, and the vapor stopped spewing from the wheel wells.

"What on earth was *that*?" Prescott asked.

"Tear gas."

"What?"

"The car's modified the way the best Secret Service vehicles are. It's armor-plated and—" A new image on the monitor made him stop. "Amazing. With their ambition, if these guys were in politics, they could run the world."

On the screen, two more crack addicts approached the Taurus.

"Turn down the volume on that speaker," Cavanaugh told Prescott.

Confused, Prescott did what he was told.

As the men came closer to the Taurus, Cavanaugh pressed another button on the remote control.

Small black canisters catapulted from under the wheel wells. Shaped like miniature soup cans, they exploded with numerous roars that shook the speaker, even though its volume had been reduced. The multiple flashes of the explosions were so bright that the camera had trouble maintaining its contrast level.

When the smoke cleared, the two crack addicts lay on the concrete.

"My God, you killed them," Prescott said.

"No."

"But they were so close to the grenades."

"Those weren't grenades."

On the screen, the two men began to squirm.

"I used flash-bangs," Cavanaugh said.

"Flash-bangs?"

"Sort of like grenades, except they don't throw shrapnel. But they blind and deafen for a while. Those guys are going to have a whale of a headache."

On the screen, the two crack addicts struggled upright, holding their ears.

"But this car *can* be equipped to launch grenades if the mission calls for it," Cavanaugh said. "And it can be modified for machine guns under the headlights. All the best dictators and drug lords have those extras. In a more luxurious car than a Taurus, of course. Believe me, Mr. Prescott, we can take care of you."

Cavanaugh looked back at the row of monitors, where one of the images showed the Taurus at ground level. Able to see partway under the car, he frowned, noticing what appeared to be a shadow under the vehicle. He pointed. "Does that camera have a zoom lens?"

"All of them do." Prescott twisted a dial, enlarging the image on the monitor. The shadow under the Taurus took the shape of a small box. Jesus, Cavanaugh thought, one of the crack addicts must have put it under there.

He blinked as the Taurus exploded.

7

The roar from the speaker was so loud that the entire room shook. On the screen, chunks of the Taurus crashed onto the concrete, smoke and fire swelling.

Prescott gaped.

A second explosion rocked the room. On a different monitor, the door through which Cavanaugh had entered the building blasted inward, smoke and flames filling the area at the bottom of the stairs. Three men rushed in, but although their hair was matted and their faces were beard-stubbled and filthy, their eyes had neither the blankness of the homeless nor the desperation of drug addicts. These men had eyes as alert as any gunfighter Cavanaugh had ever encountered.

"Is there another way out of here?"

Prescott kept staring at the screen, which showed one of the men aiming a pistol at the elevator door while the other two aimed pistols upward and stormed the stairs.

"Prescott?" Cavanaugh repeated, drawing his weapon.

Prescott kept staring at the screen.

Cavanaugh grabbed him, turned him, and shook him, "For Christ's sake, listen to me. Is there another way out of here?"

Instead of responding, Prescott lunged toward one of the electronic consoles and twisted a dial.

"*What are you doing?*" Cavanaugh asked.

Prescott stared toward a different screen.

The two men came into view on an upper portion of the stairs. They stopped and aimed upward, looking as if they thought getting in had been too easy, that there had to be traps in the building.

On the monitor that showed the entrance to the building, two other ragged men charged in through the fading smoke from the explosion. They, too, aimed pistols.

They started up the stairs, then paused as had the pair above them. Wary, they glanced behind and below them, seeming to sense danger.

"*Have you got the stairwell booby-trapped, is that it?*" Cavanaugh asked Prescott.

But on the screen, nothing exploded in the stairwell. No hidden guns went off. No flames erupted from the walls. Even so, the gunmen were obviously disturbed about something. Various monitors showed the man watching the elevator, the two that had just paused on the stairs, and the pair halfway up, who stared apprehensively toward the top as if they knew they were walking into a death trap.

Moisture dripped from their faces. At first, Cavanaugh thought it was from the rain they'd charged through.

Then he realized it was sweat.

One of the gunmen on the stairs suddenly started firing toward the upper level.

Abruptly, the other gunmen on the stairs did the same. At the bottom, the ragged figure watching the elevator kept looking behind him, as if he'd heard a threatening sound. He spun toward the blown-apart door and fired toward the rain.

"What the hell's gong on?" Cavanaugh asked.

Prescott kept twisting the dial, mumbling to himself, as if

something had malfunctioned. "*Yes.*" He spun toward Cavanaugh. "There's another way out of here."

Puzzled, Cavanaugh watched Prescott hurry toward the shelves of food. Then he frowned again at the monitors, seeing the gunmen continue firing up the stairs. Two furiously reloaded. The other pair spun to aim behind them. The man on the ground floor kept switching his aim between the elevator and the blown-open door.

A noise in the room distracted Cavanaugh, a scrape as Prescott slid the shelves to the left, revealing a door.

"Where does it lead?"

"The warehouse."

Recalling the army of crack addicts he'd seen when he'd arrived, Cavanaugh wondered how much he could count on Prescott to help. "Do you know how to handle that gun you pointed at me?"

"No."

Cavanaugh wasn't surprised. He picked up the .45 and found that Prescott had aimed it with the safety on. Worse, after Cavanaugh freed the safety and pulled back the slide half an inch, he saw that the firing chamber was empty. Releasing the magazine from the grip, he discovered that it did contain the usual seven rounds, however. After he shoved the magazine back into the grip, he racked a round into the firing chamber, ready for business.

"Do you have extra ammunition?"

"No."

Cavanaugh wasn't surprised about that, either. Because the .45 needed to be cocked before it could be fired, he left the hammer back and the safety on, a method preferred by most professionals. After shoving it under his belt, he drew his Sig.

He took one final look at the monitors, where he saw other ragged men rush into the stairwell, aiming pistols. Like the others, they suddenly hesitated, as if threatened by something the cameras didn't show in the stairway.

The image that most caught Cavanaugh's attention, however, was one in the middle, where a beard-stubbled man in grimy clothes stood outside, beyond the wreckage of the Taurus, which was still in flames despite the downpour. Drenched, the man held a metal tube that was about four feet long and looked suspiciously like an antitank rocket launcher.

"*Prescott, is there a way to tell what's behind this door?*"

"The top row of monitors. On the right."

The screen showed nothing but a shadowy metal catwalk.

"Open the door! Get out of the way!"

Wild-eyed, Prescott freed the lock and yanked the door open, veering toward the cover of the wall.

Cavanaugh aimed through the opening but saw nothing except the catwalk he'd observed on the monitor. The suspended metal walkway stretched into the shadows. The warehouse rumbled from the rain.

"Remember what I said about following orders?"

Prescott could barely speak. "Yes."

"Do you have a heart condition? Any serious illnesses that would keep you from moving fast?"

Prescott squeezed out a "No."

"Okay, when I run through this doorway, run after me! Stay close!"

On the middle screen, the drenched, grimy man outside finished arming the antitank rocket launcher. It was short enough that he could easily manage it as he raised it to his shoulder and sighted upward through the rain toward the room's bricked-in window.

"Now!" Cavanaugh said.

Charging through the door, then aiming down toward the shadows below the catwalk, he heard his urgent footsteps on the catwalk's metal. An instant later, he was relieved to hear Prescott's footsteps clattering close behind him.

Then all he heard was a ringing in his ears as the rocket exploded against the side of the building behind him. He felt the concussion, like hands slamming against his back, shoving him forward, and although he couldn't risk distracting himself by looking behind him, he imagined bricks flying into the room, smashing the monitors and electronic consoles.

The shock wave knocked him off balance, sending him sprawling onto the catwalk, his forehead banging against it as Prescott's heavy frame landed on him. The .45 under Cavanaugh's belt gouged into his side. For a moment, his vision turned gray.

The catwalk swayed.

8

Prescott moaned.

The catwalk swung farther out.

Cavanaugh's mind cleared. Inhaling painfully, he tried to squirm from under Prescott's weight. Smoke and dust from the explosion swirled over them.

"Prescott."

The big man coughed.

Cavanaugh felt the force of it. "Are you hurt?"

"Not sure. . . . Don't think so."

The ringing in Cavanaugh's ears made Prescott sound far away, instead of on top of him. "We have to stand."

"The catwalk," Prescott warned.

Its back-and-forth motion made Cavanaugh feel he was in a plane being tossed in a storm. His Delta Force training had conditioned him not to feel off balance or nauseated. But Prescott was another matter. With no experience, he had to be nearly out of his mind with fright.

Pigeons scattered in panic. Rain cascaded from holes in the roof.

"Prescott, I'll take care of you. All you have to do is something simple."

"Simple?" Prescott clung to him as a drowning man does to his rescuer.

"*Very* simple." Cavanaugh imagined the gunmen running up the stairs, about to burst into the room, but he didn't dare communicate his urgency to Prescott.

"What do you want me to do?"

"Lift yourself."

As the catwalk vibrated, Prescott tensed.

"There's nothing to it." Cavanaugh strained to keep his voice calm. "Pretend you're doing a push-up."

Prescott couldn't move.

"Do it," Cavanaugh said. "*Now.*"

Prescott cautiously made an effort at straightening his elbows. An inch. Another inch.

Cavanaugh crawled from under Prescott's bulk. He shoved his handgun into its holster and rose to a crouch, gripping the metal railings as the catwalk shuddered. Now that the dust had lessened, gray light through the broken windows was enough to help his eyes adjust to the shadows. He stared toward the wreckage-filled room they'd escaped from and saw where the catwalk was attached to the wall.

Its corroded bolts were half out.

He wondered how long it would take the gunmen to break into the room.

"Prescott, you're doing fine. Now all you have to do is stand."

"Can't."

The catwalk trembled. Cavanaugh could barely keep his balance. Rain coming through holes in the roof fell around him.

"Then crawl," he said.

"What?"

"Crawl. *Now.*"

He tugged Prescott, inching him forward.

"More. A little faster."

Cavanaugh gave another tug, and Prescott crawled farther along. Water splashed his hand.

"Feel sick," Prescott said.

"Save it for when we get off this thing." Cavanaugh hoped to transport Prescott's mind into a future scenario.

"Off this thing," Prescott murmured.

"That's right. Keep crawling. Faster. We'll soon be at the other door."

Cavanaugh peered through the shadows ahead and saw that the catwalk's bolts were halfway out of the opposite wall, too.

Metal creaked.

From below, a man shouted, "Look! On the catwalk!"

In the room where Prescott had been hiding, an explosion blew away the door through which Cavanaugh had entered. As gunmen charged in, Cavanaugh drew his pistol and fired three times, sending the assault team for cover. He fired three more times, hoping to keep the gunmen down long enough for him and Prescott to reach the opposite door. But as Prescott flinched from the roar of the shots, his sudden movement jerked the catwalk. The bolts popped from the wall they approached.

The catwalk plunged.

9

Rusted metal buckled. The end of the catwalk scraped downward against the wall, tilting, forming a slide, down which Cavanaugh and Prescott struggled not to fall.

"Grab the railing!" Cavanaugh yelled.

For once, Prescott didn't need prompting. Even in the gray

light, it was obvious how white his knuckles were from the force with which he gripped the railing.

Metal protesting, the catwalk tilted lower, more steeply.

"Pretend the railing's a rope!" Cavanaugh ordered. "Climb down hand over hand!"

With a shuddering clang, the end of the catwalk slammed to a halt on the shadowy second floor. The force with which it struck almost yanked Cavanaugh's hands off the railing.

He and Prescott hung at a forty-five-degree angle.

Cavanaugh worried about the gunmen in the room above. He hoped that the shadows made him and Prescott hard to aim at. But what about the man who'd shouted from below?

"Prescott, forget trying to climb down! Dig your heels against the metal and slide!"

Prescott's face was stark.

"Now!" Cavanaugh said. "Watch me!"

He used his shoes as brakes while he slid down on his hips, using his hands on the railing to guide him. Gratified, he heard scrapes behind him as Prescott did his best to follow.

Gunshots reverberated through the warehouse. Bullets from the room they'd left blew chunks from the wall.

At once, Prescott needed no further encouragement. He slid down so rapidly that his shoes bumped against Cavanaugh. In turn, Cavanaugh slid faster, feeling the seat of his pants threaten to tear as Prescott's shoes bumped harder against him, and Cavanaugh slid even faster.

He tumbled onto the wet floor, rolling free just before Prescott slammed to a halt. But before Cavanaugh could check that Prescott was all right, he drew his weapon and crouched, on guard against the man who'd yelled from below the catwalk.

A wall seemed to move. Immediately, Cavanaugh realized it was derelicts cowering in the shadows. He saw huge boxes where they slept and garbage bags filled with God knew what. The stench of urine and feces was overwhelming.

A few crack addicts stepped forward. From above, gunshots

made them scramble back into the shadows. Bullets whacked the floor.

The gunmen can't see us, Cavanaugh thought. They're shooting blindly. If I return fire, they'll see my muzzle flashes and know where to aim.

Water from the roof fell around him. He looked behind him, noticed a door, and dragged Prescott to his feet.

But when Cavanaugh tested the door, he found that it was locked. Mentally cursing, he searched for another way out, saw a stairway that led down to the ground level, and tugged Prescott toward it. For all he knew, gunmen would be waiting down there, but he had to take the chance.

It had been less than twenty minutes since he and Prescott had met. He had no idea who Prescott was or why these men wanted to kill him. He wasn't even sure he'd have accepted the assignment after he'd finished questioning Prescott and made a risk assessment. For one thing, he had only Prescott's word that he wasn't a drug trafficker or any of the other monsters Cavanaugh refused to protect. But none of that mattered any longer. The attack had made Cavanaugh's choice for him. He and Prescott were now protector and protected.

As he guided Prescott down the stairs into deeper shadows, he rapidly did a tactical reload, taking the partially depleted magazine from his pistol, pocketing it, and inserting a full one from his belt.

The stench became more nauseating. Prescott moved so frantically that his footsteps echoed loudly. No! Cavanaugh thought. They'll hear us and shoot! He could only hope that the rumble of the rain on the roof would obscure the noises they made.

His hope was ill-founded. Shots roared from above, blasting more chunks from the wall. Hurrying Prescott to the bottom, Cavanaugh froze at the sight of another cluster of derelicts. He aimed, unable to distinguish those who were truly homeless from those who might be a threat. Most had already cowered from the shots on the floor above and the sudden descent of strangers into their midst. The sight of Cavanaugh's pistol made them cower even more.

A few others, however, had the look of jackals waiting for their prey to become distracted.

But none drew handguns or assault rifles, even though they would have a good chance against one armed man and the client he was doing everything possible to protect.

Cavanaugh heard loud, angry voices above him and the sound of the catwalk scraping, as if some of the gunmen were trying to descend the way Cavanaugh and Prescott had. The rest of the assault team would be charging down the stairs toward the outside door. They would race through the rain, burst into the warehouse, scatter its ragged occupants, and continue hunting. Meanwhile, some of the assault team would rush to the opposite side of the warehouse, in case Cavanaugh and Prescott tried to escape in that direction, but the gunmen couldn't possibly have moved fast enough to reach there yet.

Aiming toward the ragged men, Cavanaugh motioned for Prescott to follow him toward where a rusted door lay next to an opening on the river side of the warehouse. But then he realized that even if part of the assault team hadn't had time to reach that side, a few marksmen could be watching from upper windows, ready to fire through the broken glass.

We wouldn't have a chance, he thought. Rain gusted through the opening. Gray light beckoned. A tugboat's horn blared from the river. So close. Again Cavanaugh imagined the gunmen bursting into the warehouse, scattering its ragged occupants, hunting for . . .

Scattering?

"Prescott, follow me back to where we were."

"*But aren't we leaving?*"

"When I tell you." Cavanaugh led Prescott into the middle of the area.

He faced the ragged men. "I've got a job for everybody."

They looked baffled. A few even looked as frightened of the word *job* as they were of the pistol in his hand.

Thunder rumbled.

"Your first step on the road to self-sufficiency."

They looked more baffled.

"It requires no skills, and if everything goes as planned, I'll send a truck here tomorrow with food and clothes for all of you. You can't ask for a better deal than that."

They looked at Cavanaugh as if he spoke an incomprehensible language.

"So what do you think? Are you ready to start working?"

They kept staring.

"Great," Cavanaugh said. "Now this is all you have to do. You see that opening over there? It leads toward other warehouses and then the river. What I want you to do is . . . Prescott."

"What?"

"Put your hands over your ears."

No questions this time. Prescott obeyed.

"What I want everybody to do," Cavanaugh told the group, "is keep thinking of the food and clothes you'll get tomorrow and"—Cavanaugh raised his pistol—"run in that direction."

They stared blankly.

"Run!"

When they didn't move, he fired the pistol over their heads. In the shadows, the muzzle flash was vivid, the ear-torturing roar making the group stumble back.

"*Run!*" Cavanaugh's own ears were punished as he fired twice more above their heads, and now terror made them move a little faster, desperate to get away from the madman with the gun.

The next time Cavanaugh fired over their heads did the trick. They broke into a full-sized panic and scrambled toward the exit. Bumping into one another, they charged out into the rain.

10

"Follow them!" Cavanaugh told Prescott.

To increase momentum, Cavanaugh fired one last time, so terrifying the group that, unheeding, they charged through the storm. There must have been thirty of them at least, scurrying for whatever shelter they could find. He urged Prescott to keep running with them. Hoping that the chaos would distract the assault team enough to make them hold fire, he felt the cold rain drench him as he and Prescott rushed down a concrete ramp and across a garbage-strewn parking area.

Scarecrows ran everywhere around them. Ahead, some ducked through a gap in a chain-link fence. Splashing through puddles, Cavanaugh led Prescott toward the hole. He put his hand on Prescott's head, protecting it as he shoved him through. Ducking after him, he felt frozen by more than the rain because, with just a few derelicts around them now, he and Prescott were obvious targets. The only things in their favor were the distance and the difficulty of aiming at moving targets from an elevated position.

Blam! A shot from behind them tore up pavement.

"Prescott, that warehouse ahead!"

Blam! More pavement disintegrated.

"Almost there, Prescott!"

Blam! A chunk of pavement zapped past Cavanaugh's forehead.

"Move it, Prescott!"

Cavanaugh couldn't allow himself to run as fast as he was able. He had to match Prescott's pace, shouting encouragement, grabbing Prescott's arm when the heavy man seemed in danger of faltering. Even so, Cavanaugh's lungs burned from exertion as they rounded the warehouse corner.

Shielded by the wall, Prescott bent over and shuddered, gulping air. "We did it," he managed to say. "I can't believe we—"

"Keep moving."

"But I have to catch my—"

"No time. Let's go." Cavanaugh tugged Prescott.

He studied the warehouse. Its windows weren't broken. Boxes were stacked inside. Still in business, he thought. As the rain lanced against him, he came to a door and tried it. Locked. Although it was only midafternoon, no lights glowed inside. He didn't see any movement. Not surprising on a Sunday afternoon.

He managed to yank Prescott into a half-run, bringing him to the front of the building, where they faced smaller buildings and then the storm-shrouded river. Although those other buildings had been maintained also, none showed any activity. There might be a watchman somewhere, but Cavanaugh didn't see him, and for sure, he wasn't going to shout to get the watchman's attention. That would also attract the assault team's attention. By now, they had to be converging on this area.

As the rain made Cavanaugh's clothes stick to his skin, causing him to shiver, he frantically considered and rejected options. He could pick the lock on a door and try to hide with Prescott in one of the buildings. But every door he saw had a barred window. All the assault team would need to do was look through each window. The splashes of water that he and Prescott couldn't possibly avoid leaving on the floor inside would tell their hunters which building they'd chosen to hide in.

With a hand on Prescott's arm, Cavanaugh moved along the deserted, rainy street. The seething dark clouds and the shadows from the warehouses turned afternoon into violent dusk. That'll give us some cover, he thought. But it won't be enough. Tensely aware that he and Prescott couldn't stay in the open, he looked for a hiding place. A Dumpster briefly attracted his attention, but it was full, and anyway, it would only be another trap. Eventually, the gunmen would check it.

"Have to rest," Prescott murmured. Fatigue and his weight outmatched his fear now, making him plod.

"Soon."

Thrusting him farther along the street, Cavanaugh reconsidered picking the lock on one of the doors. It would take a while for the assault team to discover which building he'd chosen. It would take them even longer to search inside and discover where he and Prescott were hiding. Meanwhile, he could use his cell phone to get help from Protective Services.

Possibly the explosion and the shots had caused someone in the area to phone the police, but the explosion might also have been attributed to thunder or a lightning strike. As for the shots, perhaps the storm had muffled them, or perhaps they were common in this run-down neighborhood. In any case, if the police did arrive, they'd be a complication more than a help. After all, since the gunmen had disguised themselves as crack addicts, could a few members of the assault team not also disguise themselves as police officers? Cavanaugh wouldn't know if he could trust them. It was safer to depend on Protective Services. He'd phone Duncan. A rescue team could arrive in . . .

When? Fifteen minutes? Unlikely. A half hour? Maybe. But not guaranteed. And how would the rescue team be able to determine which of the several buildings was the one in which they were hiding?

We have to keep moving, Cavanaugh thought. He had his right hand on his pistol and his left on Prescott's soaked shirt, pulling him through the rain. Ahead, another chain-link fence caught his attention. But this one was intact. It had a stout metal gate with a lock. Next to it, a sign on a building read WILSON BROTHERS, CONSTRUCTION CONTRACTORS. Shivering from the cold, he led Prescott closer to the fence and saw two forklifts, a dump truck, a pickup truck, and a beat-up rust-colored sedan that looked to be twenty years old.

Please, let there be gas in it. Cavanaugh removed his lock picks from a slit beneath the collar of his soaked jacket. He felt increasingly vulnerable as he holstered his pistol, chose two picks that would fit the lock, and worked both of them, one applying torque while the other freed the lock's pins. Ten seconds later, he had the gate open.

No sooner had he tugged Prescott into the parking area and closed the gate than several men raced between two warehouses down the street. He heard their urgent footfalls and angry voices as he forced Prescott down behind the rust-colored sedan, barely noticing that the vehicle's color was due to actual rust and not paint.

He tried the driver's door and found it unlocked. The construction company must have thought the fence was sufficient protection for a car that looked like junk. The voices of the men sounded nearer. If they get to the fence, if they notice it isn't locked . . .

Rain misting his eyes, Cavanaugh opened the door. He slid into the passenger seat, faced the steering column, braced his feet against it, and used both hands to yank on the steering wheel, breaking the internal lock that kept the steering wheel from moving. He pulled the hood-release lever and scrambled into the rain, hurrying to lift the hood. A bundle of wires led into the engine compartment from the steering column. Knowing the wires he needed, he pulled a safety pin from under his collar, pierced the wires so they formed a circuit, and closed the pin over them. The engine started.

The sound made the men rush closer, their footsteps and voices more audible now.

No longer caring about making noise, Cavanaugh slammed the hood and shoved Prescott into the car. "Put on your seat belt!"

He rammed the gearshift into drive and stomped the gas pedal. "Roll down your window!"

11

The rusted car surprised Cavanaugh by rocketing forward with amazing energy. Somebody had obviously cared for the engine, even though the body had been allowed to go to hell.

"Roll down your window!" Cavanaugh shouted again to Prescott, and Prescott—conditioned by now—instantly obeyed.

"Slide toward the floor!" Cavanaugh drew his pistol.

As the car struck the fence, headlights shattering, the fence slamming open to the right, Cavanaugh fired repeatedly through Prescott's open window at two nearby gunmen. They'd been coming to check the fence. As it slammed open, they'd halted in openmouthed shock and now lurched back from the impact of Cavanaugh's bullets.

The slide on his pistol stayed open. The magazine was empty. But as he steered violently to the left to get away from other gunmen suddenly appearing, he couldn't free his hands to reload the Sig with the remaining magazine on his belt. He'd have to rely on the .45 he'd taken from Prescott.

He pulled it from under his belt and dropped it on the seat, but as things were, he didn't have time to shoot anyhow. He was too busy trying to control the car. It fishtailed on the wet, oily pavement. The rain struck the windshield so hard that he could barely see the narrow street ahead. With his left hand, he fumbled for the windshield-wiper control on the steering wheel, twisted it, and discovered that only the wiper on the driver's side was functional. It only had one speed: ultrafast.

As the wiper flipped hysterically back and forth, a bullet shattered the sedan's rear window and went through the roof just above Cavanaugh's head. He sank low, trying to peer over the dashboard at the rain-obscured street, trying also to make himself a minimal target, even though he knew that the bullets aimed at the trunk had a good chance of plowing through the trunk, through the backseat, and through the front seat, possibly hitting him.

He didn't care if the assault team shot at the gas tank, which the gauge on the dashboard told him was three-quarters full. True, the bullet holes would cause him to lose fuel, but unless the gunmen were using tracer rounds, which they weren't, there wasn't any risk that the fuel would explode. That impossible phenomenon of bullets igniting gasoline happened only in urban myth. If anything, the fuel in the tank could help him by slowing any bullets that hit it and preventing them from plowing through the seats.

The better tactic would be for the assault team to shoot at Cavanaugh's tires. But even then, the damage would be much less than what might generally be expected. A blast from a shotgun or a volley from an automatic rifle could blow a tire apart. But if a tire was hit by one or two bullets from a handgun, the tire usually retained air for about five miles, a distance that would give Cavanaugh a chance to elude the assault team. If necessary (he'd been forced to do this a couple of times), he would keep driving on a wheel's metal rim.

Another bullet smashed through the rear window. This one blew through the front windshield. Cavanaugh heard it zip past. He felt the air forced away strike his cheek. But he couldn't think about how close it had come, and he couldn't think about Prescott huddling as near to the floor as the bulky man could press himself.

What Cavanaugh concentrated on was trying to see past the rain and the blur of the superquick windshield wiper as he drove faster. A long black car sped from a side street and skidded to a stop, blocking the narrow intersection ahead. Men jumped out into the storm and aimed pistols from behind the vehicle. But before they could shoot, they realized that instead of trapping Cavanaugh, they'd trapped themselves, for Cavanaugh didn't have time to stop. Their look of confidence changing to one of panic, they bolted toward buildings on either side.

"Prescott, brace yourself! There's going to be a hell of a bump."

As Cavanaugh sped toward the car blocking the intersection, he saw enough through the rain to be certain that there wasn't space on either side of the car for him to swing around it. That left only two choices. The first was to yank the lever for the parking brake and twist the steering wheel a quarter turn, spinning the car 180 degrees, facing it in the opposite direction: the so-called bootlegger's turn. He would then release the parking brake and speed from the barricade.

But that wouldn't solve anything, because the new direction would only lead back to the gunmen chasing them. Besides, the slippery pavement would make it difficult to execute the maneuver with precision. That left choice number two.

Cavanaugh checked the speedometer. Sixty. Too fast. Sweating, he eased his foot off the accelerator and tried to keep his moist hands firmly at ten o'clock and two o'clock on the steering wheel, his fingers spread for maximum grip.

It was obvious that if he hit the car straight on, he would probably kill Prescott and himself—an irresistible force against an immovable mass. But there *was* a way to survive the crash. What he had to do was change the relationship between the force and the mass.

"Here it comes, Prescott! Hold on!"

Reducing his speed to forty-five miles an hour, Cavanaugh stared past the frantic windshield wiper toward the vehicle spread sideways in front of him. He aimed toward where the vehicle had the least weight—the trunk end, which was on his right. He focused on the rear fender. At the same time, he turned so far to the right that only the area around his left headlight would strike the car's fender.

The impact sent a shock wave of punishment through him. Prepared for his head to jerk back, he hunkered down, bracing his head against the seat. Even then, the jolt to his neck was painful.

Instead of 100 percent force hitting 100 percent mass, the precise way in which Cavanaugh rammed the other vehicle reduced both factors by two-thirds. More glass shattered. Metal crumpled. The opposing car pivoted in front of Cavanaugh, its trunk end swerving out of the way, creating a gap through which Cavanaugh increased speed, stomping his foot on the accelerator.

Behind him, the assault team overcame their shock enough to fire at the receding vehicle. Cavanaugh stayed low, hearing bullets *whump* against the back of the car, some of them going through the now-almost-nonexistent front windshield. One bullet whacked into the dashboard. Another blew away the spastic windshield wiper.

As rain lashed through the gap where the windshield had been, Cavanaugh continued speeding down the narrow street. He heard sirens in the distance.

"Prescott, are you all right?"

No answer.

Between gusts of wind, Cavanaugh saw a looming intersection and eased his foot onto the brake pedal so he could make a turn. The slippery pavement caused the tires to slide as if on ice. He released his foot from the brake, simultaneously applying less force to the accelerator, letting the engine act as a brake. Even so, the intersection was behind him before he could make the turn.

"Prescott, talk to me! *Are you all right?*"

Huddled close to the floor, Prescott moved.

"Glad to know you're still with us."

As the distant sirens wailed louder, another intersection loomed, and this time, Cavanaugh was able to control his speed enough to stop the tires from gliding as he turned to the right.

Not a target at the moment, he felt marginally elated as he asked Prescott, "Are you hit?"

"No."

"Then get up here and make yourself useful."

"Don't feel so good."

"I've had better days, too. Look, I need to concentrate on driving. Take my phone from my jacket and call this number." Cavanaugh dictated it. "Then give me back the phone so I can get help."

"Yes, help," Prescott said.

"And then," Cavanaugh said, "you're going to tell me who the hell those guys are and why they're so eager to kill you."

12

"They're *not* eager to kill me," Prescott said.

"What?"

"They want me alive."

Abruptly, Cavanaugh felt a deeper chill than that caused by the rain blowing in on him. As he checked the rearview mirror to see if the assault team was in pursuit, his sense of reality shifted dramatically, making him think of the attack in an entirely different way. In the warehouse, when the gunmen had fired, Cavanaugh had believed that the shadows and the rain falling through the roof had thrown off the attackers' aim. Now he realized that the bullets had, in fact, been carefully placed, trying to stop Prescott but not to kill him. If anyone was a shoot-to-kill target, *I* was, Cavanaugh thought. It was now clear to him that the bullets aimed toward the car had been directed toward the driver's side, toward him, not toward Prescott. The only indiscriminate part of the attack had been the rocket aimed toward the bricked-over window, but that, too, could be explained. In retrospect, Cavanaugh realized that the explosive force of the rocket had been less than normal. The damage it inflicted to the building should have been far more extensive. The shell's power had been reduced in the hopes that it would stun, not kill.

"Sure." Gratified to see traffic through the rain, Cavanaugh steered from the warehouses and reached decrepit houses near a highway. "They disguised themselves as crack addicts, blending with their surroundings, hoping to catch you by surprise. When I showed up, they realized the situation was about to change and quickly adjusted their time table, attacking before they were ready."

Ahead, the sirens grew louder.

"Use my cell phone," Cavanaugh repeated. "Press the numbers I gave you."

Prescott finally did. "Here. It's ringing on the other end."

As Cavanaugh released his right hand from the steering wheel and took the phone, he decided to test Prescott by saying, "Those sirens. Don't you want me to go to the police?"

"No," Prescott said.

"Why not?"

"No police," Prescott emphasized.

Before Cavanaugh could question him further, he heard Duncan's voice say, "Global Protective Services."

"This is Cavanaugh. I'm in Condition Red."

Cavanaugh imagined Duncan sitting ramrod-straight.

The wind and the roar of the broken muffler made it difficult for Cavanaugh to hear what Duncan said next: "The location transmitter in your Taurus isn't functioning. I can't find you on the screen."

"The Taurus is history. Prescott and I are in a stolen car." Working to control the vehicle with his left hand, Cavanaugh pressed the cell phone harder to his ear.

"Give me your location."

"I'm going to voice encryption." Cavanaugh pressed a button at the bottom of the phone, which activated a scrambler. If the men in the pursuing cars had cell-phone scanners, they wouldn't be able to overhear. "I'm still in Newark," he continued. "Heading away from the river. I see a lot of traffic ahead, but I can't identify the highway."

"How many assailants?" Tension made Duncan's voice sound tight.

"Maybe eight."

"Are they in pursuit?"

"I'm not sure. I might have . . ." Speeding past more dismal houses toward the highway, Cavanaugh peered again toward his rearview mirror. He was about to finish his sentence with "lost them," when two cars skidded around a gloomy corner back there and rushed in his direction. "Yes," he said. "They're in pursuit."

Cavanaugh reached the access ramp and saw a sign. "I'm heading north on Route Twenty-one." He saw another sign. "The McCarter Highway."

"If you're leaving the river and moving north on Twenty-one"—Cavanaugh imagined Duncan scanning a map on a computer screen—"keep going in that direction. In about ten miles, you'll intersect with Route Three. Head east, then north on Seventeen. Can you make it to Teterboro?"

Duncan meant the Teterboro airport, the fourth-important airport in the New York City area, after Kennedy, La Guardia, and Newark International. Located where Routes 17 and 46 converged near Interstate 80 in New Jersey, Teterboro was twelve miles from midtown Manhattan via the George Washington Bridge. It was designated a "reliever" airstrip, which meant that corporate, charter, and private aircraft used it, taking pressure off the larger airports and the large passenger carriers they served. Because many of Global Protective Services' clients were corporate executives, the agency had an office and a helicopter at the airport, although these had logos for Atlas Avionics, a Protective Services subsidiary.

"I'm in the Teterboro office now." Duncan's voice crackled from the storm's interference. "We're doing a handover." Translation: After having been protected while in Manhattan, a client was being transferred from an armored car to the client's corporate jet, where non–Protective Services agents would take over.

When the jet left the ground, the assignment was completed. *"Can you get here?"*

"I'd better." Cavanaugh studied the fuel gauge, which had dropped from three-quarters to half indicating how much gas he was losing from bullet holes in the tank.

"Call back in ten minutes," Duncan said. "By then, I'll have rendezvous specifics."

Cavanaugh broke the transmission and put the phone down beside the .45 on the seat. He stared toward the rearview mirror and saw the two pursuing cars merge onto the highway. Because of the storm, most cars had their headlights on, but these cars stayed dark as they sped past traffic.

The sirens receded into the distance.

"Prescott, you didn't answer my question." Cavanaugh wiped rain from his face and concentrated to pass a transport truck. "Why don't you want me to go to the police?"

"They wouldn't know what to do with us. Guns. A stolen car. Christ." Prescott's face had lost some of its puffiness, tension shrinking it. "They'd question us on the street. They'd question us at the station. When they finally let me go, the people who want me would've had time to get ready again."

"True." Cavanaugh wiped more rain from his face. "But I get the feeling you've got another reason for not going to the police."

"The same reason I wouldn't go to the Drug Enforcement Administration. I don't trust anything to do with the government."

"The Drug Enforcement Administration? What have *they* got to do with . . ." Cavanaugh had a sudden sick feeling that Prescott might be a monster after all.

"The men chasing us work for Jésus Escobar." Fear made Prescott's face the color of his soiled white shirt.

Cavanaugh felt even sicker: Jésus Escobar was one of the biggest drug lords in South America. He took another quick look at the rearview mirror and saw that the cars chasing him were drawing closer. "You promised me this has nothing to do with drugs. I don't protect drug dealers!"

"I told you I wasn't a drug dealer. That's the truth. But I didn't say this has nothing to do with drugs."

"You're not making sense."

"Have you ever heard of D.P. Bio Lab?"

"No." His tires sprayed a haze of water from the pavement, as Cavanaugh sped past another transport truck.

"The D.P. stands for Daniel Prescott. It's mine—a sophisticated biotech research facility." The pupils of Prescott's eyes grew larger with fear as he stared back through the rain toward the two pursuing cars. "If you *had* heard of D.P. Bio Lab, I'd have been concerned. Most of my work is for the government."

Cavanaugh suddenly had an uneasy feeling about what he was going to hear.

"As part of the latest antidrug campaign, I was hired to do research on the parts of the brain involved with addiction." Emotion made Prescott speak quickly. "Addiction's immensely complicated. It isn't clear whether some people become addicted for psychological or physical reasons." Prescott spoke faster. "Different personalities become addicted to different effects. Passives go for depressants. Active types crave stimulants. Sometimes it's the reverse."

The pursuit cars were now a hundred yards behind the rusted sedan.

"The idea was," Prescott said, "if I could find a common denominator, a physical trigger common to all of them, in the cerebral cortex, for example, or the hypothalamus, there might be a way to stop that trigger from functioning. The addiction wouldn't happen."

The pursuit cars were now close enough that in the rearview mirror Cavanaugh could see there were four men in each. One driver had a mustache. Another had shaved his head. Their eyes had the determination of manhunters.

"And did you find it—the addiction trigger?"

"No."

Cavanaugh tried to anticipate how the gunmen would handle

this. They want Prescott alive, he thought. They won't shoot at me. Not driving this fast. They don't want to cause an accident that'll kill Prescott. Their only choice is to force me off the road.

"I didn't find a trigger that could be disabled to prevent addiction," Prescott said. "What I found instead, God help me, is an easy-to-manufacture chemical that can instantly *cause* an addiction. To itself. It's cheap to produce. It doesn't require elaborate equipment. And the manufacturing process doesn't have toxic side effects or cause explosions and fires the way some illegal drugs can."

Cavanaugh stared again toward the rearview mirror. Speeding through the rain, the pursuit cars were now only twenty yards behind the sedan.

"As soon as I reported my findings," Prescott said, "the agency I worked for became so alarmed, they terminated the research program."

One of the cars positioned itself behind the sedan while the other came up on Cavanaugh's left. They're going to try to box us in and push us off the road, Cavanaugh thought.

"Suddenly, the DEA showed up and confiscated my research," Prescott said. "They swore my lab assistants and me to secrecy. Not that my lab assistants are a security risk. I'm the only one who knows the formula."

Cavanaugh studied traffic ahead and made a quick decision.

Prescott's voice shook. His words gushed out. "But Escobar must have an informant in the DEA. My research is so well guarded there that even Escobar's people can't breach it. That leaves *me*. They want to capture me and force me to tell them the formula."

"For God's sake, why didn't the DEA try to protect you?"

"They did. But Escobar's people attempted to capture me anyhow. I think somebody at the DEA works for him and told him where I was. The team guarding me was attacked. I barely escaped a kidnapping attempt. That's when I took advantage of the confusion and slipped away, managing to reach the warehouse."

"Which you'd set up earlier. In case," Cavanaugh said.

"But I couldn't stay there forever. I'd have run out of food. I wanted people to talk to. I'm tired of being afraid."

"I'll do my best to fix that." Cavanaugh rolled down his window. In addition to the rain, he heard the car coming up next to him. "Do you know how to load a pistol?"

"No."

It figures, Cavanaugh thought. He'd been about to give Prescott one of the Sig's spare magazines and have him reload the weapon. Now there wasn't time to explain what to do. Cavanaugh was going to have to rely on Prescott's .45.

The car on Cavanaugh's left came abreast of the sedan and slammed against its side.

"Make sure your seat belt's tight," Cavanaugh said quickly.

The car struck the driver's side again. Cavanaugh heard metal crumble. Concentrating to control his steering with his left hand, he used his right hand to pick up the .45. "This pistol had better work."

He transferred the .45 to his left hand and now controlled the steering wheel with his right.

The car on the left struck Cavanaugh's side a third time, trying to force him onto the highway's shoulder.

Feeling the shudder of the impact, Cavanaugh thumbed off the safety on the cocked .45.

13

Their mass being equal, two cars can bang at each other's side for quite a while, and if the drivers are skilled, neither car will be forced off the road. The trouble is that the car banging at Cavanaugh's rusted sedan was bigger and heavier. The laws of physics were in its favor. Eventually, its weight would shove Cavanaugh's sedan onto the shoulder.

He could have shot the driver, but as the attacking car veered out of control, there was too much risk that it would strike cars behind it and kill their occupants. Moreover, the bullets could go through the driver and continue toward cars on the opposite side of the highway, possibly killing someone over there.

But there was another way to use the .45.

"Prescott, put your hands over your ears."

Cavanaugh's own ears had been ringing incessantly since he'd started shooting. Now he prepared himself for them to hurt even more.

Pressing the accelerator hard, he surged forward. Abreast of the attacking car's engine, he shoved the .45 out the window, aimed at the front hood, and fired seven times, emptying the pistol as quickly as he could pull the trigger. Under the hood, the fan disintegrated. The radiator exploded. Oil and carbon dust blew from the engine, erupting from the holes that his bullets had made in the hood of the engine. Steam from the radiator burst from the front of the car.

The slide on top of the .45 stayed back, indicating that the pistol was empty. At once, Cavanaugh pulled the weapon back into the sedan so the gunmen would know the shooting was over, so they wouldn't return fire. As it was, they had plenty to concern them without disobeying Escobar's orders and endangering Prescott's life by shooting at the driver of the vehicle Prescott was in. The power of the .45 had damaged the engine enough that the attacking car rapidly lost speed. Falling back, enveloped by more oil vapor and steam, the crippled vehicle angled toward the left shoulder.

The car behind Cavanaugh tried to compensate by speeding close to him and slamming the sedan's back bumper. Apart from sending a shudder through the sedan, this had no effect on Cavanaugh's ability to control the vehicle. Although the tactic looked dramatic, it accomplished little. When the pursuing car hit Cavanaugh's bumper a second time, all he had to do was touch the brake pedal a little, and the car behind him was reduced to doing little more than pushing him. That the attacking driver thought ramming would work told Cavanaugh that his opponent didn't have much experience with car fighting.

There was only one effective maneuver in a car fight. But first Cavanaugh had to get into position. He veered unexpectedly onto the right shoulder and pressed the brakes, applying most but not all of their force. He could tell how much force he was applying by judging the speed of the brake pulses through the pedal. Ninety-eight percent pressure gave him stopping power while at the same time allowing him to continue to control the vehicle's steering. One hundred percent would have meant that the swiftly accelerating pulses had abruptly stopped and the brakes locked, turning the sedan into little more than a couple of tons of skidding metal.

He dropped behind the pursuing car, released the brakes, and came up behind it, still on the highway's shoulder. Aiming his left front fender, he tapped the side of the opposing car's right *rear* fender in the so-called precision immobilization technique. The PIT maneuver required virtually no force, just a kiss of the left front fender.

Again, physics took over. The opposing car spun 180 degrees, rear to front, the startled occupants staring back toward Cavanaugh, face-to-face with him. At the same time, the car shifted sideways, to the right, pivoting onto the highway's shoulder. But as it continued to spin, it moved so far to the right that it crashed against a barrier at the side of the highway. Meanwhile, Cavanaugh steered onto the highway and sped forward.

"Prescott, look behind us. Are there any other cars going off the road? Any accidents?"

Prescott peered back in amazement. "No. My God, some cars are sliding, but they're holding the road. No other accidents. I can't believe you did it. You got us away from them."

"No," Cavanaugh said.

"But—"

"The PIT maneuver barely damages the other car," Cavanaugh said.

"The *what?*"

"Unless that car broke something when its side struck that barrier, those men'll soon come after us again." Cavanaugh stared toward the fuel indicator on the dashboard. The needle was now at one-quarter. "Plus, we've got too many bullet holes in the gas tank. We'll soon be on empty."

In the distance, a new group of sirens wailed.

Cavanaugh checked the rearview mirror: no sign of the second car pulling onto the highway. He peered ahead through the rain and saw an exit ramp. He was far enough along the highway that the men in the car behind him might not notice the rusted sedan leaving. Or so he hoped.

The sirens wailed louder.

"Time for a change of plan." Cavanaugh took the exit ramp, came to the bottom, saw a shopping mall on the left, and headed toward its crowded parking lot. People in other cars gaped at the smashed front end of Cavanaugh's car.

"Prescott, use your shirtsleeve. Wipe everything you touched. Smudge your fingerprints."

Counting on the rain to obscure his movements, Cavanaugh entered the expansive parking lot, but every space in the row he chose was filled. Cursing, he steered through puddles toward the next row, where all the spaces were also full.

Sure, he thought. A rainy Sunday afternoon. How do people pass the time? They go to the shopping mall.

Cavanaugh tried the next row, and the next, and the next. All were filled with vehicles.

In the distance, the sirens stopped, presumably at the car whose engine Cavanaugh had disabled.

The black car suddenly steered into the row Cavanaugh was headed along and sped toward him. Through the car's flapping windshield wipers, the three passengers and the skinhead driver glared at him.

Cavanaugh braked, put the car in reverse, and started backing away, but not before a man on the passenger side lowered the window and leaned out into the rain, aiming a pistol with a silencer on it. Cavanaugh didn't hear the shot, but he did hear the bullet's impact against the radiator.

Steam rose from the puncture. *Whump.* A second bullet hit the radiator. The assault team had learned from the way Cavanaugh had disabled the first car by firing the .45 at the engine and the radiator. The pistol the passenger used wasn't large enough to be a .45. It wouldn't damage the engine as much, but it would definitely play hell with the radiator.

Backing swiftly, Cavanaugh swung the steering wheel, pivoting the sedan 180 degrees. In the limited space, on wet pavement, he couldn't execute the backward half spin as neatly as he was capable of doing. His right front fender glanced off a parked van's taillight, sending a shudder through the sedan. Even so, in a rush, he corrected the steering and now faced the mall instead of the pursuing car. He rammed the gearshift into forward and sped along the row.

But as rain suppressed the steam from the radiator, Cavanaugh felt his chest cramp when a woman holding an umbrella stepped from between cars. She walked halfway across the open area and froze at the sight of Cavanaugh's car rocketing toward her.

14

Never look at what you're trying to avoid. Always look at where you want the car to go. Cavanaugh's instructors had drilled that rule into him at the Bill Scott Raceway in West Virginia, where

Global Protective Services and various intelligence agencies sent their operators for training in evasive driving.

"Why is it that, in many accidents, cars get hit directly on the side or the front, as if there wasn't any attempt to evade them?" Duncan had demanded from the passenger seat.

Cavanaugh hadn't been able to answer, too busy rounding a curve at 120 miles an hour.

"Why is it that if a driver hits a patch of ice and skids off the road, the only telephone pole for a hundred yards or the only tree in a field will be what that driver slams into square on?"

Again, Cavanaugh hadn't been able to answer, too busy feeling the hum and pulse of his car's tires, knowing that if the hum sounded any higher, if the pulse got any faster, his tires would lose their grip on the curve and he'd fly off the raceway.

Duncan had answered for him. "Because the driver looks at the car that veers in front of him, or the driver looks at the telephone pole at the side of the road, or the driver looks at the tree in the middle of the field, and although the driver wants to avoid them, he hits the damned things. Why does he hit them?"

"Because he looks at them," Cavanaugh had finally managed to answer, speeding out of the curve.

"Yes. You steer where your eyes lead you. If you look at what you're trying to avoid, you'll head in that direction."

Suddenly, a large cardboard box had hurtled across the track in front of Cavanaugh. Startled, he'd looked at it and almost steered toward it. With a flick of his eyes, he'd stared forward again and managed to remain on the track. His speeding car had veered only slightly as he passed where the box flew into a ditch. He thought he'd seen a rope on the box.

"Did somebody hide at the side of the track and yank that box across?" Cavanaugh had rushed into another curve.

"Eighty percent of the beginning students here see that box and follow it into the ditch," Duncan had replied. "So what's the lesson?"

"Look at where you want to go, not at what you're afraid you'll hit."

"Yes!"

Now Cavanaugh stared past the paralyzed woman toward rain splashing a puddle beyond her.

Don't move, lady.

Cavanaugh stepped on the brakes, feeling their pulses through the pedal, judging their increasing frequency. At what he estimated was 98 percent stopping power, he kept his foot steady. Any more pressure and the brakes would lock, making it impossible for him to control the direction of the sedan. But as long as the brakes weren't locked, he could steer the car while reducing speed.

He was so close to the paralyzed woman that he saw how huge the pupils of her eyes had become as he twisted the steering wheel to the right.

No! Don't look at her! Look at the rain in the puddle beyond her!

Cavanaugh felt the car threaten to slide out of control on the wet pavement. At once, the sedan shifted to the right the way he wanted. Continuing to stare toward where he wanted to go, toward the puddle, he twisted the steering wheel to the left now, veering around the woman, sensing her umbrella zip past him as his car reached the puddle and he released the brake.

For a heart-skipping moment, as Cavanaugh jerked his gaze up toward his rearview mirror, he feared that the pursuing car would hit her, but the near miss had broken the woman's paralysis. She raced toward cars at the side just before the black car sped past her, splashing water from a puddle, drenching her.

Wary of other pedestrians who might suddenly appear, Cavanaugh sped along the row heading toward the mall. He steered to the left, toward one of the mall's entrances, a group of glass doors beckoning on Prescott's side of the car.

"Prescott, open your door! We're bailing out!"

"But—"

"Do it!" Cavanaugh skidded to a stop in front of the doors. He grabbed the Sig and the .45. "Now!"

Behind him, he heard the black car speeding close as he and Prescott charged into the mall.

15

Two levels high, the place was warm, dry, and bright, packed with shoppers, loud with conversations, but all Cavanaugh paid attention to was an electronics store immediately on his left.

"In there!" he told Prescott.

The black car would stop at the rusted sedan, Cavanaugh knew. The three passengers would rush into the mall. The driver would stay with the car and use his cell phone to keep in touch with the gunmen as they tried to find where Cavanaugh and Prescott had gone. That way, the driver could be alerted to speed to another section of the mall if Cavanaugh and Prescott tried to leave via other doors.

Urging Prescott toward the electronics store, Cavanaugh shoved the .45 under his belt. Frantic to get out of sight before the gunmen rushed into the mall, he held the Sig close to him, hiding it. He ejected its empty magazine, put it in a pocket, shoved in a fresh one from the pouch on the left side of his belt, and pressed the lever that allowed the slide on top to snap forward, chambering a round. Moving, he did all this without thinking, with a sureness that came from hundreds of training exercises.

A young clerk in the electronics store looked puzzled by the haste with which Cavanaugh and Prescott entered, water dripping from them. "May I help you?"

Holding the Sig out of sight beneath his jacket, Cavanaugh

tugged Prescott past the clerk, past harshly lit rows of televisions, video tape recorders, and DVD players. "What we're looking for is in the back of the store."

The clerk hurried to follow. "If you'll show me what it is, I'll be glad to help."

"Great." Cavanaugh and Prescott squeezed past customers, approaching a counter in the rear.

The counter had a door on the left. Cavanaugh nudged Prescott past the counter and opened the door.

"Sir!" the clerk said. "Customers aren't allowed in the storeroom!"

"But this is what we're looking for." Pulling Prescott into the storeroom, Cavanaugh closed the door and locked it.

"Sir!" a muffled voice objected.

Cavanaugh spun toward palely illuminated shelves stacked with boxes containing VHS and DVD players. "Let's go, Prescott."

Hearing the knob being turned and then someone pounding on the door, Cavanaugh headed toward a metal door on the opposite wall. He'd seen the outside of that door when he'd stopped at the mall's entrance. He knew that the law required exterior doors in commercial establishments to have locks that could be easily freed so that people wouldn't be trapped if there was a fire. This door was secured by a simple dead bolt.

He twisted the lock's knob.

While the gunmen searched the mall, Cavanaugh and Prescott rushed out into the rain. At the curb, the black car, its engine running, was parked behind the rusted sedan, as Cavanaugh expected. The skinhead driver stared toward the glass doors through which his companions had hurried, again as Cavanaugh expected.

By the time the driver noticed movement next to him, Cavanaugh had run in a crouch through the gloom. Using the rusted sedan and the steam from it to conceal his approach, he drew the .45, which was useful to him now only as a blunt object he could afford to risk damaging, and slammed its barrel against the car's passenger window. Beads of safety glass burst inward over the startled skinhead as Cavanaugh aimed his Sig at him and saw that the man's cell phone and pistol were on the seat next to him, along with a Zippo lighter and a pack of cigarettes. The motor kept running.

"Out!" Cavanaugh told him.

With his gloved hands on the steering wheel, the frightened skinhead glanced toward the pistol on the seat.

"*Out!*" Cavanaugh shouted.

Terrified, the skinhead continued to stare at the pistol on the seat.

Cavanaugh pulled the Sig's trigger and blew a hole in the ceiling.

Flinching, the skinhead hurried from the car.

"*Run!*" Cavanaugh fired above the driver's bare scalp, making him race faster through the rain as he headed along the side of the mall.

"Prescott, get in!"

As Prescott obeyed, Cavanaugh ran around to the open driver's door, but before he got in, he grabbed the cigarette lighter off the seat.

He ignited it and threw it under the back of the sedan, where the lighter was protected from the rain and where gasoline from the perforated fuel tank had pooled. Immediately, vapor erupted into flames that spread along the bottom of the sedan. He hurried into the black car, put the gearshift into drive, and sped away.

Looking in his rearview mirror, he saw the rusted sedan heave as its gas tank, filled mostly with fumes, detonated. It didn't explode, contrary to popular belief. No huge fireball. No roar as if tons of TNT had gone off. Just a *whump* and an energetic burst of flame. In fact, if the gas tank had contained mostly fuel, there wouldn't have been enough oxygen for it to explode. The car would have kept burning only on the outside.

Taking one last look at his rearview mirror, Cavanaugh saw

three angry men charge out of the mall. It seemed to him that, like the skinhead driver, they wore gloves. Then he reached the street beyond the parking lot and couldn't see them any longer.

He sped toward the ramp that led back to the highway. It was a luxury to have a car with an intact windshield and two functioning wipers.

Prescott's bulky chest heaved. He clamped his hands to it.

"Are you all right?" Cavanaugh accessed the highway, staying in the right lane, trying to blend with traffic. "You're not having a heart attack, are you?"

"No. Just can't get my . . . Out of breath."

"Out of condition," Cavanaugh said. "You've got to take better care of yourself." To calm Prescott, Cavanaugh prompted him to imagine a future scenario, one in which he'd be safe. "After we make you disappear, you'll have plenty of chances to get some exercise."

"Exercise. Even *that* would be welcome."

In the distance, yet another group of sirens wailed. Although Cavanaugh wanted to get to the Teterboro airport as fast as possible, he kept his speed under the limit so he wouldn't attract attention.

"It's good to be somewhere dry." Again Cavanaugh was trying to calm Prescott.

"And warm."

"Yes." Cavanaugh's wet clothes were cold against his skin. The driver had kept the car's heater on. Cavanaugh felt air from it waft over him.

Prescott shivered.

"Turn the heater up," Cavanaugh said. "Adjust the blower as high as it'll go."

Hands shaking, Prescott fumbled at the controls on the dashboard. "You set fire to the car as—what, a distraction?"

"Partly. The police will have to waste time while they deal with the fire and try to figure out what happened."

"You said 'partly.' " Prescott's puffy forehead wrinkled. "You had another reason?"

"Our fingerprints." Cavanaugh again checked his rearview mirror. "Originally, I planned to abandon the car in the parking lot. It wouldn't have been noticed for a while. We'd have had a chance to wipe our prints before we ran from the area and called for help. But then the other car showed up and . . . This way, with the fire, we don't have to worry about our prints. Believe me, the police *would* have dusted for them, and they *would* have been able to identify us. Not a good idea when *you* want to disappear and *I* want to stay invisible."

"Cavanaugh."

"What?"

"I don't know your first name."

"I don't have one. Cavanaugh is the only name I go by. A work name. I never give my *real* name. It would endanger the people I protect."

"A pseudonym?"

"You know some of the trade jargon?" Relieved that Prescott's breathing was less agitated, Cavanaugh didn't mind distracting him by answering harmless questions. "One way for an opponent to get at a client would be to learn the identities of the client's protector's."

"What would *that* accomplish?"

"The opponent could discover where the protectors live, whether they have relatives and so on. You see the liability?"

Prescott's ample chin wavered as he nodded. "The opponent could kill the bodyguards where they live, when they're off duty, when they're not as alert."

"And the new team the client hires wouldn't be up to speed on how to maintain his security. The client becomes a viable target," Cavanaugh said.

Prescott nodded again. "Or else the opponent kidnaps the bodyguards' relatives and puts pressure on the bodyguards to lessen the client's security."

"You catch on quick. People close to me can't be threatened if the bad guys don't know who the people close to me are. Because the bad guys don't know who *I* am," Cavanaugh said.

"You have a family?"

"No," Cavanaugh replied, lying. "You referred to 'bodyguards.' That's not what I am."

"Then . . . ?"

"The technical term is *protective agent*."

"What's the distinction?"

"Bodyguards are thugs. They're what mobsters use. Crude muscle."

"But what you do, as you've proven, requires sophisticated talents. Thank you. What you went through to save me is the bravest thing I've ever seen."

"No," Cavanaugh said. "Not brave."

"I can't think what else to call it."

"Conditioned."

Between them, the skinhead's cell phone buzzed.

16

Prescott flinched.

The phone buzzed again.

"Press the answer button," Cavanaugh said. "Then give it to me."

Uneasy, Prescott obeyed.

Steering expertly with his left hand, Cavanaugh held the phone against his right ear. "Pizza Hut."

"Cute," a sandpapery voice said.

"Thanks."

"Not the Pizza Hut thing. I meant about setting fire to your car and stealing ours."

"I know what you meant."

Prescott watched intently, trying to figure out what Cavanaugh was hearing.

"This won't stop us. We'll keep coming," the voice said.

"I expect that," Cavanaugh said into the phone.

"You're not a cop. You'd have called for backup. Instead, you kept clear of police cars. You must be private security. Give it up. You're way out of your league."

"Gee, I thought I'd done pretty good so far."

"Did Prescott tell you who you're dealing with?"

"He hasn't had time to tell me anything," Cavanaugh lied. The transmission was weak. The shots had made his ears ring enough that he had to press the phone tighter against his ear so he could distinguish what the voice said next.

"If you don't know anything, we can cut you some slack. Give him to us, and we'll let you go."

"Say it again, this time as if you mean it."

The voice sounded weary. "You'd be dead now if you hadn't been near Prescott. This has to be the only time the guy we were after was a shield for his bodyguard."

"Protector."

"What?"

"I'm not a bodyguard."

"Whatever." The voice became harsher. "The next time I see you, you'd better pray you're close to Prescott. Otherwise, I'll put a bullet through your head. Does *that* sound like I mean it?"

"Is that the reason you phoned? To make cheap threats?"

The voice became silent.

Cavanaugh suddenly understood what was going on. "Lots of cheese, right?"

"What?"

"Your pizza will be ready in fifteen minutes." Cavanaugh risked taking his eyes off the road long enough to press the disconnect button.

A pickup truck loaded with junk drove past him. He lowered his window and tossed the phone into the back of the truck.

"What are you doing?" Prescott asked.

"Escobar's men didn't call just for the hell of it. They want to make certain we're with the phone."

"But why would—"

"The phone must have some kind of location transmitter in it. They'll follow it, hoping it leads them to us. Now it'll take them nowhere. For all I know, this car has a location transmitter also, but right now, there's nothing I can do about that."

"Why didn't you kill this car's driver?" Prescott asked.

"What?" Cavanaugh frowned at the unexpected question.

"Back at the mall, you took a chance when you told him to run. He might have reached for his weapon," Prescott said.

"A dead man in the car would have slowed us. I'd have had to pull him from behind the steering wheel. The other men might have found us before we could drive away."

"Would you have killed him if he *hadn't* been in the car?" Prescott asked.

"If he gave me a reason. Otherwise . . . I'm a protector, not a killer."

The rain lessened.

Cavanaugh took his phone from his jacket and pressed the re-call button.

"Global Protective Services." Duncan's voice was tense.

The phone remained in scrambler mode. "I had to switch cars. We're in a black Pontiac."

"Can you make it to the Holiday Inn near the airport? I'm here with some of your friends."

"Good," Cavanaugh said. "I can always use friends."

PART TWO

Threat Avoidance

1

The rain had lessened to a drizzle by the time Cavanaugh, following Duncan's instructions, reached the Holiday Inn on Route
17, a half mile from Teterboro Airport. Duncan waited under the
carport at the motel's entrance. He wore a raincoat and hat. His
hands were in the coat's pockets, one of them, no doubt, holding
a pistol. His trim mustache emphasized how pinched his lips
were. With his straight military posture and intense eyes, he exuded a focus that made Cavanaugh pleased to rely on him.

The moment Cavanaugh drove under the carport and stopped
next to Duncan, a gray van suddenly appeared behind them.

Prescott flinched. "They caught us."

"No," Cavanaugh said. "It's fine."

Glancing in the rearview mirror, he saw two men and a
woman, all three familiar to him, all wearing rain slickers, step
from the van. They kept their hands beneath the slickers, presumably on weapons, while they scanned the area around them,
paying particular attention to the highway beyond the parking
lot. Five seconds later, everything looking satisfactory, one of the
men approached Cavanaugh's side of the car.

With that all-clear sign, Cavanaugh pressed the car's unlock button.

Instantly, Duncan opened the passenger door and looked in. "Mr. Prescott?"

Prescott looked dumbfounded.

"I'm Duncan Wentworth. Global Protective Services. We spoke on the phone. Come with me, please."

Before Prescott seemed aware of it, Duncan had guided him from the car. Meanwhile, the woman and the remaining man flanked Prescott, Duncan leading the way, escorting him to the van.

Cavanaugh got out of the car.

"How ya doing?" The trim man who waited on the driver's side chewed gum.

"Better than I was a half hour ago."

"You can relax now. Leave the show to us."

"Looking forward to it. The car might have a location transmitter."

"By the time they find it, it'll be far from the airport. They'll never suspect how you got away."

"The pistol on the seat belongs to the assault team." Cavanaugh pulled the .45 from under his belt. "This belongs to Prescott. I have no idea where else it's been."

The man, whose name was Eddie, nodded. The rule was, you never kept a weapon whose history you didn't know. If you were caught with it, ballistics might prove that the weapon had been used in various shootings. The police would have every reason to believe you were implicated in them.

"These pieces'll soon be in pieces in a sewer," Eddie said.

Amused by the pun, Cavanaugh stepped aside and let Eddie get behind the steering wheel. "They all wore gloves."

Eddie tightened his own gloves. "No way to use fingerprints to identify them. So it won't matter if I wipe down *your* prints."

"The only places we touched are in the front seat."

"Makes it easier. Ciao."

As the black car drove from the hotel's carport into the drizzle, Cavanaugh got into the van and closed the hatch.

"Hey, Cavanaugh." The driver, who was Hispanic, put the vehicle into gear and proceeded from the carport. The drizzle made a hissing sound on the roof.

"Hey, Roberto." Cavanaugh knew the goateed man only by his first name and assumed it was an alias. "How are the tropical fish?"

"They ate each other. I'm getting a better hobby."

"What kind?"

"Model airplanes. The kind with a motor, so the planes can actually fly. I'm gonna rig them so they have aerial dogfights and shoot at each other and stuff."

"Stuff?"

"You know, tiny rockets. Maybe they could drop little bombs."

The van was configured so that two rows of seats faced each other, with a table in the middle. Cavanaugh buckled himself into a seat in back, next to Prescott and Duncan, and looked across the table toward the man and the woman who'd escorted Prescott into the van. Their rain slickers were off now, revealing Kevlar vests and holstered pistols on their belts.

"Hey, Chad," he said to the red-haired man, who was about thirty-five and had the same strong-shouldered build that Cavanaugh had. His name, too, was probably an alias.

In some elements of the security business, Chad's red hair would have been a liability, drawing attention to him. But as a protective agent, Chad often took advantage of his hair color to act as a decoy. An assassin or a kidnapper, having studied the target long enough to determine that a red-haired man was one of the protectors, would pay attention to where Chad went, on the assumption that Chad would be near his client. Thus Chad made a specialty of pretending to protect a look-alike client while the real client slipped away under escort. When Chad wanted to be inconspicuous, he wore a hat.

"I heard you got shot," Cavanaugh said.

"Nope."

"Good. I'm glad you didn't get hurt."

"I didn't say I didn't get hurt," Chad said. "I got stabbed."

"Ouch."

"Could've been worse. It was my left shoulder. If it'd been the shoulder I bowl with . . ."

Cavanaugh looked at the woman next to Chad. "Hi, Tracy."

She wore a Yankees sweatshirt and concealed most of her blond hair under a Yankees baseball cap. She had the capability of making herself look plain or gorgeous at will, and if she'd been in the Holiday Inn restaurant, if she'd put on lipstick, taken off her cap, let her long hair dangle, and pulled her sweatshirt tight, everybody in the restaurant, including four-year-old kids, would have remembered her after she left.

"I heard you quit," Cavanaugh said.

"And give up these fabulous working conditions? Besides, when would I ever see lover boy if I wasn't working with him?"

She meant Chad, but she was joking. Protectors who had a relationship weren't allowed to work on the same team. In an emergency, they might look after each other instead of the client. But on numerous assignments, Chad and Tracy had proven where their priorities lay.

The van reached the highway and headed toward the airport. Meanwhile, Duncan handed blankets to Prescott and Cavanaugh, then poured steaming coffee into Styrofoam cups for them. "We'll soon have dry coveralls for you."

Cavanaugh felt the coffee warm his stomach. "You did good, Mr. Prescott."

"Mr.? Now you call me Mr.? Ever since the warehouse, it's been 'Prescott do this' and 'Prescott do that.'"

Duncan frowned. "Is there a problem?"

Prescott's puffy eyes crinkled. "Not in the least. This man saved my life. I'm deeply grateful." With a smile, Prescott shook Cavanaugh's hand.

"Your hand's cold," Cavanaugh said.

"I was just going to say the same thing to *you*."

Cavanaugh looked down at his hands. They *did* feel cold, he realized. But not because he'd gotten soaked.

It's starting, he thought. He wrapped his hands around the warm Styrofoam cup, but the hands, which felt as if they belonged to someone else, trembled enough that some of the coffee almost spilled over.

"Your adrenaline will soon wear off," Duncan said.

"It already is."

"Do you want Dexedrine to make up for it?"

"No." Cavanaugh removed his hands from the cup and concentrated to steady them. "No speed."

Cavanaugh knew all too well the down effect that the central nervous system experienced after the high of adrenaline had made it possible to perform extraordinary acts of strength and endurance. Already, he felt uneasy urges to yawn, which had nothing to do with needing sleep but a lot to do with the uncomfortable release of muscle tension. Dexedrine would return his nervous system close to the high level at which it had functioned when he had rescued Prescott. But he hated to rely on chemicals and, as always, was determined to go through what amounted to adrenaline withdrawal in as natural a way as possible. He disliked having a client see him go through it: the slight unsteadiness, the yawns. There was always the chance that Prescott would misinterpret the unavoidable effect of being in violent action as a symptom of fear, just as earlier he had praised Cavanaugh for being brave, a virtue that Cavanaugh denied.

"No speed," Cavanaugh repeated.

2

After the control tower radioed clearance, the Bell 206L-4 helicopter rose from Teterboro Airport and headed north along the
Hudson River. Because the airport was a facility for corporate,
charter, and private aircraft, there hadn't been a need to go
through metal detectors and similar security checks, thus making it easy for the team to take aboard their weapons, which they
were licensed to carry in several states.

Like boats, cars, and firearms—to name a few items crucial to
the security profession—no helicopter fulfilled every purpose.
Swiftness had to be considered in relation to seating capacity,
cargo space, and maneuverability, along with how far and high
the helicopter could fly. Called the "Long Ranger," this sleek helicopter was designed to get neatly in and out of inaccessible or
remote areas and was popular with emergency and law-enforcement
agencies, although corporations liked it for its efficiency and
comfort. It could accommodate seven occupants, including the
pilot, who in this case was Roberto. It had a top speed of 127
miles per hour and a maximum fuel range of 360 miles, which
meant that at peak performance, it could stay in the air for approximately three hours.

Its altitude capability was twenty thousand feet, but Roberto's
flight plan called for him to stay four thousand feet above the
river. The drizzle had become a mist, and now that the sky was
clear, he was able to try to calm Prescott by giving him a view of
the cliffs and woods along the New Jersey Palisades.

But Prescott showed no interest in the view, ignoring the
ample Plexiglas windows, which Duncan explained were bullet
resistant. The Long Ranger's seating arrangement was similar to
that in the van: two rows of seats, one facing the other. While the
seats in the armored van had been designed for their sturdiness
in case of an attack, those that Duncan had ordered for the

Kevlar-protected Long Ranger were remarkably comfortable, with footrests, armrests, a tilt-back function, and soft leather.

Wearing large coveralls that still managed to look tight on his stomach and chest, Prescott ignored the view, too busy answering Duncan's questions and explaining about Jésus Escobar.

Cavanaugh remained silent. Any remarks from him would contaminate the debriefing. The team needed to hear Prescott's problem in his own words.

In the low-noise, low-vibration cabin, Duncan finally directed his attention toward Cavanaugh. "Anything to add?"

"I got a fairly good look at the men in the two cars. I didn't see any Hispanics."

Roberto, who'd been listening from the pilot's seat, said over his shoulder, "So Escobar's an equal-opportunity employer. The same as blacks don't always hire only blacks."

"It would take somebody with Escobar's resources to mount that kind of attack," Cavanaugh said.

"The way it sounds to me," Chad said, "they'd put together a careful plan, with the kidnappers posing as crack addicts, blending with the neighborhood. If Mr. Prescott had left the warehouse, they were ready to make their move, or if they got tired of waiting, they were prepared to blast their way in and take him. When Cavanaugh showed up, they got nervous that he was part of an extraction team, so they felt they had no choice except to move up their timetable."

"I'll contact the DEA and tell them to plug their security leak," Duncan said.

"For God's sake, don't tell them I hired you to make me disappear," Prescott said. "Whoever Escobar has working for him will pass that information along."

"Not to worry," Duncan said. "I don't intend to create my *own* security leak. Relax and enjoy the ride."

"Where are you taking me?"

"Where you'll be safe."

3

The helicopter followed the Hudson River two hundred miles north, passing several waterfront towns and cities, some of which were crested with smog. Beyond Kingston, it headed west into the low, rolling Catskill Mountains. Thickly wooded, they had numerous scenic valleys.

"Look." Cavanaugh pointed toward a plume of smoke rising from a ridge to the north.

"Yes," Duncan said. "It's been a dry spring."

"I've been listening to radio chatter," Roberto said over his shoulder as he worked the helicopter's controls. "The rain didn't get this far, but the lightning did, and that's what started the fire. It's small. They've got it under control."

Duncan nodded and glanced toward the sky behind them. "Is anybody following us?"

The helicopter had been modified to accommodate a sophisticated array of electronic instruments, including a powerful radar system, which was capable of isolating any aircraft following their course.

Roberto tapped numbers on a keyboard and studied the radar screen. "Nada."

"Do it," Duncan said.

Roberto crested a peak and sank into a small valley that was especially dense with evergreens.

"Look down, Mr. Prescott," Chad said. "You'll find this interesting."

The helicopter sank lower into the valley.

"What am I looking for?" Prescott said. "All I see are fir trees."

"That's what you're supposed to see," Tracy said.

"I still don't . . ." Prescott stared down through the Plexiglas.

Working the chopper's controls, Roberto pressed a button. "See anything now?"

"No, I—careful. If you go any lower you'll crash into the trees. Good God."

Cavanaugh wasn't in a position to see what Prescott did. Nonetheless, he knew what was happening. What seemed to be a section of the forest—thirty square yards of it—started moving. All of a sudden, concrete appeared.

"What the . . ." Prescott said.

"The best camouflage net available," Duncan said. "Even as low as we came, it's hard to distinguish the illusion from the real thing."

The helicopter settled onto the concrete landing pad. After Roberto shut off the engine, the group unbuckled their seat belts, opened hatches, and stepped down.

"Careful," Cavanaugh said. Feeling the wind from the still-rotating blades, he made Prescott stoop.

The group went to the left, toward a closed electrical box on a post among the trees at the side of the landing pad.

Duncan unlocked and opened the box. "We have to wait a few moments for the blades to stop or else the downdraft will suck the camouflage net into the blades."

Then Duncan pressed a switch, and a motor hummed.

Prescott watched in wonder as the net, an eerily realistic painting of the thick evergreens as seen from above, resumed motion, this time in reverse. Held up by sturdy poles that moved along motorized rails in the ground, the net shifted over the group, shut out the sky, and concealed the helicopter.

"In winter, when it snows," Duncan explained, "a sensor causes the net to retract automatically to keep the weight of the snow from damaging it. Heat coils in the concrete melt the snow. When the storm's over, the net returns to where it was. The snow on the trees melts swiftly, so the net continues to look like its surroundings."

Roberto added, "The flight plan I filed with the controller at Teterboro lists private property in these mountains as our destination. One valley's pretty much the same as another. The description isn't specific enough for anybody to be able to use the flight plan to follow us here. Even visitors, like you, wouldn't know which valley this is if you wanted to come back here."

"From the radar, we know we weren't being followed," Tracy added.

"And nobody can see the chopper from the air," Chad said. "So you can relax. This is as secure as you can be."

"But what about the helicopter's heat signature?"

Prescott's question made everyone in the group look at one another in surprise.

"You know about heat signatures?" Cavanaugh asked.

"What do you expect from a scientist? Every object gives off heat. An aircraft with sophisticated infrared sensors can detect that heat, isolate its shape, and know what's hidden under trees or a camouflage net, or in the dark."

"That's military or law-enforcement hardware," Chad said. "Anybody capable of equipping an aircraft with stuff like that is capable of equipping it with *other* fancy hardware."

"Like machine guns and rockets," Tracy said.

Prescott frowned. "Is that supposed to reassure me?"

"What they're getting at," Cavanaugh said, "is while you're worrying, why not worry about napalm and missiles?"

Prescott didn't understand.

Duncan stepped toward him. "It's a basic rule of protection that we match our security to the threat level the client faces. Escobar has a lot of money and resources, but his operation isn't sophisticated enough to be able to rig an aircraft with *that* kind of equipment in the little time his team had to try to follow us. There's no such thing as a totally secure location. Even the military command center in Cheyenne Mountain would be vulnerable if somebody managed to smuggle a suitcase nuclear weapon inside. But under the circumstances, given the threat you're facing, what Chad said is true." Duncan put a reassuring hand on Prescott's arm. "This is as secure as you can be."

Prescott glanced around, continuing to look uneasy. "Where do we stay?"

"Over there," Tracy said.

"Where? All I see are trees."

"Look harder."

"That hill? Is there a cabin or something behind it?"

"Sort of." Cavanaugh guided Prescott through the trees.

"I'll join you in a minute," Roberto said. "I need to refuel the chopper." He headed toward a pump next to a camouflaged equipment shed at the side of the landing pad.

"You mean you have *fuel* here?" Prescott sounded amazed.

"An underground tank. Every six months, we send a truck up here to refill it."

The setting sun cast shadows. A cool, gentle breeze smelled sweetly of fir needles. The group's footsteps were cushioned by the soft forest floor.

The hill they approached was about thirty feet high, with scrub brush and outcrops of boulders. Leading Prescott to it, Cavanaugh passed one of the boulders and indicated a recessed concrete passageway. "This is the cabin. Sort of."

Duncan stepped into the passageway and came to a metal door, next to which was an electronic number pad. A motion sensor triggered a faint light in the number pad as Duncan reached for it. Blocking the pad from Prescott's view, he pressed a sequence of buttons.

With a solid *thump*, the door's lock was released electronically. As Duncan opened the door, an alarm system began beeping.

"If the alarm isn't deactivated in fifteen seconds," Cavanaugh told Prescott, "the intruder gets a dose of knockout gas."

Duncan turned to an interior control panel, again blocked it from view, and pressed a further sequence of numbers.

The beeping stopped. Motion sensors turned lights on within the structure.

"Welcome to your safe site."

4

Prescott entered slowly, with even greater wonder than when he'd seen the camouflage net retract to reveal the helicopter pad.

A hallway led to a large living area on the right. The floor was polished oak. The furnishings were leather. The walls were an off-white, covered with bookshelves, impressionistic paintings, and a large fireplace.

"This is a reinforced-concrete dome covered with earth," Duncan said. "We squared off the dome's interior walls for convenience. Because of the building's strong insulating structure, the temperature tends to be a uniform seventy-two degrees in both summer and winter, with a little help from a fireplace in each room."

"Solar panels and batteries provide the electricity," Chad said. "A backup generator kicks in if necessary."

"The drinking water comes from a well under the bunker, so it can't be poisoned. On top, sunlight comes through a ventilation shaft and gets reflected by a system of mirrors that distribute the sunlight, so the rooms seem to have windows," Tracy said. "It's one of the most energy-efficient buildings imaginable."

"But with the entrance controlled electronically, if the power fails, we'll be trapped," Prescott said.

"There's a manual override on the door. Plus a second way out." Duncan pointed toward a metal door at the end of the corridor. "It has a knob, and a lever for a dead-bolt lock. But on the outside, there's nothing—no knob, no key slot, no way to pick the lock and get in."

Prescott breathed a little easier.

"Is anybody hungry?" Chad rubbed his hands together.

"That depends," Tracy said. "Who's doing the cooking? *You?*"

"None other."

"In that case, I'm starved."

Chad had a reputation for being an impressive cook. "Mr. Prescott, are you a vegetarian? Do you have food allergies?"

"I can eat anything."

Cavanaugh silently concurred, remembering the shelves of carbohydrate-rich food at the warehouse.

"Beef Stroganoff coming up," Chad said.

"Easy on the cream this time," Tracy said.

"Hey, if you're going to put restrictions on a genius at work . . ."

"I'm trying to watch my figure."

"I'm watching your figure, too."

"Can you believe the way this guy talks to me?"

"While they sort this out," Duncan told Prescott, "why don't you get settled. If you enjoy tobacco, we have a room with various smoking materials."

"No." Prescott looked horrified by the thought.

"In that case, your room—smoke-free—is the third on the left in this corridor. I imagine a hot shower and some clothes that fit you would be welcome. There's a bar. Satellite television. A sauna. You've been through a lot. Perhaps you can relieve the strain enough to take a nap."

5

"What do you think of him?" Duncan asked after he and Cavanaugh watched Prescott enter his room. Letting Chad and Tracy go ahead with their various duties, the two men crossed the living room toward a door to the right of the fireplace; it led to an office.

"He doesn't have much of a personality, but he's an ideal client," Cavanaugh said. "He did exactly what I told him. He's overweight and out of shape, but he sucked it up and did what was necessary. Sure, he almost lost his lunch from being afraid, but he trusted me and never panicked to the point of losing control. Everything considered, he kind of impressed me."

"Anything else?"

"He's smart."

"Of course. He's a biochemist."

"Likes to learn. Asks a lot of questions."

"My arrangement with him was via telephone and an electronic transfer of funds," Duncan said. "He insisted that he couldn't meet me in person."

"Now we know why." Cavanaugh paused at the entrance to the offices as Duncan went in.

"Why didn't he tell me on the phone what his problem is?" Duncan eased his tall, slender frame into an Aeron chair behind a desk.

"Maybe he didn't know if he could trust us," Cavanaugh said. "He wanted to wait until he assessed one of us face-to-face."

Duncan thought about it. "But he trusted us enough to tell us where he was hiding. That isn't consistent."

"Not necessarily. Since he couldn't come to us, he didn't have a choice about letting one of us come to *him*," Cavanaugh said. "Besides, at the warehouse, he used TV cameras to study me. If anything looked suspicious, all he had to do was shut down communications, and I still wouldn't have known where he was."

"Do you think he understands what it truly means to disappear? Is he prepared to accept the consequences?"

"He's got plenty of incentive," Cavanaugh said. "As one of his attackers told me on a cell phone, they'll keep coming. In fact, I'm sort of the quarry now, too."

"Oh?"

"The man on the phone almost made it personal between him and me."

Duncan thought another moment and picked up a phone. "I'll

speak to my contacts at the DEA and get more details about Prescott's situation."

"While you're making your calls . . ."

"Yes?"

"At the warehouse, some homeless people helped Prescott and me get away. I promised them a truck of food and clothes would be delivered there tomorrow. Maybe some sleeping bags."

Duncan smiled. "I'll make it like the Ritz."

6

Cavanaugh had his handgun apart (in addition to gunpowder residue, he'd found rainwater on some of the interior parts) and was cleaning it on a towel on the living room's coffee table. Seeing movement, he looked up as Prescott entered.

"Did you get some sleep?" Cavanaugh asked.

Prescott nodded. "I surprised myself. I felt so tense, I expected just to keep lying on the bed, staring at the ceiling."

"Was the sleep any good?"

"When I woke up, I felt wonderful for a second. Then . . ." Prescott's voice dropped. He looked awkward in jeans and a denim shirt, evidently more accustomed to suits and ties. But, unlike the coveralls he'd worn on the helicopter, at least the clothes fit his heavy frame. Duncan prided himself on keeping various sizes at the bunker.

"Where *is* everybody?" Prescott asked.

Cavanaugh wiped gun oil on the Sig's various parts, which were laid out neatly on the towel in front of him. "Duncan's making phone calls. Tracy's in the control room."

"Control room?"

"Similar to what you had in the warehouse. This place is surrounded by security cameras. Tracy's watching the monitors and a radar screen that'll warn us if any aircraft are in the area. Roberto's maintaining the helicopter. Chad's cooking."

The smell of beef Stroganoff drifted pleasantly into the room.

"What about *you*?" Prescott surveyed the jeans and denim shirt that Cavanaugh now wore. "Were *you* able to rest?"

"I had a report to write and then some chores to do."

"Like this?" Prescott indicated the disassembled weapon.

"After action, the first thing I was trained to take care of is my equipment." Cavanaugh put the barrel into the slide, then secured the recoil spring and its guide rod into place. When he compressed the spring, he made sure to point it away from Prescott and himself, lest it catapult free and injure one of them.

"What did you mean, 'conditioned'?" Prescott asked.

Cavanaugh shook his head, confused.

Prescott continued. "When I told you that what you'd done to save me was one of the bravest things I'd ever seen, you said you're not brave—you're conditioned."

Cavanaugh slid the assembled slide mechanism onto the Sig's frame and secured it. He thought a moment. "People are brave when they're terrified but force themselves to risk their lives for somebody else."

Prescott nodded, listening intently.

"Why do you care about this?" Cavanaugh asked.

"My specialty is how the human brain functions, how it releases hormones and controls our behavior," Prescott said. "Epinephrine—what's commonly called adrenaline—is one of the hormones associated with fear. The speeding and contraction of the heart. The feeling of heat in the stomach. The jitteriness in the muscles. How someone like you overcomes the hormone's effects interests me."

"But I *don't* overcome it's effects."

"I don't understand."

"In Delta Force, I was trained to use those effects, to treat them as positives, instead of the negatives people associate with fear."

Prescott kept listening intently.

"Put a parachute on someone and tell that person to leap out of a plane at twenty thousand feet, he's going to be terrified. It's a potentially life-threatening activity and one that's totally unfamiliar. But train that person in small increments, teach him how to jump off increasingly high platforms into a swimming pool. Then teach him how to jump from even higher platforms wearing a bungee harness that simulates the feel of a parachute. Then show him how to jump from small planes at reasonable altitudes. Gradually increase the size and power of the planes and the height of the jump. By the time he leaps from that plane at twenty thousand feet, he's going to feel the same speeding and contraction of the heart, the same burning in the stomach, the same jitteriness in the muscles as before. This time, though, he's not terrified. He knows how to minimize the risk, and he's experienced hundreds of similar activities. What he feels instead of fear is the sharp focus of an athlete ready to spring into action. His adrenaline is affecting him the same way it always did. But his mind knows how to control it and to appreciate its constructive effects."

"Constructive?"

"The speeding and the contraction of the heart cause a greater output of blood to reach muscles and prepare them for extreme action. The faster breath rate causes more oxygen to get to muscles. The liver creates glucose, increasing the amount of sugar in the blood. At the same time, more fatty acids circulate. Both the sugar and the fatty acids become instant fuel, creating greater energy and stamina."

"Correct," Prescott said. "You had excellent instruction."

"I was trained to *welcome* adrenaline, to appreciate what it does to help keep me alive. I was also trained to think of gunfights and car fights and all the rest of what happened today as being . . . not exactly normal, but I know what to expect. I know how to react. I can honestly say that not once today did I feel what's conventionally called fear."

Cavanaugh paused. Not once? he asked himself. What about the strange moment at the warehouse when I went up the stairs to meet Prescott?

"A powerful surge of adrenaline," Cavanaugh said, "but not fear, and that's why I don't think what I did today has anything to do with bravery. You're the one who's brave."

Prescott blinked. "Me? Brave? That's preposterous. For the past three weeks—and especially today—I've been terrified."

"That's my point," Cavanaugh said. "You can't be brave unless you're frightened to begin with. What you survived today was violent enough to unsettle even some experienced operators. I can only guess at the strength of character you had to muster to overcome the fear raging through you. You didn't freeze. You didn't panic, even though you must have felt that way. You promised me you'd be compliant, and you were. You're a prefect client."

Self-conscious, Prescott glanced down at the hardwood floor. Evidently, he wasn't used to compliments. "You might not feel afraid, but you still risk losing your life. For strangers. Why do you do that?"

Cavanaugh put on cotton gloves and began inserting 9-mm rounds into the pistol's magazine. In Manhattan, at the Warwick's bar, Jamie had asked a similar question. "Because it's what I know how to do and I'm good at it."

"No other reason?" Prescott asked.

"It's something I don't talk about with most people, because most people can't understand. Maybe *you* will because of your research into addiction."

"I'd like to try."

"Alcohol, cocaine, heroin, methamphetamines. People can get addicted to a lot of things. Some special-ops soldiers can't bear a quiet everyday life after they leave the service. They become mercenaries or contract operatives for the CIA, or security specialists."

"Or protective agents?"

Cavanaugh spread his hands in a gesture of self-admission. "It's like a race-car driver who isn't happy unless he's on a track, jockeying for position with other cars at two hundred and thirty miles an hour. The rush of adrenaline. To get it, he has to put up with periods of intense inactivity before and after each race. That's the way most protection assignments are. Intensely inactive. Even the inactivity, the constant waiting for trouble, has a rush to it, though. As much as I hate to say this, I'm addicted."

"Hate to say it?"

"Any addiction's a weakness."

The room became silent.

From a door opposite the one that Prescott had used to enter the living room, Chad appeared, wearing a white apron that contrasted with his red hair and looked slightly ridiculous on so muscular a man. He tried to sound like a butler in the movies. "Dinnah is served."

Cavanaugh couldn't help grinning. "I'll get the team."

As Chad returned to the kitchen, Prescott looked puzzled at the cotton gloves Cavanaugh wore. "Why did you put gloves on when you loaded the . . ."

"Magazine." Cavanaugh shoved it into the Sig and worked the slide on top of the pistol, inserting a round in the firing chamber. He pushed the decocking lever. "This kind of handgun ejects empty cartridges after discharging the bullets. I don't want to leave my fingerprints behind for somebody to identify them."

"Another way of being invisible?"

"If I had a coat of arms, Be Invisible would be my motto."

"What you said about addiction being a weakness," Prescott said. "It isn't always. Some thing's can't be controlled."

"I believe in willpower," Cavanaugh said.

"Sometimes, that isn't enough. The substance I discovered, for example, is stronger than anyone's will."

7

"I don't want anybody complaining because the only boneless sirloin I had was frozen and needed to be thawed in a microwave," Chad said.

The group, minus Tracy, who continued to watch the monitors in the control room, sat at a long table in a kitchen filled with stainless-steel appliances. The plates before the group had half-inch strips of beef in a beige sauce studded with mushrooms and onions on top of green noodles. A bowl of salad was next to each plate, with a napkin-covered basket of freshly baked bread in the middle.

"And I don't want anybody complaining because the green noodles aren't homemade but came out of a box."

"I can't imagine *anyone* complaining," Prescott said. "It looks and smells wonderful."

"With the right attitude like that, I'll cook for you anytime," Chad said.

"The team's on duty," Duncan told Prescott, "and can't have wine, but that doesn't mean *you* can't. I can offer what I'm told is a fine Chianti Classico."

Prescott nodded in approval.

Roberto stuck a napkin into the top of his shirt, highlighting his dark goatee. "Man, I haven't had goulash in ages."

"It's not goulash. It's beef Stroganoff," Chad said. "It was invented by a French chef who worked for a Russian aristocrat in the late nineteenth century. The aristocrat's name was Count Paul Stroganoff. As usual, the guy with the power got the attention, while nobody remembers the chef who created the dish."

"Did you ever think about getting an honest job and running a restaurant?" Cavanaugh asked.

"All the time," Chad said, "but I know I'd miss the smell of gun oil."

"Delicious." The enthusiasm with which Prescott ate was impressive. "There's something a little extra here that I can't quite place. The mustard and the sour cream, of course. But . . ."

Chad watched with interest as Prescott savored a mouthful.

"Oyster sauce? Is that what I'm tasting? Oyster sauce?"

"Two tablespoons. You know your food."

"Here's your wine." Duncan showed Prescott the bottle, then set a glass next to him.

Prescott let the dark liquid drift over his tongue, assessing it.

"I telephoned my contacts at the DEA to learn more about Escobar's tactics, but it's Sunday evening, so I couldn't reach them," Duncan said. "I'll try again tomorrow. Meanwhile, we have a number of issues to discuss." He looked at Cavanaugh, who set down his fork and started the briefing.

"You need to understand there are four stages involved in arranging for you to disappear," Cavanaugh said. "The first is a new identity and new documentation for it, especially a birth certificate and a Social Security number. You want to be confident that the government won't question your Social Security number. One way to do it is to assume the identity of someone who's been dead for quite a while, someone without any close living relatives to contradict your claim to be that person. You meet these requirements by searching old newspapers for an item about an entire family that died in a fire or a similar disaster. You then learn the Social Security number of a child in that family who'd be your age now if he had lived. Many parents get a Social Security number for their newborns. Hospitals often include the applications with their regular paperwork. In some states, death certificates include that number, and death certificates are easy to obtain, a matter of public record."

"Assuming someone else's Social Security number is illegal, of course," Duncan said. "As a consequence, we never perform that service for any of our clients. We only teach them how to do it."

"I understand," Prescott said.

Cavanaugh continued. "For a moderate threat level, it's a fairly secure way to assume a new identity."

"Not foolproof, though." Roberto wiped his mouth with his napkin and joined the conversation. "Sometimes the government gets curious about a Social Security number that hasn't been used for years and now suddenly shows up on tax returns, which means that in addition to whoever's hunting you, you've got the government on your back, charging you with a federal crime."

"Exactly," Cavanaugh said. "And Escobar's threat level is too serious for us to allow you to get exposed in any way."

"What we're going to suggest," Duncan said, "is expensive, greater than the hundred-thousand-dollar fee you and I negotiated over the telephone."

"You want to raise the price?" Prescott set down his knife and fork.

"Given what happened today," Duncan said, "I don't have a choice."

"Raise it how much?" Prescott frowned.

"An additional four hundred thousand."

Prescott didn't blink. "You did a background check on me?"

"I did."

"You know that my biotech patents made me a millionaire many times over."

"I do."

"Thanks to Protective Services, I'm not in Escobar's hands. In fact, given everything Cavanaugh and the rest of you have done so far, not to mention all this—" Prescott gestured toward his surroundings—"a half million dollars sounds like a bargain. Tomorrow morning, I'll arrange an electronic transfer to your account."

"One hundred thousand dollars of that money," Duncan said, "shouldn't go anywhere near our account. Once we teach you how to hide the electronic trail, I want the hundred thousand transferred directly to someone else." Duncan slid a piece of paper across the table to Prescott. The paper had numbers and a bank's name written on it.

"To a specialist, who has a way to get you a brand-new, previously unassigned number," Cavanaugh said.

"Doesn't a similar problem still exist?" Prescott asked. "New numbers go to young people. Won't the government question the number when it suddenly starts showing up on tax returns for a man my age?"

"New numbers also go to immigrants who get green cards," Duncan said.

Prescott gave him a significant look. "Brilliant."

"I'm assuming this specialist will invent a background for you that says you're from Canada, Great Britain, South Africa, Australia, or New Zealand. Some country that would account for your Anglo-Saxon features," Duncan said. "She'll give you—"

"She?"

"You'll find Karen quite personable. She'll give you a detailed background—where you supposedly grew up and went to school and so on—which you'll need to memorize until it seems it really is your background. She'll also give you photographs of these places and information about them that anyone who'd been there would be expected to know. You'll get a new name, of course, which you'll need to internalize until it's second nature to you. A driver's license with a picture ID. A passport. Credit cards. Sometimes even a library card. All of them perfect. Cadillac treatment. Very expensive," Duncan concluded.

Prescott looked fascinated. "But how does she manage to do this?"

"If I asked her, I'm sure she'd refuse to answer, or else she'd lie to me."

Duncan himself was lying, Cavanaugh knew. The truth was that Karen had once worked for the branch of the State Department that supplied undercover intelligence operatives with documents for false identities.

"The main thing is, she does exceptional work," Duncan continued. "She's already preparing the documents. All you need is to have her take your photograph so she can put it on your new driver's license and passport. Tomorrow, we'll take you to Albany and complete the process. By nightfall, you'll be a new man."

"You said there were four stages in arranging for me to disappear," Prescott said. "What are the other three?"

Duncan looked at Cavanaugh, nodding for him to continue.

"Eventually you'll want to change your appearance. Some of it can be easily done. Since you have fair hair, it makes sense to dye it black. You're clean-shaven, so it makes sense to grow a mustache or a beard. You don't wear glasses, so why not get a pair that has non-corrective lenses? All that's fairly obvious, and in moderate-risk situations would be sufficient, but in *your* case, some form of surgical change is advisable. We'll take you to a plastic surgeon we use. Not even your mother will recognize you after he's finished with your nose and chin."

"My mother's dead," Prescott said.

"Sorry to hear that, but on the other hand, that partly solves the biggest problem you're going to have," Cavanaugh said.

"Which is?"

"I'll come to it in a moment, after I deal with the third stage in your disappearance, which is arranging for you to have access to money. In many cases, the person who's disappearing has to give up a job. In his or her new life, money becomes a significant issue."

"Fortunately, that *won't* be an issue for you, because you're wealthy." Duncan slid another piece of paper across the table to him. "Tomorrow, after the final details of your new identity have been arranged, you'll transfer your money to this numbered bank account that we've established for you in the Bahamas. You'll note that the password is Phoenix. I couldn't resist the rebirth idea. As soon as you activate the account, change the number and the password so you're confident the money is secure, even from us."

"You'll need to establish another bank account, this one conventional, in your new name at your new place of residence,"

Cavanaugh said. "Periodically, you'll transfer funds to that second bank, preferably in amounts less than ten thousand dollars, because transactions larger than that have to be reported to the government. But don't make it *too* close to ten thousand dollars, because the DEA uses that pattern to identify drug traffickers. Seven to eight thousand would be a reasonable figure, one that won't attract the government's attention."

"You'll need a story to tell your banker to explain your income," Duncan added. "Perhaps you receive periodic installments from a trust fund. Perhaps you retired early after selling a business and for tax reasons you preferred a schedule of payments rather than a lump sum. Whatever fabrication feels comfortable to you."

Prescott took another sip of wine. "And the *fourth* stage? The one that presents the most problems?"

Cavanaugh looked around the table. Everyone glanced down, uneasy.

"Initially, a new life sounds tempting," Cavanaugh said. "An escape from your enemies. A fresh beginning. The chance to correct mistakes and start over. The trouble is, you have to make a complete break with your past. Do you have a family, Mr. Prescott?"

"No."

"No ex-wife? No children in college?"

"No. My work kept getting in the way of marriage and establishing a family."

"A lady friend?"

"No."

"A boyfriend?"

"I'm not gay," Prescott said with annoyance.

"That's remarkable. I've been protecting people for several years, and this is the first time I've dealt with someone who had no serious social connections. You said your mother was dead. What about your father?"

"Dead also."

"In other words, there's no one in the world who'll miss you if you drop out of sight."

"More or less." Uncomfortable, Prescott glanced down. "Yes."

"That makes it easier," Cavanaugh said, "because a clean break with the past means you'd never have been able to contact your parents if they were alive, or other relatives, or your friends. If you'd wished, a wife and children could have gone with you to your new life, but they'd have had relatives and friends *they'd* have missed, and eventually you or someone in your family would have been tempted to get in touch with people you cared for in your past. In most cases, if your enemy manages to find you, that's how it's done, by keeping a close watch on the friends and relatives you left behind, by checking their mail and tapping their phones and watching for any change in their routine. Fortunately, that's not going to be an issue here."

"Do you have any fantasy spot where you've always wanted to live?" Duncan asked. "When you decided to disappear, was there a place you had in mind?"

"No." Looking more abandoned, Prescott stared at his wineglass.

"Good," Duncan said. "Because, if you had, you probably would have mentioned it to people you worked with or did business with."

"Casual conversation," Chad said. " 'Gosh, wouldn't it be great to live in Aspen and ski whenever I want in the winter.' So you disappear and move to Aspen, and the next thing, Escobar's men come crashing through your back door."

"Do you subscribe to any scientific journals?" Cavanaugh asked.

"Several."

"Not any longer," Duncan said. "Escobar will find out which journals publish articles in your specialty. He'll manage to get his hands on the subscriber list. He'll make a note of which subscribers recently moved and which people subscribed after you disappeared."

"And the next thing you know," Roberto said, echoing Chad's earlier comment, "Escobar's men'll come crashing through your back door."

"Do you like to play golf?" Cavanaugh asked.

"Yes. It's one of the few forms of exercise that—"

"Not any longer. You can't ever go near a golf course again. Escobar will find a way to learn your habits. If he somehow manages to figure out where you've moved, he'll arrange to have someone watch the golf courses, waiting for you to show up. On and on," Cavanaugh said. "Do you understand what we're trying to tell you?"

Prescott gulped the last of his wine and poured another full glass. "When you say 'a new life,' you mean it literally. I have to make a complete break from my past."

"With no exceptions," Cavanaugh emphasized. "The kind of clothes you like. The music you like. The food you like. You're going to have to change *all* of it. The books you like. Back at the warehouse, you had the collected poems of Robinson Jeffers and a couple of books about him. From now on, Jeffers is one author you can't ever be caught reading."

"You make it sound . . ." Prescott's voice faltered. "Depressing."

"For many, it is, once the people who disappear finally understand the full implications," Duncan said. "You have to prepare yourself and confront the problem now. How much are you afraid of Escobar? Are you ready to do everything that's necessary, no matter how isolating, in order to keep him away from you?"

Prescott took another long swallow from his glass. "I'm tired of being afraid. Yes." His expression hardened. "I'm ready to do everything that's necessary."

"Good," Duncan said. "Tomorrow, we'll take you to meet Karen in Albany, get your photograph taken, and receive the documents for your new identity."

Tracy suddenly entered the room. "Maybe not."

"Why?" Duncan frowned.

"Three helicopters are headed this way."

8

"Helicopters?"

Duncan came to his feet at the same time Cavanaugh did. Followed by Chad and Roberto, they hurried with Tracy out of the kitchen, along a corridor, and into the control room.

Various television monitors were stacked in rows along a wall, receiving green-tinted night-vision images from cameras positioned around the helicopter and the bunker. But what the team focused its attention on was a radar screen, which showed three blips heading north, approaching the area.

Roberto studied them. "Yeah, the speed and the formation are consistent with helicopters."

"What's happening?" Prescott's strained voice asked behind them.

"We don't know yet," Cavanaugh said. "It might not be anything to concern us."

"The moment they appeared on the radar, heading up the Hudson," Tracy said, "it was obvious they were following the flight plan we filed at Teterboro."

"Coincidence?" Duncan asked.

"Maybe," Chad said. "There are a number of small airports up the Hudson, not to mention the one at Albany. They might land at one of them and go to a corporate retreat or something. Hell, maybe these are politicians flying to the state capital."

"Maybe," Tracy said. "And maybe not."

"What are we going to do?" Prescott asked.

No one turned from the radar.

"If it's Escobar's men trying to follow us," Roberto said, "the destination on the flight plan's too vague to bring them here. There are a lot of mountains and valleys. Even in daylight, those choppers could search forever and not find this place."

"Look." Tracy pointed toward the screen, where the three blips separated, moving west from the river.

"They're heading into the mountains," Chad said.

"Splitting up," Cavanaugh said, "saving time, searching one to a valley."

"But even with night-vision equipment, they're not going to see anything that tells them where we are," Roberto said. "For all they know, we landed at a farm and our helicopter's in a barn. It would take weeks for them to search all the farms in this area."

"Plus, if they flew here from Teterboro, they'll have to refuel in an hour or so," Cavanaugh said.

"Look." Tracy pointed again.

On the screen, the three blips moved back and forth over separate areas.

"Systematically searching," Duncan said.

"But they're doing it awfully fast," Cavanaugh said. "Even with night-vision equipment, they'd need to move slower to make sure they don't miss anything."

On the screen, the three blips shifted rapidly to three other areas.

"Holy . . . Nobody can do a visual check of a valley that fast, not even in daylight," Tracy said.

"Unless that's not how they're checking," Chad said.

"What do you mean?"

"Not visually."

The rest of the group abruptly understood what Chad meant. They swung to look at Prescott.

His pale face contrasted with his dark eyes, which were wide with apprehension as he, too, realized what was happening.

Cavanaugh stared back at the radar screen. "Infrared sensors? *Thermal* sensors?"

The blips moved swiftly to three other areas.

"*Dios,*" Roberto said. "That explains it. They're looking for the helicopter's heat signature. The engine's cooled, but a thermal scanner makes metal look different from wood or dirt. They'll be able to distinguish the shape of the helicopter from the trees around it."

"Plus," Tracy said, "the landing pad'll still retain heat from the sunlight the concrete absorbed all day."

"But won't heat from the houses and farm equipment confuse them?" Prescott demanded.

"No," Duncan said. "A house or a truck would have an entirely different heat pattern. Besides, this valley's so rugged, there *aren't* any farms around here. The heat signature of the landing pad will be especially distinctive in the middle of a forest."

Prescott pushed through the group and stared at the radar. "How long before they get here?"

"At sufficient altitude, with magnifiers on the sensors, they can cover a lot of miles in a hurry. At the rate they're searching, they'll be here in ten minutes," Tracy said.

"This can't be," Duncan said.

"*What do you mean, 'can't be'?*" Prescott sounded more panicked. "It's happening right in front of your eyes!"

"Even with all his money, Escobar doesn't have the resources to suddenly get his hands on three helicopters with thermal sensors," Duncan said. "That's special equipment. You need to make plans to have it available, and Escobar had no reason to expect a helicopter chase."

"So where the hell did he get thermal sensors?" Chad asked. "It doesn't make sense. Unless . . ."

"What?" Roberto asked.

"Those aren't Escobar's men." Duncan swung again toward Prescott. "Is there anybody else you're afraid of? Who else would be chasing you?"

"Nobody. If those helicopters aren't Escobar's, I have no idea whose they could be."

On the radar, the blips moved relentlessly to three other areas, proceeding closer to the center of the screen, where the bunker and the helicopter were situated.

"Whoever they are, they're sophisticated," Duncan said. "What *else* do they have in those choppers?"

"Maybe it's time to worry about those rockets we talked about earlier," Chad said.

"Moment of truth," Tracy said. "We have to decide."

"*What's she talking about?*" Prescott asked.

"Stay or go," Tracy said. "If we stay, we don't know whether they can blow their way in here. But if we go—"

"We can't leave by helicopter," Roberto said. "If they've got heat sensors, we have to assume they also have radar. They'll know if our chopper takes off."

"But what if Mr. Prescott isn't in it?" Duncan asked. "What if you take off and act as a decoy?"

"They still might shoot me down," Roberto said.

"No," Cavanaugh said, "they won't shoot. Not if they think Prescott's aboard. They want him alive. When they chased me on the highway, they could have shot me, but they didn't. They didn't want the car to crash and kill Prescott. It's safe for you to distract them."

"The rest of us could leave in the Jeep." Chad referred to one of two vehicles in the bunker's adjacent underground garage.

"*Both* Jeeps," Tracy said. "We could use one of the cars as another decoy. Some of the helicopters will scan for other heat signatures and follow us. They'll have to separate and go in three directions. If we can get to the highway—the New York State Thruway is twenty miles to the east—there'll be so much traffic, they won't be able to decide which car they're hunting."

On the radar, the blips kept moving toward the center of the screen.

The group stared at Duncan.

"If we go, they won't shoot at us because they want Mr.

Prescott alive. If we stay, they'll have him trapped. Does that about sum it up?" Duncan asked.

The group kept staring at him.

"Move," Duncan said.

9

They didn't need to discuss what they had to do next. Although they continued to wear their pistols, they'd taken off their Kevlar vests. Now, with disciplined speed, they shifted from the control room and entered a room adjacent to it. There, in the bunker's arsenal, their vests were on a table.

"You'll need this." Cavanaugh put a vest on Prescott. "In case a bullet intended for one of us heads in the wrong direction."

After buckling on their vests, the team grabbed AR-15 assault rifles from a row of weapons that included shotguns and more handguns.

In theory, the AR-15, which was the civilian version of the military's M-16, could be fired only on a semiautomatic setting, one shot with each pull of the trigger, complying with federal gun laws. But these had been modified so they could be fully automatic, numerous rounds rapidly discharging with a single pull of the trigger. If law-enforcement officers were about to examine the weapons, the automatic function could be disabled by turning a small lever on the side and pulling the lever out; an interior spring-loaded plug would then slip into place, thus making the weapon legal while at the same time concealing that it had been tampered with.

Looking ashen, Prescott reached for one.

"No," Chad said. "Leave the fireworks to us. You might shoot yourself in the foot."

"Or one of *us*," Tracy said.

"But what if I have to defend myself? I should at least know how to use one of those things."

"If the situation gets that desperate, God help us," Roberto said. "Don't touch a rifle unless we're down and there's no other choice. Brace the stock against your shoulder. Point the barrel at your target. Pull the trigger. If a shell gets stuck, yank back this knob on the side to free it."

"The AR-15 likes to kick up," Cavanaugh said. "If you're not careful, all you do is shoot toward the sky. Keep forcing the barrel down toward your target. Can you remember all that?"

"I hope I don't have to."

Chad ran to the kitchen to make sure the stove and oven were off. Everybody grabbed windbreakers to cover their Kevlar vests. At the exit, Duncan opened the door. As the group hurried along the echoing concrete passageway toward the cold mountain night, Cavanaugh heard the *whump* of the approaching helicopters getting louder.

"Good luck, Roberto." Tracy's blond hair shone briefly in the light that spilled from the closing door.

"They've got less than an hour's fuel, and my tank's full. I can outrun them." Roberto backed to the left, moving into the murky forest. "Adios."

"Come on, Prescott." His Kevlar vest feeling bulky on him, Cavanaugh headed to the right, hurrying through the darkness toward the underground garage, the entrance to which was recessed into the hill. "Stay close to me." He reached the garage and glanced toward the shadows behind him. "Prescott?"

Holding their AR-15s, Duncan, Chad, and Tracy glanced back also.

All Cavanaugh saw were the indistinct outlines of trees and bushes. "Prescott?"

The helicopters thundered closer.

"What happened?" Chad asked. "Where'd he go?"

"The last time I saw him was . . ." Duncan stared back toward the entryway. "Don't tell me he's still inside."

"I'll get the Jeeps," Tracy said.

"Prescott!" Cavanaugh yelled.

The concrete passageway prevented the helicopters from seeing the faint motion-triggered light that came on when Duncan rushed to the number pad next to the door.

"Prescott!" Cavanaugh scanned the dark trees. Behind him, he heard a muffled motor that Tracy activated, raising the garage door.

At the end of the passageway, another light appeared as Duncan hurried into the bunker.

"Maybe he's in the bushes," Chad said. "He got awfully upset when he saw those radar blips. It could be he's so scared, his bladder went crazy."

"Or his bowels." Cavanaugh said. "Or he got sick." Cavanaugh moved through the dark bushes, checking. "Prescott!"

Behind him, he heard Tracy drive the first Jeep up the ramp from the underground garage.

As the helicopters rumbled nearer, Cavanaugh suddenly realized that he hadn't heard Roberto take off with the chopper. Move, Roberto! he thought. If you don't lift off soon, you won't have a chance of getting ahead of them.

"Prescott!" Scraping branches, Chad continued to search through the undergrowth as Tracy got out of the Jeep and ran back into the garage.

Now that his eyes were accustomed to the night, Cavanaugh could see to avoid obstacles in the starlit darkness while he rushed past the bunker's entrance and made his way through evergreen branches, hurrying toward the helicopter pad.

"Prescott!"

At once, Cavanaugh saw that the camouflage net hadn't been retracted and the dark dragonfly silhouette of the helicopter still sat on the pad, its motor silent, its blades unmoving. His nostrils contracted from the sharp smell of aviation fuel. The night air was saturated with it.

Turning to run, he missed seeing a shadowy log and tripped over it, falling. Careful to keep the AR-15's barrel from jamming into the dirt, he rolled, his shoulder and his back absorbing the impact. He used the momentum of his roll to rise to a crouch, but not before he saw that what he'd tripped over wasn't a log.

Roberto lay motionless, a half-moon providing enough light for Cavanaugh to see Roberto's stark open eyes and the black pool of blood where the rear of his head had been bashed in.

Simultaneously, the darkness exploded into an eye-searing glare as the aviation fumes ignited. The flames reflected off the fuel pump's hose, which lay on the ground, spewing liquid through the forest. A long wall of fire burst up through the bushes and trees. The force of the heat thrust Cavanaugh backward.

Before he ran, he saw the blaze envelope the helicopter, the camouflage net vanishing in a crackling flash. The light from the flames was so intense that he saw individual needles on tree branches, the texture of bark on trunks. Sprinting toward the bunker, he heard his footsteps crush dead needles and then a roar as the fire erupted farther through the forest, chasing him.

"Prescott!"

Although the power of the fire's roar overwhelmed what Cavanaugh shouted, it wasn't loud enough to obscure the din of the rapidly approaching helicopters. Racing harder, Cavanaugh saw the two Jeeps that Tracy had driven from the underground garage. Holding their AR-15s, she and Chad stood next to the vehicles, staring in surprise at the rapidly spreading flames.

The next instant, Tracy and Chad disintegrated as something streaked from one of the helicopters and hit the two Jeeps, the detonation spewing chunks of metal and body parts in every direction.

The shock of what Cavanaugh had seen, in combination with the force of the blast, almost knocked him to the ground. His

sanity felt threatened, the enormity of what had happened overwhelming him. But then he saw Duncan race from the bunker,
and his conditioning took control. Tightening his grip on his assault rifle, he hurried in a crouch toward where Duncan gaped at
the flames spreading quickly through the trees.

"Prescott's not inside!" Duncan swung to stare at the crater
where the Jeeps had been. "Chad and Tracy—"

"Took that hit!"

"Son of a bitch!" The outrage on Duncan's face changed to
alarm at the sound of something else shrieking from one of the
helicopters toward the flames.

10

Charging along the bunker's entryway, they dove through the
open door a moment before a second explosion struck near the
bunker. Shrapnel and chunks of burning trees filled the space
where they'd been standing.

Duncan slammed the door shut. "I thought Escobar wanted
Prescott alive!" The bunker shook from another explosion. "How
can he be sure he won't kill Prescott along with us?"

"Roberto's dead, too!" Cavanaugh rose to his feet and ran toward the control room.

"*What?*" Holding his AR-15, Duncan rushed after him.

"His skull's bashed in!"

"What the Christ is going on?"

They hurried into the control room and faced it's monitors.
Although Tracy had left the electronics on, some screens were
blank, the fire having destroyed the cameras linked to them. As
Cavanaugh studied the remaining active screens, some of those
went blank also. But enough cameras remained undamaged for

him to see that the fire had spread fast enough to have enclosed a third of the area around the bunker on the side where the landing pad and the helicopter had been.

One camera showed the three helicopters coming into view in the distance.

Something stung Cavanaugh's nostrils. "Do you smell smoke?"

"From the ventilation system." Duncan flicked a switch. "There. It's shut off. The outside air and the smoke can't get in. We've got enough air in here for a couple of days."

Cavanaugh nodded. "We won't need to stay inside that long. Those choppers'll soon be forced to leave to refuel. They won't come back, not after the fire and the explosions send the state police and emergency crews up here."

"They can't hope to get away unnoticed. I don't understand why Escobar's acting this desperately."

"What you said earlier—maybe you were right." Cavanaugh kept staring at the green-tinted images. Some of the outside cameras were having trouble adjusting their night-vision lenses to the fierce brightness of the spreading flames. On a few, all Cavanaugh saw was a glaring green tint. "Maybe this isn't Escobar."

"Then who else—"

Haze in the room irritated Cavanaugh's throat. "I thought you sealed the ventilation system."

"You saw me do it."

"Then what's causing this smoke?"

Thicker haze drifted from a ventilation panel in the ceiling.

"I smell—"

"*Aviation fuel.*" Cavanaugh pushed Duncan ahead of him, charging toward the corridor outside the control room. At the same moment, flames burst from the ventilation panel and ripped along the ceiling.

Cavanaugh felt the heat at his back as he and Duncan reached the corridor.

In the ceiling, smoke and flames erupted from a second ventilation panel.

Pressed down by the heat, Duncan coughed. "The fire must have come down the ventilation shaft before I blocked it."

"No! Look in the control room! The top left monitor!"

Despite the haze and the fire on the ceiling, they managed to get a half-distinct view of the screens. The one on the top left showed the earth on top of the bunker. The fire hadn't reached the bushes up there, and yet smoke spewed from the ventilation shaft.

"How the hell did aviation fuel get down the ventilation shaft?" Cavanaugh asked.

More smoke spread along the ceiling.

"We can't go out the front way!" Coughing, Duncan pointed into the control room toward the haze-enveloped screens.

A monitor on the top right showed an image from a camera that was aimed along the inside of the entryway toward what should have been forest. All the screen showed now were flames.

But the screen next to it showed the back exit, where the trees and bushes remained untouched, the fire not yet having spread that far.

Stooping, Cavanaugh hurried through the smoke-filled kitchen and living room. He and Duncan reached the front corridor and ran to the right along the wall of doors that ended at the bunker's rear exit.

Duncan twisted the lever on the dead-bolt lock and pulled the door open. Ready with his assault rifle, Cavanaugh rushed with Duncan along an exterior concrete passageway toward cool air and not-yet-burned trees. But the wind from the approaching fire whipped branches, and the forest's shadows were pierced by the rippling reflection of flames crackling nearer on the right. Suddenly, Duncan slammed backward into Cavanaugh, the two of them falling, the roar of an automatic rifle filling the passageway, muzzle flashes like strobe lights as bullets ricocheted off concrete. Duncan screamed.

With equal abruptness, the shooting stopped. Amid the smell of cordite, weighed down by Duncan, Cavanaugh groaned from a pain in his left shoulder. From the trees, he heard a scrape of metal that sounded like someone trying to free a shell stuck in an assault rifle's firing chamber. The approaching blaze dispelled shadows. Astonishingly, it revealed Prescott crouched among bushes. Glancing wildly toward the fire, Prescott held an AR-15, presumably Roberto's, and furiously worked to pull back the knob on the side.

"Duncan," Cavanaugh managed to say.

No answer.

The pain in his shoulder intensifying, Cavanaugh squirmed out from under Duncan's weight. He smelled the nauseating coppery odor of blood.

"Duncan, move!"

He hoped desperately that Duncan's wounds weren't serious. But then he saw Duncan's mangled face, where at least half a dozen high-powered rounds had made him unrecognizable.

"Duncan!" Forced to drop his rifle, Cavanaugh dragged his friend back toward the bunker. He struggled to get inside before Prescott freed the jammed cartridge. The closer Cavanaugh got to the doorway behind him, the more heat pressed against his back.

The scrape of metal ended.

"No!" With one last desperate effort, Cavanaugh pulled Duncan through the doorway. Another furious volley sent bullets zipping above Cavanaugh's head. They struck the corridor's ceiling and cracked against the concrete above the door. Cavanaugh slammed the door shut just before Prescott corrected the barrel's upward tug, forcing down his aim as Cavanaugh had taught him, sending bullets walloping against the metal door.

"Duncan." Cavanaugh's left shoulder ached worse. Coughing from the smoke and the heat, he concentrated on Duncan, feeling for a pulse, but it was obvious he would never find one.

"Duncan!"

11

Anger fought with grief. Too busy raging to fear for his life, wanting only to hammer Prescott's face until it was as unrecognizable as Duncan's, Cavanaugh scrambled back. After one last look at his friend, he ran in a crouch toward the living room. He couldn't go out the rear door. The passageway was like a shooting gallery, funneling bullets toward the target. As long as Prescott keeps his aim down, I don't have a chance, Cavanaugh thought. The only reason Cavanaugh was alive was that Duncan had been ahead of him and had taken almost the full force of the barrage.

Racing through the living room, Cavanaugh fought not to choke on the smoke. A round had hit an exposed area at the top of his left shoulder, between the vest's strap and his neck. As he charged bent over through the kitchen, his hand came away smeared with red from where he'd touched the meaty portion between his collarbone and his neck. Blood welled.

He dropped to his knees and gasped whatever relatively smoke-clear air was near the floor. Stung by the heat from the burning ceiling, he hurried to the munitions room. To leave the bunker, he needed to use the front exit, but as the camera in that passageway had shown, the burning trees and bushes out there blocked his way. The arsenal had a trapdoor that led to a concrete tunnel connected to an exit near the landing pad, but since that was the area where the fire was most intense, Cavanaugh wasn't sure he could use the tunnel as an exit.

Amid spreading smoke and heat, he shoved away the table on which the Kevlar vests had been piled. He kicked away a carpet, exposed the tunnel's trapdoor, and lifted the handle. Wafts of smoke drifted up, confirming his suspicion that the tunnel wouldn't protect him. If he tried to avoid the flames by climbing down there, the fire would suck out the tunnel's oxygen, asphyxiating him before it cooked him.

Cavanaugh's shoulder was stiff with greater pain. He felt light-headed.

Need to stop bleeding. Need to do it fast. Cavanaugh thought. He lurched toward a shelf that contained several red-colored pouches: Pro Med trauma kits favored by emergency service organizations. Among other things, each kit contained a fist-sized gauze wad called a "blood stopper" because it could soak up as much as a pint of blood. But as the fire worsened, Cavanaugh didn't have time to open a kit, pull out a blood stopper, apply it, and tape it down.

All he had time for was the tape. Not surgical tape. Instead, he grabbed a roll of silver-colored tape that was next to the trauma kits and was considered part of the first-aid supplies. Duct tape. The gunfighter's friend. He couldn't count the number to times he'd seen wounds sealed with duct tape. He ripped his collar open and used his right sleeve to wipe blood from the meaty part where his shoulder met his neck. He tore off two sections of tape and pressed them crossways onto the wound. Then he pressed them harder, wincing from the pain but feeling the thick tape's sticky underside grip his skin and adhere to it.

Staying closer to the floor, Cavanaugh ran from the arsenal and into a farther smoke-filled room—a bathroom—where he climbed into the tub and turned on the shower, dousing his hair and his clothes. He soaked a towel and tied it around his head. Dripping, he scrambled into the kitchen, where he grabbed a fire extinguisher from under the sink. The bunker's lights flickered, then failed as he ran into Duncan's office and grabbed another fire extinguisher from a corner of the room.

Staggering now, he crossed the living room, which was lit only by flames, and managed to reach the corridor at the bunker's entrance. He set down the fire extinguishers and took a third one from a closet. As with the rear exit, the front door had a knob and a lever for a dead-bolt lock. After freeing the lock, he tested the knob and jerked his fingers back when he felt heat on it. Wavering, he tugged down his jacket sleeve and protected his hand as he again tried the knob, still feeling heat but no longer caring, desperate to escape from the bunker.

He pulled the door open and stumbled back, aware of the intense heat behind him but unable to resist the backward motion because of what faced him—hell.

12

The roar of the flames blocking the passageway was matched by the howl of the wind they created. The heat was intense enough to suck the remaining oxygen from the bunker, causing a fierce wind from the interior that stopped Cavanaugh's reflexive backward motion and instead pushed him forward.

Now!

As a boy in Oklahoma, Cavanaugh had once seen a fire on an oil rig that his father had worked on. Cavanaugh had never forgotten how high the flames had gushed and how powerful the heat had been. The fire had started at sunset and had raged all night, making the area around the oil rig shimmer like noon in August. It had resisted the full force of five high-pressured water hoses, until finally Cavanaugh's father, dressed in a fire-retardant suit, complete with a head covering, had driven a bulldozer close to the upward-surging blaze. The bulldozer's blade had been raised to try to protect Cavanaugh's father from the heat. A metal pole had extended from the blade, a container of explosives dangling from it, asbestos-covered wires leading back from it. Cavanaugh's father had dumped the explosives near the heart of the gushing flames, had hurriedly backed the bulldozer away, and then had leapt down, taking cover behind the bulldozer as someone else had pushed a plunger that detonated the explosives. The wallop of the blast had nearly knocked Cavanaugh down, even from a distance. The din had made his ears ring for hours, although his hands had been clamped over them. But most impressive of all, most amazing, the explosion had blown out the fire.

"Because of the vacuum the blast created, because it sucked air away from the blaze," Cavanaugh's father had explained.

13

Cavanaugh threw the first fire extinguisher into the flames beyond the entryway. Frantic, using all his strength, he hurled the second extinguisher much farther. He had no idea how long it would take the intense heat to rupture the tanks, but he couldn't afford to wait. Not daring to think, feeling heat behind him about to boil his wet clothes, knowing that he'd die if he didn't move, he picked up the third extinguisher and ran toward the inferno.

The shock wave from the first explosion hit him like a punch. Continuing to run, he hurled the third extinguisher ahead of him. The next explosion stunned him, nearly knocking him down. But he couldn't relent, couldn't hold back. He entered the roaring flames, or what had been roaring flames, for the explosions and the retardant they spewed had caused a vacuum in the fire. Then the third extinguisher detonated ahead of him, and he found himself racing, breath held, through an empty corridor in the fire, a wall of flames ten feet on each side of him. He crashed through unburned undergrowth and lost his balance, tumbling down a wooded slope, the motion putting out flames on his jacket and pants while with a mighty *whoosh* the blaze recombined behind him.

He realized that the throbbing in his legs, arms, and back must have come from rocks he'd rolled over. He didn't care. Pain was life. Pain urged him forward along a deep gully. He'd lost the drenched towel he'd tied over his head. Not that it mattered, for the fire had quickly dried the towel, and the heat on his head was from smoldering hair, which he swatted with his hands and sleeves.

He fell again, rolling. He came to his feet and staggered onward into darkness. He heard the crackle of the blaze spreading behind him. But he also heard the thunder of the three helicopters moving toward the side of the bunker that hadn't yet been enclosed by the fire.

Staring up, Cavanaugh saw the flame-reflecting unmarked choppers descend to the treetops, saw ropes drop from each chopper, saw black-clad men with compact submachine guns slung over their shoulders fling themselves from a hatch in each chopper and rappel to the ground—one, two, three, four, five men from each hatch. They slid smoothly, expertly, relentlessly down. They wore helmets with earphones and radio microphones.

Then they disappeared among the trees, and Cavanaugh stumbled onward along the dark gully, but he'd seen enough to conclude that no drug lord, not even Escobar, would have quick access to that many men who looked that well trained. The only place men got that kind of training was the military, but not just any branch of the military. The men who'd rappelled from those choppers were obviously special-operations personnel, just as *he* had belonged to special operations.

Heart pounding furiously, he saw the choppers rise and separate, moving to equidistant points near the fire, making him realize that he was far from being safe, for the hunters who remained in those choppers had to be using thermal sensors to search for anyone trying to escape from the flames.

He didn't dare run. The moment the sensors detected a human-shaped source of heat, whoever was in charge up there would radio directions to the assault team on the ground. The gunmen would converge on that sector of the forest.

To save himself, Cavanaugh realized, he had to go back, to put himself as close as he could risk to the edge of the blaze so that his heat pattern would be disguised by the fire's. He turned and stumbled up the gully toward where trees and bushes erupted into flames ahead of him. The noises they made were like small explosions and gave him hope that when the fire extinguishers had detonated, they'd been noticed only as a seemingly natural part of the fire's progress. He felt the scorched air envelop him and tried to take heart from the thought that he was now invisible to the thermal sensors above him.

But the heat was so fierce that he couldn't possibly survive if he got any closer to it. The fire moved faster, forcing him to retreat with increasing speed as bushes in the gully burst into flames and gave the impression of chasing him. In that calculated, on-the-edge-of-death pattern, Cavanaugh shifted with the fire, moving as *it* moved. His vision blurred. His skin felt parched. He'd never been so thirsty. But he couldn't think about any of that, for in addition to keeping pace with the fire, he had to concentrate on the edges of the blaze to his right and left, watching for the gunmen. He assumed that they had separated to form a perimeter around the fire, keeping pace with it as *he* was, except they'd maintain a safe distance while they hunted for anyone the thermal sensors in the choppers failed to notice.

Pursued by fire as further trees and bushes burst into flames, Cavanaugh reached a more uneven part of the gully. His knees bent. He forced them to straighten. His chest fought to take in the little air available. His knees bent once more, and this time, he lost his balance, toppling, no longer rolling smoothly. In the shadows at the bottom of the gully he banged his side against a boulder, winced, and started to come to his feet, only to tense, making himself motionless as a man holding a submachine gun emerged from trees ahead on Cavanaugh's right, following the edge of the fire.

A sharp crack of blazing wood made the gunman spin to look behind him. In that instant, Cavanaugh dove to the side of the gully, toward a narrow space between the boulder he had banged against and the gully's dirt slope. He pressed himself down, desperate to merge with the terrain, hoping that the soot blackening his clothes and face would make him appear no more than another boulder or a rotting tree trunk.

If you're hiding, never look directly at a man who's searching for you, Cavanaugh's instructors had warned. The hunter might notice the glare of your eyes, or else the intensity you radiate might make him sense, rather than see, he's being stared at. Keep your gaze slightly away from him. Study him from the side of your eyes. Use your peripheral vision to keep track of his movements.

Cavanaugh did that now. Staring toward the opposite side of the gully while concentrating his peripheral vision on the right, he saw the blur of the gunman's silhouette descend into the gully. The gunman paused, as if studying the progress of the fire. Cavanaugh braced himself to shoot if the man showed any interest in the boulder Cavanaugh tried to hide behind. The man paused a moment longer. Too long. Cavanaugh was just about to pull the trigger when the man climbed from the gully, and continued along the edge of the fire.

The flames got closer. Pressed down by the accumulating heat, Cavanaugh squirmed forward past other boulders, straining to gain some distance from the fire behind him but unable to proceed with any speed lest the gunman glance back into the gully and notice movement. The heat became so intense that, as Cavanaugh breathed through his mouth, trying to get as much air as he could, his tongue and throat felt burned.

Above him, the three helicopters remained spread out like the points of a triangle, continuing to search for the human-shaped thermal pattern of any fleeing survivor. Feeling heat on the soles of his shoes, nearly overcome by the close flames behind him, Cavanaugh squirmed faster through the boulders. He was too low to be able to see if other gunmen approached the gully. All he could do was try to solve one problem at a time, and at the moment, his biggest problem was how not to get burned to death.

He came under an outcrop of earth, which past storms had formed when flash floods raged along the gully and tore a hollow along its side. Abruptly, dirt trickled onto him from the roof, the earth of which was held together by roots. His muscles compacting, Cavanaugh again stopped moving and imagined a gunman above him, aiming his weapon, scanning the edge of the approaching fire. He worried that the man's weight would collapse the roof, that his hunter would drop on him. More specks of dirt fell as the man shifted his weight. The specks pelted the back of Cavanaugh's head.

Fighting not to cough from smoke drifting toward him, Cavanaugh prepared to shoot if the man descended into the gully. Then the smoke became so thick that Cavanaugh had to hold his breath. But the man above him had to be holding his breath also, Cavanaugh knew. The smoke would soon force the man to move. The question was, Would the man move before Cavanaugh had to? During the arduous training Cavanaugh had received in Delta Force, he had once held his breath for four minutes in a room filled with tear gas, but that had been years earlier, and no matter how determined he was now, he doubted that he could hold his breath that long. Plus, he didn't know if the man above him wore some kind of mask that filtered the smoke.

Seeing the flames get nearer, almost overpowered by the heat, Cavanaugh realized that in a very few seconds, if the man didn't move, he was going to have to roll from his hiding place and shoot, then run farther along the gully so he'd be able to breathe.

And then what? Would other gunmen hear the shots and rush toward this sector? Even if they didn't hear the shots, the man would be expected to use the radio microphone on his helmet to maintain regular contact with the helicopters and the other members of his team. When the man didn't report on schedule, the other hunters would become suspicious and head in Cavanaugh's direction.

So would the helicopters. As Cavanaugh kept holding his breath, spots beginning to swirl in front of his eyes, it seemed that the helicopters were *already* heading in his direction, so suddenly loud did they become. They were descending toward the trees.

The man standing above Cavanaugh said something Cavanaugh couldn't distinguish. The man was evidently speaking to his radio microphone, his tone urgent. The next moment, Cavanaugh heard heavy footsteps pounding the earth, rushing away. More dirt fell. The thunder of the helicopters became even louder.

Cavanaugh couldn't hold his breath any longer. The spots before his eyes thickening, he bolted from the hollow. Scrambling to escape the dense smoke, he passed one boulder and then another, reaching clear air, and filled his lungs. Despite its warmth, the air was cooler than any he'd drawn in since he'd left the bunker. His vision became focused enough for him to see the orange ripple of flames within the smoke that he'd left. But what he concentrated on, aiming his weapon, were the rims of the gully, toward which he prepared to shoot if any gunmen showed themselves.

None did. To his right, the close roar of the helicopters made him peer warily over the slope's rim. The fire showed the helicopters a hundred yards away, above the trees. The gunmen seemed to be magically levitating toward hatches in the choppers, although they were actually being drawn up by power-driven cables. It was one of the smoothest extractions Cavanaugh had ever seen. In what felt like no time at all, each of the helicopters raised five men, and even before the hatches were closed, the helicopters pivoted, veering past the fire, heading west toward the denser sections of the mountains. Their thunder receding, they vanished into the darkness. Then the only sound was the roar of the blaze, which Cavanaugh was now free to get as far away from as he could.

Staggering away, reaching cooler air, he heard explosions that rumbled from the direction of the bunker. Obviously, the fire had detonated the munitions inside. He plodded past more boulders, over fallen tree limbs, through dense bushes and intersecting evergreen boughs. His loss of blood made him so weak that he was tempted to sit and rest, but he had to keep moving, had to muster all his discipline to put more distance between him and the fire. A new sound now intruded. In the distance, he heard a faint, shrill, high-pitched wail that gained volume, coming nearer. An approaching siren. *No,* he told himself. *Several* sirens. No doubt the state police and emergency crews. From a narrow paved road that went through the nearest town, eight miles away, they'd be rushing up the barely noticeable tree-flanked dirt lane that led to the bunker, which they didn't know existed but which they'd have no trouble finding now because of the fire.

The idea of plodding toward those sirens, of reaching the lane and waiting for the headlights of the emergency vehicles, was powerfully tempting. A chance to rest. To get his injuries treated. To gulp water—how thirsty he was, his tongue so dry that it felt swollen. He'd done nothing illegal. He had every reason to go to the police and get help.

But then he imagined all the questions the police would ask him. They'd keep him in protective custody, which, from Cavanaugh's view, meant no protection at all. They'd try to guard him at a hospital and then at police headquarters, or at their own version of a safe site, which wouldn't be safe. They'd probably suspect him of being part of the massacre, and proving his innocence would take more time, causing further delays before he was released, putting him at greater risk. Prescott had wanted him and the rest of the team dead. The son of a bitch. Until Cavanaugh had a chance to clear his mind and get his thoughts straight—Who were the men in the helicopters? Were they military, as he suspected? What did they have to do with Prescott?—the most cautious thing he could do was to make Prescott and the men in the choppers believe that every member of the protection team was dead, including him. Otherwise, if they learned that he was still alive, they might make another attempt, although Cavanaugh had no idea why the hell they wanted the protection team dead. Duncan, Chad, Tracy, Roberto. The litany of lost friends made Cavanaugh want to scream. His head pounded harder from too many questions he couldn't answer. All he knew for sure was that until he understood what was happening, he had to make it seem that he had, in fact, died.

I'm a corpse, he thought. A walking corpse.

No, not walking. *Staggering.* He needed all his discipline and strength to place one foot in front of the other and keep moving. The duct-taped wound in his shoulder kept aching. The skin on his hands, face, and scalp smarted from having been too close to the flames. Nonetheless, he mustered every residue of energy he could, straining to walk straighter and with more control.

Pretend you're at boot camp, he thought, attempting a joke. Or better—and this wasn't a joke—pretend it's your first day of Delta Force training. As he recalled Delta's isolated compound at Fort Bragg, a powerful flood of nostalgia seized him. Make your instructors proud, he thought, and walked more firmly.

The sirens approached on Cavanaugh's right. Keeping a distance from them, using them to determine his direction, Cavanaugh continued working through the dark forest. I'm going to need help, he thought. I look like a war atrocity. The instant I show myself, somebody's going to scream and call the police. Who's going to help me?

He thought of the man who'd initially been part of the extraction team, Eddie, the gum-chewing, pun-making—"These pieces'll soon be in pieces in a sewer"—driver who'd taken the black car away. Wary of a possible location transmitter, he'd intended to abandon it far from the airport. Cavanaugh had worked with him several times. As soon as Eddie learned what had happened, he would drop everything and come to get Cavanaugh as quickly as possible.

But something about that plan didn't feel right. Suppose Prescott and/or the men in the helicopters had an informant in

Protective Services. Suppose they knew that Eddie had been an initial member of the team. To assure themselves that Cavanaugh and everybody else had been killed, they'd maintain surveillance on Eddie. A phone call that summoned Eddie to a town near the destroyed bunker would be an obvious indication that not everyone on the protection team had died.

Can't take the chance, Cavanaugh thought. Need to be invisible.

Then who in God's name am I going to ask?

No matter how he calculated it, he always came back to the same answer: the one person in the world he didn't want to contact and the only one he could.

PART THREE

Threat Identification

1

"Warwick Hotel." The male receptionist's voice sounded sleepy.

"Room five oh four, please." In the darkness, Cavanaugh used his cell phone, keeping his voice low. He was hunkered behind rocks and trees a quarter mile past the lights of the town he'd spent the previous four hours working toward and then passing. He'd waited to get this far before calling, because there was always the risk that the area around the fire was being monitored by a cell-phone scanner (a military version could operate from miles away) in an effort to learn if there'd been any survivors. But near a town, someone using a cell phone, even at this hour, wouldn't seem unusual. Moreover, by now, emergency personnel would be making numerous cell-phone calls, which meant that a scanner could isolate a particular conversation only if it was calibrated to identify key words, such as *dead, attack, Global Protective Services,* or Cavanaugh's name. He intended to be as vague as possible.

"You'll have to speak louder, sir. I can barely hear you."

"Room five oh four."

"It's awfully late. Are you absolutely certain you wish to disturb—"

"My wife's expecting my call."

The receptionist exhaled wearily. "I'll put you through."

Pressing the phone against his right ear, Cavanaugh listened to the repeated buzz on the other end.

"Uh . . . hello?" Jamie's voice was thick with sleep.

"It's me." Cavanaugh sank lower among the trees. The phone felt cold in his hand.

"Hello? I can't—"

"It's me." The phrase was their signal that Jamie could trust what he said, that no one was forcing him to make the call. He'd taught her never to use names over the phone. He hoped that she remembered.

"Same here." That completed the signal. "Why are you? . . . What time is it?"

That she'd absorbed what he'd taught her made him relax a little. "Late."

"My God, it's almost four."

He imagined Jamie brushing back her dark hair and squinting toward the numbers on the digital bedside clock. He wanted to tell her immediately what he needed, but the conversation had to sound normal in case someone was eavesdropping. "Yeah, I know, but you've got an early flight, and I wanted to make sure I reached you before you checked out and left for the airport. I couldn't sleep until we patched up the argument we had."

"Argument?"

Cavanaugh imagined her frowning. "Saturday afternoon at the hotel's bar. I'm sorry you got pissed when I decided to go back to work. You're right. We should spend more time together." He imagined her frowning even harder. "Remember you said you had more money than I did and you wanted to take care of me? How'd you like to spend some of that money and take care of me now?"

Jamie paused a moment, evidently trying to figure out where the conversation was going. "Love to."

"Good. This morning, check out of the hotel the same as you'd planned. But instead of flying home alone, why don't you go by car? With *me*. We'll see some country and enjoy ourselves."

"Sounds perfect." Jamie continued to hide her confusion. "Where am I going to get the car? Rent it?"

"Go over to the West Side and buy it. We're due for a new one anyhow. I never liked the way the old one handled."

"Me, neither. It's about time we replaced it. What kind should we get?"

"A Ford Taurus is nice. Nothing too flashy. How do you feel about dark blue or dark green?"

"My favorite colors." Jamie still sounded husky from having been wakened. It made him wish that he could hold her now.

"Get the high-end model." That one had a two-hundred-horsepower engine, Cavanaugh knew, fifty more than in the standard models. The extra horses wouldn't win any Grand Prix speed records, unlike the serious racing engines that Global Protective Services put in its Tauruses. But they definitely added pep, and anyway, given the millions of Tauruses on the road, anonymity was now more important to him than massive strength.

"Since we're going to be traveling for a while, I could use more clothes," he continued. His suitcase had been in the trunk of the Taurus that had exploded at the warehouse. "Slacks, a sport coat, shoes. Jeans, a pullover, a pair of Rockports. You remember my sizes?"

"How could I forget?"

"Nothing gaudy."

"God forbid. Anything else?"

"Underwear."

"I love it when you talk sexy."

"Socks. Toothbrush. Razor. A first-aid kit. You never know what might happen on the road."

"Can't be too careful."

"You have no idea," Cavanaugh said. "Bring some sand-wiches. And water. Plenty of bottled water."

The phone was silent for a moment while Jamie tried to un-derstand the significance of that. "It'll take a while."

"I figured. That's why you'll need an early start."

"Where should I meet you?"

"I'm not sure yet. I'll call you at noon."

"Can't wait to see you."

"Same here. Sorry I woke you."

"Hey, you can wake me anytime. It's better if you're next to me, though."

2

Cavanaugh pressed the button that broke the connection. He switched off the phone to conserve its battery as well as to pre-vent it from ringing and attracting attention. Then he returned the phone to his windbreaker and glanced warily behind him, lis-tening for the sounds of emergency vehicles at the town he'd passed. The fire was close enough that the state police had begun evacuating the inhabitants. He had barely been able to sneak across the road and into the continuation of the forest without being noticed in the frequent coming and going of headlights. He'd seen trucks arriving, dropping off men with shovels and chain saws, a team that looked ready to use the road as a perime-ter from which to try to establish a firebreak. Other, bigger trucks had brought bulldozers.

He instinctively crouched when he heard a propeller-driven airplane drone overhead. No doubt the plane was with the fire-fighters. Spotters in it would direct the effort to contain the blaze, he assumed. And yet he couldn't stop irrationally worrying that the plane might somehow have a thermal sensor and be another part of the effort to hunt him. Sometimes you've got to have faith, he thought.

Using the sounds of the vehicles to guide him, he moved lower through the forest. Five minutes later, he heard an approaching helicopter and again crouched before assuring himself that the assault team would never be foolish enough to return to the attack area. This helicopter has to be part of the fire-fighting effort also, he told himself. Perhaps it's going to drop water or fire-retardant chemicals. But even though he was convinced of his logic, he felt naked as he continued through the trees.

A half-moon provided enough light for him to make his way past murky stumps and evergreen boughs. His goal was the next town along the road, about five miles farther to the east, where a north-south road intersected with one that came west from the New York State Thruway. The latter road continued west to the town he'd just left. It was the route the emergency personnel were using to get to the fire. He was certain the state police would establish a blockade at the town he was approaching. They'd want to prevent civilian traffic from heading into the fire zone. Thus, Jamie wouldn't be able to pick him up unless he found a rendezvous site beyond the blockade.

Soon, the gray light of dawn allowed him to increase speed. The sun, hazed by smoke, had been up for a couple of hours when he glimpsed a gray clapboard house through the trees. Immediately, he sank to the ground and peered through the bushes. He saw a freshly cultivated vegetable garden, a shed, a small garage painted the same gray as the house. What mostly attracted his attention was a hose on a faucet at the back. If I can just crawl over there and get a drink . . .

He imagined how cool and sweet the water would taste as it trickled over his lips and down his parched throat.

He almost weakened and emerged from the bushes. A good thing he didn't, for five seconds later, a slender young woman in work boots, jeans, a sweatshirt, and gloves came out. She would definitely have seen him, reacted to the dried blood all over him, and told the authorities.

Instead, she frowned toward the smoke in the sky, picked up the hose, and called toward the house, "Hey, Pete, I can't tell if that fire they told us about is headed this way. But since you're determined to defend the old homestead, maybe you'd better put down that beer can, grab the other hose, and give me a hand soaking the roof."

Too dehydrated to sweat in the day's heat, Cavanaugh crept back deeper into the trees. At a cautious distance, he skirted the house and several others, avoiding the town. At the north-south road, he descended into a culvert. It was cool, sandy, and dry. On the opposite side, he reentered the forest, but now he took strength from the knowledge that he would soon be able to rest. He angled toward the east-west road that came from the main highway, crept to bushes at the edge of it, and peered westward toward the crossroads, seeing that, sure enough, the state police had established a blockade but that it was beyond the crossroads, within the town itself.

Fine, he thought.

He returned to the trees near the culvert. When he looked at his watch, he was startled to see that the time was ten minutes past noon. He pulled out his phone, turned it on, and pressed numbers.

Jamie's phone buzzed only once before she answered, sounding worried. "Yes?"

"It's me." He kept his voice low.

"Same here. When you didn't call at noon—"

"Everything's okay."

"You're sure?"

"Things'll be even better when you pick me up." He heard voices in the background. "Where are you?"

"Buying the car. You'd think a cash offer and no haggling

would make it go quickly, but the paperwork went on and on. Finally, they're about to give me the keys."

He held the phone tighter. "Speaking of cash . . ."

"How much do we need?"

"At least two thousand in twenties."

"I'll bring three."

"Tell the bank clerk you're going to Atlantic City. When you get everything together, head north on the New York State Thruway. About fifty miles past the exit to Kingston, you'll come to a turnoff for a town called Baskerville."

Cavanaugh had no choice—at this point, he had to mention the name of the town. He assumed that it would be referred to in so many cell-phone messages between emergency personnel that it would never be a word that a scanner would pick to isolate a conversation.

"Follow the road west," he continued. "In about ten miles, when you get to Baskerville, stop at the crossroads and turn right. A hundred yards outside town, you'll see where a dry streambed follows a culvert under the road. Stop and get out, as if you think one of your tires might be leaking and you need to check them."

"Crossroads. Turn right. Culvert. Got it. That's where you'll be?"

"That's where I'll be." He looked up through the trees as another helicopter rumbled overhead. A huge canister, presumably containing water, dangled from its belly. "Unless the forest fire gets worse."

"Forest fire?" When he didn't answer, Jamie said, "You really know how to have a good time. I'll be there as soon as I can."

"Call me when you're close. I'll leave my cell phone on."

"Are you honestly okay?"

"I *will* be. Thanks for helping."

"Thanks for asking. I never expected you would."

3

Cavanaugh put the phone in his jacket. Having finally accomplished everything that needed to be done, he glanced around the forest. Finding a depression in the ground, he covered it with dead branches, satisfied himself that the camouflage looked natural, and crawled beneath the branches into the shadowy hollow. There, amid the not-unpleasant smell of earth, he leaned back against the slope. He had a temporary sense of relief. Now all I have to do is wait for Jamie, he thought.

Despite the shade of the branches spread over him, the day became warmer. Conscious of how awkward the Kevlar vest felt, he removed it. Only then did he become aware of the shrapnel embedded in it: fragments from one of the fire extinguishers that had exploded.

He frowned at the shrapnel for almost a minute. Then he tested the duct tape on his wound, which throbbed where his shoulder met his neck. The thick silver strips continued to provide a tight seal, no blood escaping. The swelling made it painful for him to turn his neck.

He stretched his legs, or tried to—no sooner had he extended his legs than they retracted, bending toward him. Here it comes, he thought. It was happening much sooner than he anticipated. As long as he'd been in motion, working to get away from the fire, making arrangements with Jamie, finding a safe haven, his adrenaline had been his friend, fueling his weary body, spurring him on.

But now that he had nothing to do for the next few hours, adrenaline no longer served a purpose. It made him jittery. Not only did it cause his knees to bend toward him but it also made his arms want to fold over his chest. Already he felt the urge to yawn, partly because he lacked sleep, but mostly because his muscles needed to release tension. You want the high of action, you pay the price, he thought.

He hugged himself and shivered. Waiting for his body to still itself, he assumed something like a fetal position, which was fitting, because he often thought of adrenaline withdrawal as a preparation for rebirth, and birth couldn't happen without pain.

His eyelids felt heavy. Close to drowsing, he adjusted his cell phone so that it would vibrate instead of ring. He placed it under his jacket, then withdrew his handgun and held it in one of his crossed hands. Finally, all preparations complete, he drifted into sleep.

4

The tremble of the phone against Cavanaugh's stomach brought him immediately to consciousness. Years of discipline had trained him to clear sleep's fuzz from his mind and become instantly alert. He felt the phone tremble a second time as he crawled up the hollow's slope, listened for any threatening sounds, and then peered cautiously from beneath the carefully arranged branches. The phone trembled a third time while he sniffed the smoke in the air. But there wasn't any haze, and he concluded that for now he was safe.

Sliding back into the hollow, he holstered his handgun and answered the phone. "Taco Bell." That was another of their codes.

"Good. You're open," Jamie said, completing the sequence. "When you didn't answer right away—"

"Just taking a snooze." With the phone pressed to his ear, he glanced at his watch, the hands of which were close to 4:30. "Where are you?"

"Approaching town. I see the crossroads. You weren't kidding about the fire. The mountain's covered with smoke. There's a roadblock."

"In town?" Cavanaugh hoped that it hadn't been moved lower.

"Yes, in town. A policeman's turning away a couple of cars ahead of me."

"You can make the turn at the crossroads?"

"Yes."

"I'll be waiting."

He broke the connection, put the phone in his jacket, and grabbed the Kevlar vest. After another cautious look past the branches that covered the hollow, he squirmed up into the forest, reached the bushes at its edge, and studied the north-south road. Above it, as Jamie had said, the mountain was covered with smoke. The fire seemed to have headed westward instead of toward town. A helicopter flew over the smoke, dropping water.

When a van with an unflashing emergency light went past, he stayed low, waiting until the noise of its engine receded. Then he peered toward the road again, saw nothing to alarm him, and shifted into a grassy ditch, following it to the culvert. Once inside, he listened for the echo of a car stopping above him.

A minute later, one did stop.

Someone opened a door and shut it. He heard footsteps on pavement and then gravel, someone circling a car, as if checking for a flat tire.

"Where are you?" Jamie asked quietly.

He moved to the culvert's edge. "Look up and down the road. Anybody watching?"

"Not a soul."

"Get back in the car. Wait until I slip into the rear seat. Then drive away."

Cavanaugh listened to Jamie's footsteps returning to the driver's door. His heart pounded faster. The moment he heard her open the driver's door, he left the culvert, rose from the ditch toward the dark Taurus, opened the door, threw in the Kevlar vest, and climbed in after it. Lying flat on the seat, he closed the rear door.

Jamie wore a tan linen jacket. Her glossy dark hair was silhouetted against the windshield. As she put the Taurus into gear, she glanced back. Her green eyes widened at the sight of the dried blood all over him, at his torn clothes, the dirt, the soot, his singed hair, and the duct tape on his shoulder. "Oh Christ," she said.

She made him proud by overcoming her shock, turning forward, and stepping on the accelerator, keeping the vehicle at a speed that was reasonable enough not to attract attention.

"How bad?" Tense, she kept her gaze on the road.

"It looks worse than it is." His words were like stones in his throat.

He saw a flat of bottled water on the floor. Shrink-wrapped plastic covered it. Mouth dry, tongue swollen, he yanked at a tab that allowed him to peel off the plastic.

"Are you"—she took a breath—"shot?"

"Yes." He grabbed a bottle and untwisted its cap.

"Then how could it be *worse*?"

"It wasn't center of mass. Only my shoulder." Staying low, Cavanaugh dumped water into his mouth, some of it spilling over his lips, then onto his jacket and the seat. His tongue was like a sponge, absorbing it.

Jamie's voice became agitated. "Is that like saying 'It's only a flesh wound'? What *is* that? *Duct tape*?"

"Don't leave home without it."

"You patched yourself up like you're a leaky pipe? For God's sake, you could die from infection. I'm taking you to a doctor."

"No," Cavanaugh said quickly. "No doctor."

"But—"

"A doctor would have to report a gunshot wound to the police. I don't want the police involved. I don't want the authorities to know I'm alive."

"Doesn't Protective Services have doctors?"

"Yes."

"Then—"

"I can't let anybody there know I'm alive, either."

"What the hell is going on?"

Cavanaugh gulped more water. He was so parched, he could feel it flow down his throat and into his esophagus. Next to the flat of bottled water, he saw a small Styrofoam cooler. His wounded shoulder aching, he pulled off the cooler's top and looked inside.

"Pastrami on rye," Jamie said. "Potato salad and coleslaw. There're a couple of dill pickles in there, too."

Cavanaugh bit off a chunk of sandwich and chewed it hungrily. With the first swallow, though, he suddenly felt ill. He lay back, staring at the ceiling, which seemed to waver as he felt the smooth vibration of the car.

"You're serious? No doctor?" Jamie asked.

"No doctor."

"Where do you want me to take you?"

"Back to the highway. Head north. Albany's about an hour away. Check us into a motel, one of those places where you can park outside the room."

"Let me guess—nothing fancy, right?"

"On the seedy side. Where it's not unusual to pay cash and people don't like to phone the police."

"I can tell this is going to be charming."

"Did you bring a first-aid kit?"

"Something in your voice made me think I should get a big one. It's with those bags of clothes on the floor."

Cavanaugh sorted among the bags and found a plastic first-aid kit the size of a large phone book. His wound aching more, he pried the kit open and sorted among bandages, ointments, a pair of scissors, finding several two-capsule packets of Tylenol. He tore a couple of packets open and swallowed their contents, downing them with water. Drink slowly, he warned himself. Don't make yourself sick.

"I've been patient," Jamie said. "I've asked you only once."

"You want to know what's going on."

"Gosh, how did you guess?"

"I've never told you about my assignments."

"That's right." Jamie kept driving. "But this time you will."

"Yes," Cavanaugh said. "If you're going to risk your life to help me, you have a right to know what you're getting into. This time, I'll tell you."

5

The Albany motel, called the Day's End Inn, was on a side street five blocks off the highway, in a cut-rate district away from the Holiday Inns and Best Westerns. Two bars, a transmission-repair shop, and a hamburger joint were typical of the adjacent buildings. With the lowering sun casting shadows, the transmission shop was closed. A few men got out of pickup trucks and went into one of the bars. Otherwise, there was hardly anybody on the street.

En route, Cavanaugh had used some of the bottled water to rinse blood and soot from his face. He'd put on the sport coat, jeans, and pullover that Jamie had bought for him, concealing the duct tape on his shoulder. A baseball cap that Jamie had thought to include covered his singed hair, allowing him to sit up without attracting attention. He studied the drab street while Jamie went into the office to rent a room.

Holding a key attached to a large yellow plastic cube, she returned to the car.

"You paid cash?" he asked.

"Yes. I told the clerk our credit card had been stolen."

"As good an explanation as any."

"He's probably used to couples paying cash. Maybe he thinks we're having an affair." Jamie drove off the street, heading toward the back of the motel. "I understand why you don't want me to use a credit card. No paper trail. But in theory, no one knows about me, right?"

"In theory," Cavanaugh said. "I never told anybody at Protective Services, not even Duncan." In a flash of memory, Cavanaugh saw Duncan's mutilated face. His grief and rage intensified.

Jamie parked near a Dumpster at the next-to-last unit. "Then aren't you being more careful than necessary?" She shook her head. "I know what you're going to say. There's no such thing as being too careful."

Despite how he felt, he managed a smile.

Jamie got out of the car, went over to the motel unit's door, and unlocked it.

Simultaneously, Cavanaugh opened the car's rear door, picked up several packages, which would distract anybody glancing in his direction—people love looking at packages—and walked as steadily as he could into the shadowy unit.

Two regular beds had faded covers. A table had scratches. A small television was bolted to the wall. The carpet was thin. The mirror over the bureau had a crack in one corner.

"You said you wanted seedy," Jamie said.

The room smelled faintly of cigarette smoke.

"There weren't any nonsmoking units," Jamie said.

"It's fine." Cavanaugh set the packages on a table, eased onto the bed, and sank back, closing his eyes, hoping for the unsteadiness in his head to lessen. "A good place to hide. You did great."

"I'll get the water and the rest of the stuff from the car." After Jamie finished, she shut the door and locked it.

On the bed, keeping his eyes closed, Cavanaugh sensed her studying him.

"Should I leave the lights off?" she asked.

"Yes."

"What can I do for you?"

"Bring me more water. Give me more Tylenol."

"Is the wound infected?"

He swallowed the capsules and the water. "I guess"—he managed to rouse himself—"we'd better find out."

6

The hot shower cascaded over Cavanaugh, drenching his bowed head and his back. Then he tilted his head up, letting the water pour over his face and chest. He was so unsteady, he had to sit.

The shower curtain was pulled open. Silhouetted by the light from a makeup mirror outside the shower stall, Jamie lowered the lid on the toilet seat. She sat, put her elbows on her knees, and watched him.

Although the light out there hurt his eyes, it allowed him to see the blood, dirt, and soot swirling down the drain. As he shampooed his head, bits of singed hair followed them.

"You've got bruises on your legs and chest," she said.

During the drive north, he had haltingly told her what had happened. Again, she had made him proud by listening, not interrupting with outbursts, instead swallowing her emotions and asking occasional necessary questions.

"Must have been when I rolled down the gully," he said. "You could have been an operator, you know that? You learn fast. I don't know where you got them, but you have the right instincts."

Her solemnity straining her beauty, Jamie said, "The instincts come from hanging around with *you*." She rolled up her sleeves and soaped his back. "So why did Prescott want your team dead?"

"And who were the guys in the helicopters? They handled themselves the way military special ops teams do," Cavanaugh said.

"What about the assault team at the warehouse?"

"They had hardware, but their tactics were conventional. They weren't as disciplined as the guys in the helicopters. When they stormed the stairs at the warehouse, they hung back, almost as if they were afraid."

He turned off the shower. As the water dripped from him, neither he nor Jamie moved for a moment.

"I guess it's show time," he said. "You remember what needs to be done?"

"You were very clear."

"Okay." Cavanaugh took a deep breath, reached his right hand to his left shoulder, pried up the edges on the duct tape, exhaled, took another deep breath, and started to pull the strips away. The pliant tape had a sticky under-side that parted slowly from his skin. He couldn't do it quickly, because he wanted to avoid tearing and widening the wound. Each second prolonged the pain. With the tape off, blood now flowed, but not as much as when he'd first been shot, clots having formed in the meantime.

Immediately, Jamie pressed the soapy washcloth onto it, swabbing quickly but gently, cleaning away dirt and puss.

He grimaced.

"Done," she said.

He leaned forward to turn on the shower, rinsing. "I can't move my head enough to see it."

"It's a gouge across the top of your shoulder. The good news is, as much as I can tell, the bullet went through."

"Felt like it. What's the *bad* news?"

"The gouge is two inches long."

Cavanaugh nodded. As blood flowed down the drain, he turned the shower off and braced himself for what Jamie was going to do next.

Before checking into the motel, they'd made a quick stop at a drugstore to buy a bottle of hydrogen peroxide.

Jamie opened the bottle and poured it over the wound.

As the liquid bubbled and foamed in the long, deep gouge, the pain felt like razors and fire combined. He gritted his teeth and grabbed the side of the tub.

"Rinse it," Jamie told him.

His vision shaking, he turned on the shower again. More blood, mixed with foaming liquid, swirled down the drain. When he leaned back from the spray, Jamie poured another stream of hydrogen peroxide. Again the long, deep gouge erupted in bloody foam.

"Christ Almighty . . ." Cavanaugh murmured. He leaned into the spray. As more bloody foam swirled down the drain, he turned off the shower and slumped over the side of the tub, feeling Jamie towel the wound.

His jaw muscles hardened.

"The skin's red," Jamie said.

"The tape must have irritated it."

"No. This is a different kind of red. It looks like the wound's infected." Jamie soaked up more blood. In a rush, while the gouge was temporarily dry, she opened a tube of antibiotic cream, squeezed half of it along the gouge, pressed a wad of gauze over that, and sealed everything with several strips of first-aid tape.

He took a deep breath.

"Can you stand?" Jamie asked.

He slipped when he tried. Jamie grabbed him before he could fall, water from him sticking her blouse to her chest.

She sat him on the toilet lid and used the last towel, a big one, to dry his arms, chest, head, and back, avoiding the area of the wound, the thick bandage on it now pink with blood.

"I'm going to pull you up," Jamie said.

Off balance, Cavanaugh felt her move the towel over his legs, privates, and hips. Apart from the pain in his shoulder, his sensations came from a distance, as if his body didn't belong to him.

"Hang on." Jamie hooked his arm around her neck and guided him into the shadowy bedroom, easing him onto the nearer of the two beds. "You feel hot. Do you think you have a fever?"

Before he could answer, he started shivering.

As his chills became more violent, Jamie took off her slacks, got under the covers, and held him. "You need a . . ."

"No," Cavanaugh managed to say between shivers.

His eyelids felt heavier. The shadows in the room darkened. She held him closer.

7

A tug at Cavanaugh's shoulder woke him. Blinking from faint light filtering through curtains, he managed not to wince when Jamie removed the bandage from his shoulder. Her green eyes narrowed, assessing the wound.

"How does it . . ."

"As red as last night," she said.

He felt something inside him tighten.

"But at least you don't feel as hot."

"That's encouraging, don't you think?"

"The wound crusted over."

"See what I mean? Encouraging."

She applied more antibiotic cream, covered it with another wad of gauze, and taped the wound securely.

"What's the time?" Reflexively, Cavanaugh looked at the bedside clock and frowned at red numbers that told him 4:22. More troubled, he pointed toward the curtains. "How can it be light this early in the morning?"

"It's afternoon."

"What?"

"You slept all night and most of the day. Don't you remember I fed you more of the pastrami sandwich and some of the potato salad from the cooler?"

"No."

"This morning."

"No."

"A couple of times, I helped you into the bathroom."

Cavanaugh looked blankly at her.

"When the maid came to clean the room, I went outside to talk with her," Jamie said. "I told her you were sick from eating sandwiches that had spoiled in the car. I said I didn't want to leave you alone. Then I gave her money to give to the desk clerk to rent this room for another night. I called the front desk, and she did pass the money along. 'No problem,' the clerk said."

"Yes, you've definitely got the instincts of an operator."

"You need to eat again."

"Not hungry."

"That doesn't matter. You won't heal if you don't eat."

"Can't stand the thought of pastrami and potato salad."

"They've probably gone bad by now anyhow. Name something. Pizza? We can have it delivered."

He started to object.

She made him proud by anticipating. "I take that back. No deliveries. Lousy security, right?"

"Right."

"Then I'll have to go out and get something. There's no alternative. Tell me what sounds good. Fried chicken? A milk shake? *Anything*."

Cavanaugh had to make her think he had an appetite. Otherwise, she might be more tempted to get a doctor. "The chicken. Help me to the bathroom."

Afterward, she handed him shaving soap and a new razor. Scraping off his three days of beard stubble made him feel cleaner. Nonetheless, he was exhausted by the time he got back in bed.

"Will you be all right while I go out?" Jamie asked.

"If the assault team knew where we were, they'd have broken in by now." A sheet and blanket over him, Cavanaugh propped himself up on pillows. "Put the DO NOT DISTURB sign on the knob outside, and hand me my pistol."

"You wouldn't think you needed the gun if you didn't suspect there might still be a threat."

"Force of habit."

"Right," she said skeptically.

"I can't wait for that chicken."

"Right," she added more skeptically, then left.

Hearing her test the door to make sure it was locked, Cavanaugh glanced at the bedside clock, which read 4:58. There was something he needed to know. He reached stiffly for the television's remote control on the bedside table and pointed it beyond the foot of the bed, switching on the television and looking for a local station.

On Channel 6, the *Live at 5* news was starting. As Cavanaugh had expected, the fire was one of the initial stories. He concentrated on what the reporter said while watching shots of exhausted-looking firefighters working with chain saws, shovels, and hoses to keep flames away from the first town he'd reached the previous afternoon. Swooping through smoke, a helicopter dropped fire-retardant chemicals on the blaze.

"The fire was ninety percent contained by midafternoon," one of the local news anchors assured her audience, and then switched to a story about a political scandal in Albany involving a state senator who'd been arrested for driving drunk and hitting a teenaged bicyclist, breaking her legs.

Baffled, Cavanaugh stared at the television and then moved up through the channels, stopping at Channel 10, where a story about the fire was just ending. Stunned, he listened to a male reporter tell him that by late afternoon the fire had been fully contained. He went back to Channel 6, so troubled that he barely paid attention to the images on the screen. At 5:30, another edition of the local news came on, and now the story about the allegedly drunk-driving senator got most of the attention. The fire—"fully contained"—got only a half minute of attention. He switched to Channel 10, where the story about the contained fire came on just before the weather report.

He frowned.

At six o'clock, as yet another edition of the local news started, Cavanaugh heard a rap on the door, then a triple rap, followed by a key in the lock. Just in case Jamie had an unwelcome companion, Cavanaugh put his handgun under the covers and aimed it toward the door.

Jamie entered, carrying paper bags marked KENTUCKY FRIED CHICKEN.

Cavanaugh loosened his grip on his pistol.

"Any trouble?" she asked.

"Just something I saw on television."

Jamie locked the door and removed cardboard cartons from the bags. "What did you see that bothered you?"

"It's what I *didn't* see."

She shook her head, puzzled.

"Take a look," Cavanaugh said.

She sat next to him while the local news continued.

The political scandal was again the top story, followed by a report about a series of gas-station holdups. As on Channel 10, the story about the contained fire came just before the weather report; there were just a few shots of firefighters.

"See what I mean?" Cavanaugh asked.

"I hardly saw *anything*. If I'd blinked, I'd have missed the story." Jamie turned from the television and frowned at him.

"Four people killed? A secret bunker? Helicopters with rockets? And all we see on the news are some firefighters with axes in their hands and dirt on their faces?"

"The earlier reports were longer but basically the same," Cavanaugh said.

"Maybe the fire crews haven't been able to get to where it started, so they haven't found the bodies."

"Maybe," he said. "But the area where the fire started would have been the first to stop burning, due to the lack of fuel. Spotter planes would be able to see the destroyed helicopter and the two destroyed Jeeps. Chad and Tracy were blown apart." Anger made his voice hoarse. "But Roberto's body was intact. Even burned, it would still look like a body. And surely somebody in a nearby town heard the three helicopters and the explosions."

"I bought the Albany *Times Union*." Jamie went over to the bureau. "It's this morning's newspaper, so it won't have up-to-the-minute developments. But maybe it'll tell us something."

She took the paper from next to the bags and brought it to the bed.

The story about the fire was at the bottom of the first page. It had a photograph of a haggard firefighter partially enveloped by smoke. The story carried over to page eight, where it was again at the bottom.

"There." Jamie pointed toward a paragraph at the end. "Somebody in a nearby town heard explosions."

"*From propane tanks?*" Cavanaugh couldn't believe what he read.

She quoted the passage. " 'Authorities theorize that the fire detonated propane storage tanks when it reached cabins higher on the mountainside.' "

"There *aren't* any cabins near the bunker."

"So they're just guessing about what caused the explosions," Jamie said.

"Or somebody's lying. Did you notice that bit about a special team being brought in to investigate what caused the fire?"

"You're thinking of a cover-up?"

"It wouldn't be impossible," Cavanaugh said. "Somebody with influence puts pressure on the local authorities and arranges for the firefighters to keep a distance while a special team goes to where the fire started. The site's remote enough that it could be easily sanitized. No one would see helicopters coming in to remove bodies and wreckage."

"Somebody with influence? You're talking about the government?"

"I don't know who else would be powerful enough to keep everybody away from the site," Cavanaugh said.

"But what on earth did Prescott have to do with the government?"

When Cavanaugh shrugged, he wished he hadn't, the motion causing pain in his wounded shoulder. "His lab was hired by the DEA to do research on ways of stopping addiction."

"That doesn't explain why a special ops military team would be involved," Jamie said, "or why anybody would want your team dead. At the warehouse, the attackers wanted Prescott alive?"

"It certainly looked that way. They had several chances to kill the two of us. Instead, they tried to trap us."

"But at the bunker, they suddenly wanted to kill everybody."

Cavanaugh nodded again. "What made them change their mind? Or was the protection team the real target and Prescott was bait, tricking us to go with him to the bunker, where he arranged for us to be trapped?"

"But why would anybody want to kill your team? Can you think of anything you learned on a past assignment that would make you and the rest of the group targets?"

"As far as I know, I've never seen or heard anything so serious that a former client would feel threatened because I'd learned about it,"Cavanaugh said. "Anyway, Chad, Tracy, and Roberto hadn't worked on the same assignment with Duncan and me in the past six months. Even if they *had*, there wasn't any way for the attackers to know who'd be on this assignment. *Duncan* didn't know until the last minute."

"This is just an idea, but . . ." Jamie hesitated.

He waited.

"While you were sleeping, I had a lot of time to think about this. Suppose the assault teams were not, in fact, related to each other?"

"Keep talking."

"Suppose the first group wanted to capture Prescott, just as their tactics indicated," Jamie said. "And the second group—"

"Wanted to kill him, exactly as it seemed?" Cavanaugh asked.

"Kill *Prescott*. You and your team were only secondary targets. You were simply in the way."

"But that doesn't explain why Prescott wanted to kill us all. His behavior doesn't make sense if he wasn't working for the guys in the choppers."

"Who looked like a special ops team from the military," Jamie said. "You told me you saw them being hoisted back up into the choppers."

"Yes."

"You saw *all* of them?"

"Yes. I had to make sure all of them were gone."

"Did you see Prescott being hoisted up with them?"

"No."

"Doesn't that strike you as odd if he was one of them?"

"Maybe he was killed in the fire."

"And they didn't take his body?"

"Not if they couldn't get to it. That would be one of the things this special unit the newspaper referred to would want to take out of there."

Jamie glanced down at the worn carpet. "Or maybe the facts are exactly as they seem. The first group wanted Prescott alive. The second group wanted him dead. He was scared to death of *both* of them. And your team *did* have information that absolutely had to remain a secret."

Immediately, Cavanaugh felt cold—not from chills as a consequence of his fever but from the sudden intuition that Jamie was onto something. "Jesus."

"Information that made you a threat," Jamie said.

"The plans for Prescott to disappear." Agitated, Cavanaugh sat up, wincing from the pain this caused his wound. "The son of a bitch."

It was clear to him now that Prescott had realized who was in the helicopters and that he'd been certain *this* group, unlike the first one, wanted to kill him. He'd known that the assault team would destroy any vehicle attempting to leave the bunker, just as he'd been sure the attackers would have sufficient armaments to blast their way into the bunker and overwhelm the protection team. Seconds away from being killed, he'd panicked. Deciding the only way he could escape was by creating a diversion for the helicopters, he'd started the fire, desperately believing it would give him a chance to slip away, as opposed to waiting for the certain death speeding toward him. But he couldn't stop worrying that a member of the protection team would somehow survive the attack and be captured.

"I think killing us was Prescott's intention from the start," Cavanaugh said. "He had to guarantee that no one would ever know how we'd arranged for him to disappear. That way, he could be sure his secret was totally safe. He wouldn't have to lie awake night after night, fearing that his enemies had tortured one of us into revealing his new identity and where he'd gone."

"But how did he hope to escape the fire?"

"He's extremely calculating. He asks questions. He watches. He learns. I avoided the assault team by staying close to the fire so the thermal sensors in the choppers wouldn't detect my heat pattern. If *I* could figure that out, why couldn't somebody as smart as *he* is?"

"There's a big difference. You had *me* to call for help. But a man that desperate wouldn't trust anybody to come and get him.

You said he's overweight. He'd be able to walk only so far. How did he expect to leave the area?"

"Maybe he *did* call somebody," Cavanaugh said. "As soon as he was taken to a safe place, he would have killed the person who helped him—to keep that person from revealing where he was."

Jamie's eyes darkened.

"Or maybe he reached the nearest town and forced somebody to drive him. Or maybe . . ." A sudden realization caught Cavanaugh by surprise. "He can't let anybody know how he's going to disappear."

The agitation of Cavanaugh's emotions made him light-headed again. He managed to stand. "Where are my clothes?"

Jamie looked alarmed. "You'll fall on your face. What are you trying to—"

"I just realized where Prescott went." He grabbed his cell phone, pressing numbers.

On the other end, the phone buzzed.

"Quick, help me get dressed. I'll need my Kevlar vest."

The phone buzzed again.

"Answer, answer," he pleaded to the person he was calling.

The phone buzzed a third time.

"We have to get to her."

"Her?" Jamie asked.

The phone buzzed a fourth time.

A recorded female voice said, "Leave a name, a number, and a message. I'll return your call as soon as possible."

Cavanaugh canceled the transmission.

"Hurry. There's a woman here in Albany I think Prescott's going to kill."

8

As Jamie drove quickly through Albany's sunset-tinted streets, Cavanaugh needed all his energy to explain. "We gave Prescott the name and phone number of a bank, along with an account number. After he laundered his money, he was supposed to wire a hundred thousand dollars to a document forger who lives here in Albany."

Following Cavanaugh's directions, driving as fast as the speed limit allowed, Jamie rounded a curve and entered a park. The motion increased Cavanaugh's dizziness, but he didn't let Jamie suspect, for fear that she'd reduce speed. Nothing mattered except reaching their destination.

"The forger had a Social Security number, a passport, a driver's license, a birth certificate, credit cards, an entire identity kit and new name ready for him." Cavanaugh took another deep breath. "All Prescott had to do was decide how he wanted to change his appearance: dye his hair or shave it, put on a fake mustache while he grew one, whatever. Once he made a preliminary attempt to alter his looks, the forger was going to take his photograph for the passport and the driver's license, and Prescott would be ready to start his new life. We'd planned to take him to her yesterday morning."

"Who—"

"Karen Atherton. I've been trying to remember if any of us mentioned her name to Prescott. I think Duncan did. Only her first name. But that, the name and phone number of her bank, and her account number would be all Prescott'd need to find her."

Reducing her speed a fraction below the limit, Jamie passed a police car at the side of the road as she left the park. "How could her account number help him find her?"

"Prescott's hidey-hole at the warehouse was filled with electronics. I'm guessing he's as skilled with computers as I am with weapons. Knowing the bank's name, armed with an account number . . ." Cavanaugh's voice faltered.

"Are you okay?"

"Just getting my second wind." Cavanaugh forced himself to keep talking. "Armed with an account number, a hacker wouldn't take long to get Karen's name and address off the bank's Web site. But there's another way."

Continuing to follow Cavanaugh's directions, Jamie entered an upscale residential district of spacious yards with towering trees in front of remodeled nineteenth-century homes. "How?"

"He's one of the most natural elicitors I've ever come across."

Jamie was familiar with the term: someone with the essential tradecraft ability to draw information from people without seeming to.

"Pretend you work at the bank's account-information department," Cavanaugh said. "I'll pretend to be Prescott phoning you." He made himself sound impatient. " 'This is about account number five five seven six three. My wife and I got married three months ago. She called your department to change her name and address, but we haven't gotten any statements since then. I contacted the bank several times about this. Damn it, can't anybody down there help? The account should be for Karen Washburn.' "

Jamie took a second to realize what the intimidated bank clerk would probably say. " 'No, sir, Karen Atherton.' "

" 'That was her name *before* we got married. The address is Four four four Crestview Lane.' "

" 'No, sir. Two five six Morgan Avenue.' "

" 'That's where she *used* to live. That's why her bank statements haven't been getting to us. *Would you make sure the changes get made?*' " Cavanaugh lapsed out of the impatient tone. "See how easy it is?"

"Prescott's shrewd enough to manipulate people that way?"

"Hell, he manipulated *me*. What makes me feel especially foolish is I kind of liked him. At the warehouse, he was scared to death, but he never allowed himself to lose control. He did every-thing I told him to. At the bunker, he wouldn't have started the fire unless he felt absolutely cornered. It's difficult to imagine the amount of courage he needed to try to kill us."

"Courage?" Jamie looked confused. "You sound almost as if you admire him."

"Admire him? I hate him more than I've ever hated anybody in my life."

The weight of Cavanaugh's statement made them go quiet for a moment.

"The house is just around the corner," he said.

Jamie turned onto another street with big yards, stately trees, and majestic old homes. A lawn mower droned.

"There," Cavanaugh said. "That Victorian."

It had two and a half stories, with peaks, gables, and a long, wide porch, painted white, the trim gray.

"Park down the street." Cavanaugh eased down so he wouldn't be noticed. "Far enough away that if Prescott's in there, he won't see the car."

"Why is there a ramp next to the porch steps?" Jamie asked as she passed the house.

"Karen's in a wheelchair. She's crippled from a car accident."

"And yet she chooses to live in a two-and-a-half-story Victo-rian?"

"Actually, the house suits Karen fine. It has a reconditioned elevator that dates back to the 1920s. She gets from floor to floor with no trouble. She's even able to use the toilet and climb in and out of the bathtub by herself, which is why the answering ma-chine bothered me—normally, she's able to answer the phone."

"Unless she's out of the house."

"A possibility. But what if she isn't?"

"Call the police. Tell them you think a neighbor's in danger."

"The police have a sophisticated caller ID system. They'd trace the call to your cell phone, even though you've got the number blocked. If something's wrong in there, they'd link you to it."

"Then use a pay phone."

"How seriously would the police treat *that?*" Cavanaugh asked. "Would they decide the call was a prank? Would they hurry over, or would they wait until a patrol car was in the neighborhood? If they didn't get an answer, would they barge inside to make sure everything was okay? And if everything *was* okay but they got a look around, they might start wondering what Karen did with the high-tech printing equipment and the blank documents. No. Karen might be in danger right now. There's no time to try to convince the police. I have to do this."

"You make her sound more important to you than just someone you work with."

"She's the sister of a friend I had in Delta Force."

Jamie looked as if that wasn't a compelling reason.

"His name was Ben," Cavanaugh said. "He bled to death while I carried him back from a mission."

Jamie studied him.

"Karen was his only family. I promised I'd take care of her."

"Then we'd better make good on your promise." Jamie executed a U-turn at the end of the block and parked facing the house.

She and Cavanaugh got out of the car.

"You can't come with me." His Kevlar vest felt heavy under his shirt and sport coat.

"But . . ."

"If Prescott's in there things could turn ugly fast."

"I can help."

"If we had a pistol for you"—Cavanaugh had taught Jamie how to use one—"maybe you could. But I can't let you risk your life when you don't have a way to protect yourself. I'll be so preoccupied that *I* can't protect you, either. The best thing you can do is stay in the car with the cell phone in your hand. If I call and yell for help . . ."

"I'll floor the accelerator and get to the house. If I have to, I'll drive up onto the porch."

"Good." Cavanaugh smiled and held her, careful with his shoulder.

"You were talking about bravery a minute ago. I don't understand how . . . Aren't you afraid going in there?"

"Afraid for Karen. She's all I'm thinking about."

9

The sun cast long shadows. Cavanaugh's concentration made Karen's house seem bigger than the others—more so, the closer he came. There wasn't a lane behind it, only the backs of other houses—no place for him to try to sneak up from behind without attracting suspicion from the neighbors, who would probably phone the police about him. Thus his only choice was to go in through the front, as if visiting.

He noticed that despite the approaching dusk, there weren't any lights in the house. That could be a bad sign, or it could mean Karen wasn't at home, that a friend had come to drive her somewhere, to a movie perhaps. That would explain why Karen hadn't answered the phone.

But then, wouldn't Karen have left some lights on or have put them on timers so that the house wouldn't be dark when she returned? he wondered.

He reached the front of the house and proceeded up the sidewalk, passing the carefully mowed lawn on his way to the wide porch. At the sight of any suspicious movement beyond the front windows, he was prepared to draw his weapon and take cover.

Mounting the porch steps, he felt naked, but because he knew he wouldn't be able to live with himself if he didn't honor his promise to his dead friend, he forced himself to keep going. Putting his right hand under his sport coat, resting it on his pistol, he peered through the glass that formed the top third of the front door.

All he saw were the shadows of a corridor. On impulse, he turned the knob and pushed, surprised to find that the door swung open. Did it make sense that a woman in a wheelchair would leave her door unlocked?

He drew his pistol and eased inside. His wounded shoulder hurt as he raised his weapon with two hands and sighted along it, checking the dusky corridor, the stairs that flanked it, a room on the right and a room on the left.

Careful to minimize noise, he reached behind him and closed the door. Holding his breath, he listened but heard only silence. The house felt empty, but that impression meant nothing.

Where to start? Cavanaugh needed to think for only a moment before knowing the room he had to check first. He started slowly along the corridor, taking small steps that allowed him to be sure of his balance, all the while aiming with both hands. He focused his vision so that the wide notch in the sight over the pistol's hammer framed the post on top of the barrel. That post had a luminous tritium dot that glowed green in the dark. Invisible from in front of the weapon, the dot was vivid to Cavanaugh, and without hampering his night vision, it helped him line up the sights in the deepening shadows.

He passed a closed door on his right—the entrance to the elevator he'd told Jamie about—reached the end of the corridor, and scanned a kitchen that included a brick fireplace and a modern stove that imitated an old-fashioned cast-iron one. Turning to a door on his left, he stayed out of the line of fire, twisted the knob (hating the slight scrape of metal), and pulled.

The house became quiet again.

Remaining to the side, Cavanaugh inhaled—one, two, three—held his breath—one, two, three—and exhaled—one, two, three—working to control his heartbeat and his breath rate.

At once, he pivoted into view and pointed his weapon down the stairs to the basement. The shadows below were darker than in the kitchen but seemed to remain constant.

Knowing that Karen kept a flashlight in a drawer to the right of the corridor, Cavanaugh quietly pulled it out. He crouched and used his left hand to raise the flashlight above his head, pointing it down the stairs. When he turned on the light, anyone down there would be tempted to fire at its beam, assuming it was center of mass. Meanwhile, Cavanaugh would be able to shoot at the muzzle flash.

But no one fired.

Again, he listened. Again, the house became silent.

When he started down, he made a step creak. The sound sent a spark along his nerves. Inhale—one, two, three. Hold it—one, two, three. Exhale—one, two, three.

He continued down.

Unexpectedly, Cavanaugh's leg felt unsteady. Then his stomach began to feel jittery. Just athletic reflexes, getting ready for action, he told himself. Just my heart pounding out more blood.

But at the same time, a vaguely pungent smell pinched Cavanaugh's nostrils, seeming to make his heart race even faster. It was somehow familiar, but he couldn't remember where he'd encountered it before, and he didn't dare distract himself by trying to jog his memory. He had to concentrate on whatever he might find beyond his flashlight beam at the bottom of the stairs.

Halfway down, moving with greater care to keep his balance, he felt his legs become more rubbery. The pungent smell was a little stronger. His hands shook, making it difficult to sight along his weapon.

Adrenaline's my friend, he told himself. My legs are jittery because they're ready to spring into action. My heart's racing so my muscles will have plenty of blood. My stomach's hot because of all the chemical changes my body's going through, the glucose and fatty acids my liver's working to produce so I'll have instant energy. My lungs are heaving so I'll have plenty of oxygen when I need it.

He knew that what he felt was a so-called fight or flight response. But flight meant panic, and never once in his life, especially when he'd been in combat, had he ever felt the urge to flee.

Except now.

What's happening to me? Cavanaugh thought, reaching the bottom of the stairs. As the pungent smell made his nostrils contract even harder, a deep part of his mind squirmed and shouted, urging him to race back up the stairs, to get out of the house before . . .

Before *what*?

Inhale—one, two, three. Hold it—one, two, three. Exhale—one, two, three.

But Cavanaugh couldn't maintain the rhythm. No matter how strongly he tried, his breath rate became so rapid that it verged on being out of control. He felt light-headed. Flashlight wavering, he aimed it and his pistol along the dark corridor that matched the one above him. He remembered a light switch on his left, but he didn't turn it on, wanting the flashlight to blind anyone he might confront in the darkness. His wounded shoulder ached while he kept his left hand, the one with the flashlight, outstretched from his body so that if anyone shot at it, he wouldn't take the bullet in a vital area. Because his position was reversed relative to the upstairs corridor, his unsteady flashlight revealed that the closed elevator door was now on his left. Another closed door awaited beyond it—and two closed doors on his right.

The pungent smell increased with each unwilling step he took along the corridor. His stomach now felt so jittery that he feared he would vomit. His legs wanted to buckle. His body threatened to sink to the floor, his back to the wall, his knees to his chest, his arms around them, trembling.

Appalled by how his emotions wanted to betray him, he mentally cursed himself. Sweat soaking his clothes, he strained to remember every insult his instructors had barked at him, every command, every painfully acquired lesson.

Damn it, adrenaline's my friend!

Forcing his mind to focus on Karen, on the promise he'd made, Cavanaugh took another hesitant step along the dark corridor. Abruptly, he recalled why the pungent smell was vaguely familiar to him. The warehouse. He'd come across a less noticeable form of it in the abandoned building where Prescott had been hiding. When he'd sensed it on the stairs leading up to Prescott's hidey-hole, misgivings had tempted him not to go any farther and to return to his car instead. His uneasiness had been modest compared to the apprehension with which he now struggled. If not for his training and willpower, he wouldn't have been able to continue up the warehouse stairs.

Prescott!

The bastard's been here!

Cavanaugh smelled something else. Searching for its source, he angled his trembling flashlight toward the floor ahead of him. The farther door on the left led to a storage room. On the right, the farther door led to a bathroom. The one immediately on his right led to Karen's workroom, where she kept her digital cameras, her computers and special printers.

It was toward the bottom of the latter door that Cavanaugh tilted the flashlight, sickened by the sight of smoke leaking from its bottom and a slight flicker beyond it. He touched the doorknob, which felt slightly warm. A panicked part of his mind screamed, *Run!* But another part shouted, *Karen!* and made him shove the door in.

The fire almost blinded him. But that wasn't what Cavanaugh stared at. Flanked by flames that leapt among photographic equipment, computers, and printers, Karen faced him. Slumped in her wheelchair, the once pixielike redhead was motionless, her hands to her chest, her eyes as wide as any Cavanaugh had ever seen, her features contorted in horror. Her cheeks were so pale that her freckles appeared scarlet. She was only forty years old, but the twisted expression on her face made her look twice that.

Cavanaugh shoved the flashlight into a sport-coat pocket and rushed toward her, but the flames reached her before he could get near enough to pull her away. Not that it would have mattered if he'd reached her. Karen remained motionless in her wheelchair, unresponsive to the blaze that consumed her.

Dead.

But how? Cavanaugh thought, backing from the fire. He'd seen no injuries, no traumas to her face, no blood from a bullet wound, no bruising or swelling at her throat from having been choked. The fierce way she clutched her chest, it was as if she'd had a heart attack.

The flames strengthened. Stumbling back into the corridor, Cavanaugh saw that the strongest part of them came from a corner behind the photographic equipment, from the bottom of the wall, as if a short circuit had started a small fire that had accumulated behind the wall, until the flames gained enough power to burst through and fill the room. Prescott must have rigged something in a wall socket to make it seem that the fire had broken out accidentally. Cavanaugh hadn't smelled smoke when he'd entered the house because it had taken a while for the blaze to erupt from the wall. How Prescott loved to use fire as a weapon.

Lungs irritated by smoke, Cavanaugh raced along the corridor and charged up the stairs. Inexplicably, he felt an overwhelming urge to stop. The apprehension that had seized him earlier gripped him even more powerfully. His heart pounded faster than he'd ever felt it. His chest heaved so quickly that he feared his lungs would burst.

Fight or flight. He wanted nothing more than to run from the blaze, but while he hesitated on the stairs, almost paralyzed with alarm, he stared upward and at last understood why his instincts had warned him not to rush higher. The door at the top had been open when he'd descended.

Now it was closed.

Prescott had stayed to make certain the fire would spread. Cavanaugh was certain of that, just as he was certain that the door would be locked when he climbed to it. He coughed from smoke and felt heat behind him.

Get up there and break the door down! he thought.

And what if Prescott stays until the last minute? What if he still has Roberto's AR-15? He wants to make this look like an accident, but if he has to, he'll shoot.

Cavanaugh stumbled back down the stairs. Turning, he saw the blaze spread from Karen's workroom. He yanked open the elevator door, relieved to find that the burnished oak compartment was on the basement level. Like anyone whose legs were functional and who was in a hurry, Prescott had used the stairs.

Cavanaugh took the flashlight from his sport coat and frantically studied the elevator's ceiling, feeling a surge of hope when he saw the two-foot-square maintenance hatch that he recalled being there. Unlike elevators in today's commercial buildings, this compartment was modest in size, with a ceiling that Cavanaugh could touch.

He prayed that the noise from the fire was loud enough to muffle the sound he made when he lifted the hatch's cover and tilted it back. As the fire stretched toward the elevator, he pulled the door shut and closed the metal gate. No matter how much he tried to move the gate softly, its bars jangled, and all he could do was pray that the roar of the fire had muffled *that* sound also.

In the small enclosure, Cavanaugh's harsh, rapid breathing echoed loudly. Sweat poured off his face. Elevators. He *hated* elevators. He never knew when something would go wrong to stop them or what threat would face him when the door opened.

Smoke squeezed under the door and began to fill the compartment. In something like panic, an emotion that had never seized Cavanaugh until this moment, he pressed a button marked 2. If the fire had caused the house's electrical breaker box to trip off, if the elevator's motor didn't work . . .

He wanted to scream. The impulse wedged in his throat when the elevator jerked. Unlike high-speed office elevators, this one was designed to rise slowly. Shaking, he holstered his pistol. He reached up, set the flashlight on top of the hatch cover, then grabbed the hatch's rim and flexed his arms to raise himself.

Agony racked his left shoulder. The elevator vibrating as it inched higher, he heard a tear on his shoulder as the bandage yanked free from his skin. Pulling himself up, he felt warm liquid on his shoulder as his wound reopened.

But he didn't care about the blood, and he didn't care about his pain. All that mattered was getting out of the elevator. While it rose languidly higher, smoke continued to fill the compartment. Heat seeped in. Blood trickling down his chest, soaking his shirt and jacket, he felt a panic-driven surge of more strength than seemed possible. Never, not even on the most harrowing of missions, had he known visceral power of this magnitude. His pain became nothing. The weakness in his shoulder disappeared, replaced by impossible energy that urged him up through the opening as the floor that he'd been standing on began to smolder.

Breathing raspily, Cavanaugh stared down through the opening, past the smoke, toward the glowing embers of the floor. At once, he heard a muffled *pop-pop-pop*, the crack of wood splitting, bullets piercing the elevator's first-floor door and slamming against the back wall. As the elevator continued rising, inching past the door, a more rapid *pop-pop-pop* sent more bullets into the compartment, chunks of wood bursting from the door.

The shots were too muted to be heard outside the house, which meant that Prescott had to be using a sound suppressor. But sound suppressors couldn't be purchased legally. Where had he managed to find one?

Where would *I* have found one? Cavanaugh thought.

The answer was immediate. If I had to, I'd empty a plastic water container and jam it over the barrel. But I've been trained to know these things. How would *Prescott* know?

That answer, too, was immediate. Prescott had yesterday and

today to consider the problem, Cavanaugh thought. It's his business to understand physics. And one other thing: Maybe he's a natural at this.

As the elevator labored higher, the shooting stopped. Cavanaugh imagined Prescott listening to the elevator rise past him, then charging along the corridor toward the stairs that led to the next floor, his heavy footsteps pounding upward. Even overweight, Prescott could reach the next level before the elevator stopped there.

Above him, Cavanaugh heard wheels creaking, a motor working the cable that lifted the elevator. Below, the floor of the elevator burst into flames at the same time Cavanaugh heard another *pop-pop-pop,* bullets shattering the second-floor door, riddling the compartment. If Prescott had used a plastic bottle as a sound supressor, the bullets would have blasted it apart by now. He must have switched to something else, maybe wrapping a jacket around the mouth of the barrel. But the jacket would be quickly blown apart also, and Cavanaugh guessed that from now on Prescott's shots would be loud enough for someone outside to hear them.

The wheels stopped creaking. The motor ceased droning. The elevator quivered to a stop. The only sound became the crackle of flames on the elevator's floor. The rising heat was powerful enough that Cavanaugh had to move his face away from the opening.

Then another sound caught his attention, or maybe he only imagined it amid the crackling flames: the subtle scrape of hinges.

Cavanaugh shut off the flashlight. The elevator door was slowly being opened. Prescott would stand to the side. Cavanaugh was certain of that, certain that Prescott wouldn't frame himself in the doorway, wouldn't make himself a target. From the side, through the slightly opened door, Prescott would see the flames. Would he open the door farther, or would he take for granted that the bullets he'd shot into the elevator, combined with the fire in the compartment, would have done the job?

Cavanaugh's pounding heart shook his ribs. Feeling increased heat through the open hatch, he stared up toward a third elevator door, one that led to the attic. The elevator wasn't designed to rise that high, nor was the door up there intended to let passengers in and out. Half the size of the doors on the other levels, this one was intended to allow maintenance personnel into the top of the shaft to grease wheels and cables.

The door below suddenly flew all the way open. From a wary angle, Prescott would see that Cavanaugh's body wasn't crumpled on the floor. Because it wasn't possible for someone in the basement to cause the elevator to rise unless that person was inside the compartment with both the door and the gate closed, Prescott would take very little time to realize that Cavanaugh must have climbed up through the maintenance hatch. All Prescott needed to do was tilt his rifle upward toward the opening and—

Needing both hands free, Cavanaugh shoved the flashlight into his sport coat. His wounded shoulder throbbed as he grabbed the elevator cable and strained to pull himself up. At the level of the attic door, he clung to the cable with his right hand while he stretched his bleeding left arm toward the door. Desperate, he pushed it open, grabbed the edge of the doorjamb, almost screamed from the pain in his shoulder, and pulled himself into the dark attic.

The effort dislodged the flashlight from his pocket. A moment after it clattered, a roar of gunshots tore chunks from the elevator's ceiling. Bullets rammed into the top of the shaft as Cavanaugh rolled across the attic floor, jolting against what felt like a trunk. Frantic, he pushed the trunk toward the open door and shoved it into the elevator shaft. Its impact on the elevator's roof might trick Prescott into thinking that Cavanaugh had been hit and had fallen.

But those shots hadn't been muted by a sound suppressor.

The neighbors would have heard them and phoned the police, Cavanaugh thought.

It was the first mistake Prescott had made. Even if there hadn't been a fire, Prescott couldn't take the risk of staying much longer. *With* the fire, he had to leave immediately or be trapped. The neighbors had probably seen smoke coming from the house and called the fire department. Despite the noise from the fire, Cavanaugh thought he heard faintly approaching sirens: another reason for Prescott to want to leave as fast as he could.

Lying on the dusty floor, rubbing his back where he'd banged it, Cavanaugh gulped smoke-free air, although the air would soon change, he knew. To slow that from happening, he shut the elevator door, cutting off the flickering light in the shaft. He'd become so accustomed to the glare of the flames that he wasn't prepared for the almost-total darkness of the attic. At each end, the gray of dusk struggled through tiny windows. He couldn't possibly squeeze through them. The only way out was the attic door.

But would Prescott be waiting for him down there, ready to shoot? Beyond the windows, the distant sirens seemed closer. I've got to believe he decided he'd killed me and left, Cavanaugh thought. If I stay up here any longer, the fire'll trap me.

His night vision improved sufficiently for him to see bulky shapes that he guessed were large boxes. A human silhouette was a dressmaker's mannequin. He knew that the entrance to the attic was a swing-down door at the top of the second-floor stairs. Orienting himself, he calculated where that door would be. As smoke seeped from cracks in the elevator's wall, he crept around it. Feeling his way through dust, he suddenly touched folded-up wooden stairs that rested on the hinged door. Now all he had to do was push down and—

What about Prescott? What if I'm wrong and he's waiting for me?

Cavanaugh sweated. Behind him, he felt heat. He turned and saw flames through the cracks in the elevator's wall. He heard the approaching sirens.

Prescott's gone! He *has* to be gone!

Cavanaugh shoved down on the trapdoor.

Nothing happened.

He shoved harder. No result.

I must be pushing the wrong end, he thought. I'm pushing where the hinges are.

He scuttled to the other end and shoved down harder.

The door continued to remain in place.

Almost choking on dust that he'd dislodged, he stared from one end of the door to the other. The flames through the elevator walls were now bright enough to reveal that the first end of the door that he'd tried to shove down had in fact been the one without hinges. Those hinges showed clearly, mounted on parallel beams. Panicked, he scurried to the end without hinges and pressed down with all his strength, but the door refused to budge. There had to be a latch on the other side that prevented it from opening accidentally.

Smoke drifted over it.

He stomped down, trying to smash a hole in the trapdoor so he could reach down and free the latch.

The thick wood remained in place.

He spun and scanned the boxes, the mannequin, another trunk, anything that might help him. He bent over, coughing. Maybe I can unscrew the hinges, he thought. *How?* Where am I going to find a screwdriver or *something* to . . .

His eyes watered. Smoke from the shaft obscured the light from the flames in the elevator's compartment. I could fumble around up here until I drop, he thought.

Already, he was off balance from the lack of oxygen. No matter how much strength panic had given him, his body had reached a limit. If he inhaled more smoke . . .

Then don't breathe, he told himself.

His lungs protesting when he held his breath, he drew his handgun and aimed toward the wood next to a hinge. The barrel was five inches away from it, tilted so the bullet would plow under the hinge and damage the screws.

To keep flying splinters from his eyes, he turned his head before he pulled the trigger. The roar blasted his eardrums. Continuing to hold his breath, he readjusted his aim, this time toward another spot next to the hinge, and again looked away as he pulled the trigger. The recoil jerked his unsteady hands up. The roar made his ears ring.

His pistol held eight rounds in the magazine, one in the firing chamber. Afraid he'd pass out, he kept pulling the trigger, chunks of wood flying. He emptied the magazine, replaced it with a full one from the pouch on his belt, and fired eight more bullets, this time into the wood next to the other hinge. He replaced *that* magazine with the remaining full one on his pouch and continued to shoot at the hinges.

Saving his last round in case Prescott had stayed down there despite the fire, Cavanaugh holstered his pistol and stomped on the door. He heard wood protest . . . stomped again, heard wood shriek, the hinges separating from it . . . stomped it a third time, and fell, the trapdoor giving way, he and it plummeting toward the landing.

Dropping, he grabbed the edge of the opening, dangled, saw flames eating through the elevator door below him, and released his grip. Hitting the smoke-filled landing, he rolled. The impact sent a shock wave through him that punched air from his protesting lungs and compelled him to inhale smoke.

He wanted to reach a bedroom at the top of the stairs, but when he pawed across the floor, he felt only open space and realized that he was headed in the wrong direction, about to tumble down stairs toward flames that blocked the front door. His eyes stinging, he turned to make his way on hands and knees through thick smoke toward the bedroom.

But his arms didn't want to work. His knees wouldn't push him forward. Lack of oxygen made him feel paralyzed. A blanket seemed to float down over him, smothering him.

Abruptly, hands grabbed him. He felt himself being dragged into shadows, away from the blaze consuming the elevator door. Something slammed: a door behind him, blocking the smoke. The hands grabbed him again, pulling him past a murky something that was probably a bed, toward an open door, onto the balcony that he'd been struggling to reach.

Outside, the glare of flames at ground-floor windows showed him the tense face above the hands that dragged him. Jamie. Her green eyes fiercely reflected the fire as she pulled him to the left side of the balcony, onto a railed-in, motorized platform that had allowed Karen to lower her wheelchair into the backyard.

He heard Jamie's strident breathing, then the sound of a motor as the platform descended. Sirens wailed.

The platform jerked to a stop. The fire must have burned the electrical wires, Cavanaugh realized. He peered over the edge, seeing ripples of reflected flames on the lawn five feet below him.

Jamie opened the platform's gate, squirmed over the side, and let go. She landed, then braced herself and reached up as Cavanaugh squirmed over. She grabbed him as he dropped, the two of them sprawling on the lawn.

The fire reached the back windows as the sirens wailed louder.

Jamie pulled Cavanaugh to his feet and tried to keep a distance from the burning house, guiding him along the right side.

"No," Cavanaugh murmured. "The back."

"What?"

"Backyard. Gate."

The relatively clear air chased the grogginess from his mind while he stumbled away from the house, heading through the backyard. Jamie kept pace with him, holding him up.

At the front of the house, firefighters shouted. Engines roared. Ladders and other equipment banged and rattled.

The backyard was spacious. Past two hulking trees, the shadows were thicker. The glare from the flames would soon reach this far, but for the moment, they had the cover of darkness as they came to a gap in a hedge. A high white wooden gate filled the space.

"Karen had it installed"—Cavanaugh breathed—"so the kid in the house behind hers"—he breathed again—"could bring a mower through and cut her lawn."

"What if it's locked?"

"We try climbing."

Abruptly, the gate swung open. A man, woman, and teenaged boy rushed to help them.

"*What happened? Are you all right?*"

"Visiting Karen," Cavanaugh managed to say. "Looks like . . . started behind a wall. Spread so fast. Barely got out."

"*What about Karen?*"

"In the basement." Cavanaugh kept stumbling across their backyard. His sport coat hid his pistol. "Couldn't get to . . ."

"We heard shots."

"Paint cans exploding. Tell the firefighters to try to get Karen."

Silhouetted by the burning house, the man and the teenager rushed into Karen's backyard.

The woman lingered.

"Save your house," Jamie said.

"What?"

"Spray water on your roof so sparks don't set it on fire."

The woman turned pale. She ran toward a hose connected to an outdoor tap.

As she sprayed water toward her roof, neighbors crowded into the backyard, shoving, ignoring Cavanaugh and Jamie, trying to see the blaze.

10

Cavanaugh did his best to walk straight and not look injured as he made his way along a dark street two blocks over.

Headlights turned the corner behind him, coming from the direction of the fire. Worried that it might be a police car, he stepped among bushes.

But instead of the distinctive rack of emergency lights on a police car's roof, Cavanaugh saw the anonymous silhouette of a Taurus approaching at moderate speed. He returned to the sidewalk.

When Jamie stopped, he got in and slumped on the passenger seat.

She drove away at an equally moderate speed.

"Any trouble getting the car?" Cavanaugh asked.

"On the contrary. The police were glad to see me move it so they could have room for another fire truck. How bad are you hurt?"

"I reopened the wound."

Neither of them spoke for several moments.

"You could have been killed trying to save me," Cavanaugh said.

"I didn't think about that."

"You weren't afraid?"

"Only for you."

Cavanaugh looked down at his shaky hands. "Tonight, I felt afraid."

Driving, Jamie glanced from where her headlights illuminated the darkness. She gave him a quick stare. "You just had a lot to react to."

"It was more than that. Something happened to me in that basement." Cavanaugh trembled. "For the first time, I found out what fear is." He felt more blood oozing from his wound. "I was hoping we wouldn't have to do this. We passed a Wal-Mart on the way from the motel."

"Wal-Mart?" Jamie asked, bewildered.

"We're going to need some things. Trash bags. A hotplate. A saucepan. A . . ."

PART FOUR

Threat Confrontation

1

The hotplate's coil glowed. Through steam escaping from the open bathroom door, Cavanaugh could see the unit on the counter in front of the makeup mirror. A vague outline of a saucepan was visible on top of it. The pan contained boiling water, a curved sewing needle, and fishing line.

Cavanaugh was slumped in the tub while the hot shower sprayed smoke and grime off him.

"You've got more bruises," Jamie said. "By morning, you'll have trouble walking."

"I won't need to walk. We're spending tomorrow in the car."

"And maybe part of tonight?"

Cavanaugh turned his head and studied her. "You're as quick a learner as Prescott."

"Except I don't go around setting fires. We can't stay here much longer, correct?"

"Correct. There's always a neighborhood busybody who notices unfamiliar cars on the street. He or she will remind the police about it. One of the policemen will remember the attractive woman who moved the car after the fire started. Meanwhile, the

neighbors behind Karen's house will tell the police about the injured man and the attractive woman who ran out of the house
and disappeared. It'll take the police a while to get organized, but
before midnight, they're going to be looking for a man and a
woman in a dark blue Taurus. Time to hit the road."

Jamie glanced toward the pan on the hotplate. "Think it's
boiled enough?" she asked.

"Ten minutes. If the germs aren't dead by now . . ."

"Turn off the shower." Jamie blotted the wound with surgical
gauze, then coated it with Betadine germicide that she'd bought
from Wal-Mart. The gouge looked clean enough that there wasn't
a need to put Cavanaugh through the pain of more hydrogen peroxide. Quickly, she applied antibiotic cream. Then she hurried to
the pan and used tongs, which she had swabbed with rubbing alcohol, to take the needle and fishing line from the boiling water.
She set them and disinfected scissors onto antiseptic pads at the
side of the tub.

"You should have been a nurse," Cavanaugh said.

"Yeah, that's always been my ambition: to sew up gunshot
wounds. You're absolutely sure you need to do this?"

"The wound has to stay closed, and the bandage isn't working."

"We could always try barbed wire and a staple gun."

"Funny."

"Keep laughing." Jamie knelt beside him at the tub. "No matter how gentle I try to be, this'll hurt."

Cavanaugh's face felt as taut as his nerves. "I've had it done to
me before."

"I imagine."

"But the guy doing it wasn't as good-looking as you."

"Flattery's great. Tell me more sweet things while I do this."

"You're tough."

"So are you." Jamie pushed in the needle.

2

Cavanaugh woke to the rhythm of the car. As headlights flashed past, he found himself lying on the backseat on a blanket, one of the items that Jamie had bought from Wal-Mart. Then he was alert enough to see the imitation sheepskin covers on the front and rear seats, which Jamie had bought from Wal-Mart as well and which concealed the bloodstains he'd left. The car was brand-new, but already it was on its way to being trashed. Somehow he found that amusing.

"Where are we?" he murmured.

"I thought I heard you moving back there. We're south of Poughkeepsie. Did you sleep okay?"

"Yes." He slowly sat up. The headlights passing on the opposite side of the highway hurt his eyes.

"How's the shoulder?"

"Stiff. I passed out?"

"You passed out."

"And you said I was tough."

"Are you thirsty? The bottles of water are on the floor back there."

Cavanaugh peered down and saw them in the shadows. He opened one.

"Hungry?" Jamie asked.

"For a thin woman, you sure think a lot about food."

"Just for that, you can't have any doughnuts."

"Doughnuts?"

"Chocolate-covered. You can't expect me to drive all night without something to eat to keep me awake."

"What time is it?"

"Around one."

"Did you have any trouble cleaning the motel room?"

"Nope. I did what you told me and put all the bloody towels

and clothes into the garbage bags I got from Wal-Mart. I threw the bags in a Dumpster at a construction site. The towels don't have the motel's name on them, so nobody can trace them to us."

"Fingerprints?"

"I wiped the room clean and left the key, along with a tip. Just the way you told me."

Cavanaugh studied the sporadic traffic. "Tired?"

"Getting there."

"Find a place where we can switch places. I'll drive for a while."

"Are you able to?"

"I can steer with my right arm. Once we get into New Jersey, we'll find another motel."

"And then?"

"As soon as I get organized, I'm going after Prescott."

3

"Good God, what happened to this car?" the automobile paint shop's owner said.

The question was rhetorical. Red and green Day-Glo paint had been sprayed over most of the Taurus.

"Damned kids," Cavanaugh said, although he himself had done the spraying. "I leave it on the street for a half hour, and this is what I find when I get back."

"The whole thing'll have to be repainted."

"Don't I know it, and the dealership says vandalism isn't covered under the warranty. They want a fortune to repaint it."

The owner got interested. "How much?"

Cavanaugh named so high a figure that the guy would make out like a bandit even if he gave a discount.

"How does a hundred and fifty cheaper sound?" the owner asked.

"Better than I was going to have to pay. But I need the job done in a hurry."

"Sure, sure. What color do you want? The original dark blue?"

"From the day I chose that color, my wife hated it. She says she wants gray."

4

"Sam Murdock," Cavanaugh told the Philadelphia bank clerk.

"Sign here, Mr. Murdock."

Cavanaugh did.

The clerk compared the signature with the one that the bank had on file and entered a date next to where Cavanaugh had signed. "I see it's been a while since you came here."

"Last year. Too bad. I always say, when you have to go to your safe-deposit box, you've got trouble."

The clerk gave Cavanaugh a sympathetic look, obviously attributing the scrapes on Cavanaugh's face to the trouble he referred to. "May I have your key?"

Cavanaugh, who wore a suit and tie and who'd gotten his hair cut short to get rid of the singe marks, gave it to him.

"Will you be needing a cubicle?"

"Yes."

The clerk led Cavanaugh and Jamie down marble steps to a barred metal gate, which he unlocked. Beyond, in a brightly lit vault, were walls of small gleaming stainless-steel hatches. The clerk glanced at the number on the key Cavanaugh had given him. He went to a wall on the right, put the key in a ten-by-twelve-inch hatch near the bottom, inserted another key, this one from a group he carried on a ring, and turned both keys simultaneously.

After opening the hatch, he pulled out a safe-deposit box and handed it to Cavanaugh. "The cubicles are just outside."

"Thank you."

Cavanaugh randomly chose the second on the right and went inside with Jamie, closing the door. In the process, without seeming to, he checked the walls and ceiling for hidden cameras, doubting there were any but maintaining his habits all the same. He set the box on a counter and leaned over it, as did Jamie, so that their backs concealed the box's contents.

The raised lid revealed two thick manila envelopes and a blue cloth pouch, the bulging halves of which were zipped together. Cavanaugh put everything in a briefcase that he'd bought in a store down the street a few minutes before entering the bank.

Jamie opened the door. Managing to hold the briefcase in his left hand without indicating that his arm was compromised, Cavanaugh returned the safe-deposit box to the clerk, who put it back in its slot in the vault, closed the hatch, rotated the keys to their original positions, and gave Cavanaugh's key back to him.

"Thank you," Cavanaugh said.

5

In a cash-not-unusual motel, Cavanaugh waited while Jamie closed the blinds. Then he put the contents of the briefcase on the bed. The first stuffed manila envelope contained five thousand dollars in twenties.

"I see you've been saving for a rainy day," Jamie said.

The second manila envelope contained a birth certificate,

credit card, passport, and Pennsylvania driver's license for Samuel Murdock. The driver's license and passport had Cavanaugh's photograph. "A present from Karen five years ago." Memories of her made him pause. "As she reminded me, you never know when another identity might come in handy. I'm on the eastern seaboard a lot, so it's easy to come to Philadelphia once a year. I take the credit card from the safe-deposit box and use it to buy a few things so the account remains open. I also renew the driver's license."

"Why Philadelphia?"

"It's convenient. Halfway between New York and Washington, cities where I often work."

"Where do you get the bills for the credit card?"

"They're sent to a private mailbox-rental business here in Philadelphia."

"Which forwards them to a private mailbox you rent in Jackson Hole under the name of Sam Murdock but that you never told me about," Jamie said.

Because of his stitched shoulder, Cavanaugh resisted the urge to shrug. "A benign secret."

"I just love getting to know you better. Does Global Protective Services know about this other identity?"

"Nobody does."

"What's in the pouch?"

"A present for you."

"Gee."

Cavanaugh unzipped the pouch.

Jamie picked up what was inside. "What's that joke you once told me about the compliment men most like to hear from women? 'Oh, honey, I just love it when you tinker with engines and bring home electronics, power tools, and firearms.'"

The object Jamie held was a match to Cavanaugh's Sig Sauer 9-mm pistol. Like Cavanaugh's, it had been modified. Its factory-equipped sights had been replaced with a wide-slotted rear sight and a front sight with a green luminous dot that made aiming easy. All the interior moving parts had been filed and then coated with a permanent friction reducer to discourage jamming. The exterior had been comparably smoothed so there weren't any sharp edges to snag on anything. A flat black epoxy finish prevented light from reflecting.

Cavanaugh watched to make sure that Jamie followed the precautions he'd taught her. Because the Sig didn't have a safety catch, care was all the more necessary. Holding it with her right hand, keeping her index finger out of the trigger guard and the barrel pointed toward the bed, she used her left hand to ease back the slide on top, checking to see if the weapon had a round in the firing chamber. It did. She pressed a button at the side and released the magazine from the grip, grabbing the magazine as it dropped.

"Nice catch," Cavanaugh said.

After setting down the pistol, Jamie picked up the magazine and inspected the holes on the side that showed how many rounds were in it. "Seems to be full, but you never know until you check, right?"

"Right," Cavanaugh said. "It can be downright embarrassing if you assume an unfamiliar pistol has a full magazine and it turns out you're a round short when you absolutely need it."

Jamie thumbed every round from the magazine, counting.

"Eight," she said, confirming that for the model 225 the magazine had indeed been fully loaded. Some other types of 9-mm pistols held more ammunition, but their consequently large grips made them impractical as concealed carry weapons. In addition, pistols with a large magazine tended not to fit the average-sized hands of most shooters, making aiming difficult.

"Careful you don't break a fingernail."

Giving him a caustic look, Jamie reinserted the rounds into the magazine, verifying that the spring in the magazine was functional. Then she picked up the handgun and pulled the slide fully back to eject the round in the chamber. She tested the slide several times to make sure it moved freely. "Could use a little Break-free," she said, referring to a type of pistol lubricant/cleaner.

"It ought to," Cavanaugh said. "It's been in that safe-deposit box for five years."

"The family that cleans firearms together stays together."

Jamie shoved the magazine into the Sig's grip, racked a round into the firing chamber, and pressed the decocking lever on the side. That meant there were now seven rounds in the magazine. To make up the difference, she released the magazine, picked up the round that she'd earlier extracted from the firing chamber, pressed it into the magazine, and reinserted the magazine into the grip, giving the pistol its maximum capacity.

For a moment, Jamie looked as if she thought she was done, and that worried Cavanaugh, because she wasn't, but then she picked up the spare magazine from the pouch, stripped the rounds from it, said, "Eight," and thumbed them back into the magazine. "You'll notice that not only didn't I break a fingernail but at no time did my fingers leave my hands. Should I mention that we ought to get replacements for both magazines? After having been fully loaded for several years, their springs will have metal fatigue."

"An A-plus," Cavanaugh said.

6

"Let's go shopping."

"Great idea," Jamie said.

"You do the driving." Cavanaugh's shoulder still felt stiff.

"Where to?"

He showed her addresses and a map from the phone book. "A hardware store, an auto-supply place, and a gun shop."

"Fabulous."

At the hardware store, they bought duct tape, a hammer, a screwdriver, electrical wire, a toggle switch, gloves, coveralls, a section of plumber's tubing, and an assortment of screws and clamps.

"What's all this stuff for?"

"A better mousetrap," Cavanaugh said.

At the auto-supply place, they bought an air filter, two fog lights, and four chamois cloths.

Studying the cloths, Jamie asked, "We're going to wash the car? No, that can't be right. The dirtier the car, the less notice-able."

In the gun shop, Cavanaugh took her to a rack of gun belts. "It has to look like an ordinary belt but be sturdy enough to sup-port the weight of the pistol. The strongest kind has two leather strips sewn together, with the grain on one strip going in the op-posite direction from the other. The belt should fit so the stem on the buckle goes into the second hole. Which one looks good to you?"

Jamie chose soft-looking black with a square buckle that looked silver. "Goes with the studs on my pearl earrings."

"And for an accessory"—Cavanaugh turned to the bearded clerk—"do you have any Kydex holsters?" He referred to the sturdy plastic material that his own holster was made of. He liked Kydex because it wasn't affected by rain or perspiration and be-cause it was thin enough to be easily concealed.

"What kind of pistol?"

Cavanaugh told him.

"Nice." The clerk reached under a glass counter. "Here's a new model from Fist, Inc." Slightly shorter than the length of Jamie's hand, the nonreflective matte-black holster had an open top, allowing the pistol to be drawn quickly, and a tension screw at the side, which kept the pistol secure. "They call it the 'Dave Spaulding.'"

Cavanaugh recognized the name of one of the nation's best firearms instructors.

"Anything else?"

"Two magazines for the Sig," Jamie said, "and a cleaning kit."

"And a hundred and twenty rounds of MagSafe 9-millimeter," Cavanaugh added. This type of ammunition had an epoxy resin tip with shotgun pellets embedded in it. When the tip struck a target, the resin fractured and released the pellets. The destructive force was considerable, with the added advantage that the tip and its pellets wouldn't go through a target and hit a bystander. As in any good gun store, the clerk didn't ask why the customer needed so much of a type of ammunition that was never used in target practice.

Noticing fishing equipment in back, Cavanaugh told him, "I could also use a dozen lead sinkers."

7

At the motel, they unpacked the various purchases.

Surveying the objects on the bed, Jamie said, "Apart from the pistol equipment, none of this makes any sense to me."

"Where'd you put the scissors, needle, and fishing line?" Cavanaugh asked.

"In the first-aid kit. Don't tell me your stitches are coming loose."

Instead of answering, Cavanaugh took Jamie's blazer from a hanger at the back of the room. Puzzled, she watched him reverse the jacket so he could examine the lining along its right side.

"Hey," she objected as he used the scissors to cut the thread that attached the lining to the hem.

He took three lead sinkers and sewed them under the lining. Then he sewed one of the chamois cloths to the waist level of the lining. "Any bulges?"

"You could have been a tailor."

"I've got all kinds of skills you'd be surprised about."

After she put on the belt and the holster, Cavanaugh removed the magazine from the pistol, ejected the round in the firing chamber so there wouldn't be any accidents, and shoved the pistol into the holster.

Jamie put on the blazer.

He walked around her, assessing. "Good. I can't tell the pistol's there."

"Why did you alter the blazer?"

"Do you remember how I showed you to draw a pistol?"

"You made me practice often enough."

"Then I bet you can figure out the answer."

A patient sigh. "It's a good thing my Wellesley sorority sisters can't see me now." She flipped back the right side of the blazer and drew the pistol. As she raised it, her left hand joined her right, her thumbs over one another, pointing along the side of the barrel. Knees slightly bent for balance and leaning slightly forward, she aligned the sights, aiming at an imaginary target across the bedroom.

"Love your style," Cavanaugh said.

"The lead sinkers give the side of the blazer a little weight so it'll stay back when I flip it. The chamois cloth helps the blazer glide over the holster."

"Another A-plus." Cavanaugh picked up her windbreaker and began to modify that, as well.

"I can do that."

"No, this is work I can manage with my injured shoulder. You have your own work."

Jamie eyed him suspiciously. "What work are you talking about?"

8

Wearing the gloves and coveralls they'd bought at the hardware store, Jamie sat behind the Taurus, attaching fog lamps to the back.

"If I could get down there and do that without pulling these stitches, I'd gladly take your place," Cavanaugh said.

"Somehow, you don't sound convincing. Fog lamps are supposed to be on the *front*. Why am I putting them here?"

"These aren't ordinary fog lamps. They're one-hundred-watt quartz halogens with a candlepower of four hundred and eighty thousand. We'll run the wires to a toggle switch we'll put on the dashboard. Once we get the lamps pointing up toward eye level, we can blind any driver coming after us."

He opened the hood and removed the air filter that had come with the Taurus. "The standard filter's okay, but this K and N improves pickup."

He used the plumber's tubing along with hose clamps to alter the intake system. "This'll get more air to the engine and add horsepower. I phoned a specialty car-parts store in Daytona Beach and ordered a high-speed computer chip to replace the one the car came with."

"Anything else we have to do?"

"Get heavy-duty shocks. Rig the ignition so we can start it easily if we don't have the key. But first, you have to crawl into the trunk," Cavanaugh said.

"What?"

"That wasn't a kinky proposal. We just need to get some measurements."

"Actually, doing it in the trunk sounds intriguing."

"Not with this shoulder."

"I wasn't planning to do it with your shoulder. What are the measurements for?"

"A half-inch plate of steel to stop bullets from going through the trunk and into the car."

9

"Hold still."

"Your hands are cold," Cavanaugh said.

"Quit complaining and relax. This'll be over before you know it."

"You never said *that* to me before. Reminds me of the teenaged girl in a sex-education class."

"Sex-education class?"

"Yeah, the teacher said, 'Don't ruin your life for fifteen minutes of pleasure,' and the teenaged girl asked, 'Fifteen minutes? How do you make it last that long?'"

"Stop moving," Jamie said. "There. How was that?"

"Didn't feel a thing."

"See? I'm getting good at this." Using sterilized scissors and tweezers, Jamie snipped and removed another stitch. "Looks clean. No sign of infection." She cut and took out another stitch. "You'll have a scar to add to your collection."

"Beauty marks."

After removing the final stitches, Jamie surveyed her work. "Damn, I'm good. The wound's still healing. Here's a bandage to remind you to be careful."

"Oh, I'll be careful." It had been ten days since the fire at the bunker. There had been many things to do, but mostly Cavanaugh had allowed himself to rest and heal, the effort testing his patience. Despite his banter with Jamie, which he felt he owed her, his mood had been dark. In his dreams and often while awake, he suffered vivid mental images of Roberto's bashed-in head, of Chad and Tracy being blown apart, of Duncan's bullet-mutilated face. He remembered gaping at Karen in her wheel-chair, her hands clamped against her chest, her face contorted in the rigid aftermath of a death frenzy, the cause of which he was still powerless to explain. But this much Cavanaugh knew beyond question: Prescott was to blame.

"We're as organized as we're going to get. It's time to come back from the grave."

10

The sturdy black man rounded a curve and jogged faster along a straightaway through the suburban Washington park. He wasn't alone. At 6:30 A.M. other joggers were out preparing themselves for the day's stress. Because of a slight chill in the air, the man wore navy leggings and a sweatshirt. The white man who jogged up next to him wore a similar outfit, except the color was gray.

They passed bushes and trees and ducks in a pond. When it was obvious that the white man stayed next to him longer than was usual for a stranger, the black man looked over and almost broke his stride.

"Am I having a religious experience?" the black man asked. His name was John Rutherford. He'd been raised as a Southern Baptist. "Seeing visions? Receiving visitations from the dead?"

"Seeing's believing," Cavanaugh said.

"Yeah, but Thomas still doubted. He wasn't satisfied until he put his hand in the wound in Christ's side."

"I hate to disappoint you, but I don't know you well enough to let you get that familiar. Anyway, I don't have a wound in my side."

The almost-healed wound in Cavanaugh's shoulder ached

from running on concrete, but by keeping the sway of his arms to a minimum, he avoided tearing it.

"I heard you were missing," Rutherford said. "Probably dead."

"These pesky rumors. Where'd you hear this one?" As Cavanaugh kept pace with Rutherford, sweat slicked his forehead.

"The second in command at Protective Services told me. We were going to offer an assignment to your firm."

Cavanaugh nodded. The government had several superb protective-agent organizations, including the Secret Service, the U.S. Marshals Service, and the Diplomatic Security Service, but sometimes personnel shortages required that outside organizations be brought in.

"Seems you, Duncan, and three other operatives dropped off the face of the earth, along with a client," Rutherford said. "One of your safe sites was destroyed."

"Did the second in command tell you which client and which safe site?"

"No way." Rutherford's breath was slightly labored as he and Cavanaugh rounded another curve. "If he'd told me *that* much, I wouldn't have trusted your firm to work for us. I think the only reason he told me as much as he did was to find out if I'd heard anything."

"And *had* you?" A dark stain formed on Cavanaugh's sweat-shirt.

"Not a whisper."

They came near the pond again and passed more ducks.

"So what's the story?" Rutherford asked.

"Can you keep a secret?"

"If I couldn't, the Bureau would have booted me out a long time ago."

The question was rhetorical, the answer expected. Cavanaugh wouldn't have risked meeting with Rutherford if their history hadn't proven that Rutherford could be trusted.

"Provided it isn't illegal and it won't destroy my career, I'll keep any secret you want."

"The rumors are right. I'm dead," Cavanaugh told him. "You never saw me. You never talked to me."

Rutherford didn't reply for a moment. Sweat dripped from his chin as they reached a straightaway. "What about Duncan and the others?"

"If you see *them,* you *are* having a visitation."

"Killed?"

"A couple of times over."

"Who were the other protectors?"

"Chad, Tracy, and Roberto."

"God help them," Rutherford said. "I worked with them all. I knew I could trust them with my life. What happened to your client?"

"That's the problem." Cavanaugh's anger rose. "He's the reason Duncan, Chad, Tracy, and Roberto are dead."

"He got careless? He forced you to expose yourselves needlessly?"

"He turned against us."

Rutherford slowed, left the path, stopped among bushes, and waited for Cavanaugh to do the same. They faced each other. "The man you were protecting . . ."

"Deliberately attracted the bad guys to us. Then he bashed Roberto's head in and shot Duncan. After Chad and Tracy got blown up, he left *me* to die in a burning building."

Rutherford's chest heaved as he caught his breath and tried to make sense of the unthinkable. *"He worked for the bad guys?"*

"No. He was running from the bad guys."

"Then why did he . . ."

"Because we showed him how to get a new identity and disappear. He figured if he got rid of us, his escape plan was safe. One less chance of the bad guys finding him."

"There's a special place in hell for a man like that. What's his name?"

"Daniel Prescott."

"Never heard of him."

"He owns D.P. Bio Lab."

"Never heard of that, either."

"The Drug Enforcement Administration had a contract with him. He was doing research on the physical basis for addiction. Instead, he found an easily manufactured substance that *causes* addiction."

Rutherford looked mystified. "I work closely enough with the DEA. I'd know about this."

"Jésus Escobar got wind of what Prescott had discovered and tried to grab him. When a DEA protective team couldn't keep Escobar away, Prescott came to us for help."

Rutherford looked even more mystified. "Impossible. Escobar got killed two months ago. His cartel's in disarray. They're not organized enough to go after *anybody*."

Cavanaugh felt as if the ground were swaying beneath him.

"It must have been another cartel that wanted Prescott," Cavanaugh said, not believing it. The ground seemed more unsteady, his shifting sense of reality making him dizzy.

"I'd know about that, too," Rutherford said.

"A second group wanted Prescott. They handled themselves like special ops."

"The military? Why would *they* be involved in this?"

"I was hoping you could help me find out."

11

While Jamie idled the car, Cavanaugh pressed numbers on a pay phone at the side of a shopping mall's parking lot. The setting sun cast his shadow.

On the other end, the phone rang three times.

"Hello?" Rutherford's deep voice said.

"This is the Peking Duck restaurant. I'm calling to confirm that someone at your phone number just ordered a hundred and twenty-six dollars' worth of takeout," Cavanaugh said.

"The MSG you put in that stuff gives me a headache." Rutherford sounded as if he had one.

"Makes *me* feel bloated," Cavanaugh said. The exchange was the all-clear signal they'd agreed upon.

"There's absolutely no indication that Prescott or his lab had anything to do with addiction research for the Drug Enforcement Administration. That's not even something they normally get into. It's National Institutes of Health stuff."

Traffic noises in the parking lot forced Cavanaugh to press the phone harder against his ear. "You think NIH is where I should go next?"

"No. Go to the source."

"If you're talking about Prescott's lab, I spent the day at George Washington University's library. I couldn't find anything about the lab in print or on the Internet."

"*I* did. There wasn't any indication of what it does, but it's at—"

A pickup truck with a noisy muffler went by. "What? I didn't hear the next part."

"I said the lab's at a place called Bailey's Ridge in Virginia."

"Where's *that*?"

Rutherford gave him directions, then added, "Sorry I couldn't have helped more."

"You helped plenty. Thanks. I'll send over that Chinese food."

"Don't bother. I wasn't kidding about MSG and headaches."

"I'll call you tomorrow. By then, I'll have more questions."

"Fine with me."

"Same number. Same time." Cavanaugh hung up the phone, wiped his prints from the receiver, and got into the Taurus.

"Learn anything?" Jamie asked.

"Yeah, somebody had a gun to his head. Get us out of here before a bunch of cars rush toward this pay phone, looking for us."

12

"We had a prearranged code, a signal to let each of us know the other was okay," Cavanaugh said. Apprehension made his veins feel swollen as he studied traffic behind them.

Jamie listened tensely as she drove.

"A joke about a Chinese restaurant and MSG. At the start of the conversation, we both said what we were supposed to. At the end, though, when I told John I was going to send him Chinese food, he was supposed to say, 'Don't bother. I've already got plans for dinner.' Instead, he complained about the MSG again."

"Did he give you information?" Jamie checked the rearview mirror.

"Yes. The location of Prescott's lab. We've got to assume it's a trap."

"Somebody forced him to do it."

"No question." Cavanaugh's hands sweated. "But John knew he wasn't betraying me—because he warned me by not supplying all of the code."

"Will whoever's holding him prisoner . . ."

"Kill him?" Cavanaugh felt his breath rate increasing. "Once the trap was set, they'd have no further use for him. But I managed to buy him some time."

"How?"

"I told him I'd call him again tomorrow. The same hour. The same number. With more questions. Whoever's got him will keep him alive for a while longer now—in case the trap doesn't work. So they have a way to stay in touch with me."

Jamie looked over at him, assessing. "I've got a lot to learn from you."

"Look, we need to talk." Cavanaugh peered down at his hands, working to keep them steady.

"We *always* talk."

"Not about everything."

"Now here it comes. You're going to tell me this is getting too dangerous and you want me to go back to Wyoming, where I'll be safe. Don't bother. You opened the door on this. You invited me in, and I'm not leaving. I proved I can help. I proved I'm dependable, that I've got the right instincts and won't fall apart. If you want to keep this relationship, that's the price you pay. No more secrets. No more separations. Two years ago, I'd have been killed if not for you. I owe you, and, by God, I intend to pay you back."

"Agreed."

"What?"

"You don't owe me anything, but I won't argue with the rest of what you said. I'm not asking you to leave."

"Then . . ."

"I need to warn you about something."

"Warn me?"

"I told you something happened to me. In Karen's basement. In the fire."

Puzzled, Jamie waited for him to continue.

"I lost control."

"Anybody would have. You had a lot to deal with."

"No," Cavanaugh said. "Stress has always been second nature to me. It made me feel alive. Except . . ." His mouth felt dry. "Maybe now it doesn't."

Jamie looked at him more closely.

"For five years in Delta Force and another five with Protective Services, I thrived on action," Cavanaugh said. "Physical sensations most people find terrifying were a pleasure to me. I couldn't wait for my next hit of adrenaline. I loved the rush."

Cavanaugh worked to keep his breath rate under control.

"I once protected a Fortune Five Hundred executive who was a nicotine and caffeine junkie. He smoked two packs of unfiltered cigarettes and drank fourteen cups of strong coffee each day. He called the cigarettes and coffee 'rocket fuel.' He said the speed they gave him made him think better and faster and clearer. He loved the high they gave him. One morning in Brussels, while I was standing watch outside his hotel suite, I heard a noise, as if something had fallen and broken. I had another protector working with me, so while he radioed for backup and kept guarding the corridor, I hurried into the suite, where I found the client on the floor. The noise I'd heard was a breakfast cart he'd upset when he fell."

"Was he dead?"

Cavanaugh had the eerie feeling that with each sentence, he was speaking a little faster.

"At first, I thought he was. But then I saw he was blinking. His pupils were huge. I ran to the phone and called a doctor we had on retainer. Then I hurried back to the client. I didn't think he'd been poisoned—the threat he was afraid of was kidnapping, not assassination. But I had to ask him anyhow. 'Do you think you've been poisoned?' He thrashed his head *no*. 'Do you think you're having a heart attack?' I asked. Again he thrashed his head no. 'Stroke,' he said. 'Dizzy. Room's spinning. Floor's tilting.' I felt his pulse. A hundred and fifty. So then I knew what was wrong with him, although I waited for the doctor to tell me for sure."

"And what was wrong with him?"

Cavanaugh felt throbbing at his temples. "A massive nicotine and caffeine overdose. He'd been supercharging himself for so many years that eventually his body reached a limit to the speed it could take. The doctor had to give him a downer and ordered him into a detox program."

"Did the detox work?"

"It probably saved his life. But the damage had been done. His body had established its stress level. Thereafter, if he was even in the same room with someone who smoked, if he inhaled just a few puffs of secondhand smoke, he went into overdrive and nearly collapsed. If he had just a sip or two of someone else's coffee—decaffeinated, mind you, which is never totally decaffeinated—his heart started pounding like a jackhammer."

Jamie frowned. "Where are you heading with this?"

"Adrenaline." Cavanaugh's legs felt more jittery. "Right now, it's flying through me. Before I went to Karen's house, I'd have welcomed it. But now . . ." His mouth had become so dry, he had trouble speaking. "What I need to tell you, to warn you about . . . Whatever happened to me in Karen's basement . . ." He could hardly say it, would never have imagined that he'd say it. "Maybe I can't do this anymore."

Jamie didn't react for a moment. "Do you want to go back to Wyoming?"

"No. I . . . *Yes.*" Cavanaugh said. "I want to go back to Wyoming."

Jamie looked surprised.

"I'm so confused"—the word surprised him—"so afraid of what's changing inside me, I want to go back to Jackson Hole and never leave. But if I give in and hide, I'll never be any good to you or me or anybody else. How can I pretend to be close to anyone if I let John die? He wouldn't be in this mess if it weren't for me. If he gets killed . . ."

"We won't let that happen."

"That's right, by God. But I'm not sure how you're going to feel being around someone who shows signs of fear."

"Signs of being human, you mean?"

"I'll try to be as dependable as *you've* been." Cavanaugh breathed deeply, working to concentrate on what needed to be done. "Is anybody following us?"

Jamie checked the rearview mirror. "Traffic looks normal."

"Head over to the park where I met John this morning."

"What's at—"

"I phoned him at his condo. His wife died last year. He lives alone. That's where they held a gun to him when he talked to me. That's the logical spot for him to be held prisoner."

13

They left the Taurus in a parking garage and followed the shadowy jogging path to the opposite edge of the park. There, concealed by trees, they peered across a busy street toward a brightly lit condominium building.

"The sixth floor," Cavanaugh said. "On the right. The fourth unit from the end."

Jamie adjusted her gaze. "Lights in one window."

"That's the living room. John loves his view of the park."

"Not tonight. The curtains are closed."

"The window next to it, on the right—any lights in his bedroom?"

"The curtains are closed there also, but no lights. Any other bedrooms?"

"No." Cavanaugh wished they could get in the car and drive away. "After John's wife died, he sold their house and moved here. Wanted a simpler life, he said. Became kind of a hermit, reading his Bible when he wasn't hunting bad guys."

"What's the arrangement of the rooms?"

"Past the front door, there's a corridor that leads into the living room." Talking about what he knew helped distract him from what he was feeling. "As you go along the corridor, there's an archway on the left, leading into a small kitchen. An arch on the other side of the kitchen goes into the living room. To the left of the living room is the door to the bedroom."

"Bathroom?"

"Off the bedroom. On the left."

Cavanaugh's attention quickened as a shadow moved beyond the closed curtains in the living room.

"How many people are watching him, do you think?" Jamie asked.

"At least two, so one can sleep while the other's on guard."

The details of tradecraft continued to help distract him from his emotions. "He'll be tied up in a chair in the living room. That way, the bedroom's all theirs, so they can spell each other and take naps."

"But how do we get him out?"

As Jamie spoke, a man and woman approached the building's entrance and went into the gleaming lobby. Visible through floor-to-ceiling windows, a security guard stood behind a counter. He spoke to the couple, picked up a phone, said something into it, nodded, and pressed a button. That unlocked a gate on the right, allowing the couple to go farther into the lobby and reach a bank of elevators.

"For that matter," Jamie added, "how do we get into the building?"

"The law says there have to be other exits in case of an emergency. We can always go around to the back, find one, and pick the lock."

"Which you haven't shown me how to do yet."

"I've been remiss, I admit, but we don't have time to make up for that now. Anyway, in this busy neighborhood, there's always a chance we'll be noticed. We can't help John if we're in jail. Why don't we walk up to that corner store and buy some cigarettes."

"*Cigarettes?* What are you talking about? You don't smoke."

"I used to when I first joined Protective Services. Duncan put a stop to that. I can still hear him scolding me: 'How can you hope to protect somebody when you're fumbling around, trying to light a cigarette?' "

"And now you're going to start smoking again?"

14

The condo building's entrance was thirty feet from the street. Shrubs flanked a walkway. Half a dozen stone benches provided a further friendly appearance.

Cavanaugh chose the bench nearest the street, motioned for Jamie to join him, and opened the pack of cigarettes.

"Smoke?" he asked.

"What's gotten into you?"

"Give it a try. Be daring. It'll help pass the time." He handed her a cigarette and lit it, managing to keep his hand steady.

"I haven't the faintest idea how to hold this," she said.

"Doesn't matter." Cavanaugh lit a cigarette for himself.

Jamie coughed.

"Hey, I didn't say to inhale the thing. Just puff on it a little and blow out the smoke . . . Not so quickly."

"Tastes awful."

"Doesn't it, though. I wonder what I ever liked about this."

Two women passed them and glanced away in disapproval.

"These days, with so many nonsmoking areas, it's the most natural sight imaginable for two people to be huddled outside a building, awkwardly puffing on cigarettes," Cavanaugh said. "We look like we were visiting somebody in the building and got banished down here so we wouldn't stink up the living room when we absolutely had to get a nicotine fix."

A man and woman shook their heads in pity. The next couple actually looked sympathetic, as if on occasion they'd been forced to smoke outside also.

"All right, so you found a way to make us an acceptable presence outside the building," Jamie said. "Now what?"

"Do what Prescott does. Listen and learn."

People came and went, their conversations filled with references to domineering bosses, newly discovered restaurants, cheap plane tickets to the Bahamas, and women who ought to stop flirting with other people's husbands.

Five minutes passed.

"Gosh, I can't believe we're done with those cigarettes so quickly. We'd better light up again," Cavanaugh said.

"If I get yellow stains on my fingers . . ." Jamie said.

Cavanaugh gave her another cigarette, struck a match for her, and pretended to ignore two taxis that stopped at the curb. Each cab discharged four well-dressed people. After lighting a new cigarette for himself, he glanced up at the night sky, pretending to ignore the eight people hurrying past.

"What time is it?" a woman asked urgently. "Almost ten? Thank God we made it. Sandy said she and Ted'd be home from the movie by ten-fifteen."

"How's she going to manage that?" a man asked.

"Pretend she's sick, so they don't go to dinner. Isn't she clever? Her sister's going to let us in. Imagine the look on Ted's face when we all shout 'Surprise.' "

They crowded into the lobby, several of them speaking at once to the security guard, who made a phone call, nodded, and buzzed them through.

"Poor Ted," Jamie muttered as she blew out smoke.

Through the windows, Cavanaugh was able to see the console above the elevator the group used. Numbers flashed, indicating the floors the elevator passed. He was too far away to read the numbers, but he could count the times the console flashed. Seventeen. On the eighteenth, the number remained steady. Add another number for the ground floor, he told himself. They're on nineteen.

Flicking ashes from his cigarette, he noticed a car with a DOMINO'S PIZZA sign stopping in the building's delivery zone. A gangly, bespectacled driver got out, lugging an armful of pizza boxes in an insulated wrapper.

"Let's see where these pizzas are going," Cavanaugh told Jamie. As the driver came closer, Cavanaugh stood, put on a convincing smile, and said, "Hi. We thought we'd come down for a smoke and head you off at the pass. Unit six twenty-eight." That was the number of John's unit.

"Sorry. These are all for somebody else."

"All?" Cavanaugh looked at the stack. "Must be that party on the seventh floor. That's one of the reasons we came down here. They're making so much racket."

"Nope. This bunch goes to"—the delivery guy squinted through his spectacles toward a piece of paper taped to the insulated wrapper—"nineteen eleven."

"Lucky them," Jamie said. "Guess we'll just have to wait and have another cigarette."

"Shouldn't be long," the driver said.

"Sorry we bothered you," Cavanaugh said.

"No problem." Balancing the pizza boxes, the delivery guy walked up to the glass door at the entrance just as somebody came out and held the door open for him.

Jamie stubbed out her cigarette. "What was *that* about? Did you really believe those pizzas would be going to John's apartment?"

"Maybe not this time. But eventually, pizzas or Chinese or some kind of food will probably be delivered there."

"How can you be sure?"

"Because I've seen guards make that mistake too many times before. Round-the-clock watchdog duty is tedious. If the guys on the security team don't have any discipline, they keep thinking about eating. They could scrounge the cupboards and cook, but most of them aren't good at it." Except for Chad who could make anything taste delicious, Cavanaugh thought, sorrow blindsiding him. "They start fantasizing about pizza or egg rolls and chicken chow mein. If this is part of the bunch that tried to grab Prescott at the warehouse, they have a few rough edges that suggest they're the type to give in and have food delivered."

"We could wait for hours."

"If it's going to happen, it'll be sooner rather than later. My call to John was less than an hour ago. Before then, they were too preoccupied to think about food. But now they're getting a routine established."

"Won't the building's guard get curious about us hanging around out here?"

"He can't see us."

"Why?"

"The last time I was here, I noticed that the lobby's more brightly lit than this outside walkway. The glare in there reflects off the inside windows. The guard can't see out."

"But what about the camera above the door?"

"You spotted that? It's pointed toward the area in front of the door, not toward the street. When we get John out of there, I'm going to tell him to move to a building with better security."

"Is that a mind trick you use with your clients?"

" 'Mind trick'?"

" 'When we get John out of there.' You put me in the future and made me believe everything's going to be fine. It's very reassuring."

Another car stopped at the building's delivery zone, this one marked PIZZA HUT.

"My turn." Jamie looked grateful for something to do to control her nerves.

As the driver pulled pizza boxes from the car, she approached him, rubbing her hands together in hungry anticipation. "Hi. We decided to come down for a smoke and save you the trouble of going upstairs. Unit six twenty-eight. We're starved."

The pimply teenager looked starved as well, but for something other than food. He nearly dropped his boxes at the sight of the attractive woman standing next to him. "Um," he said. "Um. Lemme see." He studied a delivery slip taped to a box. "Yep, six twenty-eight."

"Wonderful."

"Two mediums? One pepperoni and black olives? The other deluxe?"

"Exactly. They smell delicious. How much do I owe you?"

Jamie added a tip and took the two boxes. "See you next time."

"Yes, ma'am." The kid blushed. "Thank you." He looked flustered as he got in the car and drove away.

"Two medium pizzas. Enough for two husky guards," Jamie said.

"Seems that way to me," Cavanaugh said, "unless there's only one guard and he's being generous to his prisoner, which I doubt."

"That they ordered food means they're feeling comfortable, right?"

"Right. They assume nobody knows they're keeping John prisoner."

"So what happens now?" Jamie asked.

"We go back to the park, find somebody sleeping in the bushes, and donate these pizzas. All we need are the boxes."

Jamie looked puzzled.

"I need to tear off the top of one box and the bottom of the other so I can stack them together to hold my Kevlar vest," Cavanaugh said.

15

The guard looked up from the counter as Jamie held the door open and Cavanaugh carried the pizza boxes into the lobby. It took a moment for his eyes to adjust to the glare of the lights.

"Hi. We're with the surprise party for Ted up in nineteen eleven," Cavanaugh said.

The guard's face was stern. "A bunch of pizzas went up about twenty minutes ago."

"I *knew* we should have brought ribs, french fries, and coleslaw," Jamie said.

"You really do think a lot about food," Cavanaugh said, trying to sound humorous in spite of the tightness in his chest.

"Tell them to make sure to keep the noise down," the guard said. "We don't want complaints from the neighbors."

"Mum's the word," Cavanaugh said.

The guard pressed a button that caused a waist-high gate on the right to buzz and unlock.

"Thanks." They went through and reached the elevators, where Jamie pressed the up button. After a short wait that felt interminable, one set of doors made a *ding* and opened.

Hating elevators, Cavanaugh entered. As Jamie reached to push the button for the sixth floor, he murmured, "Stop."

"What's the matter?"

"The guard will watch the numbers above the elevator to make sure we go to the floor we said we wanted."

"Ooops." Jamie pushed the button for the nineteenth floor.

The doors closed.

Cavanaugh's legs felt heavy as the elevator rose. He watched orange numbers on a console go from one to two to three. It seemed to take a long time to reach nineteen, enough for him to repeat instructions he'd given to Jamie before they'd entered the building.

"You're sure they'll open the door?" Jamie asked.

"For a pimply delivery kid, they'd keep a chain on the door, hand money through the crack, and tell the kid to hand in the pizzas sideways. But after they get a look at you through the peephole, believe me, they'll open the door. Undo your blouse."

"Excuse me?"

"The top three buttons."

"What kind of girl do you think I am?" Jamie undid them.

Good, Cavanaugh silently told her. Keep making jokes. It tells me you're in control.

And what about *me*? Cavanaugh wondered. Am *I* in control?

Ding. The doors opened. His breath rate increasing, he stepped out onto a new-looking beige carpet in what smelled like a freshly painted white corridor that had bright overhead lights and no one in view.

A quick look each way showed them a door marked STAIRS on their right. They pushed through and found themselves in a dank concrete stairwell even more brightly lit than the corridor. As Jamie shut the door, Cavanaugh checked for security cameras but saw none. They listened for noises and heard none. Their footsteps echoed as they descended in a cautious hurry to the sixth floor.

Outside the door, they paused.

"Can you manage this?" Cavanaugh kept his voice low. "I'll be right there next to you. Just do everything exactly as I explained."

Jamie hesitated.

"It's not too late to back out," he said.

"Sure it is," she said. "I'll never be able to force myself to go this far again."

"Maybe you shouldn't go this far at all."

"Can you save John without me?"

Cavanaugh didn't answer.

"Then give me the boxes." Jamie's pupils were large.

Cavanaugh watched her react to the weight of the Kevlar vest in them. She arranged the boxes so they pushed up slightly under her breasts, widening the gap where she'd opened the buttons.

"They'll think they'd died and gone to heaven," Cavanaugh said. "Before you knock on their door, close your eyes for a few seconds. That'll make your pupils smaller, so you won't seem on edge. Remember, if you hear a TV, it means they're careless. Good watchdogs keep the room quiet so they can hear noises outside."

Jamie took a deep breath and nodded toward the door. "Open it."

16

The sixth floor had the same type of new-looking beige carpet and freshly painted white walls as on the nineteenth. Tense, Cavanaugh followed Jamie along the corridor. As he'd anticipated, after 10:00 P.M. no one was in it.

It's still not too late to back out, he kept telling himself.

Sure it is. If I back out, I might not get another chance to save John.

Unit 628 was on the right. Pressing himself against the wall next to it, Cavanaugh heard the muffled sounds of an explosion, followed by gunshots, sirens, and pulsing music: an action program on television. He gave Jamie a reassuring look and drew his pistol.

Jamie stood in front of the door's peephole and closed her eyes. When she opened them a few seconds later, her pupils were a normal size, in no way suggesting she was under stress.

But Cavanaugh was. He made a sudden decision that he should never have allowed her to be part of this. He motioned to her that they were leaving.

Jamie ignored him and knocked on the door.

Cavanaugh motioned even more forcefully.

Paying no attention, Jamie knocked again, and this time, the TV's sound went off.

We're in it now, Cavanaugh thought. He marveled at how bored Jamie made herself look in front of the door's peephole, the pizza boxes propping up her breasts.

With a loud scrape, a lock was disengaged. Cavanaugh pressed himself closer to the wall, keeping far enough away that he couldn't be seen.

As he expected, whoever was in there opened the door only as far as a chain would allow.

"You ordered two medium pizzas?" Jamie looked at the piece

of paper taped to the top box. "Pepperoni and black olives? The other deluxe?"

"Usually it's a kid who delivers." The man had a European accent.

"No shit," Jamie said. "My husband and I own the business. Three delivery kids didn't show up tonight. Lucky me, here I am."

The man chuckled. "How much?"

She raised the boxes tighter to her breasts while she leaned down to read him the price on the piece of paper.

"Hang on a second." The man closed the door.

The moment the door swung shut and the man couldn't see what was in front of it, Cavanaugh hurried from where he was pressed against the wall. He rushed the door and ducked below the peephole. Shielding Jamie, he heard the scrape and rattle of the chain being freed.

As the door came open all the way, Cavanaugh charged toward the surprised man. Obeying instructions, Jamie upended the pizza boxes so the Kevlar vest inside protected her. The man was the same skinhead Cavanaugh had taken the black car from at the shopping mall almost two weeks earlier. Gaping, the skinhead fumbled to draw a pistol. Cavanaugh whacked his Sig's barrel hard across the man's hairless skull. Stunned, the man fell backward, pinning his gun arm. Cavanaugh leapt over him and entered the living room, aiming to the left, toward the area across from the television.

A mustached man who looked about forty sat petrified in a chair, not knowing which way to look—toward Cavanaugh's pistol or the one that Jamie aimed from the kitchen archway. The man's own pistol was on a coffee table before him.

Rutherford was bound and gagged in a chair in the far left corner. Blood on his face contrasted with his black skin. His eyes bulged in surprise, but Cavanaugh didn't have time for him now. He grabbed the pistol off the table. As he passed the mustached man, he whacked *him* over the head, as well. Then he pressed himself against a wall leading into the shadowy bedroom. After aiming in toward the side of the room that he was able to see, he darted over to the other wall and aimed in toward the opposite side of the room. When nothing alarmed him, he lunged in, shoved a bureau against the closet door, checked under the bed, and then made sure the bathroom was clear.

When he returned to the living room, the mustached man lay on the floor, moaning.

Cavanaugh hurried to the front door, locked it, then aimed toward the skinhead on the floor. He searched him for weapons, removed a pistol tucked at the back of his belt, and used the belt to secure the man's hands behind his back.

He did the same to the mustached man's hands, then checked that the front closet was empty. Only then did he run over to Rutherford, removing the gag from his mouth. "Did we get them all?"

"Yes."

Cavanaugh untied rope from Rutherford's ankles and wrists. "How bad are you hurt?" He assessed the bruises and gashes on Rutherford's face.

"I lost a tooth." Rutherford pointed toward his swollen left cheek. "They might have cracked some ribs." He winced as he took a breath.

Cavanaugh saw a box of tissues on a side table. He grabbed several and gave them to Rutherford. "Cough deeply and spit into these."

Rutherford did. "Lord Almighty, that hurt."

Cavanaugh inspected the spit in the tissue. "No blood. Lie down on the sofa." Cavanaugh helped him over to it and then pressed gently against Rutherford's abdomen and chest. "I don't feel any swelling. Have you got any pain you're suspicious about?"

"It's been long enough; if they broke anything inside me, I'd have passed out by now." Rutherford massaged his wrists, where the blood circulation had been almost cut off.

"Where's your first-aid kit?"

"Under the sink in the bathroom."

When Cavanaugh returned with the kit and a soapy wash-cloth, Rutherford was making an effort to sit up. "You haven't introduced me to your friend."

"Meet Jennifer. Jennifer, this is John."

Jamie showed no reaction to being introduced by a false name.

"Pleased to meet you. Mighty glad to be alive to have the pleasure," Rutherford said.

Cavanaugh opened the first-aid kit and paused when he found three syringes among the bandages and ointments. He held them up and then realized why they were there. "From when your wife was alive?"

She'd been a diabetic and had injected herself daily with insulin, Cavanaugh knew. Ironically, a car accident had been what killed her.

"I gave away a lot of Deb's clothes to the church. I threw away a lot more stuff, old shoes and things that she knew weren't worth keeping but she'd hung on to anyhow. Except for a few of her favorite dresses, which I kept, I didn't have any trouble parting with most of it, but somehow those syringes made me think of her more fondly than anything else. I couldn't bring myself to throw them out."

Cavanaugh put them back in the first-aid kit and began to clean Rutherford's face.

"You got my warning—my second MSG remark?" Rutherford asked.

"Nicely done."

"I'd have let them kill me before I'd have sent you into a trap."

"I know," Cavanaugh said.

"The people I asked about Prescott and his lab said they'd never heard of him." Hours of having been gagged made Rutherford sound raspy.

"I'll get you some water," Jamie said.

When she returned, Rutherford took several deep swallows, wetting the dried blood on his lips and causing it to trickle. "Then I searched our computer database." Another swallow. "I came up with nothing."

"Then how did—"

"These guys must have an informant in the Bureau. Either that or they hacked into our computer system, looking for anybody who'd made inquiries about Prescott. When I left my office to go home, they were waiting near my car in the parking area." Wincing, Rutherford fingered the side of his jaw where his tooth had been knocked out. "Somebody called my name from the next row. I turned to see who it was. All of a sudden, a van stopped next to me. While it screened me from view, three guys grabbed me from behind and shoved me inside."

"The man who shouted. The three men who grabbed you. The van's driver. A total of five?" Cavanaugh asked.

"No." Rutherford swallowed more water. "There's a sixth guy, the one who runs the show. He calls himself Kline."

"I recognize your two guards. They were with the first group that went after Prescott."

Rutherford frowned past Cavanaugh. "Jennifer, you look sick."

Cavanaugh turned toward her. "You're pale. You'd better sit."

"What I had in mind was kneeling." She went through the bedroom and into the bathroom.

A moment later, Cavanaugh heard the muffled sounds of her throwing up.

"Her first time on an operation?" Rutherford asked.

"Yes."

"She did good."

Cavanaugh nodded.

When she came back, he held her.

"I didn't let you down," Jamie said.

"You didn't let me down." And *I* didn't let *you* down, he added silently.

As the mustached man moaned on the floor, Jamie stepped over him, easing into a chair across from Rutherford. "Don't mind me. Go on with what you were saying while I try to convince myself that I'm still alive."

Cavanaugh's hands had been steady as long as he'd had something to do. Now he had to concentrate to keep them from shaking. "Yes, what happened next?"

"After these guys worked me over enough to prove they meant business, they put a gun to my head and gave me a choice—either I'd tell them why I wanted Prescott or they'd kill me." Rutherford held the wet washcloth to his bruised cheek. "I explained *I* didn't want Prescott. A friend of mine did. They gave me the same choice—tell them who my friend was or they'd kill me. I didn't use your name. All I said was 'a man who'd been part of Prescott's security.' "

Cavanaugh nodded.

"That got them extremely interested," Rutherford said. "They couldn't wait to get their hands on you."

"Sure. They thought I might know where Prescott had gone."

"I told them *you* were trying to find him, too, that you didn't know anything more than they did."

"But they didn't buy it?" Cavanaugh asked.

"No way. They put the gun to my head again and ordered me to tell you Prescott's lab was at a place called Bailey's Ridge in Virginia."

"And now four of them, including Kline, are at Bailey's Ridge, arranging a trap for me?"

"They left as soon as your phone call was over," Rutherford said.

Jamie leaned forward. "When nobody shows up, they'll wonder what went wrong. They'll come back here and hope you make contact again, as you promised."

"Yes," Cavanaugh said. "They'll want to set another trap."

Rutherford reached for the phone.

"Hey, what are you doing?" Cavanaugh reached to stop him.

"Getting help."

"No."

"But the Bureau can—"

"We don't know who else is involved in this."

Rutherford hesitated.

"You said Kline might have an informant in the Bureau," Cavanaugh said. "Suppose Kline got word we were waiting for him. This'd be the *last* place he'd come near."

17

When the intercom buzzed, Cavanaugh waited a few seconds, then pressed the button. "Yes?"

The security guard's voice was tinny. "Mr. Kline and another gentleman to see you."

"Send them up." Cavanaugh released the button and went back into the living room.

"Two of them," Rutherford said. "The other two must have stayed at Bailey's Ridge in case you showed up."

Jamie glanced at her watch. "Just past noon. Earlier than you expected."

"After being on a stakeout all night, Kline must really be annoyed that I didn't do what I said I would. Now he wants another heart-to-heart with John. Are we ready for guests?" Cavanaugh directed his question toward the skinhead and the mustached man, who were tied to chairs. It had taken the men an hour to regain consciousness. Insistent questioning had revealed only that they were contract operators and knew nothing about why Prescott was important.

On two occasions, the skinhead's cell phone had rung, Kline angrily checking in. Cavanaugh had rehearsed with the two captives, making sure they knew exactly how to respond if either of their cell phones rang. With his pistol to the skinhead's temple, Cavanaugh had watched the man's eyes as he spoke into his phone. If Cavanaugh had detected even the slightest attempt to warn Kline, he'd have shown keen displeasure.

The skinhead now wore a baseball cap to hide his gashed scalp.

"I asked you"—Cavanaugh tapped the cap—"if you're ready to receive guests."

The skinhead winced and nodded.

"I'll see you in a few minutes," Jamie said. Following instructions that they'd worked out earlier, she left the apartment. Rutherford locked the door.

Cavanaugh nervously imagined her moving along the corridor, opening the door to the stairwell near the elevator, and waiting behind it. When Jamie heard the *ding* of the elevator, she would count to twenty, the length of time they had calculated it took to walk from the elevator to Rutherford's condo. Then she would open the door and step from the stairwell, fumbling in her purse for what was presumably the key to her unit, never once looking down the hallway at the two men outside Rutherford's door. The men would notice her, but with no reason to be suspicious of a trap—after all, *they* were the ones setting a trap—they would soon be distracted by what happened when Rutherford's door opened. Jamie had looked steady as she left, having used the intervening time to practice visualization techniques that Cavanaugh taught her, imagining possible variations to the scenario they had planned, replaying them in her mind, preparing herself not to be surprised. To give her more confidence, she wore the Kevlar vest under her blouse and jacket. It made her look overweight, her clothes too tight, but her appearance was the last thing she was worried about.

"Okay," Cavanaugh told the skinhead, aiming his pistol at him. "Be a good host."

Rutherford had already freed the man's ankles and wrists. Now he untied the ropes that held the hostage to the chair.

"Remember," Cavanaugh told the man. "You'll be the first one in our line of fire." He motioned for him to cross the living room. Following, he watched the man go down the corridor and pause at the front door.

"Now all you have to do is make sure you don't give us a reason to shoot you," Cavanaugh said.

Rutherford took his position in the kitchen, ready with a pistol.

Sweat trickling down his sides, Cavanaugh waited.

Fifteen seconds. Thirty. Fifty. Cavanaugh recalled how slowly the elevator had seemed to rise. That the men hadn't yet knocked on the door didn't mean something was wrong, he tried to assure himself. Be patient. Everything's going to be—

Knock, knock. Pause. Knock, knock. That was the pattern John had heard the team agree on—the code that signaled it was okay to open the door.

Cavanaugh's stomach constricted as he motioned for the skinhead to let them in.

At that point, the start of a carefully rehearsed sequence, Cavanaugh stepped back into the living room, out of sight of the doorway. The skinhead would be very aware that Rutherford was aiming at him from the kitchen. Having opened the door, the skinhead would say, "He hasn't called," then turn and walk toward the living room, directly into Cavanaugh's line of fire. Meanwhile, Rutherford would have taken cover beside the refrigerator. Only when the men came inside and started along the corridor would Rutherford again show himself, aiming at them through the kitchen archway. The second man would notice Rutherford about the same time the first man noticed Cavanaugh in the living room. Simultaneously, Jamie would have come up behind them, drawing her pistol, saying, *"Into the living room,"* which she did now.

Caught by surprise in a three-way vise, their weapons beneath their jackets, the men had little choice but to comply.

"On the floor," Rutherford said. *"Hands behind your head."*

"Now," Cavanaugh said.

The skinhead did what he was told, sinking chest-down onto

the carpet. The other two hesitated only briefly before they imitated him, putting their hands behind their heads.

Jamie stepped in, locking the door.

"Was anybody else in the hallway?" Cavanaugh asked, aiming at the men. "Did they see your pistol?"

"Two people got off the elevator as I came in here. My pistol was next to my purse. Nobody saw it."

Cavanaugh felt a measure of relief. John had assured him that the people who lived in the building were mostly professional types, not likely to be home early in the afternoon on a weekday. Even so, someone coming along the hallway at the wrong time had been a liability Cavanaugh couldn't plan for.

"Cute," the first man said, peering up from the carpet. He was of medium height, wiry, with a thin face and military-style hair.

Cavanaugh recognized the sandpapery voice. "We've spoken before. On *this* guy's cell phone." Cavanaugh meant the skinhead. "After I took the car from him outside the shopping mall."

"You figured out the phone contained a homing device." Like the skinhead, the man had a European accent. "We followed it for hours, until we realized you'd thrown it into the back of a passing pickup truck."

"Hey, if you can't take a joke." A thought occurred to Cavanaugh. "You followed the truck? Why did you bother if you already knew we'd used a helicopter to leave the area?"

"Helicopter? I don't know what you're talking about."

The man's confusion looked spontaneous enough to be convincing, reinforcing Cavanaugh's suspicion that the team who'd tried to grab Prescott at the warehouse had not been the same team that had used helicopters to attack the bunker.

While he and Jamie continued to aim at the men on the floor, Rutherford tied their ankles and wrists.

Cavanaugh removed a 9-mm Beretta from beneath the second man's loose pullover. He felt beneath the first man's black leather jacket and found a 9-mm Browning Hi-Power. He also found a folding knife clipped to the inside of his pants pocket. Only the clip showed on the outside. By pulling upward on the clip, the owner could draw the knife instantaneously from concealment. A small ribbed projection on the back of the blade allowed it to be thumbed open one-handed in the same motion as the knife was being drawn. When open, it was almost eight inches long.

Knives had once been considered inferior weapons ("Dummy, you brought a knife to a gunfight"), but a graphic self-defense video released in the 1990s, *Surviving Sharp-Edged Weapon Attacks,* had shown law-enforcement and security personnel that an assailant with a knife could race across a distance of twenty feet and cause lethal wounds before someone with a concealed handgun could overcome his startle reflex, draw, and fire. Now some operators considered a knife as prudent a backup weapon as a pistol and carried as many as three. The knife Cavanaugh held had a nonreflective flat-black surface and had been manufactured by one of the best self-defense instructors and knife makers: Ernest Emerson. It was called the CQC-7, the initials representing "close-quarter combat." Its weave-patterned epoxy handle was designed not to be slippery when covered with water, sweat, or blood. Its serrated steel was hard and sharp enough to punch through a car door.

"Cute," Cavanaugh said, echoing what the first man had said. He closed the knife and clipped it into his pants pocket. He sat cross-legged on the floor, at the first man's eye level. "You're using the name Kline?"

"It's as good as anything."

"Tell me about Prescott."

Kline didn't answer.

"I'll tell you what *I* know about him," Cavanaugh said. "Feel free to chime in any time you feel like it."

Cavanaugh told Kline what had happened after the car chase: the arrival at the bunker, the instructions to Prescott about how to disappear, the fire, the helicopter attack, and the other fire at Karen's house. "So, you see, I want him as much as *you* do. Probably worse. We'd accomplish more if we worked together."

"But our purposes conflict."

"I'm sure we can work around our differences." Cavanaugh studied him. "You look like your arms are starting to hurt. Why don't I make you more comfortable?"

Kline frowned, puzzled, as Cavanaugh brought a captain's chair from the kitchen. Kline frowned even more when Cavanaugh raised him to his feet and thumbed open the Emerson knife.

"I'm going to cut the rope on your wrists," Cavanaugh said. "If you make any move against me, my friend here"—Cavanaugh indicated Rutherford—"who's in a world of hurt and a really foul mood because of the beating your team gave him yesterday, will shoot you."

Rutherford had gone into the kitchen and returned with an empty plastic soft-drink bottle shoved over the barrel of his pistol as a sound suppressor. "I want my tooth back."

It was a tactic that he and Cavanaugh had rehearsed, and it had its intended effect, especially the rigged sound suppressor, causing Kline's eyes to narrow.

"But why invite trouble?" Cavanaugh asked. "We're having a pleasant conversation. We want to cooperate with one another." Cavanaugh stepped behind Kline, cut the rope on his wrists, and told him, "Sit."

Kline obeyed.

Cavanaugh retied Kline's wrists, this time to the arms of the captain's chair.

"Comfy?" Cavanaugh asked. "Good. I honestly think we'd have a better chance of finding Prescott if we worked together. It's *your* turn. Tell me what you know."

Kline looked away.

"For starters," Cavanaugh said, "why do you want him so much? He told me a story about addiction research he was doing for the DEA. He was supposed to find a way to block the physical mechanism that causes people to become addicted. Instead, he claimed he found an easy-to-manufacture substance that *causes* addiction. He said Jésus Escobar somehow found out and tried to grab him to get the formula. He said *you* guys worked for Escobar. But all that turned out to be a bunch of hooey. The DEA never heard of Prescott, and Escobar was killed two months ago, so who do you guys really work for?"

Kline finally looked back at Cavanaugh. Tension made his European accent—Slavic or possibly Russian—more pronounced. "You know I can't tell you that."

"Maybe I should make you some coffee while we consider the problem."

"Coffee?" Kline tilted his head, puzzled.

"Yeah, there's nothing like a chat over coffee. John, where do you keep it?"

"Above the fridge." He and Jamie looked as puzzled as Kline did. "The grinder's next to it. The percolator's next to the toaster on the counter."

"Percolator? What I had in mind was *instant* coffee," Cavanaugh said.

"Uh, in the cupboard to the right of the stove."

Cavanaugh turned Kline's chair so Kline could watch. Then Cavanaugh went into the kitchen and opened the cupboard, finding a small box that had packets of various kinds of instant coffees. "Let's see. Hazelnut roast, vanilla roast, chocolate roast. Any of that appeal to you?" he asked Kline.

No answer.

"John, you've got to lay off this sweet coffee," Cavanaugh said. "You'll put on so much weight, you won't be able to run it off. Haven't you got anything with some heft to it? Wait a minute. What's this? Mocha Java? Now *that* sounds like a manly brew."

Cavanaugh opened two packets of it and dumped the powder into a small transparent juice glass. He put very little water in a kettle and set the kettle on the stove, turning the burner to high.

"Won't be long now," he assured Kline. "There's nothing like hot, rich caffeinated coffee to promote conversation. Are you sure you don't want to give me some tidbits right now—about why you want Prescott and about who else would be after him?"

Kline continued to look stubborn.

"Ah, well," Cavanaugh said, "I certainly respect your principles. You're definitely not a blabbermouth."

The kettle whistled.

Cavanaugh poured what amounted to an ounce and a half of boiling liquid into the juice glass. There was barely enough water to dissolve the two packets of coffee crystals. He gave it a stir, letting Kline see how dark and thick the mixture was. "Nothing limp-wristed about *this* stuff. It'll put fire in your eyes and hair on your chest."

Kline looked even more perplexed. "You expect me to drink that? What the hell good will *that* do to make me talk? I'd probably throw it up."

"Drink it? The farthest thing from my mind. And believe me, you won't be throwing it up."

Cavanaugh opened Rutherford's first-aid kit and removed one of the syringes.

Kline's eyes got bigger.

Cavanaugh inserted the syringe in the thick coffee mixture and pulled back the plunger, filling the tube, then pushed the plunger to remove air from the syringe. He started humming "Fly Me to the Moon."

"Hold it," Kline said. "You're not seriously thinking about—"

Cavanaugh interrupted him by ripping Kline's shirt open, fully exposing his neck. Now he was humming "Black Coffee" as he angled the tip of the syringe toward Kline's jugular vein.

"For Christ's sake, stop!" Kline tilted his body toward the opposite side, nearly overturning the chair.

"Watch your language," Rutherford, the Southern Baptist, said seriously.

"All right, all right. Just stop," Kline told Cavanaugh. "You can't expect me to believe you're crazy enough to—"

"Expand your mind, along with your arteries and your vital

organs," Cavanaugh said. "I'm going to set your heart racing and blow your brains out from the inside. I figure by the time your pulse gets up to about a hundred and eighty, you might even start to levitate, except you'll be tied to that chair. Now if you'll hold still . . ."

Cavanaugh put a firm hand on Kline's shoulder and re-adjusted the syringe's trajectory.

"No!" Kline tilted his body so far to the side that this time the chair did topple. With a *thump*, he landed on the carpet.

"Hey, have some consideration for the neighbors," Cavanaugh said.

"That stuff'll kill me!" Kline said.

"Kill you? It'll get your metabolism racing so fast, you'll probably self-combust."

Cavanaugh pushed Kline's head against the carpet and slanted the syringe's tip so that it pressed along Kline's jugular.

Kline whispered, trying to minimize his neck movements, sounding as if he'd swallowed ashes: "If you kill me, I can't tell you anything."

"You know what? Part of me doesn't care. Running into you twice was running into you twice too often. I'm pissed about my friends being dead. I'm pissed about Prescott trying to kill *me*. I'm pissed about what you and your men did to John. I want to get even with somebody, and if you don't intend to cooperate with *me* the way *I* cooperated with *you*, at least I'll get the satisfaction of *this*."

Cavanaugh pierced Kline's artery enough to draw blood.

Kline winced and looked as if he was trying not to shudder, but he didn't succeed, his involuntary movement causing a little more blood to leak from his artery. "The drug-addiction story was a cover. Prescott worked for the U.S. military."

"I want specifics."

"A branch of it devoted to special-weapons development." Kline licked his lips, which suddenly looked very dry. "I might need to cough."

"Better not. The syringe'll go all the way in."

"A subsection of a subsection." Kline lowered his voice even more, trying not to move his neck. "The kind of research they don't report to the secretary of defense."

"Or the kind the Pentagon itself doesn't know about? Like the LSD experiments in Washington in the 1950s or the nerve-gas experiments in Utah in the '70s."

Kline licked his dry lips again. "Yes."

"Our tax dollars at work. So what was *this* experiment about?"

"Fear."

18

The word seemed to linger in the air. It was so unexpected that Cavanaugh didn't react to it at first. He was certain he hadn't heard correctly. "Fear?"

Cavanaugh's muscles tightened and his palms became moist as he felt a premonition about what Kline was going to tell him next.

"Fear," Kline whispered hoarsely, repulsed by the pressure of the syringe's tip against his artery. "Prescott was in charge of bio-chemical research designed to create fear in any opponent the U.S. military confronted. My neck." Kline tensed. "You're shoving harder."

"Prescott. Tell me about Prescott."

Kline's brow was beaded with sweat. "He created a synthetic hormone that triggered adrenaline in such massive doses that panic was an immediate result."

Prescott's lie about trying to stop addiction and instead discovering how to *increase* addiction had been partially based on truth, Cavanaugh now realized. All that needed to be done was to substitute the word *fear* for *addiction*. His mind flashed back to the stairs in the abandoned warehouse and the pungent odor he'd smelled as he'd gone up to meet Prescott. He'd become more and more uneasy as he'd mounted the stairs, his body more jittery with each step.

"Prescott's military controllers were thrilled." Unable to turn his head, Kline strained his eyes sideways toward where the syringe pricked the artery in his neck. Sweat dripped from his face. "If the synthetic hormone could be modified into a gas and delivered in canisters dropped from planes or via rockets, it would render opposing armies helpless during an attack."

"Politicians tend to get a little nervous when they hear about chemical-weapons research, but why should that hold back a good idea?" Cavanaugh said, barely containing his anger.

He recalled how Kline's men had suddenly panicked when they'd invaded the warehouse's stairwell. Responding to an unseen threat, they had fired uncontrollably up the stairs, unable to force themselves higher. Prescott must have had canisters of the gas concealed in the stairwell. Traces of it had escaped, which explained Cavanaugh's jittery reaction.

He recalled something else—how Prescott had worked dials on a panel when Kline's team invaded the stairwell. But as frightened as Kline's men had become, their reaction had apparently not been strong enough, for Prescott had murmured in alarm to himself, as if something was wrong. Perhaps the canisters had developed a slow leak so that by the time Kline's team attacked, the full force of the weapon wasn't available.

"Prescott experimented with it on animals," Kline said. "Rats went berserk. Cats and dogs became so afraid of each other, they cowered in corners. On one occasion, it drove a dozen goats into such a panic that they raced around the walls that contained them until they dropped in shock and died."

Cavanaugh thought of Karen's basement, of the pungent smell that he now realized had caused him, for the first time in his life, to suffer fear, the effects of which continued to linger. He thought of the panic that had almost destroyed him in the fire. He thought of seeing Karen slumped motionless in her wheelchair, her hands clamped to her chest, her face contorted rigidly with horror. Now he understood what had killed her. Wanting to avoid a wound or a strangle mark that would alert a medical examiner to Karen's murder, Prescott had used the hormone to terrify her to death. Her heart and arteries must have ruptured from the massive force of terror.

"The syringe. Your hand's shaking again," Kline said.

"Tell me *everything*."

"Eventually, the temptation became too great. Prescott tried it on humans. Inner-city gangs ran in panic when a lone victim wandered onto their turf and defended himself from their attacks by throwing a small hissing canister at them."

"Then there must be a neutralizer," Cavanaugh said. "Otherwise, the person throwing the canister would become terrified also."

"Yes." Kline cringed from the pressure of the syringe against his neck.

Prescott must have used the neutralizer on himself when he was in Karen's house, Cavanaugh realized. Otherwise, the hormone would have overpowered him.

"Without the neutralizer, they couldn't have managed what happened at the World Trade Organization riots in St. Louis," Kline said.

All Cavanaugh remembered about the riots was that after three days of chaos, the authorities had finally overwhelmed the rioters and forced them into the Mississippi. "The tear gas?"

"Contained the fear hormone." Kline shut his eyes in an attempt to relieve his tension. "The gas masks, supplied by the military, had the neutralizer in their filters. The experiment was a success."

"Except that only a few military officers and Prescott knew what had really happened," Cavanaugh said.

"And a few powerful civilians with strong ideas about how

your country should protect itself. They decided to try another secret test on humans, this time on a group trained not to respond to fear. A team of U.S. Rangers on a training exercise in a swamp in Florida."

Cavanaugh recalled being troubled by a recent report about fifteen Rangers who had drowned in Florida.

Sweating, Kline kept his eyes shut. "Maybe the hormone had the wrong strength. Or maybe men trained to use weapons do just that when they're overwhelmed with panic. They started shooting at anything and everything. Most of them didn't drown—they were hit by cross fire."

Sickened, Cavanaugh found himself leaning back, taking the syringe from where he'd pressed it against Kline's jugular.

Except for Kline's labored breathing, the room became silent. It took several moments before Kline—pale, taped to the chair, lying sideways on the floor—seemed to realize that the syringe had been removed. Slowly, apprehensively, he opened his eyes, evidently not believing that Cavanaugh sat across from him, the syringe next to him on the carpet.

"Keep talking," Cavanaugh said.

"Two things happened." Kline tried to raise his head so he could look at Cavanaugh straight on. "First, my employer learned about the experiments."

"How?"

"One of Prescott's researchers was an informant for us."

"And the second thing?"

"The informant wasn't cautious about the way he spent what we paid him. Prescott's controllers became suspicious, interrogated the man, and discovered that the research had been compromised, that an unfriendly foreign government wanted the weapon. In tandem with the dead Rangers in the failed experiment, that security lapse made the military officers decide it was too risky to continue. Before anyone in your government could learn about the research and make trouble about it, they aborted the program."

Kline let the implication hang in the air.

"You're suggesting Prescott's controllers worried about him, about whether they could trust him?" Cavanaugh asked.

"Our informant knew the nature of the fear hormone but not how to produce it. Only Prescott had all the details. He was synonymous with the research. To shut down the program fully—"

"Prescott had to be eliminated," Cavanaugh said.

"Especially because his controllers knew *we* wanted to get our hands on him. He suspected the danger he faced. He fled—with us and his controllers after him, one group trying to capture him, the other trying to kill him. We managed to track him to that warehouse. Then *you* showed up, and here we are," Kline said.

"But how did Prescott's controllers learn where we were taking him?" Cavanaugh asked. Abruptly, the answer seemed evident. "They must have followed you to the warehouse."

"We were careful."

"Perhaps one of your men informed on you."

"Then why did it take so long for Prescott's controllers to try to get him?" Kline asked. "They made their move only after *you* became involved."

Cavanaugh felt his face turn cold. "*I* was followed? Someone at Protective Services told them we were helping Prescott?"

"Your firm protects the rich and powerful. It makes sense that various intelligence agencies would keep tabs on your company's activities."

Again, Cavanaugh began to lose focus on reality. He didn't know what to think, what to depend on. Then he looked at Jamie, whose beautiful yet worried gaze was directed toward him, and he knew very definitely what to depend on.

"To hell with it." Cavanaugh raised Kline from the floor and pulled out the Emerson knife.

"What are you doing?" Kline flinched.

"John's going to phone the Justice Department and have your companions picked up for a heart-to-heart chat about unfriendly foreign governments."

Kline stared at the knife. "But what's going to happen to *me*?"

"We're going sight-seeing."

"What?"

"A quiet drive in the countryside."

"With *you*?" Kline looked pleadingly toward Rutherford. "Can't you see this guy's crazy? He'll take me out to the woods. God knows *what* he'll do to me *there*. No one'll ever find my body."

Rutherford studied Cavanaugh. "Can I talk to you a minute?"

"Keep your pistol aimed at Kline," Cavanaugh told Jamie. He followed Rutherford into the bedroom.

19

Rutherford closed the bedroom door. "Are you serious?"

"I need him to show me Prescott's lab. Maybe something there will tell me where Prescott went. It's the only direction I can think to go."

"Can't let you," Rutherford said. "Kline's an FBI prisoner now."

"I haven't heard you read him his rights."

"You will in about thirty seconds," Rutherford said.

"How about in a couple of hours?"

"What are you trying to—"

"Once Kline's officially in FBI custody and the Bureau puts him in a government facility, the pressure's off him. He won't feel threatened. He won't tell you anything more."

"Kidnapping a federal agent can put him in prison for life," Rutherford said. "He'll tell us anything we want to know in exchange for a plea bargain."

"But plea bargains take time," Cavanaugh said. "Meanwhile, Prescott's trail gets colder. I need everything Kline knows *now*."

"Can't," Rutherford repeated. "If the Bureau found out I let a prisoner go, I'd lose my job."

"You won't be letting him go," Cavanaugh said.

"Then why are we having this conversation?"

"I'm *taking* him."

"What?"

"Wait two hours, then phone the Bureau. Tell them there was another prisoner but that I took him before the situation was under control. Tell them we went to Prescott's lab. Send a team out there. By then, I'll have learned everything I need from Kline."

"You *are* crazy."

"Let's just say things are happening inside me I need to stop."

"I don't understand."

Cavanaugh held up his shaking hand. "Prescott gave me a dose of the fear hormone Kline talked about."

Rutherford didn't say anything for a moment. "God."

"Kline said there was a neutralizer. Prescott has it. I need it." Cavanaugh opened the door and went into the living room, where Kline looked apprehensive. "Let's go."

"No," Rutherford said.

Cavanaugh thumbed open the Emerson knife, freed Kline from the chair, tied his wrists in front of him, and draped Kline's leather jacket over his hands. "We'll use the stairs and go out through the emergency exit. Jennifer, get the car. Meet us in back."

"I can't let you do this," Rutherford said.

"Two hours, John."

"Don't make me stop you."

"What are you going to do? Shoot me?"

Rutherford stared at him.

PART FIVE

Threat Escalation

1

While Jamie drove, Kline sat next to her. Cavanaugh was in the back, his pistol under a newspaper on his lap, ready to shoot through the rear of Kline's seat if Kline did anything to justify it.

A hundred miles west of Washington, the Virginia country-side was lush and hilly, with fewer towns and more fields and wooded areas as they went along. Occasional farmhouses, stone fences, and ponds were visible along the tree-lined two-lane road. The prevailing impression, though, was of large estates and horses grazing.

At four in the afternoon, there was little traffic. As Jamie guided the Taurus into a hollow, up a slight rise, and into another hollow, Cavanaugh asked Kline, "How far?"

"Another five minutes."

"You're certain the two men you left here to watch for me have gone?"

"You heard me phone and tell them to leave. You made it clear: You'll shoot me if you catch even a glimpse of them. I assure you, they've gone. I gave them no warning."

Jamie drove past a sign that read BAILEY'S RIDGE. "Where's the town? I don't see any buildings."

"It's not a town," Kline said.

"Then what is it?"

"A site where a Civil War battle occurred."

Past the sign, a plaque showed a map and an historical note. Jamie stopped next to it.

The map was in bas-relief, dramatizing the contour of the wooded hills in the area. Arrows indicated where Union and Confederate soldiers had fought one another in a battle that had destroyed most of a farm owned by an Irish immigrant, Samuel Bailey, killing his wife and daughter. The battle had concluded when Bailey put on a fallen Union soldier's jacket, grabbed a rifle, and led a company of Northerners across a ridge above his farm, outflanking their opponents. Bailey went on to receive a field commission as a captain and to fight in numerous other battles, eventually dying from diphtheria, never again seeing his farm and the graves of his wife and daughter.

"Well, *that's* enough to ruin my day," Cavanaugh said.

"Mine already *was* ruined," Kline said. His wrists remained tied together beneath his leather jacket. "Two hollows from here, there's a lane on the right."

Jamie drove on, went up an incline, and descended into the first hollow.

"Take this lane," Cavanaugh told Jamie.

"No, that's not the one," Kline said. "I told you *two* hollows."

"I know what you told me," Cavanaugh said, "but we're trying *this* one."

Jamie pulled off the road. Flanked by dense bushes and trees, two shadowy weed-choked ruts in the dirt were blocked by a wooden gate, the white paint of which had faded to the color of dirty chalk. What attracted Cavanaugh's attention was that the weeds in the lane looked crushed, as if a vehicle had recently gone over them.

"I don't see a lock," Jamie said. After a cautious glance

around, she got out of the car and unhooked a rusted chain from the gate, swinging it open. She drove through, stopped, and took another wary glance around before she returned to the gate and shut it behind her.

"It's so flimsy," Jamie said, getting back into the car, "if we have to when we come back, we can always ram through it."

"Park where the undergrowth conceals us from the road. We'll walk," Cavanaugh said.

After warning Kline to be quiet, Cavanaugh made him lead the way up a potholed lane that twisted through trees and bushes. He had his pistol out, following Kline at a careful distance.

Overhead branches shut out the sun. Then the branches opened, and the steep rise brought them to knee-high grass in a clearing where old weather-grayed picnic benches looked down on a valley half a mile wide. The area down there was completely devoted to pasture, no shade trees anywhere, which was odd if the pasture was intended for horses, Cavanaugh thought, but *not* odd if the trees had been leveled to create an unobstructed line of fire and to remove places in which an intruder might be able to hide.

A wooden sign attached to a post had faded yellow letters that might once have been orange: WELCOME TO BAILEY'S RIDGE.

"Looks like one of the locals tried some kind of tourist thing several years ago," Cavanaugh said.

He glanced down at indentations in the long grass, where a vehicle had recently been parked. Then he motioned for Kline to walk along a furrow in the grass toward the picnic benches. A trampled area around one of the benches attracted his attention, as did cigarette butts, the paper of which looked fresh.

"This was where your men watched for me, right?" Cavanaugh asked. He peered down at the paved road that went through the pasture. "From here, they could see pretty much everything that happened down there. Yesterday, what made you think I'd use the next lane?"

"It's the only area where the trees have been cut back from the road. Until a month ago, a chain-link fence used to be there. The dirt was disturbed when they ripped the poles out. The sanitizers tried to smooth the dirt and put in bushes, but it's obvious the landscape's been changed. Every other lane that seems to go nowhere is made of dirt and has weeds and potholes. *That* lane's as smooth and weed-free as can be. Beyond the trees, it becomes paved."

"How did Prescott and his controllers get permission to block off a historic site?" Cavanaugh asked.

"Prescott didn't need permission. This property's historic, but it isn't owned by the government. It's his."

"Is it safe to go down there?"

"Nobody's around. The lab was abandoned as soon as the project was terminated."

"But where's the lab?"

Kline pointed toward the valley.

"I don't see anything except a burned-out farmhouse," Cavanaugh said.

2

"The first time Bailey's farmhouse was destroyed was in 1864," Kline explained as they drove along the road through the pasture, approaching the burned structure. "After your Civil War, the new owner—an industrialist who'd made a fortune selling munitions to the government—bought most of the land around here and had a mansion built where Bailey's house had stood. The original cellar was incorporated into the design. Stones from the original house were used in the walls."

"You should have been a historian."

"My father was." Kline's voice was filled with regret.

They reached the scorched, collapsed building and got out of the Taurus.

Despite the devastation of the burned timbers and the blackened stones from the fallen walls, Cavanaugh was able to get an idea of how impressive the mansion had been in its heyday. He imagined pillars and two long porches, one above the other, people standing on them, waving, as horse-drawn carriages brought brightly dressed visitors. "It's a shame Prescott's controllers had to destroy it."

"*They* didn't destroy it," Kline said. "Prescott did."

Cavanaugh and Jamie looked at him.

"Prescott's controllers confined him to the mansion when they terminated his project," Kline said. "A man doesn't devote himself to researching fear unless he identifies with it. If he's paranoid, he's going to become more so when he sees signs all around him that people consider him a liability."

"Fear's his primary emotion," Cavanaugh agreed. And now, thanks to him, it's mine, he added silently.

"To protect himself, Prescott did something his controllers could never have anticipated, given how proud he was of this property," Kline said. "One night when his fear became especially intense and he was certain he was about to be killed, he burned the mansion down. Because he looked so heavy and out of shape, his controllers had misjudged him, putting a few guards on him, while the majority were devoted to keeping intruders such as myself off the property. In the confusion caused by the flames, he was able to slip away into the darkness. The fire was only half of his tactic, however. He also released the hormone as the mansion burned. Under its influence, the guards panicked and shot at what they thought were attackers coming through the flickering shadows. Several got killed by their own men—another mess that had to be cleaned up. The shots brought the guards from the perimeter. Meanwhile, Prescott stole one of their vehicles and smashed through a fence at the back of the property. He abandoned the vehicle in a nearby town, where he had a car stored in a garage that he'd rented under another name."

"Just goes to show—paranoia's a survival trait," Jamie said.

"Where's Prescott's lab?" Cavanaugh asked.

"In back," Kline said.

They rounded the jumble of scorched timbers and stones and approached a similar ruin, but this one looked as if it had been a barn.

"The fire Prescott set didn't spread this far," Kline said. "A few days later, his controllers were responsible for *this* one. It was part of their sanitizing. An efficient way to get the job done."

"The lab's underground?"

"Under the barn." Kline pointed toward where blackened wreckage had been moved to form a path across the barn's concrete floor. He indicated a hatchlike slab. "That's the entrance."

"You and your men cleared this? Weren't you afraid of being caught?"

"By whom? I told you the property had been abandoned. There's no reason to guard this place. There's nothing here for Prescott's controllers to worry about."

Kline suddenly groaned. As Cavanaugh gaped, Jamie screamed, seeing blood fly from Kline's forehead. A faraway shot echoing, Kline toppled face-forward into the dirt.

It happened so suddenly and so unexpectedly that Cavanaugh was momentarily controlled only by his startle reflex. Until now, after the tension of what had happened in Rutherford's condo, he had managed to keep his nervousness at bay. This was supposed to have been a fact-finding mission, not a confrontation. Now the unaccustomed fear that Prescott's hormone had created in him and that he had struggled to subdue took possession of him again. But his fear for Jamie was even greater. His muscles responding like tightly wound springs abruptly released, he dove toward her, pushing her down with him next to the barn's wreckage.

A bullet kicked up dirt beyond their heads, but this time, the shot was close and loud, almost simultaneous with the bullet's impact.

A second shot tore up dirt near their feet. Cavanaugh felt the sharp vibration through the ground.

At the mansion, charred boards scraped against each other, shifting, creating gaps. Blackened rocks toppled. The ruin had seemingly come to life, portions of it able to move, assuming independent shapes. One by one, black-clad figures rose from ashes, soot, and grime, their faces streaked with carbon. They aimed assault weapons.

One of the camouflaged men fired a burst at the ground next to Jamie. Dust flew. The ground shook. The roar was overwhelming.

Then the shooting stopped, and in the sudden silence, which was broken only by the ringing in Cavanaugh's ears, he managed to control his trembling arms and raise them in surrender.

Pale, breathing rapidly, Jamie imitated him.

Slowly, unsteadily, they came to their feet.

"If they wanted us dead"—his mouth dry, his words like paste, Cavanaugh murmured, doing his best to assure her— "they'd have shot us by now." He hoped he was convincing, that his voice didn't sound hollow. Heat seared his stomach.

Stepping from the mansion's ruin, the dark camouflaged figures continued to aim their weapons, which Cavanaugh recognized now as MP-5 submachine guns. Like the men who'd rappelled from the helicopters the night of the attack on the bunker, these men obviously had special-operations training. One of them stared past Cavanaugh prompting Cavanaugh to glance apprehensively in that direction.

From the woods at the back of the valley, the speck of a vehicle emerged. As it sped closer, crossing a field, it threw up dust. Then it reached the paved road, the dust drifting in the breeze, and even with the ringing in his ears, Cavanaugh could hear its engine getting louder. The vehicle was now close enough for Cavanaugh to recognize it as a big four-wheel-drive SUV, a Ford Explorer. With the sun angled in its direction, he saw the shapes of two people beyond the windshield: a broad-shouldered driver and a tall blond woman in her thirties, whose oval face and high cheekbones might have been attractive if her eyes hadn't been the coldest he'd ever seen.

As the Explorer skidded to a halt, the woman got out. She was around five ten, the same as Jamie. Her face had an athlete's tan and no makeup. Her hair was like an athlete's also, too short to be combed back. Her eyes were the blue of a glacier. She wore sturdy walking shoes, khaki pants, a matching jacket, and a beige shirt that gave her a military appearance.

While the camouflaged figures approached with their weapons, the woman told her driver, who was built like a weight lifter, "Search them."

The muscular man enjoyed his work, prodding Cavanaugh more forcefully than necessary, then pawing Jamie.

You'll pay for that, Cavanaugh thought, trying to use anger to balance his fear.

The driver found their pistols under their jackets and nodded at their nonreflective flat-black coating, evidence of the expert gunsmith work that had been done on them. The way he put them into his baggy hiking pants, it was obvious he intended to keep them as his own. He took their extra magazines and Cavanaugh's cell phone. He unclipped the Emerson knife from the inside of Cavanaugh's front pants pocket, approved of that weapon also, and clipped it into his own pocket. He also took Jamie's car keys.

"Your *names*," the woman said.

"Sam Murdock." Cavanaugh gave her the name on the ID Karen had manufactured for him.

"Jennifer," Jamie said, using the false name Cavanaugh had assigned her at Rutherford's condo. Her ID was with her purse, which she'd left under the Taurus's front seat.

"Sam Murdock?" The woman studied the wallet the driver

tossed to her. "That might be what it says here, but your professional name is Cavanaugh."

"I don't know what—"

"You're with Global Protective Services. You're the one who went to the warehouse to get Prescott."

So Kline was right, Cavanaugh thought. Somebody at Protective Services betrayed me. I was followed to the warehouse.

"Prescott?" Cavanaugh frowned. "What are you talking about?"

The woman nodded to her driver, who plunged a fist into Cavanaugh's stomach.

Gasping, Cavanaugh sank to his knees. His breath had been so knocked out of him that his vision turned gray for a moment as he struggled to inhale.

"You came here to see the lab," the woman said. "Fine. I'll show it to you."

She took what looked like a pager from her belt and pressed a button.

Behind Cavanaugh, a motor droned. He turned in that direction. Hydraulic poles tilted the concrete slab up, revealing steps that descended into darkness.

"The shots will attract attention," Cavanaugh found enough breath to say.

"Not around here. Prescott owns most of the land. The locals have been told he enjoys target shooting. Now go down to the lab, or else Edgar will throw you," the woman said.

"I'll take the first option, thanks."

Cavanaugh managed to stand. Nodding to Jamie, who looked paler and searched his eyes for assurance, he went down the steps with her.

"We stripped this place clean," the woman said, voice echoing. "Totally gutted it."

The armed men removed Surefire flashlights from their equipment belts. A little longer and thicker than a heavyweight boxer's index finger, the compact black tubes gave off an amaz-

ing amount of light for their size, revealing a long concrete corridor that had numerous openings on each side. The air was
stale.

"We destroyed all the scientific equipment, the computers,
and the files," the woman said. "We carted away the furniture.
We disassembled the heating and air-conditioning systems. We
even removed the lighting fixtures, the sinks and toilets, the car-
peting, the false ceilings, the doors, and the wall panels." Taking
a flashlight from one of the men, the woman aimed it at the ceiling, where insulated wires dangled from holes in which fluores-
cent lamps had presumably once been anchored. She pointed the
flashlight in a different direction and showed wires projecting
from small rectangular holes in the wall where light switches had
been. "It doesn't get cleaner than this. No one could possibly
guess what these rooms were used for. Hell, if the barn was still
standing, you could put hay or animals down here."

"Then why would you care if anybody wandered onto the
property?" Cavanaugh's voice reverberated. "There's nothing
here to bother anybody and get you in trouble."

"That's exactly right. There's nothing here but bare rooms. I'm
not sure you get the point," the woman said.

The armed men stepped closer, aiming the flashlights at Cavanaugh's and Jamie's eyes, backing them into the room.

"We're not here protecting anything. My men haven't been
lying motionless under that rubble merely to demonstrate their
skill and patience. We've been waiting."

Cavanaugh didn't react.

"But not just for anybody."

Cavanaugh still didn't react.

"For *you*."

3

Now Cavanaugh did react, but not in a way that the woman expected. Relying on his training, he said, "I need to know your name."

"What?"

"If we're going to reach an understanding, it helps me to know your name. To relate. To build a position of trust."

"Amazing," the woman replied.

"In that case, I bet I can guess your last name: Grace."

In darkness pierced by flashlight beams, the woman became silent for a moment. When she finally spoke again, she sounded annoyed. "Yes, all our research says you're good at using words to manipulate situations. In fact, that's what I want from you. Talk. A lot of it."

"About?"

"Prescott."

"How did you know we'd come here?"

"Teach him not to change the subject, Edgar."

Blinded by the flashlights, Cavanaugh couldn't see where the fist was directed. He expected another punch to his stomach and braced his muscles there, but this time the blow struck his face, knocking him to the floor. Stunned, briefly seeing more flashlight beams than were aimed at him, he spat blood. Again, anger helped neutralize his fear.

"We thought Prescott was dead, but we didn't find his body on the mountain after the fire," Grace said.

You punished me, but I still won, Cavanaugh thought. You're answering my question.

"So we decided to keep tabs on our rivals," she said. "*They* were still trying to find him, and they were *very* interested in anybody else who was trying to find him. Yesterday, we saw them kidnap an FBI agent. Then four of them, including the dead man outside, set up surveillance on a nearby ridge, obviously expecting somebody important to arrive. We hoped it would be Prescott, although we couldn't figure why he'd come back. But then two of the men went away. When the final two started to leave this afternoon, we interrogated them and learned about you and your interest in this place, so we did our *own* watching for a while."

"Why did you shoot Kline?"

"Was that his name?" Grace shrugged. "If he knew anything, he wouldn't have been so eager to get his hands on *you*. I didn't need him, except to make a point about how serious we are."

"But you need *me*, so you won't kill me," Cavanaugh said.

"Meaning how can we make you afraid enough to talk? Why doesn't Edgar have a heart-to-heart with your friend here. Maybe *that'll* make you talk."

The threat was like a hot needle piercing Cavanaugh's chest. Still dazed by the blow to his face, he tried to think quickly, to distract Grace from fixating on Jamie. "My team and I taught Prescott how to disappear. Then he killed everybody but me." What Cavanaugh said was only partly true. He deliberately didn't mention that a rocket from Grace's team had blown up Chad and Tracy. Maybe he could keep Grace from realizing that he hated *her* side almost as much as he hated Prescott. "I risked my life for that son of a bitch. He killed the people who'd pledged to protect him. My *friends*. Tried to kill *me*. . . . I want him as much as you do."

"Then tell us where to find him," Grace said.

On the floor, Cavanaugh raised his left arm, trying to shield his eyes from the glare of the lights. More blood dripped from his mouth. "You think if I knew where to find him, I'd have come to his lab?"

"You just told me you helped teach Prescott how to disappear!" Grace's voice boomed.

"Everything but the final step: his new identity." Cavanaugh's swollen mouth made it difficult for him to talk. "We'd arranged for him to go to a forger who'd supply him with a new name and documents for it. Prescott got there ahead of me, took the documents, and killed the forger. There's no way to find out the name and background the forger created for him."

"Where did Prescott intend to live?"

"I have no idea. We hadn't decided that yet."

"Edgar," Grace said.

This time, it was a kick to Cavanaugh's side that made him groan. Trying to absorb the impact, he rolled, but not far—a corner blocked his way.

As the reverberation of the impact ended, Cavanaugh heard Jamie's nervous breathing. "We told him to pick a spot where he'd never been, where he'd be least expected to go, a place he'd never spoken to anybody about."

"You're not making a very good case for yourself," Grace said. "Why should we let you live if there's no way you can help us?"

"I understand him."

"You understand him?" Grace mocked. "He worked for us for ten years, and nobody *here* understood him."

"Except that he's paranoid," Cavanaugh said. "And he's arrogant."

"You're not telling me anything I don't know. I think Edgar needs to have that heart-to-heart with your friend to get you to be more generous with your information."

Cavanaugh heard Jamie stop breathing. "Grace, I'll tell you the most important thing you need to know about him," he said.

"Quit calling me that! If you're trying to pretend you're delirious, it isn't going to—"

"Prescott believes he's smarter than everybody else," Cavanaugh said.

"So what?"

"I'm betting he thinks he knows how to disappear better than I taught him. I'm betting he thinks he can break the rules and be clever enough to get away with it." The idea, which had suddenly occurred to Cavanaugh, began to seem more than just a stalling tactic.

"Be specific."

Cavanaugh squinted past the nearly blinding flashlights toward where Grace's voice came from the darkness on his left. "We asked Prescott if he had a place in mind where he wanted to start his new life. He told us no, which we said was good"—Cavanaugh wiped blood from his mouth—"because people who have a place in mind often make inadvertent comments about it." He took a painful breath. "Later, somebody might remember those comments and tell the wrong people." He shifted where he lay on the concrete floor, feeling its chill creeping into him. "I've been trying to remember if Prescott made any inadvertent slips like that."

"And did he?"

"He liked wine."

"That's not a bulletin, either."

"He liked fine cooking. He could analyze it the way a chef would." Thinking of Prescott's praise for Chad's beef Stroganoff, Cavanaugh felt a mounting fury about Chad's death, about how it wouldn't have happened if not for Grace's team and the fire Prescott had started. Hating Grace, he hid his emotions by concentrating on the pain Edgar had inflicted on him: his aching stomach muscles and his mangled lips. "He said the only exercise he enjoyed was golf."

"So Prescott went to Napa Valley or the New York wine district or the Bordeaux region of France, where he eats gourmet meals when he's not playing golf—is *that* the news flash you're giving me?" Grace asked. "If you don't start telling me something useful, Edgar and your friend are going to start dancing. While he's at it, he'll step on *your* toes a little more."

"Let me finish." Cavanaugh's swollen lips throbbed. "When I met him at the warehouse, he had some books and videotapes on a shelf. Not many. But he'd been in that hidey-hole for three weeks. It stands to reason that the few things he had with him were extremely important to him, enough to keep him amused for that length of time." Cavanaugh paused, hoping to sink the hook. "Or to satisfy his fantasies."

"Fantasies?"

"About the ideal life he was planning. About the dreamed-of place he was going to see with his brand-new identity."

"What were the books and the videos?"

"That's the problem. I've been trying to remember, but I can't think of the titles." Again, Cavanaugh was partly lying. He definitely remembered Prescott's fascination with the poet Robinson Jeffers. He was trying to give Grace enough information to retain her interest while he bought time, in the hopes that he could find a way to get Jamie and himself out of there. "He had a porno book. Another book about geology. I saw an odd mix of videos. A Clint Eastwood thriller. A teenage romance starring Troy Donahue."

"Titles," Grace said.

"I told you—I can't remember."

"You will," Grace said.

She snapped her fingers. Footsteps scraping, the group backed away. Gripping the wall to get support to stand, Cavanaugh felt Jamie help him to his feet. He shambled from the room and watched the group climb the concrete steps toward sunlight that hurt his eyes.

At the top, Grace had a cell phone to her ear. "Somebody bring Dr. Rattigan . . . I don't care *what* he's doing. Get him here *now.*"

The group disappeared into daylight.

With a drone, the concrete door descended, blocking the sun. Three feet. Two feet. Cavanaugh cherished the final sliver of light. Then, with a hollow thump as the door closed, he and Jamie were enveloped by darkness.

4

The gloom and the isolation were so total that the air felt denser and smelled staler. He heard Jamie breathing next to him.

"Who's Dr. Rattigan?" Her voice was unsteady. The complete lack of light caused the echo to seem louder.

Cavanaugh's injuries, plus his fear-weakened muscles, made it hard for him to keep his balance in the darkness. "My guess is somebody with a satchelful of syringes and chemicals to help me remember."

"How hard did he hit you?"

"My smile isn't as winning as it used to be." The joke wasn't much, but Cavanaugh had to try to do something to lift Jamie's spirit. "What about you? Are—"

"I need to . . . I'm sorry, but I have to . . ."

Cavanaugh heard Jamie feel her way along a wall and into a room. An urgent tug on a buckle was followed by a zipper being pulled down, slacks being dropped, urine hissing on the floor.

"Sorry," she said. "Sorry."

"For what it's worth . . ." If he hadn't been determined to rouse her spirits, he wouldn't have admitted that his own pants were wet. "When Edgar kicked me, my bladder let go."

And that's something else he and Grace will pay for, Cavanaugh thought.

Fabric made a brushing sound as Jamie readjusted her clothes. "I don't know if I ever told you. When I was a kid, some friends—if I can call them that—locked me in a closet. I don't like the dark."

"I'm not crazy about it, either."

"I have trouble in places that make me feel closed in."

"Maybe I can make the space seem larger." The luminous dial on Cavanaugh's watch showed the rising motion of his hand as he remembered something in the upper pocket of his jacket.

Scrape.

A match flared.

Jamie's surprised face appeared in the flickering light. "Where'd you get—"

"From when we pretended to be smoking outside John's building."

"One of the few benefits anyone ever got from lighting up," Jamie said.

"Edgar's not half as good at searching people as he thinks he is. He also left us our belts."

"What good are—"

"The spike on the buckle can be a weapon."

Cavanaugh felt heat as the match burned closer to his fingers. His trembling hand made the flame waver. Finally, he had to drop it.

"Step next to me," he said. "Hold my jacket."

The sound of cloth being torn echoed in the darkness.

"What are you doing?" Jamie asked.

"Ripping off my shirtsleeves."

"Why would—"

"To make torches." Cavanaugh tugged at the fabric, which was stronger than he'd expected. Finally, he had both sleeves off. His bare arms felt a chill that radiated from the concrete around him. Quickly, he put his coat back on.

"My turn," Jamie said. She gave him her blazer. The finer material of her blouse made it easier for her and Cavanaugh to tear the sleeves off. She shoved them into a pocket.

"We'll be able to see for a while," Jamie said, "but we still won't be able to get out of here."

"Imagine you're Prescott." Cavanaugh removed his belt and shoved the spike on its buckle through the end of one of his torn-off sleeves. "Suspicious as he is, he wouldn't like feeling closed in any more than *we* do. That concrete door comes down and—"

"The hydraulics could fail," Jamie said. "Everybody could be trapped and suffocate. Prescott definitely wouldn't like to think about running out of air."

"Right." Cavanaugh struck another match and applied the flame to the end of his sleeve. Like many fabrics, it had been treated with a fire retardant. That wouldn't stop the cloth from catching fire, but it *would* prevent the fire from spreading quickly, which was what Cavanaugh needed.

He set the sleeve on the floor and pulled it with his belt. That way, he wouldn't risk burning his hand. His buckle clattered along the concrete. Meanwhile, the shimmering light caused Jamie's face to lose a little of its tension.

"A tunnel that goes to Prescott's mansion," she said.

"Exactly."

The buckle continued to clatter as they moved toward the steps leading up to the door. Next to the steps, on the right, the burning sleeve revealed a corridor. They followed the narrow passageway, only to be stopped by a door.

The door was locked.

Cavanaugh folded up his jacket collar and removed his lock-pick tools. He set the belt on the floor, tried to steady his hands, and went to work.

"Can you see to do it?" Jamie asked.

"Most of this is feel." Giving Jamie the lesson he'd promised, hoping to distract her, and distracting himself in the process, Cavanaugh explained what he was doing. Applying torque with the end of one pick, he inserted the second pick into the key slot. The lock was solid and had six pins, each of which he nudged.

In fifteen seconds, despite his trembling fingers, Cavanaugh had disabled the lock.

But when he pulled the door open, the dwindling flames revealed a solid plug of fallen stones and scorched timbers, a sight that made Jamie moan.

"It'll take hours to clean out this much debris, assuming we can do it at all," Cavanaugh said.

The flame weakened.

"Not to mention, the noise we'd make would attract attention on the surface. We'd have a dozen submachine guns pointed at us if we managed to crawl out."

The flame died.

"What are we going to do?" Jamie asked.

Without an answer, Cavanaugh attached another torn sleeve to the buckle and lit it. Hurrying, he led the way back along the tunnel. "What did Grace say about all this? What did she mention they took out of here?"

"The air-conditioning and the heating systems. Maybe we can use the ductwork," Jamie said quickly. "Maybe there's a ventilation shaft that leads to the surface."

They reached the main corridor. At the bottom of the stairs leading up to the concrete door, Cavanaugh glanced toward the ceiling, finding a two-foot-square gap where a ventilation grille had been removed.

Crouching, he interlaced his hands and made them into a stirrup. When Jamie stepped onto them, he straightened, lifting her.

She was tall enough that she had no trouble reaching the gap in the ceiling. She eased her head up through it.

"See anything?" Cavanaugh asked.

"I can't fit through it, so I guarantee *you* can't. Damn it, in the movies, the air-conditioning ducts are always big enough for Andre the Giant."

As Cavanaugh lowered her, the burning sleeve began to dim. Smoke rose. "What else did Grace say? What else did they take out of here?"

"The plumbing fixtures. The lights. The—"

"We know there's electricity." Cavanaugh glanced at the wires protruding from small gaps in the walls. "Otherwise, the system that raises the concrete slab wouldn't work."

"What switch would have activated the door from the *inside*?" Jamie headed toward wires in a gap to the right of the steps. Plastic caps covered the ends of the wires.

Cavanaugh pulled the caps off and studied the bare tips of the wires. "The switch that was here was the closest to the steps. If I press these wires together, will they make a circuit and cause the door to open?"

In the dimming light, Jamie looked hopeful. Then the spirit in her eyes faded. "There'll be guards outside. They'll see and hear the door move."

"Maybe not. If I only tap these wires together, there'll be sound and movement just for an instant. Maybe not long enough for anybody to notice. At least we'll know if these wires control the door."

"But what good will *that* do? We'll still be trapped in here."

"Until later," Cavanaugh said. "Until we think the timing's better. Then we can open the door all the way."

"Is that before or after Dr. Rattigan fills you full of chemicals to refresh your memory?"

Cavanaugh didn't know what to answer. We've got to try *something,* he thought.

As he was about to tap the wires together, the door moved seemingly on its own, the hydraulic system droning, the door rising.

Sunlight revealed the silhouettes of Grace, Edgar, and half a dozen armed men.

Cavanaugh stepped on the burning sleeve to extinguish it, then grabbed his belt and pulled Jamie into the shadows of a room. He didn't know what he hoped to accomplish, but anything was better than standing in the open. He removed the matchbook from his pocket and tore off several of the matches, along with a quarter inch of the abrasive paper, putting them in a different pocket. Then he crushed the matchbook inside his fist.

Heavy footsteps indicated that the armed men came down the steps first.

Grace and Edgar followed. "Show yourselves," Grace said. "If you make us search for you, we'll throw flash-bangs into each room."

The threat of ruptured eardrums was enough to persuade Cavanaugh to emerge into the corridor, Jamie coming with him.

"I smell smoke." Grace glanced toward the ashy remnants of the burned sleeve on the floor.

"For light," Cavanaugh said.

"How'd you set fire to the clothing?"

"Matches."

Grace gave Edgar a look of disgust.

There was enough light spilling through the entrance for Cavanaugh to see that the gunmen didn't have the distinctive bulky look that came from wearing Kevlar vests under their shirts. They wore utility belts with two-way radios, Beretta pistols, extra ammunition, and flash-bang canisters.

Cavanaugh shifted his gaze toward Edgar's baggy pants pockets. Something heavy weighed down the right side, presumably one of the pistols that Edgar had taken. The clip on the Emerson knife was secured to the outside of Edgar's other pocket.

"Toss the matches over," Grace said.

Cavanaugh obeyed.

"What did you do, run over them with a car?" Looking disgusted, Grace picked them up, their mutilated appearance making the missing quarter inch of abrasive paper seem normal. "I've got a computer in the car and access to the Internet." Grace gestured with several computer printouts. "Before the good doctor gets here, maybe you'd like to refresh your memory the easy way. Troy Donahue." The sunlight behind Grace allowed her to read from one of the pages. " 'Tall, blond, blue-eyed teenage heartthrob known for his wooden acting. Peak of popularity—late fifties, early sixties. Major hits: *A Summer Place. Susan Slade. Parrish. Rome Adventure. Palm Springs Weekend.*' Do any of those sound familiar?"

"All I saw was the box for the video," Cavanaugh said. "I have no idea what the movie was about. The female costar's name was on the box. Mention some actresses."

Grace frowned at the page. "Connie Stevens. Sandra Dee. Suzanne Pleshette. Stefanie Powers."

"Sandra Dee," Cavanaugh said, knowing he had to keep Grace patient by giving her something. "The one with Sandra Dee."

"*A Summer Place.*" Grace read the plot summary. " 'Love at a resort town in Maine.' Maybe Prescott was planning to go to Maine." She looked at another printout. "Clint Eastwood movies. You said 'thriller'?"

"It definitely wasn't a war movie or a Western."

"*Dirty Harry.*"

"No."

"*Magnum Force. The Enforcer. The Dead Pool.*"

"No."

"*The Eiger Sanction. Play Misty for Me. Thunderbolt and Lightfoot. Tightrope.*"

"No." With a rush of emotion, Cavanaugh suddenly remembered the title of the movie. He managed to keep his face blank, concealing his reaction.

"You're starting to annoy me. *The Gauntlet. The Rookie. In the Line of Fire.*"

"No."

"*A Perfect World. Absolute Power. True Crime. Blood Work.*"

"No."

"Definitely annoying me. End of list. End of discussion. The doctor'll be here in thirty minutes. It'll be a pleasure watching him do his magic on you."

Grace turned angrily and left. Edgar and the armed men followed. The concrete door again descended. Again, Cavanaugh savored the last moments of light. Again, total darkness surrounded them.

5

This time, the blackness was so palpable that it seemed to squeeze them.

Jamie sounded as if she was having trouble getting enough air. Cavanaugh's legs were so unsteady, he wanted to lean against a wall and sink to the floor. He struggled to resist. "One thing's in our favor."

"I can't imagine what," Jamie said.

"They still didn't take our belts." His attempt at bravado failed as he felt his way into the room where they'd tried to hide. He brushed his shoes along the floor and found where he'd dropped his belt. "Give me the sleeves we tore from your blouse."

"What good will *that* do? Grace took your matches. We've got no way to set fire to the sleeves."

"Actually, there's another thing in our favor." Cavanaugh hoped he sounded confident. "I didn't give Grace all the matches." He removed one from his jacket and scraped it against the quarter-inch of abrasive paper.

Nothing happened.

Jesus, maybe I didn't tear off enough of the paper, he thought. Heart pounding, he tried it again, and this time the match flared, providing enough illumination for him to see the near panic on Jamie's face, which the faint light only partially alleviated.

She pulled the sleeves from her blazer pocket. He attached one to his belt buckle and put the match to it. As if it were the flickering of their lives, they watched the fabric start to burn.

"Thirsty," she said.

"Me, too. Something else to blame adrenaline for."

"My mouth's so dry. . . . If only I could get a drink of water. If only they hadn't removed the plumbing fixtures."

Suddenly, even in the dim light, Cavanaugh saw Jamie's eyes flash as if she realized something.

"What?" he asked.

"Where would the bathroom have been?" She moved halt-ingly along the corridor.

Cavanaugh's buckle scraped, its echo emphasizing the dark closeness of their confinement as he pulled his belt and the burn-ing cloth. "What are you thinking?"

She told him.

"Maybe," he said. "We might be able to do it."

"But it all depends on water," Jamie said.

Desperate, they checked the rooms along the right side of the corridor, finally coming to the next-to-last room, where pipes projected from the walls, the vestiges of sinks and urinals that had been removed.

"Damn it, they're capped," Jamie said. "I hoped for valves that could be opened. This could've *worked*."

"It *still* can work." In the dwindling light from the burning sleeve, Cavanaugh studied a pipe that was bigger than the others. Its screw-on cap was square-shaped.

"But we don't have a wrench to loosen it!"

"Take off your belt."

"What good will . . ." Even as Jamie questioned him, she took off her belt and gave it to him.

Thankful to have the distraction of doing something, Ca-vanaugh lit the end of Jamie's other sleeve, then used its light to examine her belt's double layers of leather, the grain on one strip going in the opposite direction from the other. "Let's see how strong this really is."

He put the tip of the belt through the buckle and made a noose. Then he slipped the noose over the square cap on the pipe and tightened the belt. When the leather firmly gripped it, he pulled on the belt, putting torque on the cap. The leather dug into his hands. His arms strained. His feet had trouble keeping a purchase on the floor.

The cap wouldn't budge.

Jamie grabbed the belt with him.

They pulled. The cap made a high-pitched sound, budging a little. They braced their feet, tugging, and suddenly leaned back as the cap twisted freely.

In a rush, Cavanaugh released the belt and used his hands to untwist the cap. He hoped water would start dripping, but even when the cap came fully away, the mouth of the pipe was dry.

"There's got to be a main water valve," Jamie said. "It's turned off where the water comes into the building."

Dragging the burning sleeve, Cavanaugh followed her to the shadows of the final room on the right.

"There!"

In what was evidently a gutted utility room, the flame revealed a large pipe that came up from the floor and connected to a network of smaller pipes leading into a wall. The main pipe had a valve. Jamie turned it, but even when it was opened as far as it would go, the pipe didn't vibrate with the flow of water. Nor was there any sound of splashing from the pipe they'd opened in the next room.

"The water's been turned off somewhere else." Cavanaugh pivoted frantically toward the wall behind him. The panel on an electrical breaker box had been removed. Except for a switch on the upper right, which presumably supplied power to the front entrance, all the other switches had been removed also. Various colored wires dangled.

"This place probably uses a well," Cavanaugh said. "Which needs a pump. But the water isn't flowing because the pump isn't getting electricity."

They shifted toward the wires and tried to figure out which went with which. A few moment's study made Cavanaugh suspect that the wires hung in vague pairs. Holding two wires by their rubber insulation, he joined their exposed tips. Nothing happened. He pressed another two together. Nothing.

Jamie desperately did the same. "How much time do we have left?"

"Less than fifteen minutes."

Shadows thickened as the flame weakened.

Cavanaugh pressed another pair together and saw a spark when they connected. But the flow of electricity had no obvious effect on anything around him. He separated the wires but bent them back in such a way that he'd have no trouble finding them again.

"Faster," Jamie said. Her raspy breathing echoed.

When Cavanaugh could barely see the wires he was trying to match, he took off his jacket and tore his shirt along its seams, the chill of the concrete making him shiver. After setting fire to a section of his shirt, he rushed back to the wires, only to hear something droning under the floor and water vibrating through the intake pipe.

"I did it," Jamie said. "I found the right pair."

From down the hall, they heard water splashing out of the opened pipe in the bathroom.

Trying to control his emotions, Cavanaugh noticed an outline on the floor where a furnace had been. He focused on hooks projecting from the wall next to the breaker box. The hooks must have had something to do with supporting the furnace ducts, he realized.

Pressured by time, he returned his attention to the wires in the breaker box. "They've got to be longer."

Jamie pulled two wires from a gap in the wall, stretching them as far as they would go. She and Cavanaugh bent them back and forth rapidly to create enough friction to break them.

Meanwhile, the pump kept droning, spewing water from the pipes in the next room.

As Cavanaugh used his teeth to pull the insulation off the tips of each wire, the flame got smaller. Jamie attached another section from Cavanaugh's shirt and pulled the fire into the corridor.

"I don't see any water on the floor," she said in alarm.

They hurried toward the water splashing into the washroom and found that only the central part of the washroom's floor was covered with it.

"My God, there's a drain," Jamie said. She yanked off her blazer and pushed it onto the drain, trying to create a plug.

Cavanaugh left the burning cloth in the corridor and hurried in next to her, adding his jacket as well, pushing it onto the drain.

Tense, they watched the water collect. Feeling light-headed, Cavanaugh realized he was holding his breath.

The plug worked. The water began to spread. As it reached the entrance to the corridor, Cavanaugh got to the burning cloth and pulled it back to the utility room.

He heard a frenzied splashing sound and realized that Jamie was kicking water along the corridor, trying to make it spread as far and fast as possible. At the breaker box, he grabbed the wires that he'd bent back earlier, the ones that had made a spark. Keeping them separate, he extended them to their maximum length from the box and connected them to the wires that he and Jamie had taken from the gap in the wall, twisting them together.

The tips reached the floor.

Jamie's bare arms flashed in the light from the burning cloth as she appeared at the entrance to the utility room. "The water's spreading."

"We have to get it to here." He ran into the corridor with her and had just enough light to see that the murky floor was covered with a film of water. He helped kick it as far as it would go, guiding it toward the utility room.

Before it got there, he hurried back and raised the wires off the floor, keeping them separate, suspending them over the hooks next to the breaker box.

The water entered the utility room.

"Jamie, get your belt."

Simultaneously, Cavanaugh separated the burning cloth from *his* belt and dipped its buckle in the approaching water, cooling the metal. He put the belt's tip through the buckle and cinched it, making a circle. Jamie did the same with hers. He looped his belt over a hook. So did Jamie.

As the water spread toward the burning cloth near them, they waited in silent tension for the light to be extinguished. Just before the fire made a hissing sound, in the last of the light, Cavanaugh separated the wires that controlled the water pump.

The underfloor droning stopped. So did the splashing. The flame went out.

Plunged into darkness again, they waited.

The chill of the water added to that of the concrete. Cavanaugh shivered harder now that his upper torso was completely exposed. In the blackness, he listened to Jamie's nervous breathing.

He tried to distract her. "When this is over, I'll have to teach you about neuro-linguistic programming."

"What's *that*?"

"A way of using language to control what you're thinking and feeling."

" 'When this is over'? You're doing it to me again, making me think we'll get out of this."

"We *will* get out of this." Cavanaugh hoped he sounded confident. "Visualize what's going to happen and what you need to do. Don't let yourself get surprised by something you haven't imagined."

"I'm visualizing sunlight."

"Which you'll see very soon."

"The future tense is wonderful."

"Isn't it, though."

A rumble from along the corridor indicated that the concrete door was being opened. The sound of numerous footsteps came down the steps, echoing along the corridor. Flashlights glared, high enough that they didn't reveal the film of water on the floor.

"I've brought your doctor," Grace said.

In the utility room, Cavanaugh and Jamie remained quiet.

"Where *are* you?" Grace demanded.

No response.

"*Where are you?* Damn it, get out here! I warned you what would happen if you tried to hide."

No reply.

"Flash-bangs you want, flash-bangs you get," Grace said.

Fabric rustled. Cavanaugh guessed that the team was putting on ear protection. He felt for Jamie's hands, pressed them over her ears, then quickly protected his own ears. That would help against flash-bangs detonated a distance away, but if any were thrown into the utility room, the nonlethal concussions would be so great that hands over ears wouldn't relieve the agony.

In his imagination, Cavanaugh heard the clatter of a flash-bang hitting the floor of one of the rooms.

A muffled blast compressed the air around him. Reverberating off the concrete, the roar was something he felt as much as heard.

Another distant blast shook him.

And another, coming closer.

Cavanaugh pressed his hands harder against his ears. When yet another flash-bang detonated, Jamie leaned against him, trembling. The blasts were in rooms close enough that Cavanaugh could see the fierce glare—the flash of the immobilizing device—reflect off the corridor's walls. He assumed that Grace and her team were shielding their eyes.

The next roar was even closer. The flashlights revealed the shadows of men with submachine guns moving along the corridor. As much as Cavanaugh could tell, Grace and her team were at the water. Their earplugs would prevent them from hearing the faint splash of their footsteps, but any second now, they would look down and notice what they were standing in.

In fact, they already had. When another flash-bang didn't go off within the interval Cavanaugh expected, he eased his hands away from his ears.

"What's all this water?" Grace demanded. "Where the hell did it come from?"

Cavanaugh tapped Jamie's shoulder, feeling her respond to the signal they'd agreed on. She shoved an arm through where her belt was looped over the hook above her. Hanging, she lifted her shoes out of the water.

"Check these last two rooms," Grace ordered.

In a rush, Cavanaugh shoved his right arm through where his belt was looped over a hook. He raised his knees, hoisting himself off the water.

The next instant, he lifted the wires from the hook where they'd been suspended and dropped them into the water.

If this doesn't work . . . he thought.

He'd expected to see sparks when the wires struck the water, but he saw nothing and immediately knew that he and Jamie were doomed. *I'm sorry, Jamie,* he thought.

An eerie noise made him frown.

Uuuuuuuuuuhhhhhhh.

It came from the corridor. Low, wavering, guttural. Several similar sounds joined it.

Uuuuuuuuuuuuuhhhhhhhhhhh.

Cavanaugh abruptly understood that he was hearing men groan as electricity shot through them. *Crack. Bang.* Then a clatter. Submachine guns dropped, echoing harshly. Flashlights fell, their glare rolling across the water-covered floor, their tight seals preventing them from taking in water and being extinguished.

Uuuuuuuuhhhhhhhhhhhhhhhhhhhhhhhhhhhhhhhh.

In the grotesque shadows created by the lights pointing along the floor, men collapsed, their silhouettes twitching in the water. The stuttering roar of a submachine gun tortured Cavanaugh's ears, but he couldn't cup his hands over them, had to keep his right arm through the belt, holding himself above the water. As the weapons kept firing, bullets ricocheted along the corridor. Men screamed. Cavanaugh couldn't tell if a gunman was aiming at an imagined threat or if the electricity jolting through the man had caused him to convulse, his finger squeezing the trigger. Empty cartridge casings hit the water, some jangling on top of one another. Then the submachine gun clicked on empty, and another loud clatter indicated that it, too, had fallen to the floor.

Uuuuuhhhhh.

The thrashing shadows in the corridor began to subside.

Uh.

The corridor became eerily quiet. Dangling by his right hand, Cavanaugh used his left to raise one of the wires from the water and twist it around the hook, interrupting the electrical circuit.

"Now," he told Jamie.

6

They dropped to the water. When they rushed into the corridor, the glare of the lights on the floor revealed ten bodies. Cavanaugh grabbed a submachine gun and prepared to shoot in case anyone was faking. He saw the contorted body of a man in a business suit, a doctor's valise next to him. He saw Edgar lying facedown in the water and reached into the man's baggy pants pockets, removing the Emerson knife and the Sig Sauer he'd expected to find there. He gave the handgun to Jamie and shoved the knife in his own pocket.

Grace. Damn it, where was Grace?

Hurried footsteps directed Cavanaugh's attention toward the end of the corridor. Silhouetted by sunlight, a figure darted up the steps toward the entrance.

Cavanaugh fired.

Bullets struck the steps, but Grace had already vanished through the opening, ducking to the left. Evidently, she had pressed the remote control on her belt. The concrete door began to descend.

Cavanaugh raced toward the steps, wondering how the hell

Grace had survived. She must have been standing away from the water. Perhaps she'd been wearing rubber-soled shoes.

The concrete door sank lower. Cavanaugh heard Jamie charging behind him, but all he concentrated on was reaching the steps and lunging up them.

The gap of light was only two feet high now. He dove sideways, scraping his bare shoulders and back when he rolled. His body and then his shoes cleared the door a moment before it thudded into place.

In eye-stabbing light, he caught a glimpse of four startled men as he rolled upward and pulled the trigger, muscle memory controlling the length of time he pressed his finger against it. Tap. Tap. Tap. Three and four rounds at a time burst from the MP-5.

One man lurched back, blood spurting from his unarmored chest before he could raise his weapon. Another man did manage to raise his weapon, the wallop of bullets into his face deflecting his aim toward the sky as he fired and then dropped.

The third and fourth men scurried toward the rubble of the collapsed barn.

At the same time, Cavanaugh raced toward what remained of the burned mansion.

He dove behind the remnants of a stone wall just before the two men opened fire, bullets ricocheting. He hurt his bare chest when he landed on stones, but he didn't care—all that mattered was surviving, killing whoever blocked his way, and getting Jamie out of there.

But to open the door, he needed the remote control on Grace's belt. Where *was* she? Cavanaugh hadn't noticed her when he'd shot and run for cover. She'd disappeared to the left of the entrance, which was now on Cavanaugh's right. Her Ford Explorer was in that direction. Was she using it to hide?

A dark green station wagon, presumably the doctor's, was in front of the Explorer. Grace might be inching along them, trying to outflank me, Cavanaugh thought. Peering through a gap in the stones, he didn't have a vantage point that allowed him to see under the vehicles, where the movement of Grace's shoes might tell him what she was doing.

Likewise, the ringing in his ears prevented him from hearing faint sounds that might have warned him of what Grace or the two men were up to. His heart pounded furiously as he realized that he'd landed in a trough that one of the gunmen had made when the assault team had hidden among the rubble. To his left were similar troughs where wreckage had been removed. He crawled through them, over rubble, following the length of the collapsed stone wall. Trying to make as little noise as possible, he searched for a gap in the stones, a place through which he could study the ruins of the barn and perhaps get a better view of the vehicles to his right.

He examined the MP-5 in his hands. Its magazine was capable of holding thirty rounds of 9-mm ammunition. He tried to judge how many rounds he had remaining. He'd fired three bursts. He'd been trained to release approximately four rounds per burst. But perhaps he'd fired more. Assuming he'd shot sixteen rounds, that left fourteen in the magazine—if it had been fully loaded—and one in the firing chamber, if the gunman had inserted a round there before attaching the magazine.

Be conservative, he thought. Assume you've got only *twelve* rounds.

He flicked the selection lever from automatic to the single-fire position. He extended the butt from a slot in the MP-5's frame, trying to make it aim like a rifle. When he raised himself to peer through the gap in the stones, he saw movement in the barn's rubble, to the right and left of the closed door. But before he could shoot, bullets struck the stones near his head, forcing him down. His forehead stung. Liquid trickled from it. When he touched his brow, his finger came away with blood from where a chunk flying off the stones had grazed him.

He picked up a charred piece of board and tossed it underhand toward where he'd first landed behind the wall. He hoped that the clatter would make the gunmen think that he'd returned to that position. Peering quickly through the gap he'd just used, he saw the man on the right raise his head from cover, aiming toward where he'd thrown the board.

Cavanaugh fired, hitting the man's shoulder, knocking him down. Immediately, he ducked below the gap as a volley from over there blasted the area through which he'd been peering. More chunks of stones flew, dust rising. He felt little elation that he'd hit one of the men. The wound hadn't been center of mass. It wouldn't have been incapacitating. The man was still a threat.

Jamie, he thought. She'll go out of her mind down there. Maybe some of the gunmen aren't dead. Maybe she'll have to fight.

Stop thinking.

He squirmed farther to the left along the collapsed wall, snaking over wreckage, scraping his chest more severely. He came to the edge of the ruins and realized that the men at the collapsed barn couldn't see him if he stayed low when he shifted along this far side. If he could reach the front and creep along to the opposite side, he'd have a chance of surprising his hunters. He would also have a chance of surprising Grace if she was behind the Explorer and the station wagon to the right of the collapsed barn.

When Cavanaugh reached the front of the wreckage, he found the Taurus where Jamie had parked it. Not that it did him any good. Without the ignition key, he couldn't start the car unobtrusively enough to be able to use it as a surprise weapon. In front, the rubble was high enough for him to run in a crouch. Blood oozed from the scrapes on his chest. His tongue felt thick. He peered around the next corner, seeing the station wagon and the SUV near the ruins of the barn. Their sides were angled toward him, concealing what was behind them, but from this vantage point, he could hug the ground and see under the vehicles.

Beneath the Explorer, Grace's sturdy walking shoes were visible near the front tires. He saw the cuffs of her khaki slacks. She knew enough to crouch behind the engine, the only spot where a high-powered bullet couldn't go all the way through. Then Cavanaugh saw movement just above the hood. Near the windshield, blond hair showed as Grace raised her head slightly to peer toward the collapsed wall at the back of the mansion. The angle of her gaze prevented her from noticing where Cavanaugh studied her from the front corner.

The MP-5 had a range of 220 yards. In contrast, the Explorer was about seventy-five yards away. But under the circumstances, the distance was considerable. Cavanaugh wondered if his aim would be accurate enough to hit so small a target—the top of her head showing above the hood—with a weapon whose barrel was short and whose sights he hadn't calibrated. After everything he'd been through, his hands felt unsteady. His nervous breathing would also be a liability, making it difficult for him to keep his arms still. If he missed the shot, he'd have exposed his position. All Grace and the two men would need to do would be to separate and make a wide circle toward the front, catching him in a pincer movement.

Changing his mind, he pressed his bare stomach to the ground. In this position, propping the MP-5 against the dirt, he had a better chance of keeping the weapon steady. With both eyes open, he aligned the front and rear sights, keeping them in focus while he aimed under the Explorer toward Grace's shoes and shins. Although her feet were apart for balance, the angle from which he viewed them made them seem together, giving him a better target than the top of Grace's head. He held his breath, braced his arms, and flexed the trigger.

The *crack* of the shot was so loud that he couldn't hear the bullet's impact, but he *did* hear a scream from behind the Explorer. Staring under the vehicle, he saw Grace fall to the ground, her pain-contorted face near one of the SUV's front tires. To readjust his aim, he had to peer farther around the corner. Grace saw his movement and pointed a handgun under the Explorer in his direction. He rolled back an instant before a bullet tore away a chunk of burned wood.

"The bastard's on this side!" Grace shouted. "At the front!"

Cavanaugh rose to a crouch and hurried along the front of the ruins, going back the way he'd come, toward the left side of the mansion. Nearly sick with the shock of the fight-or-flight hormones rushing through him, he relied on all his training, all his years of combat experience, all the nerve that he could muster, and charged past the corner. A shocked gunman froze. Having responded to Grace's shout and rushed from the barn, the man was halfway along the left side of the mansion when Cavanaugh shot him with two quick bursts, tearing the man's chest apart.

Cavanaugh kept charging, reached the fallen man, verified that he was dead, and grabbed the man's weapon. He had no idea how much ammunition remained in its magazine, but at least it gave him more than he already had. Carrying both, he reached the left rear corner of the mansion. The remaining man over there was wounded and wouldn't emerge from cover unless he had a good reason. Grace was wounded also, and could move only by hobbling or crawling. She would want to remain behind the Explorer until she knew what was going on. Neither of them had any way to tell the outcome of the shots they had heard. Logically, the man over here would have yelled to them if he'd been victorious, but if he'd missed and was stalking Cavanaugh, he'd have maintained battle silence, so the lack of a triumphant shout didn't necessarily mean that Grace and her partner would conclude the man over here was dead.

Cavanaugh decided to wait, to let them bleed a while longer, before he risked showing himself.

Then, despite the ringing in his ears, he heard a drone. Frowning, he told himself that the sound wasn't possible, that it indicated the concrete door was opening, but he couldn't imagine how that could be.

The drone continued. Jesus, had Grace used her remote control to open the door? Was she trying to lure Jamie out, to use her as a hostage?

Reasoning that the last place either Grace or the gunman

would look for him was at the very bottom of the corner, at ground level, he dropped to his chest and peered around a rock. Squinting toward the ruins of the barn, he saw that the concrete door was indeed opening.

He looked behind him, suddenly not trusting his position, wondering if Grace was raising the door in order to distract him. Was she hoping to hobble around the wreckage of the mansion and sneak up on him while he concentrated on the barn, on keeping Jamie from showing herself at the open door?

After another quick look behind him, Cavanaugh once more peered around the bottom rock at the corner of the collapsed wall. The door was fully open now. Amid the darkness beyond it, something moved.

"Jamie, don't come out!"

Cavanaugh ducked back as he shouted it. The next instant, gunfire shattered several stones at the mansion's corner. Fragments flew, dust spewing. Some of the shots had been bursts from a submachine gun, but others had been single shots from a pistol, telling Cavanaugh that Grace was still behind the Explorer.

"Do you hear me, Jamie! Don't come out!"

This time, Cavanaugh's voice didn't attract shots, presumably because Grace and the gunman were saving their ammunition.

"I hear you!" Jamie's voice was faint. "I'm staying where I am!"

"If you show yourself, they'll shoot you or grab you as a hostage! That's why Grace opened the door!"

"*Grace* didn't raise the door! *I* did!"

What? Cavanaugh thought.

"Those wires you were going to press together! The ones you thought might raise the door! You were right! They *do!*"

"Stay down!"

"How many are out there?"

"Grace and one of her men!" Cavanaugh shouted.

"Where *are* they?"

"Grace is to your left! Behind the Explorer! Where you saw her park it! The man's in the wreckage behind the door to the lab! For God's sake, don't come out!"

"Is the man to my right or left?"

"He *was* on your left, but he might have moved! I'm telling you, don't try to come out!"

"I'm not!" Jamie shouted. "But I've got an idea! When I tell you, get ready to shoot!"

"Whatever you're thinking, don't do it! It's too risky!"

"Give me twenty seconds!"

What the hell is she going to try? Cavanaugh wondered.

Wary, he looped the strap of his MP-5 over his left shoulder. Then he gripped the MP-5 that he'd taken from the man he'd shot. His rationale for using the dead man's weapon was that the man wouldn't have risked leaving cover and stalking along the side of the mansion unless he'd had an acceptable amount of ammunition, but there wasn't time to remove the magazine and make sure.

Cavanaugh backed from the corner. That was where his shouts had come from. It was where Grace and the gunman would expect him to show himself. Certain that his heart would burst from the rate at which it was pounding, he shifted back twenty feet from where he'd been. There the wreckage remained low enough that if he stood, he could shoot over it.

Yet again, he glanced warily behind him. If Grace did decide to try outflanking him, how long would it take her to crawl or hobble around the mansion?

Jamie shouted from the open door, "Get ready!"

Whatever she's planning, it had better work, Cavanaugh thought.

"Count to five!" Jamie shouted. "Now!"

Baffled, Cavanaugh did so.

One. Two.

He set the submachine gun's selection lever to semiautomatic fire.

Three. Four.

Two explosions startled him. They came from the direction of the barn. Christ, they're throwing grenades at the open door, Cavanaugh thought. Furious, he surged up and fired at the wreckage to the right and the left of the door. Two more blasts went off, the fierce bangs accompanied by eye-searing flashes. Not grenades! Cavanaugh realized. Jamie's throwing flash-bangs over the back of the door.

Two further detonations shook the rubble. Smoke rose. So did the wounded gunman, who clutched his ears and rushed to get away.

Cavanaugh steadied his aim and shot three times. The bullets were all aimed at center of mass, but while one hit the man's back, the other went wild and hit his neck. The third missed entirely. No matter. So much blood flew from the man's neck, Cavanaugh knew he'd bleed to death within seconds.

"He's down!" Cavanaugh shouted to Jamie.

Bang!

Bang!

Bright, ear-torturing explosions on the far side of the barn told Cavanaugh that Jamie was now throwing flash-bangs toward the Explorer.

Bang!

Cavanaugh raced toward the front of the mansion and tried to control his frenzied breathing as he peered around its corner. Then he raced along the front and reached the corner on the right side of the mansion. Again, he checked carefully before he risked showing himself.

Bang!

Even at a distance of seventy-five yards, the flashes of the detonations around the Explorer were punishing to Cavanaugh's eyes. Reasoning that Grace must surely be immobilized by them, Cavanaugh took the chance of racing into the open, staying wide of the ruins, trying to get a view of the other side of the Explorer.

The driver's door was open. He saw Grace lurching inside, her left leg bleeding. He fired at the door, but instead of punching through and hitting her, the bullet made the walloping sound of a projectile hitting armor. Grace yanked the door shut. Her short blond hair and high cheekbones were vivid behind the windshield as she rammed a key into the ignition and started the engine.

Cavanaugh fired at the windshield but only starred it, realizing that the glass was bullet-resistant. He fired again as Grace floored the accelerator and steered from behind the station wagon, rocketing the Explorer toward him.

He fired a third time, starring more glass. Cavanaugh knew that most bullet-resistant glass couldn't withstand five rounds within an eight-inch radius. After that, the glass would disintegrate, allowing bullets to penetrate it. So he held his ground and fired a fourth time, but now Grace was racing so close to him that her glacial blue eyes seemed intensely huge.

When Cavanaugh pulled the trigger a *fifth* time, he felt the firing pin click on empty. He cursed, hurled the weapon at the windshield, and dove to the side an instant before Grace would have struck him. As the Explorer roared past, throwing up dust, he rolled across the dirt, feeling the MP-5 strapped to his shoulder dig into his bare skin.

Instead of speeding along the lane toward the road from which Cavanaugh had entered the valley, Grace twisted the steering wheel sharply and curved back in Cavanaugh's direction.

Surging to his feet, he unstrapped the MP-5 from his shoulder, but Grace was too close for him to have time to shoot.

He darted to the left.

Grace steered in that direction.

He darted to the right.

Grace pursued him.

At the last moment, Cavanaugh feinted to the left, then dove to the right. Feeling the rush of air from the Explorer speeding past him, he struck the ground, winced, and came to his feet, expecting Grace to turn sharply and come at him again.

Instead, the Explorer sped toward the rear of the valley. As its roar diminished, Cavanaugh heard something else: an approaching rumble. Gaining in intensity, it made a rapid *whump, whump, whump* sound. A helicopter. Grace had used her cell phone to call for reinforcements, Cavanaugh thought. Then he realized, No, she'd stay if the chopper was one of hers. She's trying to get away from whoever's in it.

Cavanaugh ran to the Taurus, grabbing a rock along the way. On recent American cars, the steering-wheel locks were sturdy enough that he couldn't break them by pressing his shoes against the steering column and tugging on the wheel as he had when he'd rescued Prescott from the warehouse. Now he was forced to yank the unlocked door open, unclip the Emerson knife from his pocket, thumb the blade open, and shove it into the ignition slot, using the rock to hammer the butt of the knife's handle, ramming the tip of the blade solidly into the slot. He closed the knife's handle halfway and twisted violently, gaining torque from the ninety-degree position of the handle. The blade's metal was extraordinarily hard, designed for this kind of brutal use. After one more fierce twist, Cavanaugh felt the ignition lock break, freeing the wheel.

Moving faster, he reached under the dashboard and pulled down a hidden Radio Shack switch box that he'd installed when he and Jamie had modified the Taurus: a standard precaution in case they didn't have the ignition key. The switch box was connected to the starter wires. A press of a button and the engine started.

The passenger door banged open. Cavanaugh raised the Emerson knife to defend himself, only to lower it when Jamie dove inside.

"Go!" she yelled. "Go!"

7

Cavanaugh floored the accelerator, feeling the tires bite into dirt, racing after the Explorer.

As Jamie slammed the door, Cavanaugh saw the Explorer disappear among trees ahead.

"Have you still got the pistol I took from Edgar?" Cavanaugh asked.

"Wouldn't be without it." Jamie's breathing was rapid, loud.

"Roll down your window. Watch for places where Grace might ambush us."

As the Taurus rushed past trees and dense, shadowy undergrowth, Jamie said, "A lot of choices."

The lane crested a wooded ridge, leaving the valley. At the bottom, it twisted, then straightened, ending at a T-intersection with a gravel road. Dust swirling on the right showed where Grace had turned.

Cavanaugh veered onto the gravel and hurried after her. Light filtered through the haze, reflecting off it, making it harder for him to see. He drove as quickly as he could and still have time to stop if an obstacle blocked his way. A breeze thinned the dust, allowing him to go faster. Then the air was clear enough for him to see that he approached an intersection with a paved road.

Where the gravel road continued, there wasn't any dust cloud. Grace must have turned right or left onto the pavement, but an equal number of dusty tire tracks went each way and made it impossible to follow her trail. "Pick a direction," Cavanaugh said.

"Left," Jamie said.

Checking for oncoming traffic, Cavanaugh skidded left onto the pavement and pressed hard on the gas pedal, urging the Taurus up to a hundred. Trees and fields became a blur. Cresting a hill, he was forced to reduce speed so he wouldn't be caught by surprise if Grace tried to ambush him on the other side. At the bottom of the hill, he stopped at another intersection. Here, the road was paved in all four directions.

"Pick a direction."

"Left again," Jamie said.

"Any particular reason?"

"Not much."

"Then left we go."

At the next paved intersection, with the Explorer nowhere in view, Cavanaugh stopped at the side of the road. His hands were so tight on the steering wheel that it took him a few moments to unclench them.

Sweating, he stared straight ahead. Next to him, Jamie trembled, just as *he* trembled.

"You did good back there," he finally said.

Jamie's voice was hoarse. "Thanks."

"Kept cool." He felt sick. "Didn't panic."

"Wanted to."

"I know the feeling." Sweating more, Cavanaugh kept staring straight ahead. "A neat trick, using the flash-bangs."

"I was so furious. I just told myself I wasn't going to die down there."

"Anger's a good motivator." Cavanaugh's hand shook as he wiped his grit-covered mouth. "Especially when it comes to dealing with fear."

"I brought you a present," Jamie said.

"Oh?" Dazed, Cavanaugh glanced down. Next to the Sig Sauer she'd placed on the seat was an equipment belt that she must have removed from one of the dead men in the corridor. The belt had a holstered Beretta and an extra magazine filled with ammunition.

"Thoughtful."

"The way to my loved one's heart. Who has the other Sig? Grace?"

"Probably," Cavanaugh said. "And the car keys. And my cell phone. And my wallet, with the ID Karen made for me."

"Reach under the seat."

Puzzled, Cavanaugh did what he was told and held up Jamie's purse. "I'll be damned."

The purse's zipper remained closed. Jamie checked inside. "Doesn't look like they got to it yet. I still have my wallet and cell phone."

Behind them, the sound of the helicopter descended into the valley.

Jamie glanced in that direction. "Can't be reinforcements for Grace. Otherwise, she wouldn't have run."

Cavanaugh nodded. "I'm betting it's John and a team from the Bureau."

Jamie looked relieved. "Then let's hurry back and tell them what we know."

Cavanaugh didn't move.

"What's the matter? If we don't go back, they'll issue arrest warrants for us," Jamie said. "Hell, they probably want to arrest us as it is. We took Kline away from John, and now Kline's dead. So are all those men back there. And the doctor. We've got to explain what happened."

"Can't go back."

"What?"

"Can't trust the FBI. Somebody there worked for Kline. Somebody informed against John. If I tell what I know, I might be helping the wrong people get their hands on Prescott."

"But John'll find the informant."

"How long will *that* take, and what if he doesn't? I need the antidote. For that matter, even if John *does* find the informant, even if it *is* safe to tell the FBI what I know, that doesn't solve anything, either. Prescott won't be punished."

"I don't understand."

"The government would protect him. Sure, they'd be appalled by the illegal research. Prescott's controllers would be quietly and severely punished. But not Prescott. Since the weapon exists and the damage has been done, the Defense Department would want to know everything about it, just to have it as an option. In the name of national security, they'd hide him some place comfortable, where they'd have access to his information. Prescott would get a new identity, a new life, everything he wanted in the first place."

Jamie stared at him.

"What's the matter?" he asked.

"When we first started this, people were after you," Jamie said. "They wanted to kill you. I figured that if I helped you find whoever was hunting you, we could get free of it all. We could go back to Wyoming. We could have our lives back."

"Believe me, that's exactly what I want. With everything in me, I want to go back to the way things used to be."

"Then why can't we?"

"Karen. Duncan. Chad. Tracy. Roberto. They won't be Prescott's last victims. He's paranoid enough that he'll kill again and again if he thinks anybody's looking at him wrong, if he fears his safety's being threatened. He has to be stopped."

Both of them were silent now. The only sound was a pickup truck clattering through the intersection ahead.

"You're going to need plausible deniability," he finally said.

"What?"

"*We* didn't take Kline. *I* did. I forced you to go along with me. That's your story. Play the victim."

"You think anybody's going to believe that?" Jamie asked.

"*Make* them believe it. Get yourself out of this."

"You're telling me . . ."

"Go back."

"*Split up?*" Jamie asked.

"You almost got killed because of me. I can't let you risk your life anymore."

"I'm here because I want to be."

"But I can't go after Prescott and worry about you."

"I've handled myself very well."

"Yes," Cavanaugh said. "You have."

"I'm staying."

Cavanaugh peered down at his unsteady hands. Another pickup truck clattered through the intersection.

He nodded.

"So what does that nod mean? Where does that leave us?" Jamie asked.

"Somewhere near West Virginia."

"Not funny."

"I've run out of jokes." Cavanaugh studied her grimy arms and blouse, then pressed the trunk-release button. Their suitcases were back there. "We'd better put on some fresh clothes."

"*You're* going to need more than fresh clothes."

Jamie's intense gaze made him look down at himself. He was covered with soot from head to foot. His pants were in rags. His chest was a chaos of scratches. Blood and sweat mingled with the soot.

"We've still got some bottled water in the backseat. I'll wash my face, then put on a cap, a shirt, and pants to hide the rest of this until we reach a motel."

"You reek of cordite," Jamie said.

"Some people think it's sexy."

PART SIX

Threat Reprisal

1

The motel on the outskirts of Harrisburg, Pennsylvania, was two hours north, far enough that if Rutherford ordered a search for them, it wasn't likely to be successful, especially since Rutherford didn't know Jamie's name or the kind of car they drove.

Harrisburg, the state capital, had another advantage. It was large enough to have numerous video-rental stores. The Clint Eastwood movie, whose title Cavanaugh had remembered but kept secret when Grace had read the list of Eastwood thrillers, wasn't hard to find. But the Troy Donahue/Sandra Dee film was another matter. After Cavanaugh and Jamie checked into the motel, they needed to visit almost every one of Harrisburg's video stores before they got their hands on a tape of *A Summer Place*.

"Star-crossed lovers at a resort town in Maine." Jamie read from the back of the VHS box after they returned to the motel.

Cavanaugh put the tape into a player that they'd rented. "Prescott isn't exactly a romantic kind of guy, so there's got to be another reason he thinks this movie's important."

"Maybe Grace was right. Maybe he wanted to move to Maine," Jamie said.

The tape was so old and worn that it colors were faded and its image had speckles. Obviously intended for a wide screen, the panoramic scenery looked cramped when trimmed to fit a standard-size TV. It didn't help that the screen was only twenty inches.

"Music's not bad," Jamie said.

"That's about all that isn't."

While adults had affairs, Donahue and Dee were warned that their own love was forbidden. Richard Egan acted almost as woodenly as Donahue. Ponderous scenes were punctuated by waves pounding a gorgeous pine-rimmed beach.

"Interesting house."

In the movie, a low, sleek modernistic house occupied a rocky point in a bay. Made of stone, the structure resembled the prow of a ship as waves crashed against its base.

"Reminds me of houses by Frank Lloyd Wright," Jamie said.

Amid soaring music and scenery-chewing performances, the film mercifully ended.

Cavanaugh pressed the rewind button. "Maine."

"And now for our second feature . . ." Jamie picked up *Play Misty for Me* and read what was on the back of the box. " 'Female stalker pursues disc jockey. Clint Eastwood's directorial debut. Filmed in his hometown of Carmel.' " She studied the picture on the front of the box. "Jessica Walter and a knife. Good. Slasher movies are my favorite."

"Actually, it's fairly well made. I saw it so long ago, I barely remember a thing about it, but I do recall thinking Eastwood did a decent job. It's nice and tense."

"Can't have enough tension," Jamie said.

"California. Maine. Prescott certainly had trouble making up his mind."

"Well, pop in this beauty," Jamie said, "and let's see why Prescott likes it so much."

The movie began with a long overhead helicopter shot that moved along a rugged coastline with waves smashing against rocks and windblown pine trees hugging the bluffs.

Thirty seconds into it, Cavanaugh and Jamie both leaned forward from where they sat on the bed.

"Holy shit," Cavanaugh said. "*A Summer Place* was supposed to take place in Maine, but it was actually filmed in—"

"Carmel," Jamie said.

They watched raptly as Clint Eastwood drove his sports car along the craggy coast. He and his girlfriend later took long walks along a beach.

"That's the same beach that's in *A Summer Place*," Jamie said. "The curved shape of the bay's so distinctive, I can't imagine there's another like it."

"Look for the Frank Lloyd Wright house," Cavanaugh said.

It never showed up, but that didn't matter. By the time the movie was over, Cavanaugh and Jamie were convinced. *Play Misty for Me* and *A Summer Place* had used the same location.

"What else did you notice when you first met him? You mentioned books," Jamie said.

"About photography—one looked like some kind of sex book. And geology. And Robinson Jeffers."

2

The Harrisburg library had a dark curved glass exterior and a spacious reference area with numerous computer stations. Cavanaugh and Jamie roamed the stacks, bringing various volumes to a table in an out-of-the-way area.

"Listen to this," Jamie whispered. "The bay at Carmel-by-the-Sea, as the town's really called, is at the tip of a huge underwater gorge that rivals the Grand Canyon. Geologists are fascinated by the place."

"That explains one of the books," Cavanaugh said.

"Also, the town's famous for its writers, artists, and *photographers*." Despite the emphasized word, Jamie managed to keep her voice low. "Ansel Adams lived there. So did Edward Weston."

"I know who Adams is, but who's—"

"You said you thought the photography book Prescott had was pornographic."

"It had a kind of sexy name and a nude on the cover."

"Passion?"

"What?"

"Could the book have been called *Forms of Passion*? Take a look."

Jamie slid the book across. The photographer's name was Edward Weston. The cover had been removed, but when Cavanaugh flipped through the pages, he came to the most beautiful nude he'd ever seen.

"This was on the cover," he said.

A slender young woman sat with her head bowed, her forehead resting on an upraised knee. She was naked and yet no private part was exposed. Her sensuous pose reminded Cavanaugh of an earlier photograph of a pepper that looked like two people making love. Another page showed a magnificent seashell with the same erotic contours.

"Passion." Cavanaugh stared at the photos. "For everything."

Then Cavanaugh came to landscapes of what the book said was Point Lobos, near Carmel. Page after page showed the same beautifully rugged seacoast that had been in *A Summer Place* and *Play Misty for Me*.

"Is there any doubt Prescott was crazy about this area?" Jamie asked.

A librarian going by didn't seem to notice Cavanaugh's bruised face, but she did give Jamie a stare for talking.

Looking apologetic, Jamie peered down at the books. As soon as the librarian was gone, she whispered, "You said Prescott had an interest in golf. Pebble Beach is one of the most famous golf courses in the world—it's slightly north of Carmel. You said he had a gourmet's taste for food. According to this,

Carmel has more great restaurants per block than just about anywhere. To nail down the connection, all we need to do is figure out how Robinson Jeffers fits in."

"I've already done that." Cavanaugh slid his notes across to her. "Jeffers and his wife, Una, visited Carmel in 1914 and were so struck by the area that they stayed there the rest of their lives. Jeffers bought land, hauled chunks of granite from the beach, and spent years building a stone house and a forty-foot tower. He called the place Tor House after some rock formations in England. He and Una died there."

Cavanaugh showed her a book of Jeffers's poems, drawing attention to two lines.

> I built her a tower when I was young—
> Sometime she will die—

"Prescott and I discussed those lines about the tower when I first met him, but I had no idea what they referred to," Cavanaugh said.

"Now you do."

"Now I do."

3

They drove. Because of increased security at airports due to terrorist threats, Cavanaugh was leery about trying to get to Carmel by air. At the numerous checkpoints, he would have had to show a picture ID, but Edgar had taken the fake driver's license and credit cards that Karen had created for him. Moreover, Rutherford and the FBI presumably had an alert out for persons resembling Jamie and him. Everything considered—the ease of traveling with weapons was another factor—driving had a lot to recommend it.

Plus, it gave Cavanaugh a further chance to heal. To passing drivers, the Taurus seemed just another car on the road with an ordinary couple inside, although injuries to the man's face indicated that he had recently been in some sort of accident. Those injuries probably explained why the man was letting his beard grow.

Interstate 80 took them through Ohio, Indiana, Illinois, and Iowa.

In Nebraska, studying the flat open countryside, Cavanaugh said, "Reminds me of Oklahoma."

"Oh?"

"I spent a couple of years there as a kid."

Curious, Jamie glanced at him.

"My father had the bad luck to drill oil wells after the boom was over."

He hesitated.

"I had a dog. Nothing fancy. A mutt. About the size of a miniature collie."

Jamie studied him, waiting for him to continue.

"My dad and mom and I moved around a lot while my dad looked for work. Sometimes the only job he could get was the most dangerous. Once, when I was a kid, I saw him put out an oil-well fire. He wore a suit that made him look like an astronaut. He used a bulldozer and dynamite. Afterward, he got drunk. He did that a lot. He came home that night and argued with my mom. When I tried to keep him from hitting her, he hit *me*. Then my dog starting barking, so my dad showed everybody who was boss and kicked the dog to death."

The only sounds became the drone of the engine and the hum of the tires.

"My mom left him after that," Cavanaugh said. "It took a lot of courage for her to face up to his anger. She and I were even poorer than when we'd been with him. But somehow she made do, found a decent man, even managed to send me to pretty good schools. I think my mom and my stepfather expected I'd be a lawyer or something. But I had too much anger in me. I wanted to get even for all the beat-up moms and kicked-to-death dogs in the world, so I joined the Army and went through special-operations training. I had plenty of chances to put terrorists and other bullies out of business. But I realized I eventually had to plan ahead. There's not much a special-ops soldier can do with his skills in civilian life. Become a mercenary, work for the CIA, join law enforcement, or get into private security. When one of my former Delta Force instructors offered me a job as a protector, I jumped at it. I guess it's not hard to understand why. I've got a thing about victims. I'm still trying to help my mother. I'm still trying to protect my dog."

Jamie finally spoke. "That's the longest I've ever heard you talk about your past. In fact, it's one of the few times you've *ever* talked about your past."

"Prescott pretended to be a victim and turned out to be a bully. Because of him, now *I'm* afraid of bullies. I won't let him get away with it."

Driving through Wyoming, neither of them commented when they passed an exit that would have taken them north to the Teton Range, to Jackson Hole and their home.

4

After four days, Interstate 80 brought them to San Francisco. They followed the Pacific Coast Highway south to Carmel and spent the night in a motel. But Cavanaugh had trouble sleeping, too preoccupied with what needed to be done.

"Where do you want to look first?" Jamie asked the next morning over a ham and cheese omelette in the motel's diner.

Cavanaugh had only coffee. "How can you eat so much and stay so thin?"

"I've got a high metabolism. Besides, when I'm worried, I need to eat."

"We're safe for the moment."

"That's not what I mean." They were at a corner table, their backs to a wall. The nearest tables were empty. A television droned behind the counter. Even so, she lowered her voice. "You're not being hunted any longer. This isn't following orders in combat. This isn't self-defense. It isn't protecting a client. *You're* the hunter now. If you get what you want, I'm worried about how it'll change you."

"Prescott raised a similar issue."

Jamie looked puzzled.

"After I rescued him from the warehouse, we nearly got trapped at a shopping mall. The team chasing us left a car outside. I managed to sneak up on it and shout to its driver to run away. The driver was too startled to move. I had to shoot through the car's roof before he got his legs to work. Later, Prescott asked me why I hadn't just killed the man."

"And what did you answer?"

"That the man hadn't given me a reason, that I was a protector, not a . . ."

Jamie didn't need to say anything further to make her point.

"I wonder if Prescott's counting on that," Cavanaugh said bitterly. "He can't be sure I died in the fire at Karen's house. I wonder if the son of a bitch is betting that my personality's essentially defensive, that I won't come after him for betraying me and my friends."

Jamie stayed silent.

"He'll have changed his appearance," Cavanaugh said. "He'll probably wear glasses now. He's had enough time to grow a mustache or a beard. He might even have had some plastic surgery. His heaviness will be hard to disguise, though."

Troubled, Jamie started eating her omelette again.

Cavanaugh glanced at the television behind the counter. A commercial for a weight-losing product showed before and after photographs of a formerly bulky man who was now amazingly thin. He turned toward Jamie. "When I first met Prescott, he had shelves of the most carbohydrate-heavy, calorie-rich foods imaginable. Macaroni and cheese. Lasagna. Ravioli. Potato chips. Candy bars. Chocolates. Classic Coke."

"That would put the pounds on all right."

"Suppose he went on a crash diet."

Jamie looked up.

"It's been almost three weeks since I last saw him," Cavanaugh said. "If he starves himself, if he drinks tons of water to flush his system . . ."

"A man as determined as Prescott . . ." Jamie nodded. "It wouldn't be healthy, but I bet he could lose a pound or two a day."

"Jesus," Cavanaugh said, "at that rate, he'd soon be unrecognizable."

"But even with that beard you're trying to grow to disguise your appearance, you'll be *very* recognizable," Jamie said. "Prescott could blend with a crowd and see you coming."

"Not you, though," Cavanaugh said.

"What do you mean?"

"He doesn't know you're with me. He could look straight at you and not be aware you're hunting him."

"Hunting him is what *you're* doing," Jamie said.

5

Ocean Avenue was the only Carmel street that went directly from the highway down to the water. Steep and several blocks long, it was separated by a median of shrubs and sheltering trees. Quaint shops and relaxed-looking tourists flanked it.

While Jamie drove, Cavanaugh scanned the people on the sidewalk, wondering if he'd get lucky and see Prescott.

It didn't happen.

At the bottom of the hill, they came to waves pounding a picture-postcard mile-long crescent-shaped beach of amazingly white sand. Sections of bedrock protruded. Cypresses spread fernlike branches. Two surfers in wet suits rode the whitecaps. Dogs frolicked through the waves while their owners strolled behind them. Gulls soared.

But Cavanaugh's attention was focused on the people along the beach, none of whom reminded him of Prescott.

Jamie steered left and followed a scenic road along the water. Rustic homes were enclosed by trees, some of which were Monterey pines, their guidebook said, while others showed the distinctive twisted trunks of wind-contorted live oaks.

Jamie pointed toward an outcrop on the right. "There's the house from *A Summer Place*."

It still reminded Cavanaugh of the prow of a ship, but the constant crashing of waves had not been kind to it. "Looks deserted," he said, giving it only a moment's notice before continuing to concentrate on people walking along the beach or the side of the road.

Prescott wasn't any of them.

6

They stopped on a quiet, narrow, tree-lined street that hadn't existed when Robinson Jeffers and Una had settled in Carmel.

After walking up a brick driveway, they opened a wooden gate and entered a compound.

Cavanaugh had read so much about the place, about the gaunt-cheeked, lanky Irishman's epic struggle to build it, that he'd expected something on that epic scale. Instead, he was surprised by how intimate it felt. Colorful flowers and shrubs reminded him of an English rural garden. On the left was the forty-foot-high stone structure that Jeffers had called Hawk Tower, with its chimney, staircase, battlement, and turrets. To the right was the low stone house with its gently sloped shingled roof and stone chimney.

A brick walkway led to a door, where an elderly gentleman explained that he worked for the foundation that maintained the property. "Would you care for a tour?" he asked.

"Very much."

"Have you been in an accident?" the white-haired man asked sympathetically, noticing Cavanaugh's face.

"A fall. I'm taking some time off from work, recuperating."

"Carmel is a fine place to do that."

Inside, the rooms that Jeffers had painstakingly built were small and yet somehow spacious. From the weight of the structure, the air felt compressed. A slight chill came off the paneled walls. In the living room, Cavanaugh studied the stone fireplace on the right and the piano in the far corner. Windows provided a view of the ocean.

The guide took them through the guest room, kitchen, and bathroom on the main floor and the two attic bedrooms, one of which Jeffers had used for writing.

"Robin, as we liked to call him, built the house on a small scale," the elderly man explained, "to withstand ocean storms. He and Una had twin sons, and you can imagine how much they all loved one another for them to be able to live happily in such cramped and isolated circumstances. They deliberately didn't have electricity installed until 1949, after they'd lived here thirty years."

Cavanaugh felt a curious tightening in his throat.

"Notice the poetry that Robin etched into this beam," the guide said. "They're not *his* words, however. They're from one of his favorite works: Spenser's *Faerie Queene.*"

Sleepe after toyle, port after stormie seas,
Ease after warre, death after life does greatly please.

Now Cavanaugh felt hollow.

"If you'll follow me to Hawk Tower," the elderly man said.

Considering Jeffers's somber themes of human frailty as opposed to the abiding strength of nature, Cavanaugh was surprised by the humor that Jeffers had put into the tower. Intended as a retreat for Una and a playhouse for his sons, it had a dungeon and a "secret" interior staircase in which the children could hide. From a lookout on top and from several narrow windows, the sea was always in view.

"Una died in 1950, Robin in 1962, she from cancer, he from a variety of ailments," the guide said. "Robin had bad lungs and hardened arteries from smoking, but since he never recovered from Una's death, I've always assumed that what really killed him was a broken heart. She was sixty-six. He was seventy-five. Still too young to go, some would say, and yet what a full life. I don't tell this to the children whose teachers bring them here for tours, but I'll tell *you.* In their youth, at night, Robin and Una would send their children up to sleep in one of the attic bedrooms. Then they would"—the elderly man hesitated only slightly—"make love in the guest room downstairs before going up to the other attic bedroom. The bed that they made love in is the bed that they each later waited to die in. Their ashes are buried together in that corner of the garden."

On the street, car doors were opened and shut. Cavanaugh looked past the flowers and the wooden fence toward a family getting out of a van.

"Here are some samples of Robin's verses." The guide gave

Cavanaugh and Jamie a few photocopies. "If you have any questions . . ."

"Actually, I do." Cavanaugh glanced toward the approaching family, satisfying himself that the father wasn't Prescott. "But it's not about Robinson Jeffers."

The guide nodded and waited.

"I'm looking for someone. I'm almost certain he came here recently. He's a Robinson Jeffers fanatic."

The guide nodded again, as if it was only reasonable that everyone should be a Robinson Jeffers fanatic.

"His name's Daniel Prescott." Cavanaugh doubted very much that Prescott would use his real name, but there was no harm in trying.

"Doesn't ring any bells."

"He's in his early forties. Around six feet tall. Wears glasses. He has a mustache, but he was thinking about growing it into a beard." Cavanaugh wanted to cover several possibilities.

"Sorry I can't help you," the guide said. "That description could fit a lot of men. I see so many people, they become a blur."

"Sure. He was also pretty overweight. Under a doctor's orders to drop a lot of pounds. Have you seen anybody in his forties who looks as if he lost a good deal of weight recently?"

"How would I know?"

"Loose skin around the face and especially under the chin."

"That doesn't ring any bells, either. But if I *do* see somebody like that, do you want me to give him a message for you?"

"No," Cavanaugh said. "The truth is, I'm a private detective, and I'm trying to find him."

The guide's eyes widened.

"He's got three wives and twelve kids. When he gets tired of his domestic arrangements, he runs. Changes his name. Doesn't pay child support. A real sleazebag. We think he moved to the Carmel area and plans to start yet *another* family. Lord knows when he'll abandon his *next* wife. I've been hired to find him and get him to accept some responsibility for his actions. The joke is, he's a fanatic about Robinson Jeffers, but he never learned a thing about the devotion Jeffers wrote about in his poetry."

The guide looked troubled that anybody could fail to learn the truth about Jeffers's work.

"If this joker comes by, try to notice his license plate number or get a name from him or something," Cavanaugh said. "Don't make him suspicious, though."

"I'll be as subtle as possible."

"And for heaven's sake, don't tell him I'm around."

"Wouldn't dream of it."

"I'll get him," Cavanaugh said.

"I certainly hope so."

7

Pebble Beach was just to the north. They took a roundabout route through Carmel's sleepy streets, always on the lookout for anyone who even remotely resembled Prescott.

No one did.

At a toll gate, Jamie paid to get onto the area's famous 17-Mile Drive, a picturesque route that bordered the extensive golf course, allowing a view of its greens, ponds, sand traps, and the ocean in the background. Deer roamed freely. Cypresses and Monterey pines flanked multimillion-dollar properties. Cavanaugh ignored it all, watching for Prescott.

At Pebble Beach's lodge, Jamie drove through the entrance and parked in an out-of-the-way spot, from where Cavanaugh could watch guests arriving and departing. Then she went inside, only to come back ten minutes later, looking puzzled.

"What's the matter?" Cavanaugh asked.

"If Prescott had visions of playing golf at Pebble Beach all the time, he was in for a big surprise. Unless you've got influence, you need to make an appointment to play here a year in advance."

"A *year*?"

"And if you're with a group, it's *two* years. If you're right and he'd been planning this for a long time, he might have made an appointment quite a while ago, somehow finding a way to keep his controllers from knowing what he'd done."

"A big risk," Cavanaugh said. "And he wouldn't have known his new name back then. He wouldn't have had a credit card to go with it to reserve the appointment."

"So unless he found a way to get influence here, which is hard to do in a couple of weeks," Jamie said, "you can come back in about a year and see if you recognize him."

"I had in mind a little quicker timetable," Cavanaugh said.

"There are at least a dozen golf courses in the area. Some of them might not have as long a waiting list. What did you plan to do? Go from one course to the next? Find a spot near the links and use binoculars to watch the players in case someone who reminds you of Prescott shows up?"

"If that's what it takes."

"A lot of time. Too many chances to miss him. The FBI has enough personnel to watch all the golf courses simultaneously."

"No FBI," Cavanaugh said.

"They also have the resources to run background checks on guests who haven't played here before," Jamie said.

"No FBI," Cavanaugh repeated.

8

Sheltered by a cypress, Cavanaugh sat at the northeast rim of Carmel's beach, close to where the shore rose to the grass of the Pebble Beach links. He was far enough inland that he blended with the trees and shrubs behind him. The air was balmy, the afternoon sun reflecting so brightly off the water that he had to wear sunglasses.

"All roads lead to Rome?" Jamie asked.

"And everybody in the area ends up going to Carmel's famous beach. As much as the golf courses and 17-Mile Drive, this is the big attraction." Cavanaugh studied the long crescent of white sand. Hundreds of people were on it, reading in beach chairs, splashing in the surf, strolling, jogging, or tossing Frisbees to dogs. "I can't imagine that Prescott would live in the area and not come down here. At first, he'd be apprehensive about showing himself. He'd probably stay close to wherever he's living. But eventually he'd begin to loosen up. He might even come down here for exercise. Hell, for all I know, he got himself a dog."

"The FBI could check everybody who recently bought property around here," Jamie said.

Cavanaugh continued watching the people on the beach.

"It's just a thought," Jamie said.

"I keep seeing Roberto with his head beaten in . . . Duncan with his face full of bullet holes . . . Karen literally scared to death in her wheelchair."

"The government might not be as lenient with Prescott as you think."

Instead of responding, Cavanaugh glanced down at a map of the shops in town. "The big bookstore is in the Carmel Mall. We could keep a watch on the place. Since Prescott likes books, there's a good chance he'd eventually show up there."

"Unless he buys books off the Internet."

"There's nothing like a real bookstore, though."

"In that case, he might decide to make the short drive north to Monterey," Jamie said.

Cavanaugh gave her a look.

"Just trying to investigate alternatives," she said.

"Which brings us back to sitting here on the beach and watching for him."

"Fine with me. I'll get a beach chair and a book. I can use the rest," Jamie said.

"After dark, we'll stake out the best restaurants and see if he shows up."

"I was sort of hoping we could *eat* in those restaurants, not watch them."

"Given how little he's probably eating these days, he'll want the small portions he allows himself to be exquisite. Only the top two or three restaurants in town will be acceptable to him."

"Unless he eats at home."

Cavanaugh gave her another look.

A jogger sprinted to their end of the beach, turned, and ran back in the opposite direction.

"Weight loss," Jamie said.

"You thought of something?"

"I'm going to hate myself for being honest. It'll take more than dieting for Prescott to lose weight fast. He'll need exercise. Hours and hours of it."

9

Cavanaugh waited in an art gallery while Jamie found a break in traffic and crossed to the opposite side, where a walkway led to what their map indicated was a warren of shops in the center of a block. They'd learned that one of the exercise clubs they wanted to check was on the second floor of a building over there, affiliated with a nearby hotel. The time was now 4:30. Although there wasn't any guarantee that Prescott would use an exercise club, let alone that particular club at that particular moment, Cavanaugh couldn't risk entering, just in case Prescott might, in fact, be present. Because Prescott didn't know Jamie existed, the safer course was for her to go in alone and look around. If no one aroused her suspicion, she was to tell an instructor that she was writing a health-magazine article about overweight people who'd lost a remarkable amount of weight in a short time thanks to their determination. Then she'd ask if any of the club's members fit that description.

Pretending to appreciate the gallery's paintings, Cavanaugh often glanced through the front window toward the other side of the street. The late-afternoon sun put some of the doorways in shadow. As tourists went in and out of the mews over there, he checked his watch, then feigned interest in more of the paintings.

Thirty minutes later, he was still pretending to be interested in the paintings.

He stepped outside and crossed the street. Pots of brightly colored flowers flanked the mews's entrance. Beyond them, shifting among tourists, he passed a walkway on his right. According to what he and Jamie had learned, the exercise club would be along the next walkway on the right. He turned a corner, passed more flowers, and came to steps that led up to the second floor. A sign read THE FITNESS CLINIC.

Upstairs, he scanned the lobby and the long, bright exercise room beyond it. Jamie was nowhere in view. Staying to the side of the lobby, he carefully assessed the people working the various machines. None of them reminded him of Prescott. Amid the hum of treadmills and the clank of weights, he approached a muscular man in tight shorts and a T-shirt who stood behind a counter.

"I'm supposed to meet my wife here, but I'm late," Cavanaugh said. "Do you know if she's still around? Tall, thin, auburn hair. Good-looking."

The instructor frowned. "Is your name Cavanaugh?"

"Why? Is something wrong?"

"Man, I'm real sorry about what happened."

"Sorry?"

"After your wife fainted, her two friends told me she's got some kind of low blood pressure problem."

Cavanaugh's hands and feet felt numb.

"I wanted to call an ambulance," the instructor said, "but they said she'd had fainting spells a couple of times before. Nothing life-threatening. Something about her electrolytes being low."

Cavanaugh's stomach turned to ice.

"So I got them a bottle of Gatorade from the machine over there," the instructor said. "They gave her a couple of sips and helped her stand. She was woozy, but she could walk, sort of, if somebody put an arm around her."

"Friends?" Cavanaugh could barely speak.

"Two women who came in behind her. A good thing there were two of them. The one with the crutches couldn't have handled your wife all by herself."

"Crutches?" The lobby seemed to waver.

"Because of a cast on one leg. She said she knew you'd be worried, so she left a message for you." The instructor reached under the counter and set down an envelope.

Cavanaugh's fingers didn't want to work as he fumbled to open it. The neatly hand-printed note inside made him want to scream.

Tor House. Eight tomorrow morning.

10

Grace, Cavanaugh thought. He struggled to keep control. Despite the weakness in his legs and arms, he drove at random through the area, going around blocks, making U-turns and heading back in the direction from which he'd just come. He timed traffic lights so he got through them just before they turned red, using every technique he could think of to make sure he wasn't followed. Cursing, he realized that Grace had made the connection between *A Summer Place* and Carmel. With no other direction in which to go, she was searching the area as he and Jamie had been doing. Sometime during the day, their paths had crossed. Perhaps at Tor House. Grace didn't know about Prescott's fascination with Robinson Jeffers, but that didn't matter. Tor House was one of the local attractions and had to be investigated. Perhaps Grace had been approaching it when she'd seen Cavanaugh and Jamie get in their car and drive away. That would explain Grace's choice for a meeting place tomorrow. Or had it been on 17-Mile Drive or at Pebble Beach's lodge, or had Grace seen Cavanaugh through binoculars while she scanned Carmel's beach?

This much was certain: Grace had followed him, had taken her chance to grab Jamie, and was probably following Cavanaugh now. Inhaling sharply, he realized that while he'd been away from the Taurus, Grace might have planted a location transmitter in the car, making it easy for her to follow at a distance. Cavanaugh immediately stopped at a gas station and checked the obvious hiding places in and under the car. He used a pay phone to call information and get the numbers for Radio Shack stores in the area. One—to the north, in Monterey—was open until nine o'clock, he discovered. After asking directions about how to get there, he drove the seven miles along Highway 1 as fast as he could without breaking the speed limit. Using an

FM receiver that he purchased at the store, he walked around the Taurus several times, slowly changing stations, waiting to hear the *beep . . . beep . . . beep* of the location transmitter. It would be set to one of the unused FM bands in the area. On Grace's end, the loudness or softness of the signal would tell her if Cavanaugh was near or far. But if Grace had managed to get something more sophisticated, something that used ultrasonic transmissions, Cavanaugh couldn't hope to find a comparably sophisticated device at Radio Shack to detect it.

After an hour in which he failed to discover a transmitter, he got back in the Taurus and resumed his evasive driving, frequently checking his rearview mirror to see if any headlights took the same direction *he* did. At last, fatigue and frustration wore him down. He returned to the motel room that he and Jamie had rented. Grace might use chemicals to make Jamie tell her the name of the place, but as much as Cavanaugh was tempted to spend the night somewhere else, he couldn't let himself. If Jamie escaped, she would phone the room or return to it, looking for him. He kept the lights out, wedged the bureau against the door, and sat on the floor in the corner next to the front window, his knees drawn to his chest, his pistol in his hand, not daring to sleep, ready to shoot if anybody crashed through.

11

Fog made the morning like twilight. Arriving at 7:00 A.M., an hour early, he parked a block away from Tor House. He shut off the headlights, the windshield wipers, and the engine, then stepped out into the fog. The car's heater had done little to warm him. Now the chill dampness made him tremble. Wanting to button his sport coat against the cold but needing to keep it open so he could draw his pistol, he forced himself to move. The fog thickened, shadows deepening. The echo of his footsteps made him shift to the side of the road, where fallen pine needles provided a cushion.

As he approached the street on which Tor House was located, he wasn't sure what he hoped to accomplish by arriving early. The fog prevented him from identifying any ambush sites. What am I supposed to do when Grace shows up? he wondered. Shoot? Hope to wound her? Try to force her to tell me where Jamie is? Grace won't let it be that easy, and if this *is* an ambush, she could just as easily shoot *me*.

Pausing, trying to assess the shadows of trees, shrubs, and houses before him, Cavanaugh realized that he should have listened to Jamie and not gone after Prescott. Then she wouldn't be missing and he wouldn't be standing here in the fog, as afraid as he'd ever been in his life.

No longer afraid for himself.

Afraid for Jamie.

He had difficulty making his legs work. If, in the past weeks, anger had helped him to offset fear, the need to protect Jamie now proved to be an even greater force. During the night, he'd considered doing what Jamie had wanted and asking the FBI for help, but with no time to coordinate a plan, with the risk of a hastily assembled hostage-rescue team giving itself away, there was every chance that Grace would have sensed the danger and not shown up, destroying Cavanaugh's potentially single chance to save Jamie.

As he passed murky trees and spectral homes, shifting closer to where he estimated Tor House was, the fog chilled him to the core, a sensation he would not have thought possible, given the searing heat in his stomach. Because no one lived in Tor House, he was tempted to hide somewhere on the grounds, possibly in Hawk Tower, and hope that the fog would thin in an hour, allowing him to watch Grace's approach.

For all I know, Grace is already hiding on the grounds, he thought. Maybe *she's* in the tower.

Bup-bup.

The sound made Cavanaugh's heart lurch. He stopped halfway through the fog-shrouded intersection.

Bup-bup.

The sound came closer.

Bup-bup.

Seeing motion in the fog, Cavanaugh drew his pistol.

Bup-bup.

A silhouette appeared at the edge of the fog. The noises stopped.

In the distance, the surf pounded.

"You got here an hour early, huh?" a voice asked. Grace's. "Trying for an advantage. How come I'm not surprised?"

Cavanaugh couldn't speak.

"I'm stepping closer," Grace said. "I'd appreciate it if you don't shoot me again."

Bup-bup.

Grace's tall, trim silhouette emerged from the fog. Again, she had a pseudomilitary look: khaki pants, a matching tuck-in sweater, and a photographer's jacket, the kind with numerous loops and pockets, good for concealing a weapon.

But what Cavanaugh noticed most were the crutches she held under her armpits. The rubber pads on the bottom accounted for the noise he'd heard on the pavement. A cast covered her lower left leg.

"A good thing it's the left one. Otherwise, I'd have trouble driving. Care to autograph the cast? *X* marks the spot where you shot me?"

Again, Cavanaugh couldn't answer.

"Maybe later," Grace said. "After we finish our business." The fog drifted around her short blond hair, creating the illusion that the fog emanated from it. Her high-cheekboned face might

have been attractive if her expression hadn't been so disagreeable.

She frowned at the Beretta in Cavanaugh's hand.

He holstered it.

Somewhere in the fog, a door banged.

"Let's go down to the beach, before we wake the neighbors,"
Grace said.

She swung her feet forward, set them down, and moved the
crutches. One landed slightly later than the other. *Bup-bup.*

"Shooting me is something I can understand," she said, "but
forcing me to watch all those Troy Donahue movies is unforgiv-
able."

Bup-bup.

"I couldn't tell if you were lying that the movie also starred
Sandra Dee, so I had to suffer through Donahue's greatest hits.
Rome Adventure? With so many terrorist threats against Ameri-
cans in foreign countries, someone as suspicious as Prescott
wouldn't go to Europe. For sure, the tobacco farms in *Parrish*
aren't Prescott's thing, even with all the sex-starved women the
movie expects us to believe lurk among the tobacco plants. *Palm
Springs Weekend?* It has the golf course Prescott wants, but because he built his lab in a lush Virginia valley, I couldn't imagine
him living in a desert. That left *A Summer Place* and that amazing beach, which turned out not to be in Maine at all."

The fog parted enough to reveal that Cavanaugh and Grace
had reached the scenic drive above the surf. Cold sweat beaded
Cavanaugh's face.

"But to find that out," Grace said, "I had to watch every Clint
Eastwood thriller I could get my hands on. As much as I enjoy
watching Clint shoot bad guys, a steady diet of it can be a little
much after a couple of days. I'm not sure I'll ever be able to
make myself go to another movie of his. That's something else I
blame you for."

"Where did you spot us?"

"I concentrated on Prescott's interest in golf. I knew sooner or later you'd look for him where every golfer dreams of playing: Pebble Beach. Yesterday, you showed up there."

Cavanaugh didn't respond for a moment.

The surf kept pounding.

"Shit," he said.

"Then I waited for my chance."

"How did you manage to subdue Jennifer?"

"Spare me the disinformation. The ID in her purse says her real name is Jamie. I called in a favor from a friend. My *only* friend, I might add. Thanks to you, the Justice Department is investigating Prescott's lab and everybody associated with it. At the moment, my controllers would prefer that Prescott and I *both* didn't exist. My friend gave Jamie a touch of this." Grace showed Cavanaugh a small spray container. It was sealed in a plastic bag. "The guy behind the counter seemed relieved that we got Jamie out of there. Fainting isn't the best advertisement for an exercise club. My crutches added sympathy. Nobody suspects that a woman with crutches is anything but a victim."

It seemed to Cavanaugh that his heart pounded louder than the surf. "Is Jamie safe?"

"As much as can be expected. But whether she's *going* to be depends on you. Have you had enough time to think about how much you miss her? Are you ready to do what you're told?"

Temples throbbing, Cavanaugh waited for her to explain.

"I need Prescott," she said. "It's the only way to keep my controllers from considering me a liability. If I can get him, if I can complete my assignment and deliver proof that he's dead, they might trust me again, enough that they'll let me disappear on *my* terms, rather than theirs."

Cavanaugh felt sick.

"You're going to get him for me," Grace said.

"You followed us around the area. Isn't it obvious I don't know where he is? Damn it, I don't have any better idea of where he is than *you* do."

"But you've got two good legs, and because of you, I don't. If you want Jamie back, find him," Grace said. "Find him by this time tomorrow."

"*Tomorrow?*"

"That's how much time you've got. That's how much time *I've* got. If the situation with Prescott isn't settled by tomorrow, my controllers will be so panicked, so distrustful of me, I'll never be able to regain their confidence. Find him. Here's my cell-phone number." Grace handed Cavanaugh a piece of paper.

"You want me to bring him to you?"

"Bring him to me? Hell no. I want you to kill him, then show me the body."

Cavanaugh couldn't help thinking that setting out to kill Prescott was what had caused this mess.

"Here," Grace said. "Maybe this'll help."

She gave him the sealed plastic bag containing the spray container that had made Jamie faint.

"It lasts a couple of hours," she said. "The chemical works via skin contact. Be sure you wear a latex glove when you administer it." As Cavanaugh put the bag in his jacket pocket, she added, "If I don't hear from you by this time tomorrow morning, the next thing you'll get from me will be Jamie's corpse."

They stared at each other.

The surf roared.

Grace stepped into the gloom.

As the sound of her crutches receded, the fog became colder. Shaking, Cavanaugh wanted to follow her, in the hope that she'd lead him to where Jamie was being held. But trying to follow Grace on foot would be useless once she got in her car and drove away. Even if he managed to identify the make of the car and get a license number, he didn't have a way to trace it. Moreover, he had to assume that Grace might have rented a car and would never be associated with it again. The alternative was to hurry to the Taurus and drive back to this street on the unlikely chance that Grace would not yet have reached her car. But in the fog, he'd be forced to use his headlights. She was bound to see them.

If she felt he was a threat, she might decide to cut her losses, kill Jamie, and do her best to disappear.

No, he thought. I have to find Prescott.

And then? he wondered. Can I depend on Grace to keep her word and let Jamie go?

Bup-bup. The sound of the crutches became fainter. In the fog, the dim headlights of an indistinct car swept past him on the scenic drive. The car's engine became a murmur as the vehicle stopped. A door was opened and then slammed shut. The sound of the car receded into the distance.

He raced up the fog-choked street toward where he'd left the Taurus. Kill Prescott? he thought. No way. I've got to keep him alive. That's my only hope of getting Jamie back.

But first, God help me, I need to find him.

12

"This is Rutherford," the deep voice said.

Outside a gas station, Cavanaugh clutched a pay phone. "Do you still hate Chinese food?"

Rutherford hesitated only a moment. "That was quite a war zone you left us."

"Self-defense."

"You'd be a lot more convincing if you'd stuck around to explain what happened. Do you have any idea how many agents are looking for you, how many laws you've broken? I don't suppose you'd like to tell me where you've been."

"Be glad to, since your caller ID system will tell you anyhow. Carmel."

"Nice to have the leisure for a vacation." Rutherford's voice thickened with sarcasm. "Someday, I'll take one"—several voices spoke chaotically in the background—"when I'm not up to my ears helping investigate Prescott and his lab. The Justice Department thinks it's identified Prescott's military controllers, but with the lab destroyed and Prescott missing, there's no way to connect them with the lab or to prove it was manufacturing an unsanctioned biochemical weapon. The same goes for proving the weapon was tested illegally on civilians and military personnel."

"Maybe I can help get the proof," Cavanaugh said.

"Earlier in the week, you had the chance to stick around and do that, but you bugged out."

"I've had a change of heart." He gripped the phone with such force that his fingers ached.

"How do you explain this miraculous turnaround?"

"My wife's missing." Trying to keep his voice steady, Cavanaugh explained what had happened to Jamie and what he needed to do to get her back. "Will you work with me on finding Prescott and using him as bait?"

"Work with you? Hey, you wouldn't include *us* before, so why should we include *you* now?"

"Because that's what it'll take for me to tell you where to look."

"In Carmel? I already figured that much."

"I can give you a lot more focus than that, but listen to me, if this isn't done right, she'll be killed."

The voices in the background, presumably an office, were all Cavanaugh heard for several moments as Rutherford thought about it.

"So what's the right way?" Rutherford finally asked.

"Check all the golf courses in the Carmel/Monterey area. Get the name of every golfer who contacted them within the past three weeks to make an appointment to play."

"But that could be *thousands*."

"Then talk to all the Realtors in this area. Get the names of everybody who bought or leased property around here in the past three weeks. If Prescott leased, he might have done it through someone other than a Realtor, but we've got to start *somewhere*. Compare those names to the golf lists. Look for the common denominators."

Rutherford became briefly silent again. "A lot of people to talk to. This'll take time."

"*I don't have time.* This afternoon, John. I'll call you back this afternoon." He almost slammed the phone's handset down in helplessness. As he ran toward the car, he couldn't help thinking that phoning Rutherford was exactly what Jamie had wanted him to do in the first place.

13

"Bob Bannister." Cavanaugh extended his right hand in greeting.

"Vic McQueen." The instructor put a lot of manly sincerity and strength into his handshake.

Cavanaugh let Vic crush his fingers for a few seconds and then withdrew them. "I write for a new fitness magazine called *Our Bodies, Our Health.* It's based in Los Angeles, but thanks to E-mail and the Internet, I didn't have to move from around here."

Vic nodded in sympathy with anyone who might have been forced to leave the clean air of the Carmel Valley for the smog of LA.

"My editors are pretty wild about an idea I suggested," Cavanaugh said. "I want to write an article about how quickly people can get into shape if they're really determined."

Vic cocked his head in interest. They sat across from each other in an office, where shelves supported various fitness tro-

phies and the walls had autographed photographs of Vic with
other well-built, incredibly healthy-looking people in skimpy T-
shirts: presumably celebrities in their field.

"I'm talking about worst cases," Cavanaugh said, "people
who huff and puff crossing a room, who're overweight enough
that they look like coronaries ready to happen. An article that
shows it doesn't matter what kind of wreck a person is. With the
proper motivation, diet, and instruction, that person can get in
shape, can dramatically change his or her life in a relatively
short time. Not the six months or a year you normally read
about. For people in really bad shape, six months or a year is an
eternity. They don't want to imagine suffering for months and
months. They want quicker results. What's that joke? 'The trouble with instant gratification is, it takes too long.'"

Vic frowned. "How quick are you talking about?"

"A month. I want to know if it's possible to take a guy who's
really overweight, put him on a healthy, lean diet, teach him
how to work the machines, watch over him, encourage him, get
him coming in here several hours each day, start low and build
his stamina, vary his exercises—could he lose a lot of pounds in
a month and start to look like *you*?"

"Like *me*? In a *month*? Hell no, not like *me*."

"But could he look dramatically in better shape?"

"It'd be dangerous."

"So is being a physical wreck," Cavanaugh said. "What I
want to write is a before and after kind of article. I want to show
that a health club like this can work wonders in a very short
time. The hook for the piece is: A person doesn't have to be patient to be fit, as long as there's motivation."

Vic debated with himself. "Might work as long as you
pointed out the risks of going too fast."

"I'll have you read the article before I send it in. That way,
you can make sure I've got it right. Maybe we can get some photographs of you and a couple of the miracle cases you've worked
with."

"Photographs of me? Sure."

"And what about your club members? Do any of them fit the profile?"

"Well, we had a guy in here six months ago who—"

"I had in mind somebody who started recently, so I can get pictures of him as he goes through the process."

"Nobody at the moment." Vic looked crestfallen. "Does that mean you won't put me and the club in the article?"

14

"Most of our members are in terrific condition. From time to time, we get remedial cases, but not in the past three weeks."

*   *   *

"We do wonders for people if they give us the chance, but . . ."

*   *   *

"Not in the past three weeks."

*   *   *

"I might have just the guy," the Nordic-god fitness instructor said.

Cavanaugh concealed his reaction. This was the tenth exercise club he'd visited. Having exhausted Carmel, Pacific Grove, and Monterey, he was now ten miles to the east, in the community of Seaside on Monterey Bay, near the former Fort Ord military facility. Working to seem calm, Cavanaugh poised his pen over his notepad and said, "Really?"

"His name's Joshua Carter. Not Josh. Joshua. He's very particular about that. Came in here"—the instructor thought a moment—"a little under three weeks ago. I remember because he looked so out of condition I doubted he'd stick to the program. But he's been coming here every afternoon since then. I mean

every afternoon. Stays four hours. At the start, I thought he was
going to kill himself, drop dead on a treadmill or one of the
weight machines, but he paces himself, works at a steady rate,
doesn't overdo or strain. Afterward, he sits in the sauna and
sweats off more pounds."

Cavanaugh somehow managed to keep his hand steady as he
wrote on the notepad. All the while, his heart was on overdrive.
"Sounds like he'd be perfect for my article."

"Only trouble is, you're a little late for the photographs."

"Late?"

"He's so determined, so strict about his workout and his diet,
he looks different from when he came in. I almost didn't recognize him when I returned from a three-day camping trip. I
couldn't get over the rate at which he's improving himself. The
only 'before' pictures you'll get are ones he might have at his
house."

"Well, if he doesn't have any photos, I'm wasting my time.
What are his phone number and address so I can ask?" Cavanaugh phrased the question in positive terms that pro-
grammed the instructor to act upon it.

"Let's have a look." The instructor pressed keys on a computer keyboard. "Seventy-eight Vista Linda. That's one of those
new streets that got built after the city took over the Fort Ord
golf course." The instructor wrote down the phone number.
"You know, something bothers me here. I've got to be honest."

"Oh?" Tensing, Cavanaugh wondered if the instructor had
suddenly suspected he wasn't a magazine writer.

"The more I think about it, Joshua might *not* be right for
your article. He's getting in shape so rapidly, it's not natural. I
sometimes wonder if it's not just his determination and his diet
and the help we're giving him."

"What do you mean?" Cavanaugh anticipated the answer but
made the pretense of a frown.

"Well, I don't want to get you in trouble with your magazine
if you write this article and they print it and down the road

somebody finds out a lot of the difference Joshua made in his body is due to . . ."

"Steroids?"

"All that talk about weight lifters and professional football players using them, the steroid scandals in the Olympics, the rumors about some of those women tennis players using them . . . It gives the fitness industry a bad name. Some people look at me, at all these muscles, and say, 'Sure, if you take steroids, anybody can look like that.' I swear to God I've never taken steroids in my life. They cause heart attacks and strokes. They're the opposite of every health principle that got me into this business."

Steroids would be in keeping with Prescott's biochemical background, Cavanaugh thought. "Did you ask Joshua about it?"

"He was shocked at the question. He swore he had nothing to do with that junk."

"But?" Cavanaugh asked.

"Part of me can't imagine how else he could make such a quick difference in his body."

"When I meet him, if he agrees to help me, I'll make a point of asking him. What's he look like?"

"Around six feet tall. Early forties. Still a little puffy, but not much. He's getting more trim and solid all the time. One of the reasons I didn't recognize him is, while I was away camping, he got his scalp shaved. He's growing a goatee."

The reference made Cavanaugh think of Roberto's goatee, and that, in turn, made him think of Roberto's bashed-in skull.

"Sounds like he's photogenic. Great for the article," Cavanaugh said. With everything in him, he wanted to see *Prescott's* skull bashed in, but he had to repress his anger. Getting Jamie was all that mattered, but to get her, to force Grace to return her, he had to keep Prescott alive. "What time does he usually come in?"

"Around one."

Cavanaugh glanced at his watch. Checking so many health

clubs had consumed the morning. The time was now 12:35. Time. He didn't have much time. "Joshua must have a night job or something if he's got so many free afternoons."

"Night job? I don't think he's got *any* job," the instructor said.

"I don't understand."

"He dresses real well. Has a gold watch. A Piaget or something like that. I know it's expensive because when he joined the club, he made a big deal about whether the lockers were secure. Drives a brand-new Porsche. Not a Boxter. A Carrera. Lives on a fancy street. I get the feeling he's got so much money, he doesn't need to work."

A gold watch? Cavanaugh thought. A Porsche? Didn't Prescott remember what I told him about keeping a low profile?

"Money? I'm sorry to hear that," Cavanaugh said.

"What do you mean?"

"Rich people are usually concerned about their privacy and don't like to have articles written about them. They're afraid it sets them up to be robbed or something. Do me a favor. When Joshua comes in, don't tell him about this conversation. Let me approach him in my own way. Otherwise, I might not be able to persuade him, especially if he thinks you've been talking about him. For that matter, if he suspects you told me he might be using steroids, he could get upset enough to sue you for slander."

"Jesus Christ, *sue* me?"

"Maybe even sue the club. Rich people are like that. Don't worry. I'll leave you out of it. Just don't talk to him before *I* do."

"Man, I'm out of this, believe me."

"A Porsche, huh?"

"Yeah."

"If I ever won the lottery, I'd buy one. Red. That's my favorite color."

"Joshua's is white."

15

At 12:55, a white Porsche drove into the parking lot to the right of the redwood and glass exercise club. Breathing faster, Cavanaugh watched from a Starbucks across the street and scribbled the Porsche's license number on his stenographer's pad. Pretending to enjoy a latte, he sat a careful distance from the coffee shop's windows. He watched the Porsche stop in a parking space near the club. A tall, only somewhat overweight man got out. Even from a distance, it was obvious that the man's black loafers, gray slacks, and blue pullover were designer-expensive. The man's scalp was shaved. He had a goatee. Tan, he wore sunglasses.

Cavanaugh managed to seem calm as he set down his coffee, concentrating fiercely on the man who called himself Joshua Carter. If this was Prescott, the change was startling. A puffy, awkward, pasty-faced man was becoming something else, reshaping his body. Although he still had more volume to lose, what he had already lost had modified the contour of his cheeks and jawline. His goatee and shaved head altered his profile also, giving him a burly, masculine appearance. In an odd way, he was almost handsome. Beneath his comfortably loose clothing, Cavanaugh sensed, the man was developing strength and power.

Given the time frame, that doesn't seem possible, Cavanaugh thought. Something like steroids had to be part of the self-improvement mix, or else . . . An idea struck him: Had Prescott developed some kind of hormone stimulant?

The man paused a moment, scanning the parking lot and the area around him, before he pulled a dark gym bag from behind the front seat. Was he checking for trouble or simply enjoying his surroundings? His sunglasses prevented Cavanaugh from seeing if Carter glanced warily from side to side as he walked toward the front of the exercise club. But before he opened the door, there was no question that he looked behind him along the street.

16

Fifty. Fifty-two. Fifty-four. Hands tight on the steering wheel, Cavanaugh drove along Vista Linda, noting the house numbers. The street consisted of elaborately landscaped million-dollar homes with magnificent views of what was called the Bayonet/ Blackhorse Golf Course, a name left over from when Fort Ord had been active.

Sixty. Sixty-two. Sixty-four. Even with the street's proximity to the golf course, Cavanaugh didn't understand why Prescott had chosen to live somewhere in the Monterey peninsula area other than Carmel. Perhaps Prescott was staying away from a spot that he feared might be associated with him. But if he was being extra cautious, why the hell was he wearing a gold watch and driving around in a Porsche?

Seventy. Seventy-two. Cavanaugh planned to learn what he could about the layout of Prescott's house, find a way in, and use the knockout spray Grace had given him to subdue Prescott and arrange to trade him for Jamie. He would no doubt have to by-pass a burglar alarm, and it wouldn't be easy getting in without neighbors seeing him, but he didn't have a choice.

Seventy-four. Seventy-eight was just ahead, an imposing, im-pressive two-story pseudo-Hispanic structure with a tile roof and . . .

Cavanaugh slowed, staring at the FOR SALE sign on the front lawn.

17

"Sorry to bother you," Cavanaugh said to the elderly wispy-haired man who answered the door, "but I couldn't help noticing the sign across the street."

From too much sun, the man's leathery brown face had numerous creases. His stern gaze deepened them.

"My dad's a surgeon in Chicago, wants to retire out here," Cavanaugh said. "He's crazy about golf, so I've been driving around, seeing what places are for sale. The house across the street looks perfect, but this is a newly built area, and I'm wondering if there's something wrong with the place that it's being sold so soon."

"That god-awful sign," the man said.

"Excuse me?"

"I told her to put the house on the market privately. What do we want with a sign like that making the neighborhood look junky and Realtors and people who can't afford to live here coming around, gawking, cluttering up the street? No respect. The minute Sam died, his wife couldn't wait to sell the place."

"Sam?"

"Jamison. He and I moved here the same week two years ago. He dropped dead on the golf course yesterday morning, and that damned sign was sticking up in the yard by afternoon."

18

At the nearest gas station, Cavanaugh rushed to a pay phone. He shoved a phone card into a slot and pressed numbers.

"Rutherford," the deep voice said.

"How are you coming with those lists?" Speaking quickly, Cavanaugh was surprised by how breathless he felt.

"We've got a dozen agents working the phones from Washington. We sent agents from San Francisco and San Jose down to liaise with the agent we've got in the Carmel/Monterey area. But we still haven't been able to contact a lot of the Realtors, and as for the golf courses, I wish I had a dollar for everybody who wants to play there."

"You've got to hurry. Check this license number. It's a California plate and goes with a new Porsche Carrera. White." Cavanaugh dictated the number. "Who owns the car?"

"Are you at . . ." John recited the location and number of the pay phone Cavanaugh was using.

"Your caller ID system's damned good."

"*Damned* and *good* don't go together," the Southern Baptist said. "Stay where you are. I'll contact the California DMV and call you back in ten minutes."

"Make it as quick as you can. I'll be waiting."

The instant Cavanaugh hung up, he hurried to the Taurus and drove away, certain that in a very short while, a police car sent by Rutherford would arrive, looking for him. He went ten blocks and stopped at another gas station with an outside pay phone. Time, having sped by, now dragged agonizingly. Exactly when he was supposed to, he shoved his phone card into a slot and pressed numbers. His hand sweated on the phone's receiver. "What did you find?"

"You were supposed to stay where you were."

"*What did you find?*"

"The Porsche's leased."

"What?"

"Only for a month. To someone named Joshua Carter. The company he leased it from says he gave his address as seventy-eight Vista Linda in Seaside, California. The local police department's sending an unmarked car to check it out."

Cavanaugh could barely speak. "Tell them to forget it. Carter doesn't live there."

"Doesn't live there? If you knew that, why on earth did you ask me to—"

"I was hoping you'd find a different address."

"This is crazy. I need you at the command center we're setting up. This time, stay where you are."

"Right." Cavanaugh hung up and ran to the Taurus.

19

Jesus, Prescott's so paranoid, he created a false identity within a false identity, Cavanaugh thought as he watched the exercise club from the Starbucks across the street. The son of a bitch probably did what we told him at the bunker. Checked old newspaper obituaries. Found the name of a child who, if he'd lived, would now be the same age as he was. Knowing that most parents get Social Security numbers for their children at the time they're born, and that some states, California among them, include Social Security numbers on death certificates, he went to the hall of records in the city where the child died and asked for a copy of the death certificate. With the Social Security number from the death certificate, he could get a driver's license and a bank account in the child's name.

Pretending to read a magazine, Cavanaugh sat back from the windows. The instructor had said that Joshua Carter usually stayed four hours. The time was now five o'clock. Presumably, Prescott was using his second false identity to test his surroundings. If his remarkable transformation at the exercise club attracted the wrong attention, he could abandon the easily dispensable Joshua Carter persona and go to ground, relying on the absolutely dependable, irreplaceable identity that Karen had created for him. When he came out of the club, he would revert to that identity and drive to his actual residence.

I can't hope to catch him alone in the club, subdue him, and get him out of there without people trying to stop me, Cavanaugh thought. But if I can follow him . . .

Prescott stepped from the building. Pausing in the sunlight, he stood a little straighter than when he'd gone in. His shoulders looked a little more broad, his chest a little more solid. His cheeks, flushed from exertion, seemed subtly thinner. Whatever chemical he was taking, it worked remarkably in tandem with exercise and a strict diet. He wore sunglasses and the same black loafers, gray slacks, and blue pullover as when he'd gone in. He carried the same dark gym bag as, scalp glistening, he scanned the street and turned to his left toward the club's parking lot. At the Porsche, he again looked around, then got into the car.

The moment Prescott drove from the lot, Cavanaugh hurried outside to where he'd parked the Taurus behind Starbucks. Fifteen seconds later, he followed. That length of time was critical because he'd tested both directions on the street and had concluded that fifteen seconds was a little less than the time it took, at the speed limit, to reach the stop sign at either end. As Cavanaugh emerged from the Starbucks lot, he saw the Porsche reach the intersection on the right. A moment later, Prescott turned left.

Cavanaugh headed down to the intersection, turned left, and saw the Porsche among the traffic a block away. He knew he couldn't keep up with the sports car if Prescott used its maneuvering abilities to weave in and out of traffic and turn corners with an efficiency that made up for staying within the speed limit. But Cavanaugh hoped that once Prescott was away from the exercise club, he'd abandon the glitzy persona he'd created and do his best to blend, at least as much as he could with so expensive a car.

In keeping with that logic, Prescott drove conservatively

along Del Monte Avenue, taking that main thoroughfare west into the adjoining city of Monterey, where he made two conservative turns in the congestion of five o'clock traffic and entered a two-story parking garage next to an office complex.

The exit from the garage was next to its entrance, but Cavanaugh had to make sure there wasn't a second entrance/exit and that Prescott had not entered the garage only to leave it immediately on the opposite side in case anyone was following him. The problem was, while Cavanaugh drove around the block, checking for other exits, Prescott might leave through the exit that Cavanaugh knew about. But then Cavanaugh noticed that so many drivers were leaving the garage at the end of the workday that a line of cars had formed inside, waiting to reach the checkout booth, enough cars that Cavanaugh figured he had time to drive around the block before Prescott could leave via this exit.

As he hoped, there wasn't another exit. Returning to where Prescott had entered, Cavanaugh drove into the garage and wound his way all through the dusky, exhaust-smelling lower level, but he didn't see the Porsche. Continuing to the second level, he found it in an area marked COMPACT ONLY, along with other small cars, next to a door that led into the office complex.

The location forced Cavanaugh to reconsider his strategy. In an ideal situation, the Porsche would have been away from a door and parked among larger vehicles, preferably SUVs, behind which Cavanaugh could have concealed the Taurus and taken cover, rushing Prescott when he approached the sports car.

Now Cavanaugh was going to have to park a distance away. He considered hiding in a dark corner near the Porsche, charging Prescott before he could get in the car. An alternative was to use the Emerson knife to cut chunks from the seat covers that hid Cavanaugh's bloodstains. If he shoved the chunks into the Porsche's exhaust pipes, the engine wouldn't be able to function. When Prescott got out to see what was wrong, he'd be so distracted that Cavanaugh would have a better chance of rushing him.

But *would* Prescott be distracted? Cavanaugh wondered. Or would the car's sudden failure make Prescott wary? If Prescott had a pistol, if there was a gunfight . . . I can't risk killing him, Cavanaugh thought.

Then he realized that the best way to do this was to spray some of the knockout chemical on the Porsche's door handle. When Prescott touched it and collapsed, Cavanaugh could hurry over, pick him up as if Prescott were drunk, and get him into the Taurus.

Cavanaugh put on latex gloves that he'd purchased during the day. He took the spray container from the plastic bag, got out of the car, and put his hands behind his back to prevent departing office workers from noticing the gloves. Thirty seconds later, he was back behind the steering wheel. After returning the container to its bag, he cautiously removed the gloves, careful to touch them only on their interior.

The Taurus was in a shadowy area. Office workers entering the garage didn't notice him. The sounds of car doors being opened and shut echoed throughout the garage. Vehicles pulled out of spaces and descended to the lower level. Fewer and fewer cars remained. By six o'clock, the Porsche was the only car against the wall next to the door, and the Taurus was one of only a handful across from it.

Cavanaugh moved the Taurus to a farther section of the garage, blending with the remaining vehicles.

Six-thirty. A few more office workers departed.

Seven.

When eight o'clock came and the only vehicles in the area were the Porsche and the Taurus, Cavanaugh had a premonition.

20

"Somebody's got a brand-new Porsche up there," he told the kid with a ring in his nose who was in charge of the parking garage's exit booth.

"Yeah, cool, huh?"

"Is this place safe enough for a car that expensive?"

"Somebody like me's always on duty. Nobody's tried to steal it so far."

"So far?"

"The guy who owns it pays by the month. Weird, though."

"What do you mean?"

"The guy never takes the Porsche out except in the afternoon. Half-past twelve or so, he leaves. A little after five, he comes back."

And walks away via the office building, Cavanaugh realized. Then he watches from down the street to see if anybody followed him.

21

He spotted me. I've got to assume the bastard spotted me. Cavanaugh drove from the garage, which he now realized was the dividing line between Joshua Carter and whatever identity Karen had created for him. As Cavanaugh headed back to Del Monte Avenue, he was absolutely convinced that Prescott had another vehicle near the garage, something that didn't attract attention, that blended in, the way Cavanaugh had taught him.

Cavanaugh took care not to glance at his rearview mirror. He

couldn't risk doing even the slightest thing that might make
Prescott realize Cavanaugh hoped he was being followed. As
sparks seemed to shoot through his nervous system, he turned
left and headed deeper into the historic part of Monterey. Soon,
he discovered he was on Cannery Row, where boutiques and
cafés had replaced the fish factories from John Steinbeck's day,
but he paid no attention. To his right, the sun was low over the
ocean. He paid no attention to that, either.

Follow me, Cavanaugh kept hoping. Follow me.

He tried to imagine what was going through Prescott's mind.
One temptation would be to flee the Carmel/Monterey area as
quickly as possible. But to the best of Prescott's knowledge, only
his Joshua Carter persona had been uncovered. If Prescott concluded that Cavanaugh was acting on his own, which Cavanaugh seemed to be doing, would Prescott decide to protect
the false identity Karen had created for him by eliminating the
threat to it, by going after Cavanaugh? It all depended on how
much Prescott enjoyed his new life, on how much he hated to
abandon it. Would he run, or would he protect the identity for
which he'd already killed five people?

Cavanaugh drove as steadily as possible, making no attempt
at evasion tactics. Cannery Row dead-ended, forcing him to
make a left turn and then a right, but otherwise he continued in
a direct fashion, following the edge of the ocean on his right.
The sun sank, casting crimson over the whitecaps. Never once
did Cavanaugh look in his rearview mirror. Never once did he
give an indication that he hoped he was being followed. He
passed several scenic stopping places and finally chose one that
had few vehicles. Steering from the road, he parked in an isolated area, got out of the car, and crossed the pavement, heading
toward the numerous boulders along the ocean.

There, he did something that he realized with surprise could
be considered brave, although he didn't think that the act was
anything remotely to be proud of. As he despondently reminded
himself, if he'd listened to Jamie and gone home to Jackson Hole

with her, he wouldn't need to deny all his protective instincts now. He selected two low boulders that were close enough to each other for him to sit on one while he propped his shoes on the other. With his back to the parking lot, he placed his hands on his knees and waited.

The sunset gleamed across the water. He felt a cool breeze, spray from the waves hitting the boulders in front of him. But all he paid attention to was the sound of a vehicle pulling off the road and stopping in the parking area behind him.

The engine remained on. A car door was opened and then closed. Despite the pounding of the surf, Cavanaugh heard footsteps crossing the pavement. Shoes crunched on pebbles as someone approached the boulder he sat on.

The footsteps halted behind his back.

Fear insisted on a fight-or-flight response. As Cavanaugh maintained his defenseless position, his central nervous system was on overdrive, speeding, pulsing, demanding more oxygen and an even more urgent flow of blood.

"How did you find me?" Prescott's voice shook, just as it had the first time Cavanaugh had heard it.

"*A Summer Place* and *Play Misty for Me*." Cavanaugh's palms sweated.

For several moments, the only sound came from the surf and the idling engine. "Observant."

"And you're a quick learner. In another life, you could have been an operator." Appeal to his pride, Cavanaugh thought.

"Do you always speak highly of people you want to kill?"

"I don't want to kill you anymore." Cavanaugh stared straight ahead toward the sunset-tinted ocean.

"Is that supposed to persuade me not to kill *you*?"

"You didn't come here to do that. Otherwise, you'd have pulled the trigger by now."

"Then why *did* I come here?"

"To talk to me." Cavanaugh struggled to control his breathing.

Again, the only sounds were the surf and the idling engine.

"Keep your hands on your knees. Keep looking at the water," Prescott said.

As the breeze strengthened, Cavanaugh heard footsteps on pebbles. To his right, a solid-looking figure appeared in his peripheral vision, coming around to a boulder a careful distance from him. Prescott had a jacket over his hands, concealing what Cavanaugh assumed was a handgun. "You seem to be alone."

"You had plenty of time to watch the garage. You know I was the only person keeping tabs on the Porsche."

"What did you put on the car's handle?"

"You had *that* good a look at me?"

"I hid small video cameras at the top of various support beams in the garage. They're tiny. Battery-powered. Barely noticeable. The Internet's crammed with advertising for them: 'Check up on your baby-sitter. See your neighbor's teenaged daughter sunbathing.' I watched the images on monitors in a van on the garage's lower level."

"Then you're aware I don't have help."

"What did you put on the car's handle?"

"A knockout chemical that works on skin contact."

"Why are you doing this alone? Why didn't you tell the government where you'd found me?"

"Because the government would make a deal with you, in exchange for your testimony against the military officials who hired you to develop the hormone."

"You learned about that?"

"I assume the only reason you're not using it on me now is that the breeze coming ashore would carry it away before it did anything to me."

"Who told you about it?"

"A man who called himself Kline. He led the team that tried to kidnap you."

"I know who Kline is." Prescott's voice hardened.

"You don't need to worry about him anymore. He's dead."

"Because of you?"

"No. A woman I call Grace was responsible for that."

"Grace?"

"Five feet ten. Blue eyes. Short blond hair. Looks like she goes to the gym a lot. Could be attractive if she weren't so disagreeable."

"I know Grace also. Her real name's Alicia."

"Seems too feminine for her."

"If you're a female trained in an experimental special-ops program, I suspect you lose some of your femininity."

The sun was almost gone. As shadows turned to dusk, Cavanaugh understood why Prescott had left his car's engine idling. The headlights were on, glaring at them. Prescott wanted to avoid depleting the car's battery.

"She's the one who gave me the knockout chemical I put on your door handle."

"I'm pleased you said that."

"Oh?"

"I doubt your skills extend to laboratories and formulas. Someone must have given you the knockout chemical. It goes against your claim to be working alone."

"I'm not working with Grace, believe me."

"Convince me."

"I have . . ." With effort, Cavanaugh broke his rule of never revealing personal details. "A wife."

"You told me you didn't have a family."

"Imagine that," Cavanaugh said. "Normally, I keep her away from my business. But after what happened at the bunker, she was the only person I could call for help. She came to Carmel with me. Yesterday, Grace kidnapped her. If I don't deliver your corpse, my wife will"—the word caught in his throat—"die."

"A powerful incentive to kill me."

"To the contrary." Spray from the surf sprinkled Cavanaugh's face, but his cheeks were so fear-numbed, he barely felt it. "If I delivered your body, what motive would Grace have to release my wife? Grace has every reason to hate me. I crippled her and eliminated her team."

"Crippled her?"

"Shot her leg. Put her on crutches. Her controllers have practically disowned her."

"Yes, all of that would definitely have annoyed her," Prescott said.

"So I suspect that if I deliver your corpse, she'll use my wife to pay me back for all the trouble I've caused her."

"Likely."

"I want you to help me," Cavanaugh said.

The surf pounded. The engine idled. The headlights glared.

"Excuse me?" Prescott asked.

"I have a way to solve both our problems." Cavanaugh's chest cramped.

"Keep talking."

"My wife means more to me than anything else in the world."

"More than your five dead friends?"

"More than *anything*. If something happened to her, I don't know how I could . . . Help me get her back, and you'll never have anything to fear from me. I'll never harm you. I'll never allow anyone else to harm you, either."

"You'll be my protector again?" Prescott scoffed. "And just how am I supposed to help you?"

"By solving *your* problem at the same time I solve *mine*. I phone Grace and tell her I've got you but that I'm keeping you alive until she releases my wife. I arrange for an exchange. You walk to Grace while my wife walks to me. What Grace doesn't realize is, you're not my prisoner—you're my ally."

"Why won't she suspect?"

"Because she knows I came all this way to get you. Because she believes you and I are enemies."

"And aren't we?"

"Not if you help me."

"What's to keep her from shooting me the moment I step into view?"

"She'll want the personal satisfaction of being close to you before she harms you. But just in case, you'll be wearing a Kevlar vest I've got in my car. Grace has seen you only when you're heavy. Because you've lost so much weight, the bulk of the vest will make you look closer to the way you used to be. It won't attract attention. It won't make her suspicious. I'll pretend to rough you up before I shove you over to her. I'll subdue her suspicions even further by making it look as if your hands are tied. But the binding won't be secure, and the moment you're close enough . . . Do you know how to use that pistol you've got under your jacket?"

"Every morning, I practice at an indoor range in Monterey."

Cavanaugh didn't bother to point out that shooting a target was quite different from mustering the resolve to shoot a human being. As Prescott had repeatedly demonstrated, he had no hesitation about killing. "The moment you're close enough to Grace, you break the bindings on your hands, draw your pistol, and shoot her."

"Easy to say. But suppose she has help?"

"In fact, she does. One other operator. She claims she's been so disowned that she can't find more help than that."

"She could be lying."

"We pick a trade-off spot we can get to before *they* can. That way, we can watch for surprises. No matter what happens, you've got me to protect you."

"You're actually serious about this?" Prescott asked.

"Grace hates you so much, she'll never stop hunting you. You'll never feel safe. You'll always hear footsteps behind you. If you want to keep your new identity, you've got to stop her. Help me get my wife back, and I'll help you get rid of Grace."

"And afterward? If we're successful, if you get your wife back, you won't do anything to harm me?"

"That's right," Cavanaugh said.

"In spite of what I did to your team? That's one hell of a leap of faith. Give me a reason to believe you."

"I'll give you the best reason in the world," Cavanaugh said. "My word."

For the first time, Cavanaugh took his gaze away from the dark horizon. In the glare of the headlights, he turned and looked squarely at Prescott, at the almost unrecognizable mannish features, the pronounced cheeks and jaw, the goatee, the shaved head, and the developed shoulders.

"I give you my word. Help me get my wife back, and you'll never have anything to fear from me."

"Your *word*?" Prescott made it sound like a brand-new concept.

"And my love for my wife."

"How do I know this wife even exists? How can I be sure this isn't some trick?"

"I could have shot you in the parking lot outside the exercise club. I kept you alive because we need each other."

Prescott's dark eyes reacted.

"But if that's not good enough, will you believe Grace?" Cavanaugh asked. "The phone at the motel where I'm staying has a speaker function. When I call Grace and you hear her voice, when she talks about my wife, will you believe me *then*?"

22

His handgun aimed beneath the jacket in his hands, Prescott followed Cavanaugh into the motel room, then told him to lock the door and close the curtains. Cavanaugh moved carefully, keeping his hands away from his sides, even though he had left his pistol and his Emerson knife in the Taurus, as Prescott had instructed.

With the curtains closed, Prescott put his jacket on a chair, revealing that he'd followed Cavanaugh's example, even to the extent that his pistol was the same kind he'd seen Cavanaugh carrying: a Sig Sauer 225.

"This is how we met," Cavanaugh said, "with you pointing a handgun at me."

The pupils of Prescott's eyes were as huge and dark as they'd been at the warehouse.

"Remember the conversation we had about adrenaline?" Cavanaugh asked.

Prescott nodded, drawing his tongue along his lips. "At the bunker."

"I told you that someone who masters adrenaline, who prefers the 'fight' option, can't be called brave. But someone like you, who somehow functions in spite of being afraid, who wants to run away but instead faces his threats head-on, *is* brave."

"Don't flatter me. All I want is to be free of my enemies."

Cavanaugh pointed toward the bureau. "I'm going to open this drawer and show you something."

"Do it slowly."

Using only the fingertips of his left hand, Cavanaugh pulled out the drawer. "Bras. Panties. I gave up cross-dressing a long time ago."

"What?" Prescott's cheeks turned red.

"In the bathroom, you'll find a woman's toilet kit. Hair spray. Lipstick. Facial cream. A dinky razor. I don't want you to have any doubt that I'm traveling with a woman."

"All right, I'm convinced," Prescott said, uncomfortable. "The question is, Has she been kidnapped?"

From his shirt pocket, Cavanaugh removed the piece of paper Grace had given him. He went over to the bedside phone, touched 9 for an outside line, touched the button to activate the phone's speaker function, then called the cell phone Grace had said she'd be using.

Sitting on beds across from each other, he and Prescott, who still had the pistol aimed at Cavanaugh, listened to a buzz.

A second buzz.

Just as Cavanaugh started to worry that Grace would be out of touch, a stern female voice answered, "Hello."

Cavanaugh looked at Prescott, as if to ask, Do you recognize it?

Prescott's lips became pale.

The cell phone reception had some static. Good, Cavanaugh thought. She won't notice the slightly hollow sound a speaker phone causes.

"It's me," Cavanaugh said.

"I hope you're calling with good news."

"I've got Prescott."

"Dead?"

"I want to hear my wife's voice."

"I asked you if he's dead."

"And *I* said I want to hear my wife's voice."

Cavanaugh heard more static, then muffled, annoyed voices in the background.

At once, Grace's sharp voice returned, saying, "Tell him you're okay."

No response.

"For Christ's sake, *tell* him!"

"I'm"—Jamie's pain-tight voice made Cavanaugh's throat ache in sympathy—"all right."

"There," Grace intruded. "She's fine. Now what about Prescott?"

"What the hell have you done to her?"

"Nothing that I can't make more painful."

Cavanaugh had a sudden harrowing image of Jamie with blood all over her face.

"The sooner you get her back, the sooner she gets tender loving care," Grace said in a mocking tone. "Prescott. You said you had good news. Is he dead?"

"No."

"Then that isn't good news at all. Why haven't you killed him?"

Cavanaugh looked at Prescott, silently asking, Do you see? I was telling the truth.

Prescott's shaved head glinted with sweat.

"Because I want to make sure I'll get my wife back," Cavanaugh said.

"You don't trust me to keep my end of the bargain?"

"Not if I deliver a corpse to you. What motive would you have to give her to me? Now I've got something to trade. When I see my wife, you can see Prescott. When you let my wife go, I'll let *him* go. After that, you can do whatever you want with him."

"Damn it, this isn't what we agreed."

"But it's the way it's going to be."

The transmission became silent, except for an electronic hiss.

"I don't like being pressured," Grace said.

"You ought to feel delighted. You told me you had until tomorrow morning to regain the trust of your controllers. This way, you're ahead of schedule. Just give me my wife, and you can have Prescott. Both our problems are almost over."

Grace lapsed into silence and finally let out an exhausted, frustrated sigh. "Where do you want to make the exchange?"

For a third time, Cavanaugh looked at Prescott. On the way to the motel, they'd discussed the logistics of the trade-off if Cavanaugh could convince Prescott he was telling the truth and if Prescott chose to go forward. Prescott, who had spent a lot of time researching the Carmel area, had made the suggestion.

Cavanaugh now told her, "About fifteen miles south of Carmel on Highway One, there's a road that heads into the mountains. A sign says HISTORIC SITE."

"Just what I need: culture. What's the historic site?"

"A stone chapel a hermit built in 1906. He was a banker whose family died in the San Francisco earthquake. Most of the place collapsed a long time ago. Hardly anybody goes there."

"And how exactly do you know about this place?"

"I've been to Carmel before," Cavanaugh said, lying. "Once, when I drove up from Los Angeles, I saw the turnoff and decided to check it out."

"And I'm supposed to feel confident meeting you there?"

"Hey, you're the one who's got help. All I want is to get rid of this son of a bitch and get my wife back. What you do with Prescott up in the hills, with no one to bother you, is your business. I thought you'd appreciate the privacy."

Another frustrated, weary exhale. Grace's suspicions fought with her need to regain the confidence of her superiors. "When?"

"An hour."

"Can't get there by then. Make it two." Grace broke the connection.

23

Cavanaugh deactivated the phone's speaker function and put the handset onto its cradle. Numb around his mouth, he looked at Prescott and the weapon Prescott aimed at him. "So?"

Drawing an unsteady breath, Prescott seemed to perform an astonishing act of will, mustering his resources, somehow looking more compact and solid in the process. He studied the numbers on the bedside clock—10:20. "She's lying about needing two hours to get there."

"That's right."

"She'll get there as soon as possible," Prescott said. "To set up a trap and make sure *you're* not setting up one."

"Right again. I keep telling you: You missed your true profession."

"There isn't much time," Prescott said.

"So what are you going to do, keep running, always looking over your shoulder, or end your problems tonight?"

Prescott stared at him or, rather, stared *through* him, as if Cavanaugh weren't there, as if Prescott peered at a bleak horizon that consisted of unending days and nights of being hunted.

At last, he stood. The dark of his goatee contrasted starkly with the pallor of his cheeks. Sweat oozed from his scalp. He looked as if the next two words were the hardest he'd ever spoken. "Let's go."

PART SEVEN

Threat Elimination

"Take off your shirt. Put this on." Cavanaugh reached under the cover on the Taurus's backseat and pulled out the bullet-resistant vest he'd hidden beneath it. "Your shirt's loose enough that it won't be obvious you're wearing the vest. Then put on your jacket to conceal your pistol."

The Taurus was parked in a shadowy area at the back of the motel's parking lot. Using the car for concealment, Prescott did what he was told. The brief glimpse that Cavanaugh got of Prescott's reduced stomach and developed chest muscles surprised him.

When Prescott put on his jacket, Cavanaugh grabbed a roll of duct tape from the rear floor. "Now get in front. While I drive, wrap this around your ankles."

Prescott looked suspicious.

"Make it appear secure," Cavanaugh said. "Then use this." Cavanaugh opened the driver's door and picked up the Emerson knife from where Prescott had insisted he put it, along with his pistol, near the car's pedals. With his thumb against the tab on the back of the blade, Cavanaugh flicked the knife open and gave it to Prescott. "Cut the tape on the inside so the force of your legs can break it if you need to."

Prescott continued looking suspicious.

"This close to you, don't you think I could have taken that pistol from you and killed you?" Cavanaugh asked. "While you're with me, you're safe. Wrap the tape around your ankles; then use this knife. Be careful. The blade's sharp."

Cavanaugh got into the car, picked up the pistol on the floor, holstered it, and waited for Prescott to join him. Prescott had to muster more resolve before he got in.

Immediately, Cavanaugh drove two blocks to a brightly lit grocery store he'd noticed when he and Prescott had gone to the motel. OPEN 'TIL MIDNIGHT, its neon sign read. He ran in and came back five minutes later with a paper bag, which he emptied on the seat.

As Cavanaugh drove away, Prescott peered down at four objects: a bottle of colorless corn syrup, a bottle of red food dye, a plastic bowl, and a large plastic spoon. "What are *these* for?"

"Stir some of the corn syrup and food dye together in the bowl." Cavanaugh steered toward Highway 1.

"For God's sake, why?"

"Without a professional makeup kit, that's the best way to imitate scabs and drying blood."

They joined headlights moving south on Highway 1. Despite his impatience, Cavanaugh stayed exactly at the speed limit. The dashboard clock showed 10:40. Needing to be at the rendezvous site as quickly as possible, they'd already lost twenty minutes.

Prescott finished stirring the mixture and reached into his jacket, pulling out a gray metal tube.

Cavanaugh tensed. "Is that . . ."

"The hormone?" Prescott nodded. "You were right. I didn't use it on you at the beach because the breeze would have blown it away from you. If I twist the cap, there's a safety delay of twenty seconds. Then the pressurized contents are released."

"You plan to use it at the rendezvous?"

"Position us so the wind's at our backs."

"Suppose that's not possible. If I get a whiff of that stuff, I won't be able to help you. Or what if Grace and her partner react the way the Rangers did in Florida? Instead of running, they might fire in panic. Jamie might get shot."

Prescott didn't respond.

"No," Cavanaugh said.

"But—"

"Put it on the seat."

Prescott stared at him.

"Do it," Cavanaugh said. "Leave it there."

Prescott put the tube on the seat.

"Because of that stuff, for the first time I understand what fear is," Cavanaugh said. "Is there a neutralizer?" He hoped the question seemed casual.

"Of course. Otherwise, even with the safety delay, the weapon might affect whoever triggers it."

"The antidote doesn't take away fear?"

"Only the fear the hormone causes."

"I want you to give it to me," Cavanaugh said.

"I can't."

"Why?"

"I don't have the antidote with me," Prescott said. "But even if I *could* give it to you, it wouldn't make a difference right now."

"What are you talking about?"

"You'd still be afraid for your wife. Once you love somebody, you start fearing something might happen to that person. Fortunately, that's one fear I've managed to avoid. Now you'll get to find out."

"Find out?"

"What it takes to be brave."

2

They passed Carmel, moving farther south, the headlights of traffic dwindling until there were only occasional vehicles as they
reached the mostly unpopulated area around Point Lobos.

Soon, through the shadows of trees, Cavanaugh saw the lights
of isolated houses. "What's this place?"

"Carmel Highlands. It's a small community of houses on a
bluff above the ocean."

Cavanaugh saw a road on the right leading into it. Headlights
piercing the shadows, he steered onto the road and parked
among the trees.

He shut off the headlights. "I couldn't do this earlier because
there was too much traffic. A policeman might have seen your
face and stopped us."

Cavanaugh took the plastic spoon, dug it into the mixture in
the bowl, and smeared the red-tinted corn syrup across the left
side of Prescott's mouth, onto his left cheek and temple, and like
a gash across his shaved skull. Exposed to the air, the mixture
had started to coagulate, making Prescott look as if blood had
thickened on his face.

When Cavanaugh switched the headlights back on, the glow
from the dashboard allowed him to study the effect. "It looks like
you belong in the emergency ward."

"But I can smell the corn syrup."

"By the time you're close enough to Grace for her to smell it,
she'll be dead."

"I have to be sure."

"What do you mean?"

"Do it for real."

"I don't know what you're—"

"Cut me," Prescott said.

"*What?*"

"My scalp. Scalp wounds are terrific bleeders. The coppery smell will disguise the corn syrup."

"Jesus," Cavanaugh said.

"Do it." Prescott flinched as Cavanaugh raised the Emerson knife.

Cavanaugh could only imagine the control Prescott needed in order to remain still while he cut a two-inch slit across the top of Prescott's forehead.

Blood streamed.

Cavanaugh wiped the side of the knife over Prescott's face and the drying mixture.

Prescott now looked like the living dead.

"Hold out your hands," Cavanaugh said.

The hands shook as Cavanaugh twisted duct tape around Prescott's wrists. Inserting the Emerson knife between Prescott's wrists, Cavanaugh carefully cut the inside of the tape in front and back. He made the tape look intact from a distance but weakened it so that Prescott would have no trouble snapping it.

"Okay?" Cavanaugh asked.

Prescott tested the tape on his wrists, almost pulling it apart. His breathing trembled when he inhaled. "Okay."

Cavanaugh reversed direction and returned to Highway 1, continuing south. On the right, the moon cast a glow over the ocean. On the left, there were only occasional lights in the mountains. Except for the Taurus, the road was deserted.

"Around the next turn," Prescott said, his voice strained.

"You know this area fairly well."

"When I started losing weight, I avoided crowds until my appearance was sufficiently changed. I spent a lot of time hiking around here."

As Cavanaugh rounded the curve, the Taurus's headlights revealed the HISTORIC SITE marker. He steered to the left onto a bumpy dirt lane that went up through murky trees.

The lane reached a moonlit meadow, then zigzagged up through more trees. A few times, furrows in the lane caused the

Taurus's underside to bump across stones and dirt. Overhead, branches blocked the moonlit sky. Bushes scraped the car.

"Soon there'll be another meadow," Prescott said. "The chapel's built against a slope on the opposite side. Not that there's much to see." Prescott's breathing was more rapid and strident. "Except for a little tower with a cross on top, everything's collapsed."

"Count to three slowly as you inhale."

"What?"

"Hold your breath for three counts. Then exhale for three counts. Keep doing that. It'll help. Now slump down before they see you. Pretend you're unconscious."

Pale even in the darkness, Prescott obeyed.

Cavanaugh listened to the exaggerated, measured pattern of Prescott's breathing. Simultaneously, he felt each jounce of the car along the lane as if it were the lurching of his heart. He turned a sharp corner and emerged from the dark trees into another meadow, this one illuminated not only by moonlight but also by the sudden glare of headlights where Prescott had said the chapel would be.

"Damn it, she's here ahead of us," Cavanaugh said.

3

He didn't slow, didn't react as if he was alarmed, just kept following the lane, heading toward the headlights. "Ready?" he asked Prescott on the floor.

"It's a little late to say I want to back out."

"Five minutes from now, you'll be safe. I'll have my wife, and you'll be free."

"That trick with the future tense did wonders for me when

you were rescuing me from the warehouse," Prescott said. "Yes. Five minutes from now, you'll have your wife, and I'll be free."

Hearing Prescott say it, Cavanaugh felt some of the magic of the words. "Let's see if you're as good an actor as you are a bio-chemist."

"And let's see"—Prescott held his breath for three beats—"if you're as good a protector as you promised to be."

The Taurus came closer to the headlights. Grace stood on crutches next to a car whose popularity and hence ability to blend made it a favorite among security specialists: a Mercury Sable. Behind the vehicle, the cross on the chapel's tower caught the glare of Cavanaugh's headlights. Collapsed walls lay below it.

He stopped eighty feet from Grace's car, out of practical night-time pistol range. There was always the chance that she had someone with a rifle hiding among the trees, but the shooter would need a night-vision scope to aim properly, and Cavanaugh doubted that Grace could have gotten that sort of sophisticated equipment this late and so quickly. Besides, the glare of both sets of headlights would interfere with most night-vision equipment, which worked by magnifying the illumination from the moon and the stars and which would be overpowered by the head-lights—in effect, blinding a sniper.

Cavanaugh left the engine idling and the headlights on as he got out. The night was cold, exaggerating the already-cold feel-ing in his chest.

Squinting from the lights, trying to keep his voice steady, he called to Grace, "You got here early." It reminded him of the start of their conversation at fog-enshrouded Tor House that morning. His voice echoed off the surrounding wooded slopes.

"You don't sound surprised any more than I'm surprised that *you* tried to get here early," Grace said. "Open all your car doors."

Cavanaugh did. The only reason for Grace to tell him to open the doors was for someone among the trees at the side to be able to see if anyone was hiding in the car, he knew. It made him worry that he'd miscalculated, that a sniper was indeed concealed on a slope and that the night-vision scope the sniper had was one of the few sophisticated enough, based on heat detection, rather than light magnification, not to be compromised by the headlights.

Sick, he opened the left rear door, rounded the back of the car, opened the right rear door, and then came forward to open the passenger door. Again he stood next to the headlights, hoping that instead of revealing him, they gave him cover.

But he suspected that his worst fears were about to come true, that the plan wasn't going to work.

Please, God, help me get Jamie back, he thought.

At once, Grace said something that changed everything and gave him hope. "Where's Prescott?"

Why would she say that? Cavanaugh wondered. With all the doors open, Prescott would be visible to someone on the side. A sniper, seeing the car's interior, would use a walkie-talkie or similar two-way radio setup to tell Grace that Cavanaugh hadn't brought help.

"He's half-unconscious on the front seat." The bit about opening the doors was a bluff, Cavanaugh realized, his pulse speeding with hope. She wants me to think there's a sniper in the trees. But there isn't. Otherwise, Grace would have been told where Prescott was and that he was the only person in the car.

"Drag the bastard out."

"Not until I see my wife."

Looking impatient, Grace raised a hand from one of her crutches and motioned to someone hidden among the collapsed walls of the chapel.

Two figures rose and emerged into the headlights. One shoved the other. The one doing the shoving was a solidly built woman. Except that her short hair was dark in contrast with Grace's blond hair, she and Grace looked remarkably similar in height and physique, perhaps because they had both belonged to the same female special-ops training group that Prescott had referred to.

The person being shoved was Jamie. Her hands were tied in front of her. She lurched forward, stooped, as if in pain. When she looked up, Cavanaugh saw blood on her face. Anger made his muscles feel on fire. He wanted to scream.

"Drag Prescott out," Grace said.

Cavanaugh went to the passenger door and made sure that Prescott had followed orders—the metal tube remained on the seat. When he hauled Prescott from the car, Prescott landed so hard, he moaned.

With equal force, Cavanaugh tugged him around to the front of the car. In the headlights, in full view of Grace and the woman pushing Jamie, Cavanaugh kicked him several times in the side, feeling his shoe collide with the bullet-resistant vest under Prescott's shirt. While the vest protected his vital organs, Prescott would nonetheless have felt the shock of the impact. Again Prescott groaned. He rolled with the fourth kick and came to a stop, clutching himself.

"On your feet," Cavanaugh said. "There's no way I'm dragging you all the way over there."

Cavanaugh unclipped the Emerson knife from the inside of his pants' pocket, thumbed the blade open, and slashed the duct tape around Prescott's ankles, freeing it. The moment he folded the blade and reclipped the knife inside his pocket, he yanked Prescott upward. Prescott's head jerked from the force with which he was raised. Cavanaugh stood behind him, holding his shoulders, trying to steady him as Prescott listed to one side and then the other.

"You want him, you got him," Cavanaugh told Grace.

"What do you think you're doing?" Grace demanded. "That's not Prescott."

"The hell he isn't."

"Prescott doesn't look like—"

"He lost weight as part of his disguise. I'll prove it's him. Hey, jerkoff, say something to her."

Prescott kept swaying.

Cavanaugh drove a kidney punch into the back of Prescott's bullet-resistant vest. To save his knuckles, he held back the force of the impact at the last second, when Grace wouldn't be able to see the blow.

Prescott groaned and bent forward.

"I told you to say something to her!"

"Uh . . ." Seeming in pain, Prescott raised his head. "How's it . . ." He coughed, as if something inside him were broken. "How's it going, Al?"

"It *is* him." Grace said. "Jesus, look at his face. What did you do to him?"

"Gave him some payback for what he did to my friends. Now it's *your* turn to give him some payback. Let my wife go. I'll let Prescott go."

Balanced on her crutches, Grace looked at her companion and nodded.

The companion pushed Jamie past the car. Silhouetted by the headlights, Jamie stumbled forward.

"*Your* turn," Grace said.

Cavanaugh shoved Prescott ahead. As if he were a marionette being manipulated by the strings of a spastic puppeteer, Prescott listed this way and that, his legs barely able to support him.

"Jamie, just a little farther." Cavanaugh watched her stagger toward him. "You're going to be fine. All you have to do is reach me."

Meanwhile, Prescott wavered toward Jamie and her companion.

Abruptly, he collapsed to his knees.

Cavanaugh went to him and yanked him to his feet. "Keep moving, damn it. People are expecting you. I've got better things to do than hang around, waiting for you to put one foot in front of the other."

Again, he shoved Prescott, who seemed even more controlled by a spastic puppeteer.

As Prescott tottered nearer to Grace and her companion, they seemed appalled by his grotesque appearance.

Jamie stumbled closer, her green eyes now distinct in the headlights.

For a second time, Prescott halted, about to collapse.

"Move!" Cavanaugh went to him, once more shoving him. They were now midway between the cars.

As Prescott reeled forward, Jamie and Prescott passed each other. Lips bleeding, she looked horrified by the damage that had apparently been done to Prescott's features.

Almost over, almost free, Cavanaugh thought, praying. For all he knew, Grace would shoot at him now that he seemed preoccupied with Jamie. Everything depended on the next few seconds.

"Let's go home," he told Jamie. About to put an arm around her, he motioned for her to keep moving toward the car.

But activity beyond Prescott caught Cavanaugh's attention. Balancing on one crutch, Grace raised the other crutch to strike Prescott across the face as he lurched in her direction. Meanwhile, Grace's companion aimed a handgun at Prescott.

I gave my word, Cavanaugh thought.

As Grace swung the crutch, Prescott fell to avoid the blow. The crutch whistled over his head. He hit the ground, his hands out of sight beneath him.

Now he's snapping the duct tape, grabbing the pistol under his jacket, Cavanaugh thought.

Grace balanced herself to swing the crutch again.

The moment Prescott rolled to get away from it, his movement much quicker than his presumed dazed condition would have allowed, Cavanaugh drew his pistol.

Three shots from three different weapons were so near in time, they were almost indistinguishable as Grace's companion shot Prescott in the chest. Shuddering, Prescott shot Grace in the head while the crutch hurtled toward him, whacking the ground beside him. Cavanaugh heard screaming as his bullet hit Grace's companion in the chest, jolting her backward. A fourth shot, this one again from Prescott, stopped the screaming when the bullet hit the woman's face and dropped her.

The smell of cordite hung in the air, wisps of it floating in the headlights.

Ears ringings, nerves on fire, Cavanaugh spun toward Jamie, relieved to see that she'd dropped to the ground the moment the shooting started. *"Are you okay?"*

"Yes."

"You're sure?"

"Yes."

He spun toward Prescott. "Are *you* okay?"

Lying on the ground, needing to catch his breath from the bullet's impact against the Kevlar vest, Prescott didn't answer right away. Presumably, he also needed to adjust to the realization that the crisis was over, that he didn't have to continue to be terrified. "Yes."

"I kept my word," Cavanaugh said. "I helped you. I protected you. Because *you* helped *me,* you have nothing to fear from me. As much as I hate you, I'll never come after you again."

Prescott nodded, continuing to lie on the ground and catch his breath.

"If you didn't remember to wipe your fingerprints from the cartridges before you loaded them, find the empty shell casings and take them with you," Cavanaugh said.

"I remembered."

"Use Grace's car to get away from here. When you abandon it, remember to wipe your prints from everything you touch."

"I won't forget."

"Then our business is finished."

Facing Prescott, continuing to hold his pistol, Cavanaugh backed toward Jamie, helped her to stand, and continued backing toward the car.

"Are you okay?" he asked her again. "Do you need a doctor?"

Prescott remained on the ground, holding himself where the bullet had struck the vest and no doubt bruised him.

From behind Cavanaugh and Jamie, the Taurus's headlights cast their silhouettes. Its engine kept idling.

"I don't think anything's broken," Jamie managed to say.

Cavanaugh reached the Taurus and guided her toward the passenger door.

Suddenly, Jamie trembled harder against him. Cavanaugh's legs felt weak. A pungent smell coming from the car filled his nostrils and sent his heart racing. His mouth became drier. His breath rate soared.

The metal tube on the seat, he realized. Prescott twisted the cap before I dragged him out of the car!

As the hormone spewed from the Taurus, Cavanaugh grabbed the tube off the seat and hurled it toward Prescott. *Toward where Prescott had been.* While Cavanaugh had been distracted, Prescott had scrambled out of sight.

As Cavanaugh spun toward Jamie, urging her into the Taurus, a shot from the darkness slammed her against him.

"No!" The hormone crammed his lungs. Terror overwhelmed him. Unable to stop shaking, he held Jamie with one hand while he used the other to fire toward where he'd seen a muzzle flash. He thought he saw a blurred shadow ducking behind Grace's car. Exposed in the glare of its headlights, he shot at Grace's car, trembling, missing the right headlight, shooting twice more. The lamp exploded, the right side of the car going dark. But before he could shoot at the other headlight, Prescott returned fire, the bullet passing so close that it made a snapping sound over Cavanaugh's head.

Aware that the open passenger door was useless as a shield against a bullet, Cavanaugh lifted Jamie urgently into the passenger seat, appalled by the blood spreading along the right side of her chest.

A bullet punched a hole in the windshield.

Cavanaugh bent over her. The Taurus's engine now provided

effective cover as he ripped her blouse open. Her lung wheezed. The pungent smell of the hormone almost made him gag as he grabbed the roll of duct tape from where Prescott had dropped it. Frantic, trembling harder, he tore off a section and pressed it over Jamie's chest, sealing the entrance wound.

Her lung stopped wheezing.

He tore off a second piece and pressed it over the exit wound on her back. Flinching from several more bullets whacking through the windshield, he crawled over Jamie and slammed the passenger door. Then he hunched behind the steering wheel, yanked the Taurus into reverse, and tried to put strength into his legs, flooring the accelerator. As the tires spewed up grass and the car rocketed backward, he released the accelerator and twisted the steering wheel a quarter turn. The car pivoted 180 degrees and suddenly faced away from Prescott. Desperate, Cavanaugh yanked the gearshift into drive and sped away, the force of his acceleration slamming the rest of the doors.

Hunched to avoid making his silhouette a target, he was so busy concentrating on his driving that he could barely fumble for the buttons that lowered the windows. He managed to get some of them down a few inches, starting to clear the air, when a bullet blew a hole in the rear windshield. As glass flew, he hunched farther down, shaking as if he had a fever. Then Prescott lowered his aim, his bullets hitting the trunk. Obviously, he hoped that they would plow through both seats and strike Cavanaugh. Instead, they walloped against the sheet of steel that Cavanaugh had installed against the back of the trunk.

Speeding toward the dark trees at the end of the meadow, Cavanaugh felt no confidence from knowing that Prescott had almost emptied his pistol. Prescott still had Grace's weapon and her companion's.

Looking in the rearview mirror, Cavanaugh saw the remaining headlight on Grace's car bob into motion, the Sable pursuing.

The son of a bitch, Cavanaugh thought, fumbling to secure his seat belt. I promised to protect him!

The Taurus's headlights entered the trees, revealing a sudden downward turn that Cavanaugh's impaired reflexes barely anticipated.

I gave him my word I wouldn't hurt him!

Trees scraping the car, Cavanaugh struggled with the steering wheel and entered another sudden turn. Looking in his rearview mirror again, he saw the occasional flash of a headlight through gaps in the trees. The car sped closer.

With Jamie wounded and the hormone shocking his nervous system, Cavanaugh knew that Prescott had the advantage. As if to prove the point, a sharp downward turn almost toppled Jamie off the seat. Cavanaugh had to reduce speed again so he could take his right hand off the steering wheel, grab Jamie, and secure her safety belt.

The murky trees vanished, the Taurus's headlights illuminating another meadow. In the rearview mirror, the single headlight rushed closer. Cavanaugh heard the impacts of more bullets hitting the steel plate in the trunk.

Racing across the gloomy meadow, he fumbled for the toggle switch that he'd clipped to the bottom of the dashboard. Instantly, he squinted from a glare in his rearview mirror, the fog lamps that Jamie had installed in back blazing toward Prescott's car. One-hundred-watt quartz halogens, they were tilted up to blind a pursuing driver, a candlepower of 480,000 hitting Prescott's windshield.

Cavanaugh sped farther across the meadow. Checking his rearview mirror, he saw the fog lamps gleaming so brightly toward Prescott's car that its remaining headlight wasn't visible. He imagined Prescott raising a hand to shield his eyes, reducing speed, trying to regain his sight.

I lost him, Cavanaugh thought. I need to get Jamie to a hospital.

She moaned.

Dear God, please don't let her die.

Another section of trees loomed. At once, the Taurus shook

as Prescott's car slammed it from behind. The force was so great
and surprising that Cavanaugh was thrust forward, jerking
against his safety belt. Jamie's head jolted back and forth. No!

Instead of easing back because he couldn't see, Prescott had
used the blazing fog lamps as a target. His eyes almost useless,
able to see *only* the fog lamps at the back of the Taurus, Prescott
had rushed toward them. Colliding with the back of the Taurus,
he was now so close that the fog lamps reflected off the front of
Prescott's car. Their light filled the inside of the Taurus, gleaming
off the rearview mirror, blinding Cavanaugh.

Cavanaugh flicked up the rearview mirror, deflecting the
glare. Fighting to control the steering wheel, he felt Prescott's car
again strike the back of the Taurus. Prescott evidently hadn't
learned anything from the chase away from the warehouse. The
vehicle Cavanaugh had stolen had been struck repeatedly from
behind—with little effect. Bumpers got damaged. Passengers got
jolted. But the car remained capable of moving.

Again, Prescott's car struck the Taurus, its closeness neutral-
izing the glare of the fog lamps. Or maybe he's trying to smash
the lamps, Cavanaugh thought. Needing to reduce his speed to
enter the looming dark trees, Cavanaugh felt the constant pressure of Prescott's car against his and realized what Prescott was
doing. Jesus, he's trying to push me so I can't control my steering. He's trying to shove me into the woods.

Despite the risk, Cavanaugh had no choice except to increase
speed. While he did, the reduced glare behind him indicated that
Prescott had, in fact, managed to destroy one of the fog lamps.
Then Cavanaugh had time to think only about braking and steering through the trees. Skidding around the first turn, he banged
a fender. A bullet blasted through a window. Others struck the
steel in the trunk. Then one hit the remaining fog lamp, and the
glare behind the Taurus vanished. The only illumination back
there was Prescott's single headlight.

Abruptly, the trees opened, and Cavanaugh swerved to the
right, entering the darkness of the Pacific Coast Highway. His

tires squealed as he pressed a trembling foot on the accelerator and sped north toward Carmel.

Jamie moaned again.

"Stay alive," he begged.

Behind him, Prescott skidded onto the narrow highway. To Cavanaugh's left, moonlight glowed off the ocean. To his right, tree-covered hills receded into the distance. No lights of cars or houses beckoned. He raced around a curve and had trouble coming out of it. The steering felt mushy, as if something was broken. Then Cavanaugh feared that the problem was his tires. If Prescott had managed to shoot one of them, it wouldn't have exploded, but it *would* have started leaking air, going soft.

Already, Prescott was gaining distance on him. When Cavanaugh entered another curve, the faulty steering forced him to go slower. Rushing behind him, Prescott rammed the Taurus's back end, sending a shudder through Jamie, making her gasp. Cavanaugh didn't dare think about her. All he could allow himself to focus on was trying to drive.

The mushy steering got worse. Passing the lights of houses, Cavanaugh hoped he had a chance. On a straightaway, he floored the accelerator, attempting to gain distance, but the softening tire kept the Taurus from responding.

Headlights appeared. As a minivan sped past, Prescott again rammed Cavanaugh, backed off, sped closer as if to ram him again, then veered unexpectedly into the left lane, about to come abreast of the Taurus.

No! Cavanaugh thought.

As he'd learned from Cavanaugh, Prescott tapped his right front fender against Cavanaugh's left rear fender. Aided by Cavanaugh's faulty steering, the so-called precision immobilization technique caused the Taurus to spin to the left. While Prescott's car rushed safely onward, Cavanaugh found himself gaping in the direction from which he'd just come. Headlights flashing, the Taurus hit a guardrail next to a low bridge, broke through, listed down a slope, turned onto its side, its roof, its other side, and righted itself as it dropped. Cavanaugh felt a sickening shock as the car struck water.

4

"Jamie!"

She'd been jerked against her seat when the car flipped and fell. Now she groaned beside him.

Stunned, Cavanaugh tried to clear his mind. As the Taurus began to submerge, the pressure of the water against the side made it impossible to open the door until the car was filled with water and the pressure was equalized. During the chase, he'd managed to lower the windows a few inches. Now he touched the button that would take the driver's window down all the way. Hoping to shove Jamie through the gap and then go after her, he was dismayed when the window didn't budge.

Cold water soaked his shoes as he unclipped the Emerson knife from inside his pants pocket and slammed its butt against the safety glass on the driver's side, shattering the middle of the window into pellets. He pounded the knife's butt against the rest of the window, trying to clear its edges, when a dark shape made him stop. Moonlight, in combination with the Taurus's fading headlights, revealed that the dark shape was a boulder.

Turning toward the passenger window, Cavanaugh saw a boulder on that side also. The Taurus had landed upright in the water in a trough between shelves of rock. On each side, there was no way to get out through a broken window, no matter if in front or back.

Kick through the front windshield, Cavanaugh thought. Instantly he became aware that when the car had rolled, its roof had been pushed down, crushing the windshield and the window over the trunk, making the space too narrow for him to squeeze Jamie through.

The cold water now reached Cavanaugh's knees. As the Taurus continued sinking, the headlights and the lights on the dashboard flickered. Trembling from the cold, Cavanaugh pulled Jamie into an upright position, trying to give her air for as long as possible. His feet felt numb.

Doors. Blocked by boulders.

Windows. Can't get through them.

The roof.

Cavanaugh thumbed the Emerson knife open, slashed at the roof's liner, and yanked it down. The roof was buckled inward. Its support struts had widened, creating enough space for someone to squeeze through, provided a gap could be created in the roof itself.

Gripping the knife so its blade pointed in the same direction as his thumb, Cavanaugh stabbed upward into the metal. Among operators, the Emerson knife had a worldwide reputation as a hard-use tool. Its edge was razor-sharp and chisel-ground, its metal astonishingly strong, its point engineered for maximum durability. Its serrations were designed to cut along metal. It could pierce a car door, and Cavanaugh knew of instances in which it had struck through the fibers of a Kevlar vest.

Indeed, its sharpness, its strength, and the force with which he hit the roof caused the blade to go through. He sawed, withdrew the knife, pounded it into the roof again, sawed, and withdrew the knife, straining to cut a hole. As the cold water reached his groin, he punched the knife into the roof again and again, the impact of the blows jarring his arm and his shoulder, radiating through his body.

He jabbed the knife through the roof yet again, groaning from the pain it caused him. Alarmed, he saw that Jamie had listed sideways, drooping toward the rising water, which was now at his stomach. In a frenzy, he propped her upright again, then pounded the knife at the roof, straining to make a circle. His breath echoed loudly. He saw its vapor. The water reached his chest. Again, he stabbed the knife toward the roof, but the resistance of the water robbed him of strength, and this time the blade didn't pierce the metal.

The lights went out. In darkness, as the Taurus sank farther, Cavanaugh inwardly screamed. With the water restricting his movements and without lights to see where he was cutting, he would never be able to get through the roof. He felt Jamie slide sideways toward the water and again propped her up. He touched her face. Close to tears, he thought, *I'm sorry.* If I'd loved you enough, if I'd listened, we'd be home right now. I didn't protect you well enough. So sorry.

As the water rose past Cavanaugh's nipples, a fierce anger possessed him. God help me, there has to be a—

Immediately, he pushed the trunk-release button. He kicked off his shoes, squirmed over the seat, and splashed into the back. Trembling from the cold, he yanked away the seat cover and drove the Emerson knife into the back support, hacking at it. Tearing, ripping, he widened a hole and shoved at the steel plate that he'd put against the rear of the trunk. Then he took a deep breath and swam underwater into the submerged trunk. The weight of the water had kept the trunk from opening. He pushed at the hatch, but although he'd used the trunk-release button, nothing happened. The trunk must have been damaged when the car rolled, he realized. He pushed harder. Lungs aching, he twisted the knife against the latch, pried, levered, and felt something give. Shoving up with his back, he forced the lid up.

Breathe. Need to breathe. Desperate, he swam back through the hole in the rear seat, reached the car's interior, and raised his head, only to bump it in the darkness. Exhaling, his lungs made a roaring sound, amplified by the confined space. He frantically estimated that there were barely five inches between the rising water and the roof. Without pause, he inhaled as much air as he could, then plunged under the water, groping into the front seat, finding Jamie and raising her into the airspace.

Her moan filled him with a hope. You can't moan if you're not breathing. He pulled off her shoes. Then he turned her to face him, opened her battered mouth, and breathed into it, trying to fill her lungs, to give her enough air that she could survive what he was now forced to do, which was to pull her over the seat and swim with her through the hole in the backseat. He tugged her into the trunk, braced his feet against the floor, and shoved upward, clearing the open lid, fighting to rise with the current.

He had a powerless, disorienting sensation of being buffeted this way and that.

One thousand.

Two thousand.

Three thousand.

Four thousand.

He seemed to hear explosions as he and Jamie broke through the surface—the impact of waves hitting rocks. As Jamie gasped, he gripped her around the shoulders and kicked through the water, using his free arm to fight to swim.

A flashlight's glare almost blinded him. It was aimed from a bridge about twenty feet above him, from near the bluff over which the Taurus had fallen. *Prescott,* Cavanaugh thought. Now he's going to finish it. Struggling to swim toward boulders, Cavanaugh waited for the bullet he would never feel, which would blow his skull apart. He knew that Jamie would drown, if Prescott didn't shoot her first. Their corpses would be caught in the current and swept out to sea.

Close. We came so close.

"You son of a bitch!" Cavanaugh managed to yell.

"What? I can't hear you!" a man's voice yelled back, not Prescott's. "Try to reach those rocks!"

Cavanaugh didn't have the strength to answer.

The flashlight kept blinding him. "When I saw the broken guardrail, I stopped and spotted your car going under! I called the police! Swim closer! I've got a rope in my truck!"

5

An oxygen mask over her face, an IV blood line going into her left arm, Jamie lay on a gurney that two nurses wheeled urgently through electronically controlled swinging doors toward a brightly lit corridor flanked by operating rooms. Two surgeons quickly followed. A clock on the wall showed it was 12:35. Watching the doors swing shut, Cavanaugh tightened his grip on the blanket wrapped around him.

"I heard you stopped the bleeding with duct tape," a voice behind him said.

Cavanaugh turned toward Rutherford, whose husky dark features looked pale with fatigue. Like Cavanaugh, he still bore the marks of the beating he'd received.

"We're going to have to start teaching that at the Academy," Rutherford said.

Cavanaugh's hollowness made it difficult for him to speak. "Good to see you again, John."

"Hard to believe, given how much trouble you took to avoid me."

"When did you get in?"

"This evening. As soon as it was obvious you were jerking us around again, several of us decided to go sight-seeing in Carmel. In fact, I received your second phone call in a Bureau jet somewhere over Ohio."

"You told the police to report any incidents involving people who matched our description?"

"It seemed a reasonable tactic. Trouble has a way of happening to you." Rutherford nodded toward the doors to the surgical area. "Is she going to be all right?"

Cavanaugh glanced down at his hands. "They don't know."

"I'm very sorry. We could have tried to help you get her back."

" 'Tried.' A lot to coordinate. No time to do it. The govern-

ment would have cared more about keeping Prescott than helping me. I couldn't risk it."

"Did the doctors tell you when they'd have word about her
condition?"

"Four to five hours."

"A long time to wait," Rutherford said. "You can spend it in
jail, or you can spend it with us. Do you think you're ready now
to help us get Prescott?"

6

The squad room in the Monterey police station had two rows of
desks at which weary-looking Justice Department and local law-
enforcement officers sat, listening to Cavanaugh. Throughout,
phones rang. Each time one was answered, Cavanaugh tensely
expected it would be word from the hospital. It never was.

"We'll get a sketch artist working on the description you gave
us. The airports along the coast have already been alerted,"
Rutherford said.

"I don't think he'll leave the area," Cavanaugh said. The overhead lights were painfully bright. "To the best of Prescott's
knowledge, we're dead."

The possibility that Jamie might, in fact, be dying at that moment made Cavanaugh hesitate.

Somehow he continued. "I told Prescott that the government
didn't know I'd tracked him to Carmel. He believed me. After all,
if I was working with the government, I wouldn't have been
alone. In his arrogance, Prescott might decide he'd finally covered his tracks. He might do the unexpected and stick close to
home. Where's the list I asked you to make?" He referred to the
names of men who had bought or leased property in the

Carmel/Monterey area within the previous three weeks and who had also made appointments to play golf at the best courses.

Rutherford handed Cavanaugh several sheets of paper. "This is what we've got so far. It doesn't include men who've rented property without using a broker. We're checking past 'For Rent' ads in the local papers to try to contact property owners who made direct arrangements with new renters."

The overhead lights seemed harsher as Cavanaugh studied the list. "There're more than I expected."

"It's a popular area."

"How come there aren't many names in Carmel itself?"

"Expensive real estate. Not many people can afford it. The location's so prized, very few sell."

Cavanaugh kept scanning the names. Noting occupants in Pacific Grove, Monterey, Seaside, Carmel, the Carmel Valley, and the Carmel Highlands, the list went on and on.

"It's going to take a lot of personnel to check all this," Cavanaugh said. "And a lot of time and effort not to make Prescott suspicious if you get close to him."

"We were hoping we'd save some of that time and effort if any of those names caught your attention," an FBI agent said.

"When Karen was preparing Prescott's new identity," Cavanaugh said, "she wouldn't have picked an unusual name. Nothing that stood out. And nothing that anybody would associate with Prescott's former life."

The group looked more weary.

"Unless Karen got a bad feeling about Prescott," Cavanaugh said.

They glanced up.

"If Karen knew she was in danger," Cavanaugh said, "she might have chosen a name for Prescott that meant something to me and led me to him."

"You?" an agent asked.

"She had every reason to expect I'd go after anybody who hurt her."

"You and she were that close?"

"Her brother and I were in Delta Force together. He bled to death in my arms."

The group became silent, sobered.

Cavanaugh scanned the list. "His name was . . ." Cavanaugh tapped his index finger on a name. "Ben."

Rutherford came over and stared at the name he indicated. "Benjamin Kramer."

"The Carmel Highlands." Cavanaugh remembered steering onto a road that led to the Highlands and asking Prescott the significance of the name. "It's a small community of houses on a bluff above the ocean," Prescott had said matter-of-factly. The bastard lives there, Cavanaugh thought. Without knowing it, I was close to Prescott's home.

"How strongly do you believe there's a connection?" Rutherford sounded like he wanted desperately to believe. "It could be a coincidence."

"I didn't notice it at the start because Ben never used the formal version of his name. He was always just Ben. But Prescott has a thing about nicknames. He insisted that his first name was Daniel, not Dan, and when he created the Joshua Carter identity, he was firm to the staff at the exercise club that his name was Joshua, not Josh. On this list, some people used abbreviations to identify themselves—Sam, Steve. In contrast, Benjamin seems awfully formal."

"What about the last name 'Kramer'?" an FBI agent asked.

"Before Karen had the car accident that put her in a wheelchair, she was engaged to a guy named Kramer. As soon as the creep found out Karen was permanently crippled, he broke the engagement. Ben said the only good thing about Karen's accident was it kept Kramer from marrying her."

"Let's find out where this address is. Who's familiar with the Highlands?" Rutherford asked.

"My aunt lives down there." A female detective grabbed a phone.

Rutherford turned toward another detective. "Does your department have detailed maps of the communities around here?"

"A computer program and a satellite image from the Internet."

"Let's get a precise location of the house."

A phone rang. As a detective answered it, Cavanaugh hoped but also dreaded that this time the call would be from the hospital, but it turned out to be about another matter.

Someone put a CD-ROM disc into a computer. A layout of the few streets in the Carmel Highlands appeared on the screen. The detective typed the address. "There. At the end of this ridge. Directly over the ocean." A magnified satellite image showed the tops of homes, the patterns of vegetation, and the contours of streets. The detective zoomed in on the property they wanted to know about.

"A big lot," Cavanaugh said.

"In the Highlands, some of them are an acre and more."

"Sprawling house."

"Compared to the shadows these other houses give off, it looks like it has only one level."

The female detective finished talking to her aunt and set down the phone. "Everybody knows everybody down there. When this guy moved in, she took him a fruit basket to welcome him. He was overweight. Gruff. Said he was dieting. Couldn't eat fruit because of the fructose in it. That's the word he used—*fructose*. The few times she's seen him since then, he'd slimmed down. Shaved his head. Grew a goatee. She says she can see through the trees to his house. The lights are on."

"At one-thirty in the morning?" an FBI agent asked.

"Maybe he leaves them on when he's not home."

"Or he could be packing," Rutherford said, grabbing a phone, "in which case, there isn't much time to trap him."

7

On edge from tension and lack of sleep, Cavanaugh stood behind one of the three police cars that formed a barricade at the entrance to the dark street. Increasingly worried about Jamie, he'd phoned the hospital before he'd arrived, but there had still been no word about her condition. Next to him, Rutherford and his team used night-vision binoculars to scan the handful of shadowy, widely separated houses and then concentrated on the one at the end of the block. Perched on a bluff, its low-sprawling profile would have been silhouetted against the whitecaps of the ocean if not for the numerous outdoor lights that glared around the house's perimeter. Several of the windows were illuminated also.

"I still don't see any shadows moving behind the curtains," an agent said.

"Maybe Prescott's gone, and the lights are supposed to make us believe he's there," someone else said.

Despite dry clothes, Cavanaugh crossed his arms over his chest, trying to generate warmth, continuing to feel the chill of what had happened to Jamie—and another chill: fear. "You don't see movement because it's not in Prescott's nature to go near windows."

Movement attracted his attention, figures emerging from trees and shadows, policemen escorting a family up the street toward the protection of the barricade. Wakened with a phone call, warned not to turn on their lights, they had been directed to leave their house via a back door, where the heavily armed officers had been waiting.

"Is that the last of them?" Rutherford asked.

"Six houses. Six families. All clear," a detective told him.

Behind the barricade, next to an open van, equipment made scraping sounds as shadowy black-clad figures put on two-way-radio gear, equipment belts, armored vests, night-vision goggles, and helmets, ten members of a SWAT team looking like starship troopers while they checked their pistols and assault rifles.

Rutherford went over to them. Cavanaugh followed.

On the far side of the van, a middle-aged male civilian, one of Prescott's neighbors, showed the SWAT commander a diagram he'd made of the interior of Prescott's house. The muted red flashlight the commander used to study it couldn't be seen beyond the van.

"How recently were you in there?" the commander asked.

"Five weeks ago. Just before the previous owner moved. Jay and I were very close. It's a damned shame he got sick."

"Any construction work since then? Workmen showing up? That sort of thing?"

"None that I saw."

"Okay, so we've got a living room past the front door," the commander said. "Media room, spare bedroom, and bathroom to the right. To the left, the kitchen, two more bedrooms and bathrooms. A home office. Friggin' big house. These are French doors leading off the living room?"

"Yes. There's a terrace in back. A waist-high wall looks over the cliff to the water."

"What's this area in back of the garage?"

"Laundry room."

"And *this* next to it?"

"A darkroom. Jay and I like—" The man became more somber and corrected himself. "*Liked* to take photographs, until Jay got sick."

The commander showed the diagram to his team and explained the procedures they would use to enter. When there weren't any questions, he nodded to Rutherford. "Ready when *you* are."

"I need to emphasize we want him alive," Rutherford said.

So the government intends to make a deal with him, Cavanaugh thought.

"Is he armed?"

"To the best of our knowledge, he has an AR-15 converted to full automatic. He also has probably more than one 9-millimeter pistol."

"If he fires at us . . ."

"You have tear gas. You have flash-bangs. If you absolutely need to defend yourselves, do your best to wound him."

"He also has a Kevlar vest," Cavanaugh said.

The SWAT team turned toward Cavanaugh and studied him as best they could in the shadows.

"You're the bodyguard?" the commander asked.

Cavanaugh ignored the reference. "I've had several run-ins with him. He's extremely dangerous."

The commander looked toward Rutherford. "You said the target was a biochemist."

"That's correct."

"A wanna-be who thinks he's a runner-and-gunner."

"And who's killed five people that we know of," Cavanaugh said. "He's intelligent. He has an aptitude for this. Don't underestimate him."

"We'll toss him so many flash-bangs, he won't hear for a week."

"Were you told about the weapon he developed?" Cavanaugh asked.

"Some kind of fear thing?"

"An aerosol-delivered hormone."

"Hormone?" The commander gave Cavanaugh a "Get real" look. "Most of my team's been doing this for seven years. A biochemist is almost a vacation after some of what we've rammed into. We've sort of gotten accustomed to being afraid. To handling it, I mean."

"I understand," Cavanaugh said.

The commander studied Cavanaugh as if he couldn't possibly have a background that allowed him to understand what members of a SWAT team felt.

"But unless you've experienced this thing, you can't realize how powerful it is," Cavanaugh said. "If you smell something pungent . . ."

"It'll be his bowels letting go when he panics at hell on earth storming into his house," the commander said.

"I think I should go in first," Cavanaugh said.

"*What?*" Rutherford asked.

"I know what to expect." Cavanaugh dreaded the emotions he would feel when he confronted the smell of the hormone, but he couldn't let these men go first. They had no idea of what would happen to them. "I've got a better chance to—"

"Look at yourself," the commander said. "As messed up as you are, you're in no shape to go in there. This guy already beat you once tonight, so what makes you think he won't do it again? I'm sure you're a good bodyguard, but this is a case where professionals should do the heavy lifting." The commander turned to his men. "Let's go."

As angry as Cavanaugh felt, he gave them credit. When they separated into two groups and shifted past the barricade, heading through the trees and shadows on each side of the street, they looked as trained and experienced as any SWAT group he'd seen. In a very few seconds, they were invisible.

Slowly, one by one, the lights went off in Prescott's house.

"What the . . ." someone said.

"Maybe he's finally going to bed."

"Or the lights are on timers," a detective said.

"You've got to stop this," Cavanaugh told Rutherford.

In the van, a policeman with headphones murmured, "The commander says they'll wait ten minutes and see what else happens. If the target is, in fact, going to bed, all the better—Prescott'll be nice and sleepy when they burst in."

Colder, Cavanaugh stared at the outdoor lights of the now-dark house. He felt the apprehension he'd have suffered if he'd been with the SWAT team.

Ten minutes passed. At 4:40, the man with the headphones leaned from the van. "They're entering."

Cavanaugh watched dark figures emerge from the shadows. Rapidly, they reached the glare of the outdoor lights. Racing across the front lawn, two of them carried a compact battering ram, whose handles they gripped and crashed against the front door, breaking it in. Cavanaugh assumed that the other half of the team was using a similar battering ram to smash in through the back. Weapons ready, the helmeted men charged inside. Strobe lights flashed behind the curtained windows. A siren blared.

The shooting and screaming started.

8

"My God, what's happening?" Rutherford said. *"What's that siren? What are those strobes?"*

"Prescott," Cavanaugh said.

The shooting and screaming worsened.

"Call for backup!" Rutherford yelled to the radio operator in the van. He drew his pistol. "We've got to get in there! We've got to help them!"

"They're shooting each other," Cavanaugh said.

"What?"

"Anything that moves! If you go in there, they'll shoot you, too!"

"But we can't just let—"

The shooting stopped. The screams diminished as the siren persisted. The strobes continued to flash behind the windows, their pulse so rapid that it made Cavanaugh nauseated to look at them.

"For God's sake, don't go in there until I tell you," he said. "Somebody give me a pistol!"

"You're not authorized."

Cavanaugh grabbed a flashlight from the van. As he did, he noticed a pump-action shotgun lying on a table and grabbed it also.

"Hey!" the radio operator said.

Before anyone could stop him, Cavanaugh hurried past the barricade. He reached the rustic house on the right and moved from tree to tree through the darkness, darting across the big lots toward a utility pole that Prescott's outdoor lights illuminated against the night sky.

The pole was to the right of Prescott's house, and the closer Cavanaugh came to the strobes and the siren, the more he slowed. When he reached the final house on the right, he veered along its murky side and crept through its narrow backyard, where a waist-high stone wall separated him from a cliff that dropped to the ocean. The siren almost overwhelmed the pounding of the surf as Cavanaugh came to a tall redwood fence that separated this property from Prescott's. Past the fence, the utility pole stood next to Prescott's house.

A large gray transformer capped it.

Cavanaugh considered climbing the fence, dropping to the ground, and searching for the exterior breaker box, which would usually be next to the electrical meter. A switch inside the box would shut off the power to the strobes and the siren. But the thought of raising his head over that fence and not knowing what might confront him made him hesitate. Besides, he took for granted that the box would be locked and that Prescott would have rigged some kind of device to incapacitate anybody who might try to open it and cut off power to his house. Given the time pressure, there was only one choice.

He pumped a shell into the shotgun's firing chamber, aimed at the transformer on top of the pole, and pulled the trigger, absorbing the recoil against his shoulder. With a roar, a ten-inch gap appeared in the transformer, buckshot reaming it. But the siren and the strobes persisted. He pumped out the empty shell, chambered a full one, and fired a second time, the roar of the shotgun accompanied by a roar and flash from the transformer, sparks falling as the strobes and the siren stopped.

Prescott's house became totally dark.

Wary, Cavanaugh shifted through shadows along the fence and crouched at its end, peering around it toward the front of Prescott's barely visible house.

Hurried footsteps sounded along the street.

Urgent voices came nearer.

Suddenly, Rutherford crouched next to him. "Okay, since you know so much about this, *now* what?"

"Before anybody goes in, we have to break all the windows."

"Break all the—"

"So the breeze from the ocean can clear the air inside, get the smell of the hormone out of the house. Otherwise, anybody who goes in will panic enough to start firing at shadows, and anybody still alive in there will do the same."

Two FBI agents joined them. Across the street, police officers and other agents took cover among murky trees and bushes.

The only sound became the muffled pounding of waves at the bottom of the cliff.

A moan drifted out the front door.

"Tony?" Rutherford shouted to the SWAT commander.

No answer.

"Tony, can you hear me in there?"

Still no answer.

That didn't mean anything, Cavanaugh knew. If Tony was all right, he might not want to give his position away by answering the shout.

Again, a moan drifted from the front door.

Rutherford pulled a walkie-talkie from his belt. "Anything from their radios? Over."

The walkie-talkie crackled. "Nothing."

Cavanaugh heard sirens in the distance. "Anybody who isn't dead will bleed to death if we don't get them to a hospital."

"And Prescott can pick us off as we try to go in for them." What Rutherford said next seemed to come out of nowhere. "Do you know what Baptists believe?"

Cavanaugh assumed he was talking to calm himself. "No, John. Tell me."

"Humans are sinful."

"Truth to that," Cavanaugh said.

"Our only hope is God's mercy."

"Truth to that also."

"Well, God have mercy," Rutherford said. He darted toward a pine tree in front of Prescott's house.

Cavanaugh wanted to follow, but his legs unexpectedly resisted. Imagining the smell of the hormone, he felt an impulse to back away, to get as far from the house as possible.

Rutherford said something into his walkie-talkie. As the sirens wailed closer, the FBI agents and the police officers shifted toward the house.

"God have mercy is right," Cavanaugh said. Hearing another moan through the open front door, he bolted from the fence. Punishing himself for having almost been a coward, he raced across Prescott's lawn, reached a space between two windows at the front of the house, pressed himself against the stone wall, and smashed each of the windows with the butt of the shotgun.

Next to him, he heard other windows being smashed, the agents and police officers following his example, using the butts of shotguns to shatter the glass while pressing themselves against the front wall. A half minute later, the windows in back were shattered, as well.

As Cavanaugh waited for Prescott to shoot, an ocean breeze drifted through the house, fluttering curtains.

"What's that smell?" a police officer said.

"Get away from the house!" an agent yelled.

"Take cover! I saw something move!"

"Don't shoot till you're sure of the target!" Rutherford yelled.

A policeman raced from the front of the house.

Two agents followed, scrambling toward the barricade of police cars at the end of the block.

Cavanaugh tried to hold his breath.

Then he had to inhale, the breeze carrying the pungent smell to him. Even diluted, it shocked his brain. Instantly, sweat burst from his body, soaking him. He'd have run if panic hadn't paralyzed him. With tortuous slowness, the breeze took the last of the hormone from the house. But even though the only smell was now one of salt and kelp from the ocean, Cavanaugh continued to tremble.

"Living room's clear!" someone shouted from inside. Because the team in back had followed the breeze into the house, the hormone hadn't overcome them.

"Media room clear!"

"Guest room clear!"

"Bathroom clear!"

Beyond the broken windows, flashlights zigzagged, moving through the house. Agents and policemen slipped in through the front. More flashlights zigzagged.

"Second bedroom clear!"

"Second bathroom clear!"

"Office clear!"

As the litany continued and the search team shifted toward other rooms, Cavanaugh eased through the front door. In place of the hormone's pungent smell, the air was filled with cordite and the coppery odor of blood.

"Move the barricade! Get the ambulances down here!" Rutherford yelled into his walkie-talkie.

Cavanaugh saw him hunched over a body on the floor. A flashlight showed blood on a SWAT uniform. The man had been shot in the face.

As Cavanaugh moved from room to room, he saw more bodies, more blood. Thank God, some of the men were squirming, moaning, their armored vests having saved them from center-of-mass damage. But the wounds to their arms and legs might still cause them to bleed to death.

Through broken windows, he saw the flashing lights of two ambulances approaching the house. He shifted his attention to the array of strobe lights mounted at the corner of every room, sirens next to them.

"Master bedroom clear!"

"Master bathroom clear!"

"Garage clear!"

"Laundry room clear!"

"Darkroom clear!"

Amid the glare of more flashlights, ambulance attendants rushed into the house and hurried from body to body, doing their best to keep the wounded alive.

"You were right," Rutherford said. "They shot at each other."

Cavanaugh pointed. "The way the strobes were set up, the flashes probably looked like automatic gunfire. Maybe they even created a flashing image of somebody with a weapon. The sirens would have engaged a startle reflex. Wherever those guys turned, they couldn't tell the difference between a threat and their own men. All it took was for one of them to panic because of the hormone and start shooting. Others would have followed suit. Scared beyond any extreme they'd ever experienced, they cut each other down in a cross fire."

"Professionals," Rutherford said.

"Just like the fifteen Rangers who lost control and shot at each other in the swamp. Damn it, where's Prescott?" Cavanaugh asked.

Reinforcements arrived, more flashlights filling the darkness as two dozen agents and police officers searched the house repeatedly.

"No basement, no attic," Rutherford said.

"It's a sloped roof. There'd be some kind of space under it," Cavanaugh said.

"Two agents checked every inch of it twice. Prescott isn't up there."

"As the SWAT team approached the house, he shut off the lights," Cavanaugh said. "He rigged a motion sensor for the strobes and the siren."

"Then he slipped out the back way," Rutherford said. "Check the neighboring properties. Search the houses. Get squad cars on the streets and the highway. If he's on foot, he can't go far."

"Well, that's the problem," an agent said.

"Problem?"

"There aren't any cars in the garage. Maybe he's got a vehicle hidden around here."

For the first time, Cavanaugh heard Rutherford swear.

Rutherford's walkie-talkie crackled. A voice Cavanaugh recognized as belonging to the van's radio operator asked, "Is that bodyguard with you? Over."

"Right next to me. Over."

"Tell him we just got a phone call from the hospital."

9

Cavanaugh sat in a corner of a blindingly bright room in Intensive Care. Across from him, Jamie lay unconscious, her face pale, EKG electrodes attached to her chest, a hospital gown and a sheet covering her, an IV tube leading into her left arm, a respirator tube going down her throat. Behind her, pulse, blood pressure, and heart monitors flashed and beeped.

One of her surgeons, a slender Hispanic, turned from examining her. "She's remarkably strong."

"Yes," Cavanaugh said.

"I'll know more in twelve hours, but her vitals are encouraging. We've got reason to be optimistic."

Staring at Jamie, Cavanaugh nodded.

"She'll have you to thank," the surgeon said. "She probably would have died before she got to the hospital if you hadn't stopped the bleeding with duct tape."

"No," Cavanaugh said. "She doesn't have anything to thank me for at all."

The doctor looked curious.

"If I'd listened to her," Cavanaugh said, "she never would have gotten shot."

The heart monitor beeped.

"Can I stay in here?" Cavanaugh asked.

"Normally, we don't allow . . ."

Cavanaugh looked at him.

"Yes," the surgeon told him.

"The lights," Cavanaugh said, squinting from their brightness. "Can you put something over her eyelids?"

"As soon as we're finished in here, we'll dim the room."

"What about for now?"

"I'll have a nurse bring a washcloth."

"Thank you."

Thirty seconds later, Cavanaugh was alone with her.

The respirator hissed, wheezed, and thumped, Jamie's chest going up and down.

"I'm sorry," Cavanaugh told her.

His muscles ached. His eyes felt as if sand scratched them. Closing his lids to shield his eyes from the stark overhead lights, he leaned back in the plastic chair and managed a fitful sleep, even when nurses came in to check Jamie and replace her IV.

10

Around two in the afternoon, Cavanaugh drove a borrowed un-marked police car along Highway 1 and stopped at the side of the road just before the Carmel Highlands turnoff that would even-tually lead to Prescott's street. He got out of the car and stayed close to the trees at the side of the road as he walked toward the turnoff. The afternoon was pleasant, with a gorgeous sky, but Ca-vanaugh paid attention only to the high branches on the trees just in from the turnoff. He approached them slowly from an oblique angle, craning his neck, taking off his sunglasses to get a better look at the trees.

When he didn't see what he wanted, he raised binoculars and scanned the branches. Continuing to remain carefully to the side, he paid particular attention to where the branches met the trunks. After ten minutes, a high Monterey pine—on the left, about forty feet in from the turnoff—became the sole object of his concentration. He focused the binoculars on a gap in the branches and nodded.

11

Near the entrance to Prescott's street, Cavanaugh stopped again, got out of the car, and stayed well to the side as he approached the turnoff. Now that his eyes were practiced, he took only five minutes to find the miniature TV camera, its lens about the size of a flashlight's, attached by a metal strap to the crook of a branch in a Monterey pine about thirty feet in from the entrance. The strap was painted the brown of the trunk. The camera was the same type that Prescott had said he'd hidden in the parking garage to watch for anybody who might be following him. "The Internet's crammed with advertising for them," he'd said. "Check up on your baby-sitter. See your neighbor's teenaged daughter sunbathing."

Or watch the police stake out your house and try to catch you by surprise, Cavanaugh thought. Last night, Prescott saw every move we made from when we drove into the Highlands to when Rutherford set up the roadblock here to when the SWAT team snuck up on the house. Cavanaugh recalled how the lights in Prescott's house had gone off a few seconds after the SWAT team had started to approach it. Sure, he thought. Prescott hoped that a brightly lit house would be a deterrent and buy him some time, but when he saw the police move toward it, he proceeded to stage two, shut the lights off, set the motion detectors for the strobes and the siren, then filled the house with the hormone.

Staying out of the camera's sight, Cavanaugh returned to the car. When he drove onto Prescott's street, he peered toward the end of the block and for the first time got a clear look at Prescott's house, which was low, modernistic in design, and made from flat sections of stone set on top of one another. Flanked by shrubs, a curved driveway led up to the front entrance. The door to the double-car garage was open. Yellow tape with POLICE CRIME SCENE DO NOT CROSS on it went from tree to tree, encircling the property.

Other things caught Cavanaugh's interest. On the right, a large truck had a platform raised next to the utility pole, two workmen replacing the electrical transformer Cavanaugh had shot the night before. In the driveway, a bearded man in coveralls was removing sheets of plywood from a pickup truck. Half of the broken windows in front of the house had already been covered with the wood. To the left, parked along the street, pointing in Cavanaugh's direction, were two police cars and an unmarked car that Cavanaugh recognized as the dark sedan belonging to Rutherford and some of his fellow agents.

Cavanaugh made a U-turn in front of the house, doing it

slowly, taking the opportunity to study the corners under the house's eaves without seeming to. Small boxes with peepholes might have been birdhouses, or they might have been receptacles for miniature TV cameras hidden under the eaves.

After parking in front of the police cars and walking toward the house, he saw Rutherford come out and study him wearily.

"Is your wife's condition any better?" Although Rutherford had changed his suit and shaved, he looked haggard. The lingering bruises on his face made his black skin seem pale.

"She's still unconscious." Cavanaugh made himself continue. "But the surgeon says her life signs are better than he expected. We're more hopeful."

"Good." Rutherford sounded genuinely relieved, despite the betrayed tone in what he said next. "Incidentally, I just found out her name's Jamie, not Jennifer."

"I'm sorry."

"Of course."

"I figured if I kept her real name a secret, in the long run she wouldn't be involved," Cavanaugh said.

"But she got involved anyway, didn't she?"

"Yes," Cavanaugh said, "she got involved."

"Why are you here?"

"There's nothing I can do at the hospital. The waiting . . ." Unable to finish the sentence, Cavanaugh looked around. "I hoped you could use my help."

"I don't see how. Prescott's long gone. Either he had a vehicle hidden in the area or he managed to steal one," Rutherford said. "We've got an alert out to every community north and south of here. Highway Patrol. Airports. Marinas. Train depots. Bus stations. Name it. We've staked out the car he left at the scenic lookout in Pacific Grove when he made contact with you. We're also watching the van he told you he kept in the parking garage where he stored the Porsche."

As the repairman nailed a plywood sheet to another broken

window, Cavanaugh nodded toward the open front door. "Is the lab crew finished?"

"They didn't find anything useful. We confiscated Prescott's computer and all the documents he had. Maybe they'll point us in his direction."

Entering, Cavanaugh heard voices from various rooms to the right and left, FBI agents and detectives presumably making a final inspection of the house. In daylight, the building's sprawl was dramatic. Its expensive modernistic furniture matched its architecture, although bullet holes had destroyed most of the chairs, sofas, tables, and lamps. The walls and framed black-and-white photographs of the Carmel region had been similarly destroyed. Broken glass lay everywhere. Through the shattered rear windows, an ocean breeze dispelled any lingering odor from the bloodstains amid the chalk outlines on the hardwood floor.

Cavanaugh stared at the strobe lights mounted in a corner. Their variously colored compact bulbs had been discreetly arranged to look like an abstract artwork and wouldn't have attracted suspicion if seen through a window.

"Is the casualty count still the same?" he asked.

"Five dead. Five critically wounded. In stable condition. It looks like they're going to pull through."

"Something to be thankful about."

Cavanaugh crossed the living room, heading toward the French doors, then ducked under more yellow crime-scene tape and stepped out onto a flagstone terrace that had shrubs and flowers in pots. Preoccupied, he peered over the waist-high stone wall toward where a forty-foot cliff dropped sharply to the crashing surf. Spray rose toward him.

"We have boats searching for a body in the water, in case Prescott was crazy enough to have tried climbing down there," Rutherford said.

"It's worth checking."

Doing his best to seem casual, Cavanaugh turned from the cliff and glimpsed two more birdhouses mounted under the eaves, one to the extreme right, one to the extreme left. They were angled toward the opposite corners. If miniature TV cameras were in them, as Cavanaugh was certain, their position would have allowed Prescott to see anyone coming around either side of the house.

When Cavanaugh reentered the house, the repairman hammered another sheet of plywood over a broken window. Four detectives headed out the front door. Two FBI agents waited for Rutherford.

"We'll stay and lock up after the electricity's back on and the windows are sealed," Rutherford said.

Cavanaugh nodded.

He checked the office, the bedrooms, and the bathrooms. He went into the garage and inspected the laundry room and the photo-developing room.

All the while, Rutherford followed him.

After Cavanaugh returned to the front of the house and studied it some more, he finally shook his head from side to side.

"See, I told you," Rutherford said.

"At least you can't blame me for trying."

"Right. This is one time I can't blame you."

"I should have stayed at the hospital."

12

"No, sir. No change," the nurse said.

*   *   *

"May I help you?" the sinewy, mustached gun-store clerk asked.

"I need a shotgun."

"Any specific kind?"

"A Remington 870 twelve-gauge pump."

"Yeah, that's certainly specific. You wouldn't happen to be with law enforcement?"

"No. What makes you ask?"

"Just that most police departments prefer that model. It's also the shotgun of choice for U.S. special operations."

"Is that a fact," Cavanaugh said.

* * *

"I need the strongest hacksaw you've got and several blades for it," Cavanaugh told the clerk at the hardware store.

* * *

"I need a wet suit," Cavanaugh told the clerk at the diving shop.

* * *

"I need an inflatable boat that'll accommodate an outboard motor," Cavanaugh told the clerk at the military-surplus store.

13

In the motel room, Cavanaugh stared at the makeup kit Jamie had left on the bureau. When he phoned the hospital, he was again told there was no change.

He pulled the mattress off the bed and used clamps that he'd bought in the hardware store to secure the shotgun to the bed frame, stabilizing it so the barrel protruded. Then he picked up the hacksaw and started sawing four inches off the barrel's eighteen-inch length, reducing it to the compactness that many police departments preferred. The effort took him an hour and several blades, but he wasn't conscious of the time passing—he had a great deal to think about.

After another phone call to the hospital ("No change"), Cavanaugh opened two boxes of federal double-aught "tactical" buckshot. He liked that ammunition because the large pellets gave him a compact pattern over a long distance.

To make the pattern even tighter, he thumbed open a new Emerson CQC-7 knife that he'd bought at the gun store and used its blade to cut around the plastic shaft of each shell. He chose a spot about two-thirds down each of them, at the dividing line between the gunpowder and the pellets that would be discharged when the gunpowder was ignited. He had to be careful not to cut so deeply that the plastic cylinder would break in two while he worked on it. At the same time, his cut had to be deep enough that two-thirds of the shell would break away when the shotgun was fired. The blast would thus propel not only the pellets but the plastic shaft in which they were contained. The consequence would be that the pellets would not spread but would remain in a tight clump, causing near-explosive force when they hit their target.

14

After dark, Cavanaugh drove along Highway 1 to a low bridge located just south of Point Lobos, near the Highlands. The terrain there suited his needs. It was also where Prescott had forced the Taurus into the water. He parked along the side of the road, waited for a break in the passing headlights of traffic, then lugged the collapsed rubber boat down the slope to the water. After using a pressurized canister to inflate the boat, he anchored it to a rock and made two more cautious trips back and forth from the car, bringing the small outboard motor and a buoyant waterproof bag containing his equipment. He had put on his wet suit in the motel room. Now all he had to do was take off the sport coat that disguised what he was wearing. Rubber gloves and diver's boots protected his hands and feet as he pushed off from the rocks. He started the motor and headed out to the moonlit sea, staying a hundred yards offshore, following the contour of the bluffs of the Highlands, the speckled lights of houses guiding him.

When he came abreast of the bluff upon which Prescott's house was positioned, he shut off the motor and switched to a paddle, heading in silently. With the electricity restored, several lights around the outside of Prescott's house provided a beacon. But the waves and the undertow made it difficult to control the boat. Sweating from exertion, he had to alternate between port and starboard as he paddled closer to the cliff.

Then he got so close to the surf pounding the rocks that the boat would crash and overturn if he went any nearer. Spray chilled his face. After putting on the wet suit's rubber hood, along with flippers and a face mask equipped with a snorkel, he gripped the buoyant bag that contained his equipment and eased over the side. For an instant, the water was shockingly cold, nearly robbing him of the ability to move. Then the water seeped into his wet suit and formed a thin layer between the wet suit and his skin. Almost immediately, his body heated the water to its own temperature, so that only his face felt cold. The undertow was frighteningly strong, however. Using all the power in his arms and legs, he struggled through the turbulent waves, tugging his equipment bag via a strong nylon cord looped around his left wrist. A wave lifted him, threatening to smash him against the looming rocks. His heart raced sickeningly fast, making him almost change his mind and thrash back to the boat before the current could carry the boat away.

But he couldn't allow himself to back off, couldn't give in to his fear. If he did, he knew it would be the first of *many* times when he would give in to it. The surf took him under, lifted him, dropped him. With a mighty exhale, he blew water from his snorkel and stared through his water-beaded face mask. Judging the surf, he worked his legs and his arms, straining to avoid rocks projecting from the ocean. A wave slammed him against the cliff.

If not for the buffer of his wet suit, the granite would have flayed his shoulder. Wincing from the impact, he grabbed for an outcrop, was swept away, then was caught by another wave and again slammed against the cliff; but this time, as he groaned, his gloved hand caught a fissure in the rock. He gripped harder and pawed with his other glove. Finding a higher fissure, he pulled himself up before the next wave struck his legs and almost tugged him off the cliff.

As he dangled above the thunderous water, Cavanaugh released one hand from the cliff and pulled off his face mask and snorkel. Breathing greedily, he dropped the mask into the waves, then kicked off his flippers and dropped them also. He crammed his rubber-protected feet into a niche, hung for a moment, sucked more air into his lungs, then slowly began his ascent through the darkness. Spray flew around him. He'd cut off the tips of his rubber gloves so that his fingers would be better able to grip outcrops, but the remainder of the gloves interfered with his mobility. He soon had to release his hands, one at a time, use his teeth to pull off each glove, then drop them to the waves beneath him. Instantly, his palms were cold, but not enough to immobilize his grip, his fingers continuing to grab and hold.

He pulled himself higher. The cord looped around his left wrist was attached to a spool that had a release switch. He'd pressed the switch just before he reached the rocks, allowing the cord to unwind as the waterproof bag floated in the crashing surf. Thus, he could climb without the weight of the bag dragging him back. Higher. He had the sense that his fingers were bleeding. They didn't matter. Only not giving up mattered. He reached for a handhold, shoved his feet into another fissure, reached again, and touched the rock wall at the top, gaining energy from knowing that this part of the ordeal was almost over.

The miniature TV cameras hidden under each corner of the eaves were aimed toward each other. They could show someone creeping around either corner, but the limited field of vision afforded through holes in the birdhouses made it impossible for them to provide a view of the waist-high wall above the cliff. Cavanaugh raised himself, balanced on the wall's foot-wide rim, and pulled the cord looped around his wrist, hoisting his equipment bag. Water dripped from the bag as he set it down. Throughout, he studied the back of Prescott's house. Harsh lights illuminated the corners and the French doors across from him. Like the shattered windows, the doors were covered with sheets of plywood. A padlock secured the doors. Yellow crime-scene tape was stretched across them. A police department sign nailed to the plywood warned that trespassers would be prosecuted.

Cavanaugh unzipped the waterproof bag and pulled out the sawed-off shotgun, along with a nylon bag of shells that he hitched over his right shoulder. He removed the Emerson knife and clipped it to the neck of his wet suit. He took out a pouch of his lock-pick tools. Finally, he threw off the wet suit's hood and reached into the bag for night-vision goggles that he'd found at the military-surplus store while buying the Zodiac boat. He draped the goggles around his neck.

Ready, he dropped to the terrace, sank to the flagstones, and squirmed across them toward the French doors, the bottom of which was another area that the angle of the TV cameras couldn't reach. When he came to a crouch, he at last risked being seen as he hurriedly picked the lock. He opened the doors, rushed into the dark house, shut the doors, put on his night-vision goggles, and aimed the shotgun.

His goggles gave the dark interior a faint green illumination as he checked the wreckage of the living room and then shifted left into the media room, then the guest bedroom and bathroom. These areas weren't his main interest, but he had to make sure they weren't a threat. Satisfied, he crept toward the opposite side of the house, broken glass scraping under his rubber-protected feet. The vague smell of cordite still lingered in the air. At once, Cavanaugh knew that the TV cameras had at the last moment revealed him crouching to pick the padlock and enter the house—

because the smell of cordite was overpowered by the sudden pungent stench of the hormone.

Until now, Cavanaugh's wet suit had been comfortably warm. Now the sweat that squirted from his body raised his temperature so much that he felt as if he were in a sauna. Almost dizzy from the heat under his wet suit, he risked taking his right hand off the shotgun for the few seconds he needed to pull down the wet suit's zipper, exposing his chest. The effort made no difference.

In Karen's basement, he had thought he'd endured the full force of the hormone, but now, as the smell became almost unbearable, he understood that he had no idea how powerful Prescott's weapon could be. His legs threatened not to support him. His stomach felt simultaneously scaldingly hot and polar-cold. His pulse was so fast, he came close to fainting.

Part of him wanted to roll into a ball and pray for this nightmare to end. Another part compelled him to pivot in an increasingly rapid circle, pointing his shotgun anywhere and everywhere. His body heat misted the faint green images of his night-vision goggles. Surrounded by every imaginable threat, seeing through fear-narrowed vision, he spotted a man with a pistol aiming at him from the corridor that led to the master bedroom. He came within a millisecond of pulling the trigger, then realized that the man with a pistol was merely a shadow, that this was how the Rangers and the SWAT team had reacted.

Cavanaugh's only advantage was that he'd suffered the hormone's effects and knew what to expect. Even so, as the pungent smell became strong enough to make him taste bile, he heard unnerving noises that he realized were pathetic whimpers forcing their way from his throat. The heaving bellows of his lungs made the whimpers come and go, come and go, each time stronger, building to a scream that he repressed by racing along the corridor to the master bedroom.

Charging inside, he didn't dare think, didn't dare hesitate or second-guess himself. The huge bedroom had an arcade video game next to a luxurious reading chair. A large flat-screen plasma TV was mounted to the wall at the foot of the bed, a cabinet of electronics next to it. To the right of the TV, a sliding door led into a closet. That afternoon, Cavanaugh had looked into the closet and seen Prescott's designer jackets hanging on a rod, cedar shelves of expensive tank tops, T-shirts, and sweaters behind them.

Now he shoved a bureau from the side of the room and rammed it into the closet so hard that he broke off the pole that supported the jackets. He yanked down the electronics cabinet and the plasma TV, shattering its screen. With the closet blocked and the wall at the foot of the bed fully exposed, he pulled earplugs from his bag of shotgun shells and put them on. His shaky fingers could barely do the job. The pungent smell was so overpowering that he came close to bending forward and retching. Cursing, he stepped back, raised the shotgun, and fired at a spot three feet from the ceiling. Nearly knocked back by the recoil, which his shuddering body could barely support, he was gratified that the almost-severed plastic shell separated from its base when the gunpowder detonated. Like a miniature rocket, the main part of the shell and the buckshot within it roared toward the top of the wall, blasting apart on impact, creating a fist-sized hole, through which the buckshot burst like shrapnel. An eerie pale light was visible through the hole.

Cavanaugh yanked the pump on the shotgun's forward grip, ejecting the remainder of the empty shell, chambering a full one. In a fury, he fired just below the ceiling again, aiming toward an area three feet to the left of the first hole. Another miniature rocket seemed to blast a fist-sized hole in the wall. And another. Each hole revealed more of the eerie pale light. The Remington 870 held four shells in its magazine and one in the firing chamber. Cavanaugh rapidly discharged all five, blasting more holes in the wall, working his way downward. The odor of cordite helped to mask the stench of the hormone as he fumbled for more shells and forced his trembling fingers to shove them into the slot under the shotgun. Despite his earplugs, he heard muffled screams behind the wall just before he started shooting again.

He moved the pattern of the fist-sized holes lower, soon reaching five feet down from the ceiling. Prescott screamed more fiercely behind there as Cavanaugh reloaded again and fired, the holes showing even more of the light. The bedroom was filled with a haze of gun smoke. Reload. Fire. Reload. Fire. Now Cavanaugh lowered his aim to three feet above the floor. Prescott's screams came from down there, where he'd taken cover as the descending movement of the blasts pressed him toward the floor.

"You had me believing you'd gone!" Cavanaugh shouted. His fear and the earplugs caused his voice to sound as if it came from a disorienting distance.

"Then I spotted the miniature TV cameras outside the house!" Cavanaugh pumped the shotgun and blew yet another hole in the wall, keeping it three feet above the floor, forcing Prescott to huddle in panic down there. Wood and plaster flew. More of the glowing light was exposed.

"So many cameras!" Cavanaugh's shout was primal.

"Cameras need monitors! *So where the hell are the monitors?*" As Cavanaugh blasted yet another hole in the wall, the hormone made his bladder want to let go.

"*Where's the walk-in closet that ought to go with a bedroom this huge?*" Cavanaugh pumped the shotgun and fired. The glow of the monitors streamed through the increasing holes, revealing where they were stacked on shelves against the far left side of the enclosure, away from his shots.

"It couldn't have been hard to put up a wall inside the closet! Something you could pivot like a door and lock on the other side!" Again Cavanaugh pulled the trigger. He knew that the neighbors would hear the shots and phone the police. He didn't care. By the time the police arrived, his business would be finished.

"What did you do, use the van from the parking garage to bring in construction supplies?" Again, Cavanaugh's shotgun roared. "Your neighbors wouldn't have realized you were dividing the closet! Shelves for the monitors! A ventilation duct connected to the main system! A cot! Preserved food! A portable toilet! Like the first time I met you! You were in a hiding hole then! You're in a hiding hole now!"

Cavanaugh pulled the trigger and blasted the middle of the wall. So much light from the monitors now glowed through the holes that it compromised his night-vision goggles, forcing him to raise them to his forehead. "Everybody was so impressed by the huge TV on the wall, they didn't realize you were hidden back there! A couple of days from now, when the police stopped searching for you around here, you could have left the house after dark! You could have stolen a car and been in San Francisco before anybody realized the car was missing! Nobody would have made the connection with you, especially if you remembered to wipe your fingerprints the way I taught you!"

Cavanaugh's hands and face dripped with sweat as he pumped out a final empty shell and started to reload.

Abruptly, he was stunned by a chaos of bullets erupting from the ravaged wall. Wood and plaster flew as an assault rifle fired an automatic volley from the other side. *Roberto's AR-15,* Cavanaugh thought, diving to the floor. His earplugs only partially muffled the stuttering clamor. Chunks of the wall spewed across the bedroom, bullets rupturing the headboard and the wall behind Cavanaugh. Lamps and picture frames shattered. Amid the widening gaps in the wall and the increasing glow of the monitors, Cavanaugh saw the staccato muzzle flashes.

At once, the shooting stopped. Cavanaugh thought he heard a curse, the scrape of metal, the struggle to release a jammed cartridge. The next instant, what was left of the wall burst apart, Prescott shrieking, his muscular body ramming through the cluster of holes. His upper torso was bare, except for the Kevlar vest he'd pulled over it. The glow of the monitors reflected off the sweat on his powerful-looking arms and shaved scalp. Even in the dim light, his eyes blazed. The sharp contours of his jaw and chin radiated the fury of a cornered predator. Throwing the assault rifle while he charged, he leapt over the broken TV and dove toward Cavanaugh. The impact was so great, Cavanaugh felt air being slammed from his lungs. The Kevlar vest's rigid structure reinforced the solidity of Prescott's body, stunning Cavanaugh to the point that his mind turned gray. Then Prescott's powerful hands clutched Cavanaugh's throat, sending a further shock through his nervous system. Breathless, Cavanaugh felt the bones in his throat bending inward, about to snap. He slammed his hands across Prescott's ears so hard that Prescott screamed in pain and fell back.

Gasping for air, Cavanaugh rolled toward where he'd dropped the shotgun. But Prescott kicked his hands away and got to the shotgun first, pulling the trigger. Even with the earplugs Cavanaugh wore, the noise of the shell rocketing past him was overwhelming. The shell hit the arcade video game, the cylinder of buckshot exploding on impact, blowing the machine into pieces. Because Prescott was unfamiliar with the mechanics of the shotgun, he took too long to pump out what was left of the cartridge, giving Cavanaugh time to charge. The collision sent the two men crashing against already-shattered French doors. Plywood nailed to the doors' exterior gave way, Cavanaugh and Prescott smashing through onto the brightly lit terrace.

The floodlights hurt Cavanaugh's eyes as Prescott scrambled back and raised the shotgun.

"It won't do you any good." Cavanaugh's voice wavered, fear coursing through him. The strong, cool ocean breeze surged into his mouth and up his nostrils. "I had time to reload only one shell before you crashed through the wall."

"Right," Prescott said.

Cavanaugh unclipped the Emerson knife from the top of his wet suit and thumbed open its blade. He took several deep breaths. The clear air wouldn't take away the effects of the hormone, but it stopped them from getting worse.

"Dummy, you brought a knife to a gunfight," Prescott said.

"An old joke."

"But I'm the one laughing." Prescott pulled the trigger.

Nothing happened.

"School's back in session," Cavanaugh said.

As Prescott gaped at the empty shotgun, Cavanaugh removed the plugs from his ears. He heard sirens in the distance.

"How'd you like to learn about knife fighting?" Cavanaugh lunged with the knife.

Prescott jumped back.

"Part of it has to do with balance." Cavanaugh lunged again.

Prescott dodged to the side.

"Part of it has to do with dexterity." With dizzying, eye-blinking speed, Cavanaugh flicked the dark blade back and forth, up and down.

Prescott raised the shotgun as if about to swing a baseball bat.

"And part of it has to do with knowing which areas of the body to cut, depending on if you want a quick kill," Cavanaugh said, "or a slow one."

Prescott stood his ground. He inhaled violently, unintentionally warning that he was about to act. Then he charged.

As Prescott swung the shotgun, Cavanaugh ducked, nicked Prescott's right arm, and skipped back before Prescott could swing again.

Prescott looked shocked that his arm was bleeding.

The sirens wailed closer.

When Prescott glanced in their direction, Cavanaugh darted forward and nicked Prescott's other arm.

Furious, Prescott swung the shotgun again and gasped when Cavanaugh ducked it, then plunged the Emerson knife through the Kevlar vest into Prescott's stomach.

Weak-kneed, Prescott stumbled back in shock, staring down at the bloody knife Cavanaugh pulled from the bullet-resistant vest. Blood trickled from the bottom of the vest, crimson spreading down Prescott's sweatpants. Prescott's eyes widened in denial, communicating that he couldn't believe what had happened was possible.

"The wound's too shallow to kill you for a while," Cavanaugh said. "You've still got a lot of bleeding to do."

"How did . . ." Prescott's question was a gasp.

"Surely a smart guy like you can figure that out. The vest's made of polymer fibers. It's designed to resist only the blunt force of a bullet."

"The knife's sharp enough to slip past the fibers?"

"You pass the quiz." Cavanaugh jabbed again.

But Prescott had used the pause to regroup. Instead of lurching farther back, he surprised Cavanaugh by throwing the shotgun and charging, pinning Cavanaugh's arms to his side before Cavanaugh could do anything more than nick him again. With his hands clasped behind Cavanaugh's back, Prescott flexed his muscles, tightening, squeezing.

Cavanaugh felt as if metal coils were around him, contracting ever tighter. He couldn't move his chest, couldn't work his lungs. Staring at Prescott's frenzied eyes a couple of inches away from him, he suddenly felt light-headed. The floodlights on the terrace seemed to dim. His arms were so tight against his sides that he couldn't use the knife. He was so close to Prescott that he couldn't raise his knee to kick him in the groin.

In desperation, he hooked his right leg behind Prescott's left ankle and yanked. As Prescott toppled backward, Cavanaugh pushed, landing on him, knocking the wind from him.

Prescott's arms loosened just enough for Cavanaugh to pull free. They rolled away from each other and scrambled to their feet.

Cavanaugh jabbed with the knife.

Prescott dodged back.

Cavanaugh jabbed again.

Prescott dodged farther back, hit the waist-high wall, and went over.

"No!" Cavanaugh shouted.

Rushing, he grabbed Prescott's left arm just before he would have dropped out of sight.

Prescott dangled, his shoes scraping against the cliff. He could barely speak. "Please . . . don't . . . let . . . go."

"My shoulder still hurts from when you shot me." Cavanaugh stretched over the wall, clinging to him. "I'm not sure how long I can hold you."

Prescott jerked his other arm up and grabbed Cavanaugh's hands. Far below, the waves pounded the rocks. "Scared."

"I know," Cavanaugh said. "Thanks to your hormone, I'm so frightened, I'm not sure I can control my hands."

As if demonstrating the point, Prescott's blood-streaked arms began to slip through Cavanaugh's grasp. "For God's sake," Prescott said.

"Where's the antidote?"

"What?"

"Tell me where the antidote is."

Sirens blaring, cars stopped in front of the house. Doors slammed.

"Tell me where the antidote is. I'll let you live."

Prescott's arms slipped farther.

Cavanaugh's trembling hands weakened.

Prescott gasped.

Wincing, Cavanaugh gripped tighter. *"Where's the antidote?"*

"Put your hands where I can see them!" Rutherford yelled from the side of the house, aiming a pistol at Cavanaugh.

"I guess I'd better do what the man says." Cavanaugh made a motion as if to release his hands.

"No, wait!" Prescott said.

"The antidote! Where is it?"

"In the house!"

"Keep talking." Cavanaugh clung with all his might.

"Where I was hiding! Behind a monitor! In a red aerosol container!"

"It better not be bug spray, or I'll make you wish I'd dropped you!"

"Pull him up!" Rutherford rounded the corner, accompanied by FBI agents and police officers, all aiming pistols. A similarly intense group rounded the opposite corner, pistols and shotguns aimed.

Still hanging over the wall, clutching Prescott, Cavanaugh asked, "What's going to happen to him, John? Will the government make a deal?"

"Not anymore. Too many people know what happened last night. The newspapers and TV stations all along the coast are asking questions. So are the cable news channels, the networks, the East Coast papers. If the government bargained with a multiple killer in exchange for what he knows, there'd be even *more* questions. He'll be punished."

"Whatever it is, it won't be enough. Prescott, listen to me," Cavanaugh said, pulling him up. "In prison, you'd better let yourself go to pot again, because a buff guy like you will attract a lot of romantic attention from the inmates. Or maybe you'd better take a new batch of muscle stimulant and buff yourself up even more so you can fight off all their advances. You're just beginning to understand what fear is."

15

In the mercilessly bright lights of the ICU room, Cavanaugh sat sleeplessly next to Jamie, watching for the slightest flicker of her eyelids, the slightest twitch around her mouth. The respirator had been removed from her throat. Her chest rose and fell on its own. The flashing, beeping monitors for her pulse, blood pressure, and heart rhythms showed steady improvement.

"Twenty-four hours, and no setbacks," her surgeon said. "An excellent sign."

Cavanaugh nodded, hoping.

"Why don't you go away for a couple of hours and get some rest?" the surgeon suggested.

"If it's all right with you, I'm staying."

At 6:37 in the morning (Cavanaugh noted the time precisely), Jamie's green eyes finally opened. She looked groggy, dazed, in pain. But when she recognized him, her bruised face managed a look of affection.

"Can you understand me?" he asked.

She nodded almost imperceptibly, the effort tiring her.

"In case you don't remember, I'll tell you often," Cavanaugh said. "As soon as you're able, we're going back to Wyoming. We're heading home. We're staying."

Groggy, she tried to study him.

"If I'd agreed to go home when you wanted, you wouldn't have gotten shot. I don't know how to make it up to you, but somehow I will."

With effort, she asked, "Prescott?"

"I found him."

Worry clouded her eyes.

"He's alive. John has him in custody," Cavanaugh assured her.

The beeping of the monitors filled the silence between them.

"I want to prove to you how sorry I am," Cavanaugh said. "You're more important to me than anything. From now on, there's nothing I won't do for you."

Her eyelids weakened.

"I'm sure that's too much for you to understand right now. But I'll be here the next time you wake up, and I'll tell you again. I'll keep telling you." Cavanaugh had trouble with his voice. "Until you forgive me."

Cavanaugh touched her hand.

Jamie's fingers nudged his, almost too faintly to be noticed. But it was enough.

"I'll be here," Cavanaugh said. "Feel how steady my hand is." The antidote was working. "I'll watch over you."

She nodded, her closed eyelids relaxing. As she drifted back to sleep, her bruised lips formed what might have been a smile.